Bedivere: The King's Right Hand

Book One

Wayne Wise

Wayne Wise

Published by:

Wayne Wise

http://www.wayne-wise.com/

Cover Art by Dave Wachter

www.davedrawscomics.com

Cover Design by Marcel Walker

http://www.marcelwalker.com

DEDICATION

For my own Round Table of friends...
Kings, Queens, Knights and Wizards all.

Wayne Wise

PROLOG

I walked through the haze toward the lake. The moisture on my face was a mixture of the heavy mists that always swirled around the edges of Avalon and my own tears. I was there on a final mission. I was there to discharge the last wish of my King.

It has been two score and more of years since that dark day, and I am older than I ever dreamed possible. Now, when I have finally been convinced to sit and write of the events of my life it is still that single day, the last day, that first comes to mind. With everything that happened before and since, it may prove to be the defining moment of my life, the way in which I am remembered. Even now stories are being told of the golden age of Arthur the King, and of the men who served him and the women who loved him. Tales of Lancelot and Gawaine are on the lips of every bard and storyteller in the land. The truths and lies about them could fill many books. I'm sure, in time, they will.

And though I was there at the beginning, and to my eternal grief, at the very end, there is only one story told about me.

I sit at an oaken desk in a small stone outbuilding. Quills and bottles of ink are arrayed before me. Though it is summer now, and the cool interior of the room is welcome, by the time my hand cramps from writing this account it will be the dead of winter, or even beyond. Cords of wood for the fireplace have already been stacked against the building's wall. My host is ever thoughtful, and knows better than anyone the needs of a man wrestling with his muse.

The quill feels strange in my hand. It has been a long time since I have had need to write. My skills are as rusty as my old armor, though the task fits me better now.

It took quite a bit of cajoling from my hosts to make me start this task. I am not a storyteller, I protested. I have always thought myself a simple man blessed to be surrounded by those greater than myself in a time of great events. My friends disagreed. They said no one was more qualified to tell the true story of Arthur's reign. No one else had seen it in its entirety. I said I wouldn't know where to begin. My old friend laughed and said "at the beginning."

That seems obvious enough. But, now that I am here with quill in hand, it is the end that I remember most.

I walked through the mist. The sword, in my hand for the first and last time, was heavy. Much heavier than I would ever have believed. In Arthur's hand it moved like skyfire, like wind, like the thoughts of God. None of us, even I who was there from the beginning, ever truly knew the burden he carried at all times. The weight of the sword was the weight of expectation, of duty. The day he drew it he lifted the weight of all of Britain on his shoulders and never set it down again, no matter what it cost him.

And the cost was great, his life being the least of that price, at least in his own eyes.

And at the end, as I struggled toward the water's edge, eyes blurred by grief, I briefly endured the weight he had carried his entire life and realized it was too much for me to bear. The sword, the responsibility, was not meant for me. It was meant for no other but him, at least in this time and place. I knew that always, and was content in my role as friend and advisor. Others coveted what he had, seeing only the rewards, only the power, only the love. They never realized what he carried. They couldn't see the strength it took every day.

His last wish recognized that truth; there was no one left who could take up the sword and carry its weight. It wasn't arrogance on his part. It was his duty as King, and perhaps an acknowledgment of his one failure; he left no one behind as great as himself.

His final order to me was to take the sword from his dying hand and return it to its source, the great lake of Avalon. Did this act of his condemn us to the chaos that has overtaken our kingdom since? Or would it have been worse if someone else, someone weaker had been allowed to wield the sword? Are the slow incursions of foreigners on our soil and the loss of our sovereignty worse than the iron rule of a tyrant? I had hoped history would be the final judge of that, but now I doubt any true records of our history will survive this dark age that has descended.

It pains me now, to remember how I failed him in those final moments. Even then, seeing the great wound his son had dealt him, I hoped he would survive. I was blinded by denial that all we had built was gone. Blinded too by my love for him and my inability to let him go. Blinded by my faith that evil could not win. Somewhere in the jumble of my thoughts, I believed he could be healed. Merlin had done it before, but Merlin was gone by then. I hoped for Percival's return, though Bors' tale gave me little hope for that. Surely the Grail they had found could restore the king. Even if that was an old wives tale, Percival himself was the only one of us who I believed could wield the sword of kingship. I know now that he had been given his own burden to carry.

In protest I took the sword from Arthur and left his side to carry out his last wish. In my hopes and denials I hid the sword at the lakeside until his hand was healthy enough to carry it again and then returned to his side.

"What did you see when you threw it into the lake?" he asked me through agonized breaths.

"It splashed into the water and sank," I answered. I saw pain in his eyes that had nothing to do with his wound. I left his side and returned to where I had hidden the sword. Still I could not let it go. I could not admit that my dearest friend was leaving our work undone. Selfishly I could not accept that he was leaving me.

"Well?" he asked when I returned. I could not meet his gaze.

"Bedivere," he said, "in all the years of my life you are the one who has always been steadfast. You swore to never leave my side and you never have, but now that is what I ask of you. Do this for me. I know you do not understand, but it is the right thing to do. You, of all of us, have always held true to that."

Though his words were not spoken sharply, shame filled me then. Wordless I left his side again and this time I carried out his wishes.

I have always been a simple man. Tristan once accused me of having no imagination. That may be true. I could never have imagined the very things that I helped bring about. I was content to serve my King, to serve his vision, and to know that he was also my friend. Over the years I heard stories from the other knights, stories of the strange and the miraculous, but I myself never witnessed more than my own mind could explain.

Until that last black day when I returned Excalibur to Avalon.

I returned to Arthur then and held him until his final breath left, and then held him still until the women came to claim him. I stayed by his side as they washed and prepared the body. I walked beside the bier until we came to the lake. I walked in water beside the boat until I could walk no more and then I watched as my King, my friend, finally went to a place I could not follow.

It has been over twenty years since that time, and nearly that long since I have set foot in Great Britain. Without Camelot there was no place for me there. I, who had never gone on a knightly quest, wandered the world for most of that time, aimless. Finally I settled here, in lesser Brittany, with old friends I thought long dead, who were kind enough, loving enough, to give me a home even though I had done them grave disservice years ago. It was they who prompted this account, prodding with the thought that my lack of imagination may be my prime qualification for telling the true story of Arthur, he who was King.

CHAPTER ONE

I took a ride this morning before coming here to write. The horse was old, and not very spirited. We are a good match. A slow walk around the grounds and then back to the barn where I brushed him down and gave him some oats.

The smell of horses and barns, though it is an aroma that would accompany me throughout my life, always reminds me of my boyhood in the steadfast of Sir Ector. The distinct scent of hay, wood and leather, oats and dung, mixed with the wonderful fragrance of the horses themselves still remind me of carefree days when my only responsibilities were easy and well defined. My first chore was mucking out the stalls when my arms were barely strong enough to carry the buckets from the well. From there my duties progressed to the feeding and grooming of Ector's stock.

There were two distinct sets of animals, kept in separate areas and accorded different treatment. The first were the workhorses, stout, strong, and tired. It fell to these creatures to plow the fields and pull the wagons. They were the peasants of the equine world and bore the brunt of our agricultural survival. Ector made sure they were treated well and instilled in all of us who dealt with them a respect for the role they played.

Of course it was the second group that captured my love and admiration. The warhorses were sleek and strong and their days were filled with learning to carry a warrior into battle. Their feed was a different mix, as was the tack they wore and the exercise and training they received. They moved with an aristocratic air compared to their working class cousins. They saw little actual action, at least during my youth, but Ector maintained that someday strong warhorses would be needed again and saw it as part of his duty to maintain a healthy and well-trained stock.

Unlike many boys I never complained about my chores. Kay sulked and grumbled loudly to anyone who would listen, whose number didn't include his father Ector. Even when he began training to be a knight he could not hold his tongue or hide his disdain for simple chores he felt beneath his status.

My manner was a trait I shared with my older brother Lucan. Ten years separated us, and he was always a man in my memory. At twenty he was quiet and easily overlooked. Even then Ector's household would have been chaos without Lucan's steady hand and organizational skills. Though he had trained to be a fighting man, as all able boys were, Lucan's talents ran more toward managing details than fighting prowess. Where other men would have chafed at being stuck with the household duties Lucan was burdened with, he thrived.

The difference in our age assured we would never be close. I loved Lucan, in a distant familial way. We shared a life, and duties, and while we were always cordial we didn't live in each other's hearts. Arthur was more my brother than Lucan.

The summer I was ten it fell to me to brush and groom the workhorses every evening after dinner. Daylight lingers long in June and July and I found the task relaxing and enjoyable and I fell asleep most nights smelling of horse, pleasantly tired and satisfied. If this was my role as part of our community so be it. Even then I believed each member of a society must do his part for the good of all. Since I loved the horses it was easy to hold this opinion. My ideals may not have fared as well in a task I found less agreeable.

It was just dusk one beautiful night when I finished my chores. The horses were all in their stalls and I was putting the last of my tools in their proper places when the barn door banged open, momentarily silencing the song of the night creatures.

"Bedivere, where are you?" Arthur yelled as he ran into the barn. "Come quickly. Lailoken has returned."

Throughout the long years of my life I have heard others tell of the first time they saw Arthur. The accounts varied, of course, depending on the circumstances. Some were introduced to him at formal functions of the kingdom, while others first glimpsed him in battle, covered in blood and sweat. What seemed to hold true in every story of this I ever heard told, is that Arthur arrested their attention with his mere presence. People sensed greatness about him immediately. It garnered him much love and admiration, but also created fear and jealousy.

I never gave it much thought, for I have no memory of our first meeting. We were raised together, as milk brothers when we were but babes and my mother suckled the orphan foundling who had come into Ector's care. He was simply always present for me, so I was always surprised at the impression he made on others.

Now, when I think back on my life much of my childhood is a blur of images, an endless succession of meals, and chores, and play, and Arthur is a part of all of it. Yet that one night in the barn stands out. Perhaps it is simply an old man placing too much emphasis on something that meant nothing at the time. Maybe it is because some of what we overheard later that night and the events of the following day were my first introduction to the ideas that would shape the rest of my life. All I know is that when Arthur called my name and told me our itinerant teacher Lailoken had returned once more it was as if I saw my lifelong friend for the first time.

I turned from the table where I had just laid the horse brushes to see him framed in the doorway, silhouetted by the last red rays of the setting sun. The light picked up the red in his usually brown hair. A halo of bright light appeared around his excited and smiling face. Over the years since then others have told me what I saw was a vision of Arthur wearing the crown of the High King. Merlin himself asserted this, as did Nimué. At the time a thought such as that could never enter my mind. I rubbed my eyes at the sudden brightness and when I opened them again the barn door had closed and Arthur was simply a boy again.

"Did you hear me?" he asked, running the length of the barn and grabbing my arm. "Lailoken is here." His smile and happiness were infectious. Lailoken was Arthur's teacher and they shared a great bond. I think Arthur saw him as more of a surrogate father than he did Ector. Lailoken was always kind to me but we were not close. To tell the truth he frightened me. He represented a wider world than the one I knew, a world where danger and dark things lurked on the borders. I knew someday I would need to find my way in the world outside our valley but I was not as anxious or restless for it as Arthur.

"Come on," Arthur urged, though even in his excitement he made sure to take care of business first. "Are all your chores done? Can I help you finish more quickly?"

"I'm through," I laughed. "Where were you with your offers of help an hour ago?"

"Finishing my own. I had just carried the last of the water into the longhouse when I saw Lailoken arrive. Come, he's in audience with Ector, and Ector has been drinking."

He pulled at my arm and tugged me through the door. Once outside I planted my feet, checking his forward progress.

"We can't go into their private audience," I protested, my natural caution and reticence attempting to throw a shield against his recklessness. "Not without an invitation. We're not adults."

"I know that," he said as he towed me along by my sleeve. "There's a crawl space in the eaves. We can climb the oak that sits behind the longhouse and slip in unnoticed. Lailoken tells such wonderful stories. Haven't you ever wondered what he says when we're not around?"

I had. My mother often said "little pitchers have big ears" when she was trying to stop an adult from saying something in front of us she thought we should not hear. Like all children I wanted to know more about the secret world adults conspired to keep from us. Still, this was not quite enticement enough.

"We should be in our beds soon," I said. "If we're not there they will look for us, and then our gooses will be cooked."

"Ector will give us extra chores," Arthur countered, whispering now that we stood at the foot of the oak. "So what? It's a worthwhile price to pay.

And with that he shinnied up the tree. My eyes followed him into the branches and when he reached down a hand to help me up, I took it in my own and followed where he led.

We scrambled across a massive limb and touched down lightly on the roof. Arthur crawled forward and with no hesitation lifted a loose section of tile and crawled into the opening. It was obvious he had been here before and knew of this secret entrance. I wondered if he had created it, though that sort of sneakiness seemed out of character for him. I discovered later it had been Kay who had shown it to him.

I clambered into the hole and quietly crawled through a narrow space, Arthur's moving feet mere inches from my face. Dust swirled in our wake and I gripped my nostrils shut to stifle a sneeze.

I could hear muffled voices below me; Ector's rang out, loud with ale, punctuated by his raucous barks of laughter. It was only when we reached the end of the passage that I was able to make out

Lailoken's softer chuckle and deeper voice.

Arthur put a finger to his lips to assure my silence, and then gestured through a narrow crack. From this hidden vantage point I could see only Ector's legs and the mongrel dog sleeping at his feet. Lailoken, however, was in full view and a bolt of apprehension shot through me, fear that he would see us.

As always he wore stained traveling leathers. The great green cloak I always pictured him in was nowhere to be seen. He was not wearing his wide-brimmed hat either so I saw his wild, unkempt hair. It was steel gray at the time, shot through with streaks of pure white. Small feathers and talismans were woven into ragged braids. His beard looked much the same. He looked ancient to me then, though all adults seem ancient to boys still wet behind the ears. I guess now he could not have been much more than forty, and perhaps even younger. I have known men whose hair began to go gray in their teens. They always looked older than their years.

In my nervous scrutiny of the scene below me I had failed to actually listen to what was being said. But then a name significant to me lodged in my ear and drew my full attention.

"Bedwyr held him as he died," Ector said.

My eyes grew large and I turned to Arthur, silently mouthing the words, "My father." Once again Arthur raised a finger to his lips and motioned for me to listen.

"Hard to believe it has been nearly ten years." Ector paused and we heard him take a large draught of ale. "I miss him still."

"Bedwyr? Or Uther?" Lailoken asked.

"Both, though I was speaking of Bedwyr mostly. Kings come and go in this land, but true friends are hard to find. A toast to Bedwyr Bedrydant, he of the mighty sinews, a true man."

I never knew my father, and had heard very little about him. My mother simply did not speak of him for the heartache was more than she could bear. I knew he and Ector had ridden together with King Uther, but those times seemed distant to me, more the stuff of legend rather than something a real person could have actually experienced. One person's life experience is merely a story to those who hear it later, and stories change in the telling. After Uther's death Ector and my father returned to this valley and attempted to live their lives peacefully. Bedwyr was a blacksmith by trade. My mother still rents out his forge to the smith who replaced him after a Saxon ax took his life when I was but a babe.

"And how is the little Griflet?" Lailoken asked and I nearly gasped out loud to realize they were talking about me. Bedwyr's old war shield carried the device of a Griffin Rampant, his personal symbol, and the nickname by which he was known by Uther's troops. Ector used the diminutive Griflet to refer to me in his rare sentimental moments.

"He's a good boy," Ector said. "Careful and conscientious in his chores, eager to please. He and Lucan are much alike in that way, though their leanings are very different. If only Kay could be more like both of them in that regard. Bedivere follows instructions well, but has little initiative of his own. He will make a good soldier but he will never be a leader of men."

"That is as it should be for our purposes," Lailoken said. "He will learn to be more decisive as his self confidence grows. How is he with Arthur?"

"Absolutely smitten," Ector laughed, and I hoped Arthur could not see my blush in the darkness.

"Loyal?" Lailoken asked.

"Absolutely. Though they are the same age Bedivere looks up to Arthur and follows his lead in everything. They are well matched."

"Does he follow Arthur blindly?"

"No. Bedivere has more in the way of caution and common sense, which tempers Arthur's tendency to leap without looking. Arthur is often more concerned with what is possible, and in his excitement disregards the dangers in the moment. Bedivere is not as good at seeing what lies ahead, but he is far more cognizant of the here and now. He does not follow blindly, but Arthur is hard to deny when his heart is set on something."

"How so?"

"He has a way of getting what he wants, of getting people to obey his wishes without appearing to ever command. He does this not out of deceit or will. In truth, I don't know if he even knows he does it. The boy has a way of making people love him, simply by being who he is. As a result, everyone attempts to please him."

I chanced a look at Arthur and saw an abashed glow spread across his cheeks. I knew that what Ector said was true, though I could never have stated it so. It was obvious that this was a new thought to Arthur.

"Good," Lailoken said. "It is this quality we need. Its lack proved to be Uther's undoing."

"True," Ector replied. "Uther was respected, and even feared, but very few loved him. In the end that fear and respect could not hold the other kings together."

"No. Fear only causes boundaries and resentments. Britain is carved into too many factions. As long as each kingdom is envious of the other we will always be at risk. The Saxons will overrun us all if we cannot find some way to break down these age-old feuds and petty scrambles for local power."

"You have talked of this before. How do we do what has never been done?"

"Britain needs a king, a true High King of the entire land. A sacred king, like those in the past who were married to the land and husbanded it to greatness. One who can see that all of our fates are entwined, one who puts the good of his subjects before his own desires and need for power.

"This king we wish to forge," Lailoken continued, "must be a strong sword against his enemies, with a sword's ability to cut through layers of meaning and expose the heart of any matter. He must make clear decisions, for the health and safety of all his subjects and not only a privileged few."

"Some will claim he is merely your sword, your bid for power."

"Undoubtedly. That is why we must forge more than simply a sword. A sword, however necessary for protection, divides. We must also forge a crown. It is the circle that protects the land."

"Like a scabbard for the sword?"

"More like a shield. The crown must be protected. The King must stand inside a circle dedicated to his ideals, each link of this circle bound by personal loyalty."

"Oaths to the king."

"More than oaths," Lailoken said. "Oaths can be broken. Each bound by loyalty borne out of love. It is love that unites and breaks down boundaries.

"Love can also cause fear and resentment," Ector said. "Remember, Uther claimed he genuinely loved Igraine. That night at Tintagel proved to be the beginning of the end for him."

"Uther did love Igraine. But he was, for all his strengths, ultimately a selfish man. His love was also selfish. That led to his end, and perhaps to a new beginning for the rest of us."

"I think about those days a lot," Ector said. I saw the top of his head as he stood to refill his mug. Lailoken gestured that he was content with the drink he had. "Mistakes that were made. How we might have done things differently. If we had known Uther's plans that night we might not have engaged Gorlois, though I guess his death didn't lead to anything his continued life wouldn't have."

"Do you think Gorlois would still have been loyal to Uther after being his cuckold?" Lailoken asked.

"That's the part I've never quite understood. If you knew Uther's obsession with Igraine would end his rule, why did you help him? You did help him into Tintagel that night, didn't you? There have been many conflicting stories."

There was silence between them then as Ector resumed his seat. Hiding in the rafters I thought they were simply done talking. I didn't have the life experience to understand that some events simply defy easy description, or that one person's experience and memory can conflict with another's. In my naiveté I believed that history was a simple matter of fact. That what happened was true and the same for everyone. I didn't know that individual memory clouded those facts and gave them new meaning. No one is ever aware of every detail of anything; so we make them up, fill in the gaps. For big events this is even truer. The impact something has on your own life gives great weight to it, and simple facts do nothing to help one understand the meaning of those events.

That's why story survives when history vanishes.

I do not know what really happened the night that Arthur was conceived, though I have heard many stories, from many sources. I have heard the tale from both Merlin and Vivienne, who was Lady of the Lake at that time. I tend to believe their versions of events, though they certainly had their own agendas as well. Some say Uther slipped into the castle and raped Igraine in a fit of drunken lust. Others say the two were madly in love and finally that love drove them to betray their duty to the land. God knows I have seen *that* story unfold often enough in the years since then. A favorite campfire story is the one where Merlin casts a spell to make Uther look exactly like Gorlois so that he could sneak into the castle. There are those who like the sense of magic and mystery to this tale, but I find it hard to credit. I never knew Uther Pendragon, but based on the stories told of him by everyone it is hard to imagine him sneaking around to do anything. He was a man of great passions who took what he wanted and the consequences be damned. It was his greatest strength and greatest failing.

Whatever the truth of that storm-tossed night it set in motion the fate of an entire era.

The death of Gorlois broke apart what little success Uther had in uniting the various factions that existed at that time. King Uriens took his troops and went home, as did Cradlemant and Malaguin. Cornwall fell into the hands of Marcus Conomouros, a soldier who took it by force while Gorlois' troops were leaderless. Meliodos of Lyonesse, who had been thinking of joining the union of kings, retreated to his peaceful kingdom and treated with no one. King Lot of Orkney took Gorlois and Igraine's oldest daughter as wife and left for his northern realm.

Six months after the death of Gorlois a fleet of Saxon ships landed on Britain's southern shore and there was no one to left to stop them. Uther died trying.

My father and Ector were two of the very few survivors of that battle. Ector once told me that Uther died in Bedwyr's arms.

Which of these stories are true? It's impossible to say. The true facts will never be known, and each story contains truth for the one who believes it.

Lailoken coughed and took a long, slow sip of his mead before speaking again.

"Uther's union was finished before that night. By then it was simply a matter of finding new threads and to begin weaving anew. Besides, by then I had received a vision."

"Of Uther's heir?" Ector asked.

"Yes. And of the kingdom he will build."

"I don't know much about magical visions," Ector said as he raised his mug, "except those brought on by good drink. But for some reason, I believe in yours. Perhaps it's just the fancy of an old man who still hopes the future can be better than what has gone before."

"There's nothing magical in that. That's exactly the kind of vision we all need to have."

"How are the other boys?" Ector asked.

"Boys still. I believe that most of them will someday be good men, the kind of men it will take, but there is still a long way to go."

"Ten year olds will be men soon enough. You've spent time with them. Tell me, are they going to be the men we need?"

"I understand your concern Ector. You have more of an investment than most. I believe Kay and Bedivere, thanks to your tutelage, will be fine warriors and good men."

My mouth dropped open to hear Lailoken speak of me by name and to discover Kay and I were part of some plan. I glanced at Arthur in the dark, but he gave no notice. His solemn face was directed to his teacher. I realized then that he had not been mentioned by name. It must have hurt him to be left out.

"My thanks," Ector said, "though I wonder about Kay."

"He's simply feeling his first burst of manhood, Ector. We old men tend to forget how it is to chafe under the weight of feeling like a man without yet being one. He will rein in his behavior soon enough.

"As to the others... it is still hard to say. I have my hopes..."

"What of your visions?"

"A few, but vague. They can all change depending on what we do in the meantime. Uriens has no true heirs, but his bastard son Owain is a strapping lad who is already gifted with a sword. He will have no illusions of ever ruling in his father's stead, unlike the cousins in Orkney."

"Ah yes. Lot's brood."

"Lot still believes he should be high king of Great Britain and refuses to bow to all others, yet he never stirs from his cold, stark lands, except for the yearly attempt to draw the Sword. He does nothing to actually lead his people. Morgause fills the head of Gawaine, their oldest, with tales of Lot's prowess and of how Gawaine will someday succeed him as king. She still hates everyone she believes was involved with Gorlois' death. If she can't be the daughter or wife of a High King she is determined to be the mother of one."

"And Gawaine?"

"He is a good lad, if rambunctious. Even surrounded by Lot's arrogance and his mother's bitterness he is big-hearted and takes great joy in life. He feels the weight of Lot's expectation but shows no great interest in pursuing it. He likes to fight and play, not think and deliberate. He could be one of the pillars of what we plan if we can win his loyalty. It is this I speak of with him when I get the chance; that loyalty to a greater ideal is the true mark of a man and a knight."

"And how do you, of all people, ever get near enough to Morgause's son to speak to him?"

"Like everywhere else. They see me as a wandering teacher. Lot cannot be bothered to look too closely at a lowly holy man and Morgause never saw me closely enough when she was young to make the connection."

"They have a dozen children now, don't they?"

"Only four," Lailoken laughed. "It is the second one, Agravaine, that concerns me. Like his father he is ambitious with little talent, brooding, no sense of humor, and jealous of Gawaine. The other two are but babes."

"It's a shame Leodegrance has no sons," Ector said. "No man is nobler of heart or more loyal."

"Don't underestimate the role daughters will play simply because you have none."

Ector waved a hand to dismiss the idea. Arthur and I were glad. We were more interested in hearing about other boys who would be warriors than we were of girls.

"What of Tristan?" Ector asked.

"He is a difficult child. He seems lost in thought much of the time. A dreamer, though if he takes to the sword the way he has taken to music he will be formidable."

"His parents deaths were a shock to all of us who knew and loved them," Ector said. "I know he can't remember them, but they are an absence all the same. It can't be easy for him being raised in Conomouros' home. Lyonesse and Cornwall should be his by right of birth, but King Mark will never allow it."

"Mark has the makings of a good man," Lailoken answered. "But his best intentions are too often overshadowed by his insecurity. Cornwall thrives, but I fear it may be in spite of Mark. He may have made the attempt at High King if the Irish raiding his shores didn't keep him busy.

"But my greatest hope is for King Ban's son in Benwick. He shows all the promise of a great warrior and a noble soul. I look into the mists and see that he may be the greatest knight in the realm. But..."

Here Lailoken paused and shook his head.

"But?" Ector prompted. Lailoken's voice came out in a strange croak, a tone I had never heard before.

"He will be bound to the King by love, but love will break them all."

"I don't understand why we need the outsiders," Ector went on, unaware of Lailoken's pause.

"What?"

"Why do we need help from the continent? Benwick will never be part of Britain."

"A true king knows the benefit of allies. The continent is a shield for us, and a necessary point of trade. With the right connections our small kingdom could one day span the world."

"You think big. That's a lot of weight on the shoulders of boys."

"Like you said, they will not be boys forever."

I felt a tug on my sleeve. Arthur was nodding to me that it was time to leave. He crawled silently through the eaves in front of me. I chanced a glance back through our peephole, and though the angle was bad, I swear I saw Lailoken wink at me.

Back on the ground outside Arthur was strangely quiet. I felt both anxious and happy to know I was included in the plans of men, though I could not begin to imagine the depths of what we had overheard. I started to say something to my friend but he shushed me with a finger over his lips.

"Go home, Bedivere," he said. "Go to bed. I'll see you tomorrow." With that he rushed away toward his home. I trudged back to mine, upset that I may have done something to offend Arthur.

CHAPTER TWO

The sun sat at its sweltering peak the next day before I finished my morning chores. My mother had been waiting by my bedside wearing a face of relief, worry, and anger when I attempted to sneak in late. I didn't get the thrashing that many boys would have received, but my share of the workload increased dramatically over the next few days.

Though tired from chopping kindling, I walked briskly through the woods on a well-trod path, alternating bites between an apple and a hard chunk of cheese. Arthur was probably already at our hideout, a small clearing near a pond, where we often went to play or loaf. I hoped he was in a better mood than the one I had left him in. His silence was unusual; Arthur was always one of the most cheerful people I've ever known. He was always the center of the universe, and I was so pleased that I had been included in the previous nights conversation that I didn't understand then how being left out had depressed him.

I heard the plinking splash of rocks on water before I came out of the woods. Arthur stood at the ponds edge, a pile of flat stones at his feet. He cocked back an arm and threw with a sideways motion. The rock spun flat across the pond, skipping at least a dozen times before sinking. Light from the noon sun splintered on the overlapping waves and ripples. A satisfied smile creased his face for a moment to quickly be replaced by the same serious expression I had seen the night before.

He heard me exit the woods. I learned very early that it was impossible to sneak up on my friend.

"Bedivere," he said in greeting. He picked up another rock and weighed it in his hand, finding just the right grip before flinging it over the water. I stooped and picked up one of my one.

"Arthur," I said as my fingers attempted to find the balance point like he had shown me. I threw the stone, too hard and at too sharp an angle. It skipped once and rose into a high arc only to plunk noisily and sink when it came down.

"That was something last night, wasn't it?" I said. I could see his mood, but my own interest in what we had heard overrode my caution.

"Yeah."

"Sounds like Ector and Lailoken have big plans. I think they want to create a new High King." Arthur looked at me like this was the most obvious statement in the world. I turned my eyes down and looked for a better rock.

"I think we're going to be trained to be the new High King's knights," I said as I discarded a misshapen stone with no hope of skipping.

"You, maybe," Arthur said. "I wasn't mentioned as part of this plan."

"You too," I said, though I knew no such thing. "The king will need an army of knights."

"All of whom will be the sons of nobles. You and Kay, certainly, as sons of Uther's men. Lucan, probably. These other boys they talked about were almost all the sons of kings. I'm an orphan foundling. I may be a fighting man, or even a squire one day. I'm pretty sure Ector has me lined up to be Kay's squire when the time comes. Kay will love that. He already likes bossing me around too much. If he ends up as a knight of the new king I may be part of the court but only as a servant.

"Besides, it seems Lailoken wants me to be a scholar, like him. Why else would I get lessons from him? But I'll never be a knight. Bastards don't inherit much."

I had no response to this, so I threw another rock with no more success than my first try.

Given everything that has happened in the decades since it may be hard to imagine that we never guessed who Arthur was, or what was planned for him. We were boys then, and Uther and the whole idea of knights and warfare were distant. Uther and his men were legends to us, larger than life figures whom we could not quite imagine as living, breathing people. Even Ector, who we knew was once a great warrior, was now a balding middle-aged man with a paunch and the gout. He was too human in our day-to-day for us to see the man he once was. Arthur was afforded no special treatment, other than his sessions with Lailoken. I certainly didn't have the ability to imagine my friend, who I had mucked out horse stables with, could be the son of the former High King of Britain, and destined to one day wear the crown. If Arthur ever harbored these thoughts or fantasies he never shared them with me.

He threw another stone, and then turned to me without seeing its multiple skips. A smile lit his face as he put a hand on my shoulder.

"Well," he said, "if you're going to be a knight you need to learn to use better weapons than rocks. Come on. Let's begin our training now. When the time comes we'll already be the greatest warriors in the land."

He ran to the forests edge and began scouting the ground under the trees. By the time I joined him he had found two sturdy lengths of wood. Wordlessly he tossed one to me. My hand shot up and snatched it out of the air. He had chosen well. The stick was well balanced, and about the right length to double as a sword. He raised his own in a salute to me. I smiled and touched my stick to his.

With boyish yells of enthusiasm we flailed away at each other in a mock duel.

Though we lacked finesse and anything resembling real skill, we were no strangers to the basics of sword fighting. After all, we had watched men train with weapons pretty much every day of our lives at that point, and this was not the first time we had practiced on our own. Most of what we did was to block and parry each other. Even then we knew this was not completely a game. Actually hitting each other caused real pain and damage. A few small bruises were fine, and could be ignored, but a broken wrist or a punctured eye was to be avoided.

Still, at the time, in our naiveté, we thought this was what warfare was all about. Now, as a veteran of far too many battles and witness to far too many senseless deaths, I can say there is a lot less giggling and laughter when lives are actually at stake. It is the nature of boys it seems, to believe fighting and violence are fun, and the nature of old men to finally know better.

Arthur was the better swordsman, though I occasionally foiled his expectations. We each took our turns at being the evil Saxons, being repelled by the forces of a united Britain. We danced around the pond, weaving in and out of the tree cover, tripping over branches and stones and falling to the ground. Our mistakes would have cost us our lives many times over in real combat. Instead, we climbed to our feet and resumed with renewed vigor.

I don't know how long we fought but it seemed forever. Finally we collapsed in exhaustion on the soft moss-covered ground in the shade of a giant oak. We were swathed in dirt and twigs. Grass stains insulted our clothing and dust turned to mud on our sweat-sheathed skin. We laughed and threw clumps of dirt at each other. Whatever tension Arthur felt had dissipated through our exertion.

"So," he said when we had regained our breath, "do you think you will make a good knight some day?" There had been a far-off look on my friend's face, but when he asked me this question his gaze became direct, focused entirely on me. I knew this was not to be an idle conversation between boys, but the first hint of the types of things men discuss. After a pause to collect my thoughts I responded.

"I don't know. I hope so. We have a lot to learn."

"I think you will," Arthur said and I could not help but beam from the compliment. "You are loyal, and trustworthy. I think any king would be lucky to have you as his right hand man."

Arthur didn't notice the pleasure I took at these words.

"Lailoken has told me that Uther's failure was that his men, no matter how skilled they were as warriors, were never completely loyal to him. That was because he was never completely loyal to them. Lailoken says that Uther put his own needs ahead of the Kingdom, and in that way he was the same as all the other petty kings. A king must know that he represents the land, and that his men are an extension of himself, his equal as men."

"How does a king do that?" I asked. "People must bow down to a king. How can his subjects be his equals?"

"I'm not sure, but Lailoken says that is the task of great men; to rule from among them. He says most kings believe that it is they themselves who deserve the tribute and respect, and for that they forget that they simply represent the land and the people they rule. The power comes from them, and any law that does not promote their well-being is wrong. Knights are the sword a king uses to enforce the law of the land, not a weapon drawn against his people's throats."

"If I were a knight," I said, "I would protect the innocent... women and children, and the sick, and all who need it."

"Would you protect them from your king if he were not an honorable man?"

I didn't know how to answer this. It was an idea beyond my

ability to process. It seemed Arthur was asking me if I would betray an oath to my king if I disagreed with him.

"Are you asking me if I would be a traitor?"

"If a king has betrayed the trust of his people does he deserve the continued loyalty of those sworn to him? They have sworn an oath to what he represents, not to the man himself."

It was obvious Arthur had given this much thought. I assumed it came from his sessions with Lailoken.

"If I were a knight," I said again, "and I swore an oath to my king I would try to live up to that oath." And here I foundered, trying to frame my thoughts. "Unless, the king became a tyrant and foreswore his own oaths to the... to the people and the land in the interest of his own power. Then, as a knight, sworn to the idea of a just king, my oath and my duty would be to protect the land, even if it was from a bad king."

"So, you are saying, that your beliefs, your ethics, would be more important than the man you served?"

"Yes, though if I had the ear of the king I would do everything I could to help keep him true to his oath before trouble arose. That would be the duty of any of his advisors."

"And that is why you will be a good knight, and more importantly, a good man." Arthur climbed to his feet. I could see by the glint in his eyes that, though still serious about our topic, his playful mood had returned. I started to stand as well, but he stopped me with a gesture.

"Kneel," he said.

I didn't know what he was up to, but his smile said to trust him, and trusting Arthur had always been the easiest thing in the world for me. I knelt before him in imitation of the ceremonial gestures I had witnessed. I knelt before him as I had been taught to do in religious ceremonies, with reverence. The sun lit a fire in Arthur's hair as he raised his stick-sword in the air and gently brought it down upon my right shoulder.

"Do you, Bedivere, son of Bedwyr, swear to uphold the laws of the kingdom?" he intoned. "Do you swear loyalty to the rightful king of Britain and its people, to follow his lead as long as it is righteous, to be his sword in matters of war, to be his shield, to be his conscience, to be his right hand in all matters? To follow him until the end of his days as long as his rule is just and fair? To serve the office and not the man?"

I felt the weight of the wood on my shoulder and knew that we were no longer simply playing. Something sacred had descended on the woods. It may be that, as a boy, this was my first real taste of the responsibilities of an adult. It may be that I simply took this act as seriously as only a boy at play can. When I related this story to a priest years later he believed that God had come into that clearing and ordained the act. Merlin has told me that it had been written in the stars and that my answer was a part of a tapestry just beginning to be woven.

I hadn't yet answered when Lailoken appeared. He stepped into our clearing as if he were made of the forest itself. His cloak was mottled shades of green and brown. Leaves and twigs were woven into his gray hair and beard. His eyes seemed to shine with an otherworldly light. Lailoken always scared me just a little. It seemed he could see into me somehow, and knew the guilty secrets I kept hidden in the dark corners of my mind. My first instinct was to leap to my feet and pretend we were not playing at being adults. But something kept me on my knees.

"Be careful how you answer, Bedivere, son of Bedwyr," Lailoken said. "The future of the world is at stake when you make such an oath."

I was surprised that he did not think we were being disrespectful in our play. He was not being facetious, nor was he attempting to belittle our drama. I looked at him for the briefest of moments and saw the import of what we did on his face. I turned back to Arthur and answered.

"I do so swear."

Arthur glanced at Lailoken for guidance. Lailoken gave a barely perceptible nod. Arthur raised the stick sword from my right shoulder to my left and then back again.

"I dub you Sir Bedivere," he said, "first knight of the realm."

I stood then, full of pride. I felt lighter in spirit than ever before though the weight of what I swore now rested on my future. We boys weren't sure what came next so the solemnity of the moment lingered.

"So, Sir Bedivere," Lailoken said, eyes no less serious for all the merry sparkle that danced in them, "how does it feel to be the King's right hand?"

Foolishly, I looked at my right hand. I had no answer to give. I was full of boyish pride, but in truth I felt no different. I had no real idea of what a High King was. I had simply spoken of the loyalty I felt for Arthur. Though I had given that feeling words, it was the same thing I had always felt.

CHAPTER THREE

As I feared when this project began, it has been many weeks since I was last able to put quill to parchment. Starting at the beginning is all well and good, but once you begin, what comes next? When recounting a life, especially one as complex and eventful as Arthur's, what do you choose to tell? What do you leave out? Which small events, innocuous at the time, became the basis for all that came after?

I came here, to this small but comfortable room for days and stared at the paper, remembering a thousand anecdotes; no doubt I have forgotten a million more. I began each day with short walks that grew gradually longer as I avoided my task. I began to blame the weather for my indolence. The heat of August on the continent makes me lethargic.

But the children kept asking me for more stories. They would follow me on my walks and ask me about my life. Was Arthur really seven feet tall? Was Guinevere really the most beautiful woman in the world (other than their own grandmother, of course)? Was I really there when Lancelot slew a giant?

Apparently *someone* is telling stories.

Tristan was always more bard than warrior, though his skills at the latter were among the finest in the kingdom. Yes, in spite of the many tales of Tristan and Isolde's deaths, they are still alive. They are old and happy and as much in love as they ever were. The story of how they came here is part of my tale, though getting there will take awhile. Suffice to say that not all stories end the way one expects.

His grandchildren sit in rapt attention when he spins tales to them. I envy his talent with words. I listen as spellbound as the little ones, and, once they are abed, he and I continue the storytelling. We reminisce and compare memories, laugh at old adventures and cry over old wounds. Simply being in this place, here where I first killed a man, where I lost so much, has stirred my memory. He has helped me to remember, and to focus on what was important.

The Round Table did not exist then, not as a physical object, or even as a cohesive idea, except perhaps in Merlin's head. I'm not sure even he fully foresaw what the Round Table was to become. By the time of the golden age of Camelot, no actual table was large enough to seat all of Arthur's companions. But we were a company still, no matter how many of us there were. That great company had to start somewhere. It was in the early summer of my seventeenth year when those of us who were to form the first core of what was to become Arthur's Knights of the Round Table all met for the first time. It was the first time Arthur and I ever left our home in Ector's valley. It was a summer of travel and discovery. It was the summer we were first tempered in actual combat and the summer of my greatest wound.

It was the summer Arthur became King.

Much of the seven years that followed the day by the pond when Arthur "knighted" me are a blur. Our chores continued to grow and our time for play grew shorter and shorter. When we turned twelve we began our training as warriors in earnest. Each day was spent in some formal instruction designed to turn us into fighting men. Wooden practice swords were traded for sharp blades. We learned the intricacies of armor, and shields. At that time most of our strategy in warfare was still based on the old Roman way. The shield wall was a tried and true way of standing against an enemy. Each man held a shield and a short sword. We learned to form a wall by interlocking the shields, and then stabbing at the enemy from underneath and over top. Soldiers behind the shield wall would stab over the wall with long spears. When done correctly it was a nearly impenetrable defense, one that allowed Rome to conquer most of the known world. Each man would learn to fight in each of the positions. Each man was completely dependent on his fellow soldiers, so we learned to trust each other and to fight as a unit.

But even the best shield wall could at times be broken, so we learned how to stand alone and fight as individuals. We dueled with swords, a far more serious game than the one Arthur and I had played with sticks. We fought with axes, the Saxon's weapon of choice. We learned to parry and attack, to fight with a shield and without, to use two swords, or a sword and a knife. In battle it is easy to lose your favorite weapon. To survive, a good warrior must be able to fight with whatever is at hand.

We learned to ride. Cavalry, as we know it now, didn't really exist when I was a boy. Ector had some vague notions about mounted warfare, and it had certainly been used at different times throughout history. Rome experimented with it in the later days of their doomed Empire. But the strategies and skills that would later make Arthur's Companions the finest mounted warriors in the world had not been developed.

I like to think I played some small role in developing those tactics.

I was never comfortable in the shield wall. It was too close, too confined. Though I learned to fight, I never really had the body mass to hold my position against a concerted onslaught. But on horseback I felt like a young centaur, a single living organism of horse and man.

My natural love of horses blossomed over the years, and more and more of my assigned tasks involved taking care of and learning to train them. I had an uncanny knack for getting them to know what I wanted and to respond to my subtlest command. Truth be told, for the most part I have always been more drawn to horses than to people. They are simpler creatures. A little love and care, sufficient food and a safe place to sleep are all they really crave. People should be happy with as much, but we seem destined to muck it up and make it all more complicated than it really should be.

I have been told, over the years, that I was the finest horseman in Arthur's time. Like in so many other things I would have to defer that honor to Lancelot. But as a horseman, and a warrior, Lancelot was the best on his own. He was coldly efficient at everything he did, and had little patience for the weakness or inexperience of those around him. As a result he never really learned to work with others. While his individual skills outstripped us all, he was never comfortable fighting as part of a group.

It was a routine afternoon in May when the first inkling that our routine was about to change came. Arthur and I sat at a large oaken table in the armory. I was brushing rust from the hundreds of tiny links of chain that made the mail we all wore. Arthur worked oil into the cleaned links. There are more tedious jobs, I'm sure, though none come immediately to mind. We were not being punished with this task. Clean and rust free armor would save our lives many times over in the years to come and it is the responsibility of every warrior to know how to care for his own gear. It is a task learned by all squires. Still, even knowing the reason and the practicality did not make us long for the task to be over any less.

"When we are finished," Arthur said as he hung a now clean hauberk on a wooden rack, "we will saddle our horses and take a long ride. After an afternoon in this stuffy building I could use the breeze on my face. A swim in the pond would be good as well."

"You're covered in enough oil that you will float," I said as I picked at a stubborn spot of rust. Arthur's plan was sound. Once the armor was finished we were free for the day.

"As long as I don't slide off my saddle before we get there." Arthur's voice then took on a teasing note. "You should go to the kitchen and ask Laudine for a skin of wine or ale for our retreat. She wouldn't refuse you. I don't think she would say no to anything you asked of her."

I saw the twinkle in his eyes as I dropped my own to my task. I could feel the blush rise over my cheeks. At seventeen we were both virgins, but Arthur was able to talk to anyone with confidence. I was sure Laudine was sweet on me, based on looks and smiles and words that meant more than they seemed. I was too shy and awkward to know what to do with those feelings. Though there have been women in my life since those adolescent times, my shyness with the fair sex is a trait that has never changed. The stories of many of the Companions are those of great loves and passion. That is not my story.

"You could ask," I deferred.

Arthur rolled his eyes and was about to launch another good-natured jab at me when the door to the armory slammed open. Kay stood there in his practice mail, covered in mud. His face was a thundercloud.

"Wart! Attend me!" he yelled. Wart was the name Kay called his foster brother when he was angry. In later years, when the issues of manhood were well behind us, I heard Kay use the name with true affection. That summer, when Kay was nineteen and still unsure of his skill, and Arthur was his assigned squire, the name was meant as an insult. I watched our plans for the evening dissolve as Arthur rushed to his brother's side.

"What happened?" Arthur asked, genuinely concerned as Kay limped into the armory. Kay lifted his helmet from his head and flung it the length of the room where it crashed against the wall. No one was allowed to treat his equipment so, but neither of us dared to chastise Kay when he was in this black mood.

"I fell!" Kay snapped. "Now loosen my armor. I want out of this wet mess."

Arthur unfastened the large leather belt and then helped lift the heavy hauberk over Kay's head. Kay stood while Arthur unfastened the various pieces of armor and brought them to our worktable to be cleaned.

"This is Eiddelig's fault," Kay ranted. "He started the joust before I was ready. I was barely up to speed and hadn't even set my lance."

Arthur chanced a glance at me and rolled his eyes. It was Kay's custom to blame his mistakes on others. We knew his tirade would continue until he had purged his system.

"Another moment and I would have been set," Kay continued as Arthur unfastened his boots and greaves. "And then, out of nowhere, that old druid of yours appears on the edge of the lists and completely distracts me. If I hadn't been looking at him that braggart wouldn't have unseated me."

"Lailoken is here?" Arthur's face lit up as it always did when his teacher arrived. "When was this? I wasn't expecting him for another month."

"An hour ago. No more than that," Kay said. "Hey, Wart! Where do you think you're going?" Arthur had dashed toward the door, but stopped short at Kay's imperious tone.

"To greet him," Arthur said in measured tones. "Like I always do."

"Not until my armor is clean," Kay said.

"But..."

"And, my horse needs brushed down and tended to as well."

"But..."

"No buts. You're my squire. When I give you an order, you follow it."

"But it will be well after dark by then. Dinner will be over and Lailoken will be off with Ector."

"Do you think Father will allow you to shirk your duty to me just to be with your teacher?" Kay crossed his arms and smirked. "Would he allow anyone else to walk away from their chores just to dally with a friend?"

"No," Arthur grudgingly admitted.

"Or," Kay continued, and here he began to smirk, "you can simply choose to be a scholar and spend your time with books and quills and old men. You won't need the skills of a warrior then and all of this will be unnecessary. Go now, and I'll tell Father to assign another squire to me. One who wants to be a warrior and a man."

"I'll stay." Arthur's voice was level, but I could hear the frustration that underlined his statement.

"Then get to it," Kay said, throwing the last of his soiled outerwear on the floor at Arthur's feet. "The sooner you start the sooner you will finish. Maybe Lailoken and Father will still be up by then." Kay turned his back on Arthur and strode out of the hall, slamming the door behind him. The echo resounded with the finality of truth.

As much as I hated the way Kay treated Arthur, in this case he was not only well within his rights to give orders to his squire, but he was right in what he said. None of us were afforded extra privileges. Even Kay, as son of Ector, had served his time as squire and not been given any special treatment.

To Arthur's credit he said nothing against Kay. He simply gathered his foster brothers' discarded armor and the tools and rags he would need to clean it. He sat down at the table and began his work.

"I can help you," I said. "The job will go more quickly that way."

"Thanks Bedivere," Arthur said. "But Kay is right. This is my responsibility, not yours."

"Aren't you the one who is always talking about helping those less fortunate?" I asked. "I see no one in this armory less fortunate than you right now. How can I not take this chance to do the right thing?"

His eyes sparkled and a grin lifted one corner of his mouth as he passed me a muddy greave.

Even with my help it was very late by the time we finished. Laudine, gods bless her, noticed our absence in the dining hall. She took pity and snuck a rasher of bacon, a pot of stew and half a loaf of bread to us. It wasn't the first time a squire's chores had kept him from a timely meal. She smiled and blushed as Arthur thanked her effusively and began to tell her about my growing prowess as a swordsman. I smiled and blushed and stuttered and could barely meet her eyes.

It was just dark by the time we finished the armor and the grooming of Kay's horse. The night was clear and still warm when we left the barn. A lot of people were still out and about. That wasn't that unusual on a summer evening, but something felt different. There was energy in the air. A barely concealed excitement underscored the snatches of conversation we overheard. The closer we came to Ector's longhouse the more we felt it ourselves.

"I hope Lailoken is not closed off in the study with Ector," Arthur said. "I really don't want to wait until morning to see him."

"There's something going on," I said, referring to the activity and snatches of conversation we heard. "Lailoken has brought tidings of some kind. I wonder if the Saxons have returned."

"I doubt it," Arthur said. "It isn't fear we are seeing around us. If the Saxons were back we would still be in the armory preparing."

Neither of us had ever actually seen a Saxon, or any of the invading tribes from the continent we tended to lump under that name. We knew people of Saxon blood, of course. Even by the time of our youth enough of the invaders had come to our shores to intermarry and settle here. Nearly every British settlement had some Saxon blood tending the soil. Uther's final battle did not stop the barbarians from coming to our shores, but the cost he had inflicted in lives and gold had slowed them down for a time. Though we were not many days ride from the River Glein, which ran into the sea, a deep, thick forest surrounded our valley. We had spent many relatively safe years secluded in its green depths.

We saw a number of people sitting on the portico of Ector's hall as we rounded the corner of the longhouse. Ector's loud laughter rang out. My brother Lucan was tapping an ale keg that sat on a small table nearby; the second one from the look of things. Morvawr and Turmyr, Ector's senior men at arms, stood nearby. They were relaxed and obviously not on duty. Lailoken chuckled softly in a large wooden chair next to Ector. He held a tankard of ale and thick white foam clung to his mustache. Most surprising of all, Kay leaned against a column, smiling and drinking as well.

We paused, not sure what was happening, and even more uncertain if we were welcome. Ector saw us then and stood, beckoning us.

"There you are!" he yelled. "Come on lads, join us. There's ale and stories, and a great adventure ahead of us. Enjoy tonight, for tomorrow we begin to prepare, and that means work for everyone."

We mounted the steps to the porch. I can't speak for Arthur, but I was more than a little surprised, and very nervous. We had never been included in this sort of informal gathering before. Ector and the others, except for Kay, had always been adults to us, figures of authority. To be included in this circle of men felt strange; it felt heartening, but also a little intimidating.

I pulled a draught of ale for myself and one for Arthur while he greeted Lailoken. We perched on the railing and sipped at the thick, bitter brew.

"Get a good night's sleep, lads," Ector said. "It may be your last for awhile."

"What's going on?" Arthur asked. He directed his question to Ector, as was proper, but his gaze kept returning to his teacher. I watched as Lailoken openly appraised Arthur, and then fixed his eyes on Kay. Something clouded his visage as he looked at him. I shuddered when those piercing gray depths swept toward me. I quickly looked away, unable to bear the scrutiny.

Ector slapped his thigh and boomed.

"What's going on? We're traveling, son. I thought perhaps I would never leave this vale again, but the time is finally upon us."

"Traveling?" Arthur smiled and glanced at me. "Where? When?"

"As soon as we can make preparations," Ector said. "By the end of the week, at least. There is much to be done. If the two of you had made it to dinner," and here he looked at Kay, "you would have already heard the details.

"We are traveling to little Brittany, on the continent, to visit King Ban of Benwick and renew our alliances there."

"King Ban?" Arthur said. "We'll be taking a sea voyage?" My stomach clenched at the very idea.

"A short one, yes," Ector said. "Ban is an old friend. His kingdom has provided a buffer against the barbarians for many years now. It has been too long since we have had personal contact."

"Who all is going?"

"Representatives from many of the petty kings. There will be a great many of us before it is all over. We're meeting Leodegrance and Lot along the way. Mark is sending an envoy to meet us at the coast before we depart. Several representatives of the smaller kingdoms of Brittany will meet us in Benwick."

"Yes, but... who's going from here?" Both Ector and Lailoken smirked at Arthur's impatience.

"We have not drawn up all the lists, but as many as we can spare." Ector took a long sip of ale, draining his mug. He motioned to Kay for a refill. "Lucan will essentially run the estate while we are away. The crops are planted, though there is still much to do to make sure they come in this fall. The tenant farmers will be staying of course. We need to leave men here to protect the settlement, though I fear they will be mostly bored while the rest of us are away. We will take as many of the household troops as we can."

"And their squires?" Arthur asked.

"Of course," Ector laughed. "Who else will do the work on the trip? Don't worry boy. You and Bedivere are going."

"Are you going, Lailoken?" Arthur asked.

"I'm sorry, Arthur. I have other responsibilities this summer," Lailoken said. We both watched as Arthur's disappointment showed. "I will be with you for the first part of the trip, but I will not accompany you as far as the Shrine of the Sword."

I'm sure my face lit up with as much wonder as Arthur's. We had grown up hearing tales about the Shrine of the Sword and of the magical lake of Avalon, on whose shores it stood.

Deep in a forest on the southern reaches of the land of Cameliard was Avalon itself, an island in the middle of a great lake. This was the home of the Lady of the Lake, the high priestess of the old religion, and her many acolytes. The stories of the magic there were told around every hearth in Britain, and had been from the beginning of man.

But a new mystery, a beautiful sword, plunged deep into the

heart of a great stone, had appeared there within living memory. Writing covered the stone, ancient runes and Latin both. Each said the same thing; "Whosoever pulls this sword from this stone is the rightful King of all Britain." Along with the great circle of standing stones near the old Roman hill fort Sorviodunum and the island of Avalon itself, it was among the most famous, and most magical of places in all of Britain. Unlike its ancient counterparts though the stories said the Shrine had appeared only months after the death of Uther, right around the time of my birth, actually. All children of my generation could repeat the story by heart.

And here I must urge caution. What I recall here is not true history. This is the story we heard as children. Since that time I have heard many different versions, each with some small variation on the basic information. Even those who were actually there remembered things differently. I believe the truth lies somewhere between the words.

Each of the scattered kings of Britain, the story said, those who had once followed Uther and now ruled their own small provinces, received a summons from Merlin. Merlin was reputed to be a great wizard, and the stories that were told about him even then are too numerous to recount. Whatever the truth of his powers, he had been Uther's most trusted advisor. Whether it was out of respect for Merlin's position with Uther or fear of his power I do not know, but most of the petty kings answered the summons.

They gathered in a clearing in the great forest near the shores of Avalon with their retainers on a bright summer day. Tensions ran high as each king stated his position and the reasons he alone should become the High King of Britain. Lot and Uriens were close to bloodshed when Merlin appeared.

It is said a bolt of lightning struck the clearing from a clear blue sky. Thunder shook the glade and when everyone looked to see what the lightning had hit, Merlin stood there in a nimbus of light accompanied by his familiars. Some say a crow, but others have told me it was a hawk, or an owl, or a great bear. He held a sword in his right hand. Streaks of skyfire arced along its length. In front of him stood the stone.

"Listen to me, you petty kings of Britain," Merlin said in a voice too much like the thunder. "This land is under attack from without and in danger from within. All around us our shores are breached by barbarians. Saxons from the south and east. The Irish in the west. Scots and Norsemen in the north. Each of them wants our crops, our daughters, and our land. And here we stand, more interested in killing each other over ancient feuds than we are in protecting our ancient home. The Romans came and ruled us because we acted like children fighting over scraps thrown from a table. Now that they are gone we still act as children.

"No more.

"Britain needs to be united. For all of our varied past we must see that we are one people. If we cannot stand to together we will all die alone. Our warriors must be a shield to our kingdom, a protective circle within which we will know peace and prosperity. There must be a man in the center of that circle, one who wears the crown that is

Britain, one who we can all follow, one who wields the sword of justice.

"This is that sword!" Merlin declared. He slashed at the air and thunder rumbled again. "This sword is Excalibur; forged in the Otherworld by Gofannon, smith of the gods. The heart of this land has been folded into its blade. I am but a courier. I bring this weapon here to give to the one hand worthy to wield it. Only he who is destined to be High King may use this blade."

At that point, it is said, Lot had the temerity to speak. He stepped forward, hand extended expectantly.

"Then hand the sword to me, wizard," Lot said. "Clearly no one else here has the right."

"That right would be mine!" shouted Uriens.

"Your right is no greater than my own!" Malaguin cried as he pushed his way to the front of the throng.

"The blood of Britain and the blood of the Romans both run in my veins," Conomouros said. "Who better to bring back the glory of our past?"

"Shut up, Mark!" Lot sneered. "Rome raped us then abandoned us. You have no right."

"What does a northerner like you know about the Saxon predations on our southern shores?" Uriens shouted at Lot. "Will you continue to hide in the Orkneys when the invaders sail?"

"Men have died for lesser insults," Lot said, and his hand went to his sword.

"Enough!" Merlin shouted. The force of his voice rumbled in the clearing. The petty kings stepped back from a power they did not understand. When silence returned, Merlin continued.

"This is why none of you are fit to carry this sword. Each of you is divisive. None of you can heal this land. Each of you is a wound in the heart of Britain."

At this Merlin raised Excalibur above his head plunged it into the stone that stood before him. There was a flash of blinding light, and each of the kings would later report they heard what sounded like a scream of agony from the very ground they stood on. When their vision cleared Excalibur stood lodged deeply in the stone. Steam hissed around its blade and red, molten rock poured out like blood from a fresh wound.

"Your foolishness will be the death of Britain," Merlin said. "This land will bleed until he who is rightful High King is able to draw that blade. Only then will healing begin." A cold wind blew through the glade, whipping Merlin's cloak around him.

And then he was gone.

Many stories have been told of that day. Leodegrance is the only person I have spoken with about it who was actually there (other than Merlin, of course). While he confirms most of the events, he assures me there wasn't a bear.

After Merlin's departure the kings stood, stunned by what they had witnessed. Finally it was Lot, of course, who went to the sword and gripped the handle. His hand recoiled from the heat. Undeterred, Lot grabbed the sword again and pulled.

The sword didn't budge. Lot pulled and pulled and grew angrier and angrier. Each of the kings tried with no better luck. Eventually, unable to decide what to do and unable to agree on anything, they all went home.

I find much of the tale hard to swallow. Thunder and lightning from a clear blue sky? A sword plunged cleanly into a solid piece of rock? The land screaming when it was struck? These all seem to me, still, as fanciful stories blown all out of proportion from the truth of what actually took place. I was not there, and today no one who was is left alive to speak the truth of what happened.

But I have held that sword. I have felt its power.

It didn't take long for the story to circulate. The women from Avalon built a shrine around the sword. People from all over Britain began to make pilgrimages there. Many tried to draw the sword. All failed. The following summer the petty kings returned, and annually after that. The attempt to draw Excalibur became more ritualized each year.

Merlin had disappeared.

Oddly enough, though there continued to be disputes, open warfare between the kings ceased. It was if by some common agreement, they were waiting. The sword, even then, was acting to unite the British people. It symbolized something better. Its existence reminded everyone of Merlin's words. It made everyone realize our island nation was wounded and needed to be healed.

In the face of continued Saxon raids and difficult times, it represented hope.

Of course I had thought of none of this while sitting on Ector's porch in my seventeenth year with a mug of ale in my hand. I was young enough then to still believe in magic. It took becoming an old man to believe it once again.

CHAPTER FOUR

Rain patters on the roof of my room this morning. The day is gray and I am forced to write by the light of a candle instead of the sun and warmth that usually accompanies me. My right arm aches, as it usually does in weather such as this; I am used to it. It is the aches and pains of age that still feel new to me. Every day it seems I discover new ways to remind me I am not the man I used to be. In my youth and manhood I would ache after a hard days work, or exercise with my sword, and certainly after a battle. But my muscles were hard and I was always able to shake it off. This morning I realized it winded me to walk here, and the only burden I carry is that of the years on my shoulders.

I'm getting fat.

Oh for the days when my body was mine to command and not the other way around.

We began preparations for our journey early the next morning. Planning for the traveling needs of a large group of people is not an easy task. Though we really didn't expect trouble on the road, nonetheless we needed to be ready. Armor and weapons were prepared and extras of everything were packed. Clothing, tools, gifts for those we were about to meet, medications and first aid supplies, a million and one tiny details were considered. It is impossible to plan for every eventuality on a trip of that magnitude, yet any one small factor forgotten could cause delay and hardship.

Not only did we have to plan for the comfort and health of the people who were going, but of the horses as well. The warhorses that would be ridden by the fighting men, as well as the packhorses and those who pulled the wagons we would leave behind at the shore when we crossed the Channel to the continent. Extra horses to replace those who tired out or fell ill or injured. Plenty of grazing would be available for them at that time of year, but several wagons were given over to hauling oats and straw just in case.

Ector was a master at planning. I learned then that he had been Uther's seneschal. This was not the first time he had organized the movement of people. I took naturally to the task, as did Kay, surprisingly. Ector recognized my proficiency and interest, especially in the deployment of the horses. I spent many hours with him that week, watching and learning skills that would serve me well throughout the rest of my life. Since then I have planned the movement of thousands of men and horses in the campaigns that would win Britain for Arthur.

The day we left dawned cloudy and humid. Heavy mist clung to the ground. Everything felt damp and clammy. Arthur and I sat astride our horses near the head of the entourage. Even though the details of troop placement and traveling order had been well established, Ector still shouted instructions and governed every detail. I saw him wince periodically; pain from his gout I assumed. But in those moments as he governed from horseback I saw the echo of the warrior he had once been.

Arthur watched him intently. I knew my friend well enough to know that nothing of the process escaped his notice, from the strategy inherent in the organization of the move, to the way Ector commanded without being imperious. He was making notes to himself about how to lead. It was a habit instilled in him by Lailoken and I don't think Arthur even knew he was doing it. It came as naturally to him as breathing.

Lailoken, sitting on a dumpy mule, watched Arthur as closely as Arthur watched everything else.

Finally, after much confusion and jostling, everyone was in place. Silence settled over the homestead. Ector gave the procession the once over, looking for last minute changes. He smiled to himself as everything met with his approval. He turned to Arthur, Kay, and I.

"Ready, boys?" he asked. The excitement on our faces was all the answer he needed. He waved an arm in the air and shouted.

"Forward!"

With that word, the great trip began. Those who remained behind were arrayed along the road out of the vale. They cheered and waved goodbye to loved ones. I saw envy on the faces of many of those who were not going. My mother openly wept, much to my embarrassment. We had not spoken of it, but I knew she was thinking of my father. She had lost her husband to a Saxon ax, and now her youngest son was preparing for the life of a warrior. She knew it was the way of things, and that men needed to learn to fight to protect our home from the invaders. It didn't stop her from grieving the past as well as what may come. Lucan wrapped a protective arm around her narrow shoulders.

Laudine broke from the throng as we rode by. She came to my horse and handed me a package. It was still warm from the ovens and smelled sweet and sticky and wonderful. When I leaned down to take the parcel from her she stood on tiptoe and brushed her lips across mine. They were also sweet and sticky and wonderful. I blushed furiously as Kay whooped and teased. Arthur simply smiled. I tried my best to ignore Kay as I waved goodbye to Laudine.

I never saw her again.

The clouds thickened quickly that morning and we were not an hour from home when they opened up and released a soul-drenching rain. The wind swelled and drove the precipitation sideways. We had all packed cloaks, steeped in wax and oil to make them waterproof, but none of us were mentally prepared to be that cold and wet in the first days of June. The worst of the squall was over quickly, but the rain settled into an all day affair. The storm slowed us down enough so that by nightfall we were still miles from where we had hoped to be. It was the first of countless days of sodden discomfort on horseback I was to endure in my lifetime.

We made camp that night in a wet clearing with no hope of a fire or hot food. I helped take care of the horses while others pitched tents and dug latrines. Once the camp was established and guards were posted we settled down to cold rations. Laudine's sweets were the high point of the evening.

After our rather meager meal we sat huddled under cloaks. Though we were wet and chilled, this was still our first adventure away from home, and our excitement was undiminished. Arthur and I sat with Kay and Eiddelig and talked well past the time we should have been asleep.

I may have given the impression before that Kay was imperious and insufferable. He certainly could be, but that was not his nature all the time. He could be warm and genuinely funny, and underneath his sometimes harsh treatment of Arthur there was genuine love. Many of his faults at that time could be chalked up to youth. They are all easy to forgive knowing now the man he eventually became.

"What do you think Lot will be like?" Arthur asked.

"Old," Kay said. "Old and mean, like a hungry dog."

"Or a wolf," Eiddelig added. "I wouldn't dismiss him too quickly. He didn't become a king of men by being a weakling or a complete fool."

"Easy to be a king in the Orkney's," Kay laughed. "All of his subjects are sheep. Actual sheep. Any mutt can look like a wolf up there."

"I hear it's a hard land," Arthur mused.

"Only for the sheep," Eiddelig laughed. "They live in constant fear of either the stew pot or being some warrior's bride. Of course, it makes complete sense. Have you seen any Orkney woman? They all look like their men, right down to the beards."

None of us, Eiddelig included, had ever met anyone from the Orkneys.

"I've heard Queen Morgause is beautiful," I ventured.

"She's a cow," Kay said. "Though I guess that looks good compared to the sheep. Better beef than mutton any night."

"She was Igraine's oldest daughter," Arthur said. "Everyone knows Igraine was beautiful. How can her daughter be anything but?"

"Maybe once," Kay said. "But she's been spread under Lot for years now. She's borne forty-seven children to the old goat. Whatever beauty she may have been, she's a cow now."

We were still laughing and talking the talk of untried boys when Ector and Lailoken came by our tent.

"Still awake, lads?" Ector said. "You should all turn in soon. Tomorrow is a long day, and I have a task for you. We are far enough away from our own land that I want to start sending scouts out ahead of the main body. I don't anticipate any problems, but it is always good to know what lies ahead. I have chosen some other, experienced men to go, but I think it's time you boys started earning your keep. Have your gear and rations ready and be ready to ride out at the crack of dawn tomorrow."

"Really?" Kay said.

"Yes, Kay." Ector said. "All four of you. Warok will be the senior member of the scouting party, and you will all listen to his every word as if it came straight from the mouth of God. Do you understand me?"

We all nodded our eager assent.

"Kay?" Ector asked, making sure his willful son understood that he was serious.

"Yes, Father," Kay said, embarrassed to be singled out.

"All right then," Ector said. He looked at Arthur and I and added, "And you two will listen to Kay and Eiddelig as though they were Warok, right?"

"Yes," we both said.

"Good." Ector clapped his hands together. "You two get to sleep. Kay, Eiddelig, I have some specific instructions for you before I go."

We all stood. Arthur and I stayed behind and gathered up our belongings in preparation to retire. Lailoken stayed with us while the others walked a short distance away and conferred.

"Are you ready for this?" Lailoken asked. He nodded approval to our affirmative reply. He gestured for us to sit with him. We did so and then waited for several minutes in anticipatory silence. Lailoken stroked his beard and stared into some inner distance. He was still as a stone, a part of the land on which we sat. He exuded silence like a palpable thing. The sounds of the night, bugs and birds, water dripping from wet leaves and the wind through the trees, all seemed to still. There was no magic here, simply the anticipation of our focus on that old man.

Finally he spoke. His voice was soft, yet resonant. He spoke to Arthur and I (though I suspect it was mostly to Arthur), but his words carried a gravity that made me think he was speaking to everything that was. At the time I didn't really understand half of what he said. Only later did much of its meaning become clear.

"This may be the most important summer of our lives," he said.

"There have been plans in motion for many years now. Forces at work, pieces put on the board. It is time to start moving those pieces. Britain can no longer wait. The forces of our enemies are gathering on the horizon of time. The relative peace we have known is coming to an end, and we will be dealing with what is coming for many years. If we are to survive those years we must be a united kingdom. There must be a High King. The sword must be drawn. If not this year, then the next. It is still early, but we cannot wait much longer."

He looked up at us then, coming out of his reverie.

"You boys will be a part of what is to come," he said. "Whether you are ready for it or not. It is your time. You are doomed to live this part of history, and whatever role you play, be warned; dark days lie ahead.

"But there is hope. Hope that we can be one people. That we can see beyond the trifling feuds and slights of the past. That we can stop fighting wars against each other that should be over and begin to fight the war that is bringing death us all.

"This journey will hopefully be a new beginning for Britain. You boys will be meeting many others on this trip. You will meet many of the kings, some of whom still hold hope they will be the one. I tell you this now. None of the petty kings will ever draw the sword. They are still too invested in old wounds to heal this land. The hope lies with their children. You boys... you men will meet many of the sons and daughters of the old kings during your travels. If my work has been done well, they will not be mired in the past, or chained with the aspirations of their sires.

"Talk with them. Get to know them. They are your future allies. They are the men who will stand with you in the shield wall against the invaders. They are your companions, your brothers, your family, the mothers of your children. You are all the future of Britain, but without unity there will be no Britain. Make them your friends before old disputes can make them your enemies. If we can achieve that, then by summer's end the land can begin to heal and grow strong.

"Now then," Lailoken said as he rose to his feet. "We should all get some sleep. I too have an early morning."

"Everyone does," Arthur said. "Breaking camp is time-consuming."

"I'm afraid I won't be here for that," Lailoken said. He held up a hand to forestall Arthur's query. "Other duties call me away. I will not see you again until after you return from Benwick."

"But..." Arthur began.

"No, Arthur, there is no helping it," Lailoken said. "You will be fine without my counsel. It is time you started to listen to your own advice." He glanced at me then. "Tempered of course by listening to the wisdom of trusted allies. You will be fine. You do not need me at this time."

"I will always need you, Lailoken." Arthur hugged the old man and then watched as he walked away into the dark. Without another word Arthur and I retired to our tents.

Since then I have developed the soldiers skill of being able to sleep anywhere, at anytime. The body learns the value of rest when it doesn't know when it will have the opportunity again. That night, however, I barely slept a wink.

We were up well before dawn. The sky was clear, but the air was a thick miasma of morning mist, promising humidity for the day. Arthur and I helped Kay and Eiddelig don their riding armor, and then we dressed in our own, less complicated gear. Mail shirts over thick leather jerkins. Stiff leather bracers on our forearms and tall leather boots. We each had a helm attached to our saddles if needed. The rest of the camp was just beginning to stir when Warok appeared. Warok was Ector's horselord, though he hated that term. He used the title Marshal when he used any title at all. I had spent a lot of time with him, and most of what I knew about horses at that time I had learned under his tutelage. He surveyed us and then commanded us to mount and ride out.

While I was excited about my first military foray, limited to scouting as it was, it felt strange to me not to have prepared my own horse. Usually I would have been responsible for Eiddelig's mount as well as my own, but since we were riding out as well, other, younger boys had saddled the horses and prepared them for the day.

Before mounting I rubbed Butter's forehead and whispered greetings into his soft ear. He nickered back at me, and stood still while I swung into the saddle.

Yes, my horse's name was Butter. Not very awe-inspiring I realize, but he was my first horse and I named him for his rich creamy color when I was twelve and he was but a foal. He served me well for years and sired a line of colts envied the world over.

We ate while we rode, oatcakes and a chunk of ham. Water

skins hung from our saddles. By the time the sun finally rose over the horizon to our backs we had covered several miles.

There were twelve of us in all. We four were the youngest and least experienced of the scouts, so we stayed close to Warok. The other horsemen spread out, creating a line with us in its center. No one of them ever strayed so far as to be completely out of sight of at least one other. The morning was pleasant, and we really didn't expect any trouble. The few bandits who roamed the hills would never attack a group of mounted men, and we would already know about any large group of Saxons this far inland. Still, Warok never let us forget the seriousness of what we did. This was a relatively safe training exercise, but it would not always be so. Warok constantly asked us to appraise our surroundings and watch for the smallest details. He would question us about which areas we passed would have been the best places for an ambush or a trap, and chastised us when we didn't recognize them ahead of time.

Arthur showed a good eye for this sort of thing, and when Warok put him to the test he provided solid answers with a head for strategy. Arthur would outline his reasons why a foe would choose a likely spot, then provide swift answers for how to respond if he was on the receiving end of those tactics. He wasn't always right, and Warok would point out the flaws in his reasoning, but all in all, his instincts were sound.

Kay didn't fare as well. Neither did Eiddelig or I for that matter. At first Kay would scowl when Arthur got something right that the rest of us had missed, but as the morning wore on I began to see looks of grudging respect on his face.

"There." Arthur said, and pointed to a place along the side of our trail.

"Why?" Warok asked.

"There's a small rise and then a dip behind it," Arthur reasoned. "The small scrub around the top could hide a number of men. If they were quiet, they could easily surprise anyone passing by."

"What about a group like us?"

"Not so easily. We're spread out," Kay said. "They couldn't surprise everyone."

"True," Warok said. "What about if we were grouped together?"

"With all of the noise we're making," Arthur said, "we would never know they were there until it was too late."

"They would be foolish to attack us though," I said, the first opinion I had ventured.

"What?" Arthur said. "Why?"

"Bedivere is right," Warok said. "But I'd like to know why he thinks so."

"Well," I said, and then pointed to the area behind the brush-covered rise. "We're mounted. Even if we couldn't fight we could easily outrun them on this side of the rise, before they ever reached our position. We can't really see what's on the other side, so I can't be sure, but it looks like a pretty steep hillside, covered with a lot of rocks. If we decided to fight back there's no place for them to run to, or to hide. We could run them down in seconds."

"Excellent," Warok said.

"I never even considered the advantage of the horses," Arthur said. "It's so obvious." I was more pleased with Arthur's approval than with Warok's.

Three days passed in this fashion. We reported back to Ector on a regular basis and I was surprised at how long it took the rest of the train to cover the ground we had scouted. The wagons and those who walked slowed our progress to a crawl. Men on horseback could make the trip in a fraction of the time.

Each night we followed the routine of setting up camp, eating, posting guards and sleeping. Since Arthur and I were on scout duty and needed to rise early we were excused from picket duty at night.

On the fourth day out we had paused with Warok to study a potentially dangerous stretch of ground. Kay was giving a surprisingly good analysis of the strategic possibilities of the area when the sound of a running horse drew our attention. A lone rider approached, one of ours. We moved forward as a group to meet him. He drew along side Warok.

"What is it, Kynon?" Warok asked.

"The Roman road," Kynon said. "We found it. It's about a mile ahead."

"Good," Warok said. "Any sign of other travelers?"

"Not recently. The others are gathered at a springhouse along the side of the road. Fresh water and shade." Kynon smiled. The summer heat was getting to all of us in our extra gear.

"Let's join them, then," Warok said. He whistled a shrill tone and the other outriders we could see wheeled their mounts toward us.

Our paths converged and we traveled on to the Roman road. I had heard much of these great feats of engineering, but had never seen one. At that time, though they were beginning to deteriorate from lack of maintenance, the Roman highways were still mostly intact and provided the easiest traveling across Britain.

Even though Arthur attempted to keep the roads in good repair during his reign it was a task beyond us. The stonemasons who cut and fit the blocks were long gone, and it seemed the knowledge of how to rebuild those roads had gone with them. Today, while you may still see their remnants, the desiccated veins of the Roman Empire, most of them are gone or well past using. Even then, on the day I first saw them, decay had set in. Still to my inexperienced eyes, used as they were to animal trails and dirt paths rutted out by wagon wheels, they appeared to be the engineering work of gods.

Though we stayed vigilant we were all allowed a break to drink, eat, and rub cold water over out faces and heads. A large oak grew over the springhouse and the shade was more than welcome. The horses were allowed to graze on the bountiful grass. After a short break Warok called four of the riders, including Kay and Eiddelig, to his side.

"Don't tire your mounts," he said, "but return to Ector and let him know the way to the road is clear. Escort the party back here."

"What about them?" Kay asked, gesturing to Arthur and I.

"They can stay," Warok said. "You won't need their assistance for your task. Those of us here need to check along the highway to our north. Since we're traveling south we don't need any surprises coming up behind us in the next day or so. Now go. The sooner Ector gets here, the sooner we can get to the Shrine."

Arthur and I took time to explore our location after the riders left. We had never seen the kinds of artifacts that adorned the rest stop. A Roman mile marker stood next to the road, its Latin markings scoured to illegibility by centuries of rain. A pile of rocks—Kynon told me it was called a herm—was piled outside the springhouse. Remnants of food, a few copper coins, small carvings and other objects littered the ground next to it, offerings from pilgrims to the spirit of the well. There was a small shrine with a worn sculpture of the Virgin Mary with similar offerings strewn about.

Warok had assigned four of the men to stay at the springhouse to await Ector's arrival. Arthur, Kynon and I were ordered to mount up. We were going to ride north along the road for a few miles to see if anyone else was traveling.

"Uriens' train should be traveling this way from Gorre," Warok said as we clopped along the stone road. "If he can be bothered to make the trip. There is no sign that a group as large as his has already passed this way. We may meet his group or his outriders."

We hadn't traveled far when his words proved prophetic. From over a rise in the road, just out of sight, we heard voices. They were loud, engaged in some sort of banter. Whoever it was, they were not trying to hide their passage.

Warok called us to a halt with one upraised hand. As part of our training we all learned the art of silent communication. With a few well-practiced gestures Warok conveyed his plan. Kynon and Arthur moved quickly to the far side of the road and took cover behind a stand of trees. Warok and I did the same on our side. Drainage ditches ran along both sides of the highway giving us plenty of cover yet allowing us a clear view of the top of the rise where the men would approach. If the party were a group of Uriens' scouts, or other non-threatening travelers, we would greet them. If they were bandits, their number and arms would determine if we would confront them or ride for reinforcements.

The second option proved unnecessary. Nine men rode into sight, still chatting carelessly. They were Britons, at least. They were armed, mainly with swords, though a couple of them carried spears. They were armored and well dressed enough to assume they weren't brigands.

From the corner of my eye I saw Warok scowl in disgust. I'm fairly sure my expression matched his, and for the same reasons. These men rode the sorriest looking bunch of horses I had ever seen. Obviously they had never been trained as warhorses. My immediate assessment was that they pulled wagons and plows far more often than they had men on their backs. They may have been saddle broken, but they were not used to the task.

It seemed to me the men were no more used to riding than the horses were to carrying them. They all looked awkward in the saddle, not seated well, and sore from the experience.

Warok signaled for me to follow as he lightly spurred his horse from behind our cover and onto the road. Arthur and Kynon joined us from the other side. Warok had one arm held up in greeting and his other extended to his side, far from his sword, indicating we approached peacefully. The rest of us, likewise, made no motion toward our weapons.

The men halted ineptly, surprised at our sudden appearance. A few of them started to reach for their weapons, but their apparent leader shouted them down before any steel was drawn. There were a few moments of confusion as they attempted to bring their mounts into some semblance of order. It would have been laughable if it weren't so pitiable.

"Hello," Warok shouted. "I am Warok, Marshall to Sir Ector, former seneschal to Uther the King. We bring greetings from Ector who travels on the road behind us on the way to the Shrine of the Sword."

"Greetings, Warok Horselord," the leader shouted back. Warok rolled his eyes at the title, but I could see the men visibly relax. We rode forward, still cautious, but openly friendly.

"I am Ivor," their leader said as we approached. "We are the advanced scouts for King Uriens of Gorre. The King's train is on the road behind us. We also travel to the Shrine."

"Good to meet you, then," Warok said. "There is a springhouse not far ahead where my companions wait. We are meeting Ector and the rest of our party there. Shall we wait here with you for Uriens?"

I noticed Warok didn't use the term king when referring to Uriens. It was probably due to his plainspoken nature more than any intended insult. Ector had as much right to the title of king in his own lands as Uriens, but he was one of a very few of Uther's landed men who didn't claim the name. There was a frown on Ivor's face, but he didn't make an issue of it.

The small talk continued. Ivor sent two men back to inform Uriens of the situation. I spent the time observing the first people not of our homestead I had ever met. They were much like us in dress. Ivor, though easily understandable, spoke with an accent, at least to my ears.

The men with him were all in their mid-twenties, except for one. I had noticed him first not because of his age, which was nearer to my own, but because he was having more trouble with his mount than any of the others. The horse seemed agitated by something, and would not stand still. The rider tried too hard to control him. For every movement of the horse he overcompensated, pulling too hard on the reins and throwing his body weight around. His every action distressed the poor creature even more. He was trying to manhandle the beast, and any test of strength with a horse is doomed to failure.

Suddenly the horse reared onto its two hind legs. The rider cried out and slipped down to the side of the saddle as his mount took off at a gallop. He lost his helmet when the horse jumped the ditch and darted across a field. Though he was holding on it was obvious he would never regain the saddle. At any moment he was going to slip to the ground, to be trampled or dragged.

Without hesitation Arthur and I spurred our own horses into action. We leapt the ditch and sped across the field in pursuit. Our horses were in much better shape, and trained for this. Both Arthur and I were completely at home in the saddle. We closed to distance in seconds.

"You grab the reins!" Arthur shouted. "I'll try to grab the rider!"

I nodded and then leaned forward and surged ahead. The rider hung on the left side of his saddle. He held onto his horses' mane with only one hand. The other armed flailed wildly, further unbalancing him. I rode along the right side, bringing Butter next to the frightened horse. I started talking then, soothing words that usually worked when Butter was jittery. The reins flapped around the air like battered wings. I swiped out with my left hand and got lucky. I missed the reins, but snagged the bridle. Though I was in danger of being dragged off my own mount I held on and began to slow Butter down with my right hand on the reins and with the subtle pressure of my legs.

By this time Arthur had flanked them on the other side. He reached down and grabbed the rider by his leather belt and pulled hard. The rider loosened his grip and was flung over the withers of Arthur's horse. They wheeled away, leaving me to control the runaway animal.

I gradually slowed our pace, holding the bridle, but not forcing him in any way. I murmured a constant stream of soothing words and sounds. Little by little the horse calmed. Finally we came to a stop. His eyes were still wide and his breathing was labored. The smallest misstep and I feared he would panic again. I slipped from Butter's back and stroked the other horses' neck and face, still talking to him. He began to calm. I reached into my saddlebag and pulled out an apple from a store I kept for Butter. I offered it slowly, and though he was still a little skittish, he gulped down the fruit. Butter nudged me with his head, jealous and expectant.

"You'll get yours too," I said, and rubbed between his eyes. "Good boy."

I turned my head to see what had happened to Arthur. I saw his horse grazing perhaps fifty paces away. The man we had rescued sat on the ground, arms resting on his upraised knees, head held in his hands. Arthur squatted next to him, a hand on his shoulder. I gently pulled on the reins of the once frightened horse and walked toward my friend. Butter followed on his own.

As I neared them I got my first good look at the man we had saved, though calling him a man may be an overstatement. At that time I was not yet comfortable referring to myself as a man and though not a boy, this youth was not much older than myself, if at all. He was burlier than either Arthur or I, broad across the shoulders and chest, with thickly muscled arms. His dark hair was cropped very short, little more than a shadow on his skull. The face under it, though, was still very boyish. A few dark hairs struggled, futilely, to be a mustache.

He looked up as I approached and I saw his face was flushed. Anger darkened his countenance as he leapt to his feet.

"That stupid beast!" he yelled. His hand went to his sword hilt as he stepped forward. I felt his horse tense and pull back on the reins. "It nearly killed me! I should gut it where it stands!"

"You'll have to go through me to touch this horse," I said. I dropped the reins and rested my hand on the pommel of my sword. It was out of my mouth before I even thought. I saw Arthur cock an eyebrow at me.

The youth stared at me. Rage colored his features, and I saw that he was embarrassed by his predicament as much as angry. He knew he was one to our two, and that fighting us was not a good idea in any case under the circumstances. I stood my ground. I was not going to let him harm an animal whose only sin was fear.

"Fine," he finally said, and stepped back. I took my hand away from my sword. "But you can walk him back. Lousy thing. Only good for plowing and pulling wagons. It's not natural being on the back of a horse anyway. I swear I'm never riding a horse again. I'll walk all the way to Benwick first."

He was blowing off steam, but this last proclamation drew a smile from Arthur.

"You do know there's an ocean between here and there, don't you?" he said.

"So I'll get my feet wet, as long as I don't have to get back on one of those things."

We couldn't help ourselves. Arthur and I broke out into peals of laughter. For a moment I thought he was going to go for his sword again, but his look of irritation turned quickly to a smile. He rolled his eyes, shook his head and joined us in our mirth.

"Thank you," he said when we had stopped. "Both of you. You may have saved my life there. I'm Owain." He stuck his hand out. Arthur took it and shook.

"Arthur," he said. "And this is Bedivere." I shook hands with him as well.

"Arthur?" Owain said. "You're Ector's foster son, aren't you?"

"Yes," Arthur replied, clearly surprised. "How did you know that?"

"Myrddyn has mentioned you."

"Myrddyn?"

"One of my teachers."

"Owain," I mused. I knew the name rang a bell. Suddenly I remembered Lailoken mentioning that him the night we had spied on him. Once again, before I could stop myself I blurted out, "Of course. You're Uriens'..."

I paused, realizing I had almost spoken an insult.

"Bastard?" Owain said. "It's okay, I know. Uriens recognizes me as his and treats me well enough, though I'll never inherit anything from him. Not that there will be anything to inherit the way he's going."

"What do you mean?" Arthur asked.

"Let's just say Britain is lucky he never managed to pull that stupid sword from the stone and become High King."

Our conversation stopped then as we once again approached the highway. The men there cheered us and teased Owain good-naturedly. Warok clapped me on the back and treated me to a rare smile.

"Couldn't have done better with that horse myself," he said.

No praise could have pleased me more.

CHAPTER FIVE

Though I knew him for years after that first encounter Owain and I were never really friends. We were much too different in character. He never got over his dislike of horses, and as Arthur's cavalry grew we saw less and less of each other. I respected him and his abilities. I trusted him as one of the most gifted of the Companions. He was, I guess, my counterpart with the infantry. While Lancelot and I developed new strategies for mounted warfare Owain became the unbreakable center around which our ground troops grew.

But on that long gone day we were but three boys on the verge of manhood, impatient with our youth and blissfully unaware of what our futures held.

Warok, Arthur and I rode back to the springhouse while Kynon stayed behind as our representative. We arrived shortly before the main body of Ector's company. Warok informed him of our encounter and of the impending arrival of Uriens. Though only mid-afternoon it was decided we would make camp and await Uriens arrival. There would be no more traveling that day.

Arthur and I set about our duties, helping Kay and the older soldiers establish a perimeter, dig latrines, set up tents, and of course, tend to the horses. The previous days' rain was long gone and the humidity of the morning had passed as the day wore on, turning into a pleasant early June evening. Cook fires were built in preparation for our guests and in no time, thanks to a group of our skilled hunters, the aroma of fresh game sizzled around us.

Hard work kills time and it seemed to me we had just arrived back when Kynon came riding into camp. After a quick discussion Ector turned to his assembled travelers and spoke in a loud clear voice.

"King Uriens of Gorre and his entourage will be here presently," he said. "They are less than a mile along the road from here. Tonight they are our guests, and tomorrow they are our traveling companions. We will treat all of them with respect. I might not recognize Uriens as my sovereign, but I do remember him as a fighting man of valor. There will be no mischief in this camp tonight. Whatever old slights you remember or new ones you encounter, this is not the time or place to address them."

He turned his gaze on his assembled troops.

"That means all of you," he admonished. "You've been trained to fight, and part of that skill is knowing when not to. If any one here causes strife, do not think to blame the ale, for believe me, *I* will not."

He had barely finished when Uriens and his followers appeared on the road. The horsemen we had met led the procession, followed by more than a few wagons. There were armed foot soldiers marching along both sides of the road. A large number of the party walked behind the wagons. Near the middle of the train was a coach, much larger and more ornate than the others, pulled by slightly better looking horses than were otherwise present. I assumed Uriens was inside.

I smiled when I saw that Owain was one of those who were walking.

"It's a shame," Arthur said.

"What is?" I asked.

"That Ector even had to give that speech," he replied. "It's Britain. We're all Britons. We shouldn't have to wonder about those we meet, or caution each other not to fight. Did you feel it when we first met his riders? Do you feel it now?"

"Feel what?"

"Fear," Arthur answered. "Mistrust. There is an excitement among us now, but only because the initial contact has been made. This is the first time most of us are meeting anyone we don't already know. We rarely have visitors in the vale, and certainly never in this number. We should be free from suspicion and doubt among our own people."

I agreed, in principle at least, but I had no idea how anyone could achieve that. Gorre seemed as far away from me, and everything I knew, as any of the barbarian lands. How was anyone supposed to think of them as "our own people"?

Warok cast a sharp glance at the warriors as Uriens coach neared. We stood at attention and tried to cover our excitement with our discipline. We recognized that it was important to show our strength even if we had been cautioned not to use it.

Once the procession came to a complete halt Uriens' foot troops came to attention in two lines, creating a corridor of men leading to the royal coach. Four large men ran to the next wagon in line and unloaded an ornate chair held aloft on two poles, creating a sturdy litter. The men carried this to the door of the coach and set it gently on the ground.

I had never seen anything like this. I was curious and a little appalled. I had heard stories of ancient kings in foreign lands who did not deign to let their feet touch the ground. Was Uriens that arrogant? Did his people willingly carry him around to feed his ego, or was he so much of a tyrant they were afraid not to? Was his ego that immense?

The door opened and one of the soldiers extended a hand inside to help Uriens disembark.

I wasn't prepared for my first look at King Uriens of Gorre. I had heard that he was a big man, tall and broad, with legs and arms thickly muscled. Ector had said that Uriens was perhaps the biggest man he had ever known. As he clambered from his coach I realized it wasn't his ego that was immense.

I tried hard, out of discipline and respect, to keep my face composed. I'm not sure I was completely successful. I wasn't alone. From the corner of my eye I saw the look of shock on Ector's face.

"Dear God!" I heard Kay mutter, followed immediately by Warok's hissed command to silence.

Uriens was fat. Whatever muscle he may once have had was covered in rolls of flesh. His face and countless jowls were sheened with moisture. His breathing was louder and more labored than that of the runaway horse I had calmed earlier in the day. He was so pale that he looked like an enormous fluffy cloud spilling out of the coach. He gave no indication of being cloud-like in mass, however. There was nothing light about him. He ponderously settled into the chair, parts of him overlapping and sticking out.

Once settled, the four men strained to lift him. They each used both hands to lift and I could see the effort reflected in their faces. The litter sagged in the middle. Slowly, King Uriens, who once and maybe still, believed he was the rightful high king of all Britain, was laboriously maneuvered to a place of honor under the shade of the springhouse oak.

Ector stepped forward to greet the king, but he did not bow.

"Uriens," he said. "It does my heart good to see you again after so many years. It has been too long between meetings of old companions of Uther." He extended a hand in friendship.

Uriens looked at the hand a moment too long, seemingly confused by the common gesture of equals, as if he was not used to anything but obeisance. He looked up at Ector and studied him for a moment longer.

"Ector," he finally said, and there was the barest hint of a question in his voice, as if he wasn't sure. "Yes, Ector. Good to see you again. What's it been? Fifteen years?"

"Nearly seventeen," Ector said. "The day Merlin plunged the

sword into the stone."

"Yes, yes," Uriens said. "Then both of you simply disappeared. Why did you never come to the annual gatherings at the Shrine?"

"I never laid claim to the title of High King," Ector said. "That sword is not meant for my hand, and I've always known it."

"But you'll be there this year, I take it?"

"Yes," Ector confirmed. "We should all be back from Benwick in time for the festival and the annual attempts."

"Oh yes, Benwick," Uriens said while mopping his brow with a sweat-stained cloth. "Do you intend to make that voyage personally?"

"Yes," Ector said. "I think it's important."

"Of course," Uriens said, disinterest clear in his voice. "I'll be sending representatives but I don't think I'll be going personally."

"Good. He'd probably sink the boat," Kay whispered, earning him another chastising glare from Warok.

"I plan on staying at the shrine while everyone is away," Uriens continued. "Enjoy the hospitality of the ladies of the Lake. Nowhere is more restful than Avalon. By the time the other kings return from Benwick, or arrive from elsewhere I will be rested and strong enough to wrest that infernal blade from the rock and finally claim my rightful place."

I happened to be looking at Owain as Uriens spoke. I saw him roll his eyes and shake his head. He wasn't alone in that action among Uriens' people. I sensed that this was an oft-repeated discourse.

"Well, yes, perhaps," Ector said, "if the gods will it, the sword will go to the rightful King."

"Gods, bah!" Uriens spat. "The only rightful king is the one with the strength of arms and character to take it."

"Which hasn't happened since Uther," Ector replied, momentarily forgetting his own admonition to ignore ancient feuds. "But," he went on before Uriens could start again, "That is not in my hands, and I am willing to pledge allegiance to whatever hand holds that sword. If that happens to be you, Uriens, then so be it. For tonight, however, we are but old companions met on the road, sharing a journey. My cooks have prepared a modest meal. Come, break bread and share meat at my table and we'll remember more glorious times. I know the youngsters in my train want to hear tales of your exploits from your own mouth. They only know the things I tell them, poor storyteller that I am."

Uriens grunted, mollified. I thought Ector was a better storyteller than he let on, based solely on that performance. He smiled at Uriens acquiescence and signaled for the evening's festivities to begin.

We left formation and helped Uriens' entourage set up camp and picket their horses. It was an easy task, and his people seemed grateful for our help. They were anxious to exchange news and stories, tall tales and jokes. There was much swearing and ribald exchanges among the fighting men, as there always is, testing each others' mettle and wits and the limits to which we would go. In groups of men, especially those who don't know each other well, there seems to always be subtle warfare taking place.

Arthur and I came upon Owain hammering the last pegs of a

large tent into the ground. His thick muscular arms gave me some idea of what Uriens may have been like as a younger man. How was it possible for anyone to drown his muscles in that much flesh? While Uriens was an extreme example I was unaware then of the predations of time and age on all of us.

He smiled when Arthur greeted him and wiped his brow with the back of his hairy forearm. I could see a resemblance to his father around his eyes and the shape of his nose, but I doubted if Uriens ever smiled.

"Ah," Owain said. "My rescuers. Come to help me out of another fix? You're too late, I'm afraid. This tent put up a mighty struggle and nearly ran off with me, but I managed to tame it before any harm was done. I may not be a horseman, but tents... they know not to cross me." I saw that any anger or embarrassment he had felt the day before was mostly gone. His easy humor at his own expense raised my opinion of him.

"Unpredictable beast, the tent," Arthur said. "It's why we hobble them. So they won't run off in the night. Britain would be overrun with wild packs of them if we weren't vigilant. Good job with that one." When Owain laughed his eyes lit up. I was once again impressed with Arthur's natural ease with others. Yesterday he had saved a stranger. Today he had made a friend.

"Join Bedivere and me tonight at dinner," Arthur said. "If you don't have other duties."

"Bedivere eats at a table?" Owain said. "I thought perhaps he liked horses so much he would simply graze with them." I saw that though he joked, some small measure of his anger at the horse remained.

"Careful, Owain," I said with enough of a smile that he knew I continued in the same vein he had started. "I'm enough like the horses that I won't let you ride me either. And at dinner, I am partial to the oatcakes and apples, so guard your share."

He snorted when he laughed, and any tension left between us disappeared.

"I'll share your table if you'll have me," he said. "Aren't you sitting with Ector's other soldiers?"

"Yes," Arthur said. "But I thought it would be a good idea, since we will be traveling together for a few days, for the soldiers of both groups to get to know each other. We may have to fight side by side, and it makes sense to me that we may be more willing to do so if we feel we are all part of the same group. I mentioned this to Ector and he agreed. Warok has already spoken to Ivor and arranged it. We are to be scattered among each other at the tables."

"You're right," Owain said. "It is a good idea. I would never have thought of that."

I wouldn't have either, but in that moment I began to see how we could begin to put our differences behind us and become one people. Arthur saw it before anyone.

As Ector's foster son Arthur could have sat at the head table, but instead he joined the rest of the common troops for dinner. I think the prospect of listening to Uriens , or even worse, watching him eat, was at least part of the reason.

It was the first real meal we had eaten in days and we attacked it with delight. Not that we acted like barbarians. There was a measure of order to the proceedings. We were not a people bereft of manners. There was a moment of silent respect while the few Christians among us said their private blessings, then we dug in.

It didn't take long for camaraderie to set in. Food, comfort, and not a little ale always helps. It's a good thing we wouldn't need to hunt again in this area anytime soon, for the noise of our revelry surely scared away any game for miles.

Dusk had arrived and we were savoring a last mug of ale while servants cleared the platters when a young messenger approached our table. He stood by Owain, flush with nerves.

"What?" Owain asked as he turned to the page. The boy leaned in and whispered to Owain, obviously nervous about speaking aloud at a table he perceived as filled with men.

"Thanks," Owain said. "Tell him we will be right there." The page nodded and scampered off. Owain wiped his mouth on the back of his sleeve and stood.

"Well, it seems my father has summoned me to his side. Arthur, Bedivere... he wants to see you too."

"Why us?" I blurted.

"I don't know," Owain said. "But we should go. He's not very patient."

Arthur looked at me and shrugged, then stood and went to Owain's side. I quickly swallowed the last of my draught and joined them. I can't really account for the nerves I felt. I guess it was because it was the first time I had been summoned to the presence of a king. Whatever my personal feelings about Uriens, he was a man who wielded great power, and had for years. He had once been a serious contender for the role of High King and had stood shoulder to shoulder with Uther. His name was legend to us and at that point I had yet learned to separate the stuff of story from the truth of reality.

"What do we do when we get there?" I asked. "Do we kneel? What?"

"No," Owain said. "It's not a formal court summons. Back in Gorre he would certainly expect that. But, we're in a field, and you're not his subjects. He wouldn't presume to make you kneel in front of Ector."

We made our way to the main table. Torches threw dancing shadows over the features of everyone there. As we approached I recognized Ector's hearty laughter and was relieved that there seemed to be no tension hanging over the meal. We stood within sight of Uriens and the other nobles at the table and waited to be recognized. Ector saw us first and bade us forward with a wave of his hand. We stepped into the light as every eye at the head table fixed on us. I've rarely been more uncomfortable.

This close I was able to get a better look at the king of Gorre. His skin, thick with overlapping jowls, was a sickly gray color in the torch's illumination. His eyes looked milky; viscous matter had built up in their corners. His scalp was covered in brown spots and showed through long strands of thin oily hair. His beard, like the little hair he had, was dirty gray. He looked old to me, unhealthy and infirm.

"Uriens," Ector said, "I would like to introduce you to two of my finest young men, though I am at least a little biased in their favor. This is my foster son, Arthur, a foundling I have raised as my own since he was but a babe."

"A foundling, you say?" Uriens said as he studied Arthur. "No doubt left behind by one of the Saxon raids. Mighty generous to take an unknown bastard into your own home Ector."

I saw a quick look of perturbation, there and then gone, sweep over Ector's features.

"Yes, well," Ector said, "it was a good decision. He has been a good boy, well on his way to becoming a good man. I'm proud to call him son."

I couldn't help but believe this last was a subtle dig at Uriens treatment of Owain. I felt my stomach roil as their attention turned to me.

"And this is Bedivere Bedrydant, son of Bedwyr," Ector said.

"Ahh, the Griffin's son!" Uriens boomed in genuine pleasure. "Your father was a fine man, if a little blinded by his love of Uther. If you grow to be half the man your father was Ector is lucky to have you.

"Now then," Uriens continued, "I understand that yesterday the two of you rescued my son from an unruly horse." Uriens stayed silent until we nodded in acknowledgement. Owain, though silent, looked mortified. Uriens was inscrutable in his silence and the longer we stayed the focus of his attention the worse my discomfort grew. Finally he spoke and my discomfiture turned to sudden rage at his words.

"Yes, well, the offending horse has been put down before anyone else could be harmed," Uriens said. I felt Arthur tense beside me and saw a warning look from Ector. Owain's eyes had snapped open in shock, and though he didn't like horses I could see that he was stunned as well. I swallowed my anger and restrained my instinct to lash out. My face went blank with the soldier's discipline that had been instilled in me, but anyone who saw me should have been able to read my reaction. Uriens didn't seem in the least bit aware.

"I wish to reward both of you," Uriens said. "What would you like from me?"

I wanted to tell him I wanted that poor horse back. I wanted him to promise to never harm another one. I wanted him to apologize for his cruelty and to recognize the sheer wrongness of what he had done. Instead I said nothing. Arthur was equally silent.

"Come, come," Uriens said. "There must be something you desire. No? Well then, how about this? I, King Uriens of Gorre, say here in front of these witnesses, that I am indebted to both of you, Arthur and Bedivere, and at any point in the future you may ask of me a boon and I am honor bound to grant it if it is within my power. How does that sound?"

I stood silent, still unable to trust my tongue not to betray me. Arthur finally spoke and accepted for both of us.

"Thank you, King Uriens," he said, "though our actions were not done with reward in mind. We saw a fellow Briton in trouble and simply acted the way we would have for anyone. The way we hope any of our countrymen would do for us."

"Well said," Uriens said. "Though my oath still holds. I will honor a boon to both of you." With that he turned back to his ale and conversation with his retainers. It was obvious we were dismissed. We gave a small bow and retreated. Ector nodded his approval of our behavior as we passed.

We were barely out of earshot when I started.

"How dare he have the horse killed?" I said, much too loudly.

"Bedivere, I'm sorry," Owain pleaded. "I swear I had no idea he would do that."

"That fat, heartless..."

"Bedivere! Shh!" Arthur grabbed me by the arm and placed a hand over my mouth. If it had been anyone else in that moment I would have slapped them to the ground. "Not here," he said. "If someone hears you and word gets back to Uriens there will be trouble. Let's take a walk and get you somewhere you can calm down."

Arthur grabbed a skin of wine from a nearby table and we crossed the road away from the springhouse. Kynon stood watch but only smiled as he watched three young men wander away from their elders with good drink tucked under their arms. We ducked into a stand of trees and walked well into their midst until we came upon a clearing dotted with large, quarried stones left over from the roadwork.

Night had descended, but the air was clear and warm. The stars were a horde of celestial fireflies swarming around the bright fire of the moon, making it easy to see. Arthur and Owain sat on the stones and leaned back to peer into the unfathomable beyond.

The sharp pain of my anger had passed, but the dull throb of its passing remained. I paced, still furious, at Uriens casual cruelty and at my own helplessness to change anything. Neither Arthur nor Owain attempted to calm me down. I believe they both felt my anger was justified and I think they knew nothing they could say would help. Eventually I relaxed enough to join Arthur on the large stone where he sat. He handed me the wineskin and I took a long pull of the thick, potent liquid.

We sat quiet for some time, each of us occupied with our own thoughts. Night birds cried and insects whirred. The murmur of voices from the campsite hovered in the distance, unnoticed except for an occasional boisterous burst of laughter.

"Do you see why my father should never become High King?" Owain finally said into the silence. Neither Arthur nor I responded, but when Owain turned his head to look at us he saw he had our attention.

"Killing the horse is just another example in long line of how he governs," Owain said. "If something does not follow your orders, or does something you do not approve of, you simply get rid of it. He's not a tyrant. I don't mean to imply that he kills all of his rivals or anyone who disagrees with him. It's just that he never allows anyone to rise in power or influence. He fears his kingship will be taken away, so he makes sure that anyone who may be a threat never gets the chance. Anyone who shows any initiative, leadership or real talent gets reassigned to a job he is less suited for. As a result the best men for a career are never allowed to do it.

"Uriens has no head for management, or finances. He knows strategy and war, and that is all. Our little kingdom is in a shambles. We're broke, our crops are failing, and there is no one capable of putting it right. At least no one Uriens will allow.

"And he's too damned bullheaded to see it!" Owain said, his voice rising. "He can't admit to any faults because he believes it would seem a sign of weakness. In the meantime Gorre is falling to ruin. I'm glad I'm not his legitimate heir. At this rate there will nothing left to inherit."

Owain stopped. He glared at us, and then dropped his eyes to the ground. I think he was embarrassed to have said so much against his father and his king, and was perhaps afraid we would judge him disloyal.

"Do you know what he plans he has made for Gorre in the event of his death?" Arthur asked. "You say you are not his heir. Does he have one?"

"No," Owain laughed. "I'm the closest thing he has, and he won't recognize me in that way. Once again, he fears anyone who might replace him, so he denies he will ever need to be replaced."

"Doesn't he fear losing Gorre when he is too weak to defend it?" Arthur asked. "My teacher, Lailoken, has told me Uriens fought hard to claim the throne he has. It seems strange to me he would simply let it fall into the hands of one of the other petty kings that easily."

"You don't understand," Owain said. "Uriens still fully believes that he is destined to be High King. He thinks that someday, perhaps this year, at the annual meeting at the Shrine of the Sword, he will wrap his old palsied hand around the hilt and draw it from the stone and all of Britain will simply kneel to his will."

"What if someone else draws it?" I asked.

"I wish someone would," Owain snapped. "Maybe then Uriens would give up his stupid dream."

"It doesn't sound like he would to me," I said.

"No," Owain agreed, "he wouldn't want to. But what could he do? Fight the new High King? With what? We have a decently trained infantry. Uriens was good at that if nothing else, but there is no real leadership. Like in everything else, he hasn't allowed anyone to truly excel there, and there is no real organization or loyalty. You may have noticed. My father is not a likeable man."

"What would you do?" Arthur asked.

"If the new High King was someone I could believe in more than Uriens, I would pledge my fealty and do as he bid. I don't want Gorre, and there is no one else to rule it except outsiders. If anyone could bring us more prosperity than we currently have, they're welcome to it.

"But I don't think it will ever happen," Owain concluded. "The greatest men of a generation have tried and tried to pull that damned thing out of that stone. There's no one left."

We nodded. Neither Arthur nor I knew anyone who was likely to be High King either.

As I write these words all these decades later I wonder how

much of this conversation I really remember and how much I've filled in based on everything that came after. The conversation seems prescient somehow. I do know we discussed Uriens unsuitability as a king of any kind. I know Owain said he would follow whoever became High King and not his father. That struck me at the time because I could not imagine throwing my former allegiances and family to the side so easily, though I know now it wasn't easy for Owain either.

Luckily, it was a decision I never had to make.

CHAPTER SIX

My memory of the first timed I glimpsed Camelot is vague. Our scouts had informed us we were within a half days' ride to Avalon and we were flush with anticipation of the wonders we would see. As much as I like horses I needed a few days break from riding as well. I imagine the rest of our party was likewise tired and ready for a brief rest.

We were traveling on the Roman highway. A large forest bordered the left side of the road. On our right there stretched a large field that had been cleared of trees a long time ago. Scrub brush and weeds, tall grass and heather rippled in the summer breeze. Sun glittered off the surface of a narrow river in the distance. A large hillside sat in the crook of a wide bend in the river. On top of that hill were the ruins of a large fortress. I may not have seen it at all if Arthur hadn't pointed it out.

"What's that?" he asked.

"An old hill fort," Ector said. "It sat like that the first time I came here over twenty years ago. Local lore says it was a small wooden fort built long ago. By who, no one knows exactly. The Romans expanded it and used it for many years. This is a peaceful area, thanks partly to the influence of Avalon. When the legions were recalled to Rome this was one of the first outposts to be abandoned. Camelot, I think it's called. Means something like 'at the bend of the river'. This is the southern tip of Leodegrance's land, Cameliard. That river snakes throughout the length of his kingdom."

Arthur nodded, his curiosity satisfied. That quickly, thoughts of the hill fort that would someday be home to all of were forgotten as we continued our trek to the Shrine of the Sword.

Unlike Camelot, I can never forget my first sight of the lake and island of Avalon. I have seen many bodies of water in my life, but none so beautiful. I, who have no poetry in my soul, cannot begin to describe what bards and storytellers have failed to portray.

Our entourage topped a rise on the Roman road and there, spread before us in a wide valley, was a lake of the clearest water I have ever seen. Light danced across its surface like jewels or stars. Trees lined the shore around the lake, the terminus of a deep thick forest through which our journey led. At that time of year everything was green, more shades than the gods have names for.

The island was just visible through a thin mist. I could make out the tops of buildings, carved it seemed from purest granite and marble. Tiled roofs shone red in the morning sun. I could see several boats tethered at a long dock, some of them carved to resemble great swans.

A breeze skipped across the water, carrying with it the scent of fragrant cooking, flowers, and above all, apples. No matter how many times I went there, or at what time of year, there was always the scent of apples.

All of these words, and what I have written is drab and gray compared to the reality of Avalon.

Of course, it could simply be an old man's memory focusing on the happy recollections of something that is gone.

Still, I know no one who ever went there who didn't feel at least some portion of what I describe. There are many who claim it was a place of magic, a location where the veils between this world and the next were thin. For most of my life I believed it was simply a beautiful place and the peace one felt there was due to the seclusion and safety of the locale. The Lady of the Lake and her acolytes made everyone welcome and their behavior lent a sense of the Otherworldly to any gathering there. But I saw nothing I would call magic.

Until I returned the sword to the water there and became the last mortal man to ever see Avalon on those shores.

The view of the lake disappeared as we left the straight Roman road and meandered down a narrower trail through the great forest. We could hear the soft lapping of water on the shore to our right as we passed between the trees. Excitement fluttered in my chest as we approached the first real destination of our summer-long sojourn. The Shrine of the Sword lay close by and soon I would get my first look at Excalibur, the fabled sword of the High King.

Butter sensed the presence of other people ahead of us before I saw any signs. He snorted and shook his head, but it was not a signal of alarm. Within moments I heard the sound of voices, a great many of them. They were not voices raised in protest or anger, simply the cacophony of the everyday magnified by numbers.

We came out of the woods into a large clearing. Thick trees surrounded us on three sides and the lake reclined before us on an open shore. It was my best look at the island yet, but it was not the splendor of Avalon that drew my attention. A small shrine sat at the edge of the lake. A tiny roof balanced on four columns built of oak and polished marble. Vines of ivy and holly wound around the pillars. I saw something inside the enclosure, small from my perspective but still unmistakable. Light reflected from a bright blade that protruded from a dull rock, calling the eye to look upon it.

"There it is," I said to Arthur, who rode at my side. He nodded, but said nothing. His face had never looked so solemn.

When I finally pulled my stare away from the shrine I was able to take in the whole clearing. This was the location of the annual attempt at drawing the blade, so over the years it had grown from a wilderness into a regularly used campsite. Several permanent buildings were evident, built of wood and rock. There were small roofed pavilions, cooking pits, stables and paddocks for horses, and sleeping bowers for the soldiers who regularly accompanied their lords.

At least one of the other groups of travelers to Benwick had already arrived. People were everywhere, milling about and working. Many of them looked up at our arrival and waved or shouted greetings. Tents, tables, and campsites were arrayed around the perimeter. The scent of cooking filled the sweet-smelling air.

Mixed among the travelers I saw a great number of women assisting the organization of the campsite. They were all clad in similar white shifts and of all ages, from small girls who followed their elders, to ancient crones sitting in circles around the cook fires. These were the acolytes of Avalon, followers of the old ways and the Goddess, said to be the keepers of the secrets of magic and healing.

I don't know about actual magic, but as a young man inexperienced with women I know I was spellbound. Their shifts were thin, showing bare shoulders and far more of their lithe legs than any of the girls I knew back home. Suddenly I was uncomfortable in my saddle in a way that my mail shirt and riding leathers made difficult to adjust.

A group of seven of them, mostly young, came to greet us. They stopped in front of Ector and curtsied, and then one of them stepped forward. She was, quite simply, the most beautiful girl I had seen at that point in my life. She was nineteen, perhaps twenty, older than me by a few years at least. Her skin, though darkened slightly by the summer sun, was pale, soft looking over tight muscles. Her hips and breasts were full, though not overly so. Her hair was black like a rook's wing and pulled back in a loose braid. I was close enough to see her eyes. They were the impossible blue of sky reflected on an icy lake, and like the sword in the shore, the reflection there drew your attention and held it fast.

Her voice was husky when she spoke.

"Welcome to Avalon, Sir Ector," she said, and then gestured to the coach behind us. "I see that King Uriens has arrived as well. The

Lady Vivienne sends her regrets that she is not here to meet you personally, but there is much to do today and she is pulled in many directions. She will come by and greet you during the evening meal. I have been instructed to help get you settled in and to take care of any of your requests."

"Thank you," Ector said. "Where should we make camp?"

"Arrangements have been made and a site chosen, if it suits your needs," she answered. "I can escort you there, and one of the other girls can take King Uriens' party to his site. There is fruit, bread and cheese, and fresh water to tide you over until dinner. We have provided shelter and fresh grass and oats for the horses."

"That will be fine," Ector said. "I see we are not the first to arrive."

"Leodegrance came yesterday," she replied. "Scouts have also arrived from King Lot's party; he should be here by mid-afternoon. I don't believe any of the rest of the petty kings will be arriving until the festival of the Sword later this summer." Ector nodded his understanding.

The girl signaled for four of her group to attend to Uriens and they made off to offer help and instructions. She smiled at Ector and then swung her gaze to take in our entire party. I felt my heart lurch as her eyes momentarily met mine, but she passed quickly on to Arthur.

And then she stopped. I don't really know what passed between them. No words were spoken, but their silent communion lingered. I saw both of them flush and the attraction they shared was immediate and obvious. Reluctantly, I thought, she returned her attention to Ector.

"Follow me," she said. "And if you need anything while you are here please send word to me. I have been assigned as your liaison.

"My name is Morgan."

There are many more tales of Morgan the Fey than there are about me, or about most of Arthur's Companions. Some are true, some are lies, and most fall in that nebulous area in between. We all have a need, it seems, to fill in the details about events we weren't actually witness to. Most of Arthur's relationship with Morgan took place in private, and what was said and done in those moments are lost to their memories. I only know what I witnessed and what little the two of them confided in me.

Was she a witch? The Christians certainly thought so, but then they believed all other religions were evil. She was a priestess of the old religion and whatever powers they may have had were hers to command. I never saw anything from any of the ladies of Avalon, beyond their knowledge of herbs and medicines, I would classify as true magic. Did she help engineer the downfall of Camelot and the death or Arthur? Maybe, but if so I have to believe it was inadvertent. She was a part of Merlin's great and ultimately flawed plan just like the rest of us.

She was there that last day when all was lost. She was one of the women who washed Arthur's body and placed it on the boat that took him to Avalon. She respected my grief, and the grief I saw in those magnificent eyes was as real as my own. In those last moments

Morgan and I were the only family he had left.

She loved him.

But on that day at Avalon when their eyes first met, she was simply a beautiful young woman, and Arthur a youth in the first flowering of his manhood.

We followed Morgan to the area reserved for us. Arthur and I, and probably every one of us who had never been the Avalon before, wanted nothing more than to go to the shrine and see Excalibur for ourselves. But there was much to do before we could be excused. Unlike Uriens, most of whose party would be staying for weeks, we simply had to set up camp in much the same fashion we had been doing on the road for days. If anything, the task was made easier by virtue of the structures present, and the help of a myriad of the women of Avalon, though this latter was enough of a distraction that many tasks went more slowly than they should have. Throughout the process I was with Warok at the corrals while Arthur and Kay helped Ector establish the order of the campsite.

Once the horses had been groomed and fed I was free to explore as I wished. I washed the residue of travel from my hands and face, changed out of my riding armor into more comfortable, casual clothing, and went in search of Arthur. We had each agreed not to go to the shrine without the other.

Ector was at his pavilion, greeting a small group of people from the other camp. Arthur was there, standing close to Morgan. I sped up my pace, anxious to meet new people. Ector saw my approach and smiled.

"Come on, lad, don't dally," Ector said. "I want you to meet another of my old comrades. A few minutes earlier and you would have already heard the introductions."

"I'm sorry, sir," I began. "The horses..."

"Never apologize for taking your duties to the horses seriously, son," Ector said. He turned to face his guests and continued, "This lad has been a member of my household since birth. Like Arthur, while he is not my actual son he is as close to me as my own. This is Bedivere, my future horse lord, son of our old friend Bedwyr. Lad, this is my oldest true friend, King Leodegrance of Cameliard."

Stunned as I was to hear Ector refer to me as his future horse lord I almost missed Leodegrance's greeting.

"So this is the Griflet?" Leodegrance said. "You're never going to have your father's size, are you?" I saw from the twinkle in his eyes that he was teasing me.

"That's not a bad thing," I said. "I understand the horses had trouble carrying both him and all of his muscles at the same time." Leodegrance laughed and clapped me on the shoulder, and then extended his hand to shake mine.

Leodegrance was tall and very thin. Pure white hair flowed back from a high forehead. His neatly trimmed beard was the same pale shade. His long face was all angles. The scores of wrinkles there had been carved more by smiles than by worry so that he looked amused at everything around him. As I got to know him over the years I became convinced that the amusement was real. Ector had told us that while Leodegrance had ridden with Uther and stood in combat against the Saxon invaders he was always more of a scholar than a warrior. I could see the quick intelligence in his happy eyes.

Leodegrance introduced me to his retainers, none of whom I remember now. Lastly he came to a young girl I had failed to notice before she stepped out from behind one of the men.

"This," Leodegrance beamed, "is the light and joy of my life, my only child, my daughter Guinevere."

Guinevere looked into my eyes and then quickly dropped her gaze. Her face flushed as she curtsied, but then she boldly locked her gaze on me again. She was thirteen at the time, and if she had begun to show any of the outward signs of womanhood the flowing gown that covered her from ground to neck hid them. She was thin like her father but not yet tall. Her dark blonde hair fell straight and loose over her shoulders, long enough to come nearly to her knees in the back. I don't believe it had ever been cut. Like Morgan, her eyes were blue, though softer and somehow more welcoming. She wore the Christian crucifix around her neck.

At the time I barely registered her beauty. Though it is not unusual for girls of that age to marry and bear children, surrounded as we were by the bare skin and overt sensuality of the acolytes of Avalon, Guinevere looked like a child herself. It would be years before I recognized what an amazing woman she was. Years before I fell in love with her body and mind. Years before she offered her heart to me, an offer I could not accept.

"Now then," Ector said, "Leodegrance and I need to discuss arrangements for the trip to the coast and Benwick, so if you young people will excuse us. I'm sure you're all dying to see Excalibur. Morgan, could you show them the Shrine?"

"Of course," Morgan said. "Follow me." Arthur, Guinevere and I walked in her wake. It wasn't until we were well out of site of Ector's pavilion that Morgan reached out and took Arthur's hand. Guinevere noticed and looked up at me. She blushed again, a reaction she was prone to then, and quickly looked away. I think she wanted to take my hand in the same way, but shyness and propriety won out. Arthur had the obvious affection of an exceptionally beautiful and to my mind exotic woman, while I was becoming the object of an adolescent crush. Not for the first time, and certainly not for the last, I was jealous of my closest friend.

There were no guards around the Shrine. Thieves were not feared here for obvious reasons. By tradition the petty kings had agreed to meet once a year to parlay and once again try for the High King's crown, but anyone was welcome to try to pull the Sword from the stone at any time. So far it had resisted all efforts.

We entered the Shrine. There before us was the object that had inspired a million stories and embodied the hope of all Britain. It was awe-inspiring.

The blade was bright silver and reflected the light in a prism of colors. In spite of standing outside in elements for a decade and a half there was not a spot of dirt or rust anywhere along its length. Some have seen this as proof of its magic. I thought it more likely that the ladies of Avalon tended to its condition. The cross guard looked like gold, though gold is much too soft to be a good material. The handle was wrapped in finely tooled black leather. A bright round moonstone was set in the pommel.

The stone itself grew from the ground. It was dark in hue, rough with many cracks. Tiny green plants and mold thrived in the fissures. The sword was sunk in its middle and on close inspection it was difficult to see where the blade ended and the stone began. There was a layer of black rock that appeared to have bubbled up out of the fissure and ran over the sides and dried there like blood or candle wax.

Guinevere crossed herself and then clutched her crucifix. Arthur and I stared at this object that symbolized both the wound that kept our land divided and the faith in its future. Morgan simply smiled. She had grown up with this wonder, had watched pilgrim's reactions to it her entire life. It was as commonplace to her as the stables back home were to me.

"Anyone care to try?" she asked. None of us answered. At that time none of us believed we had the right.

"I don't understand," Guinevere said. "It's a sword. Swords are objects of war and violence. They cut and divide. How is that supposed to unite Britain?"

"It's a weapon against the Saxons," I said, stating the most direct and simple answer. "They are a threat to all of us. Someone must take up the sword of war against them before they overrun our entire land."

"But there are so many of them," she persisted. "How can one sword make a difference?"

"It can't," Arthur said. "Not if it was simply one more sword in the fight. It's more than a sword. It is a symbol for what we must be."

"A symbol?" Guinevere said. I could see her turning the idea over in her mind. "My teacher, Father Emrys, has talked with me about this. When we were discussing Plato and his story about the cave. It's not a real cave, but a way of talking about something else."

I admit to being surprised, though perhaps, since she was the daughter of a well-educated man I shouldn't have been. It was rare enough for anyone to be taught to read—though Ector had insisted on it for all of us—but especially for a girl. From the sound of it, she hadn't spent her time on frivolous reading either. Arthur and Morgan both seemed more amused than surprised, but then I knew Arthur had been exposed to the same kinds of lessons from Lailoken. I assumed the acolytes of the lake were also better educated than the average person as well.

"Exactly," Arthur said. "A sword is used not only to attack in warfare, but to defend, and I think that's an important meaning. It's also used to cut things, to separate them. My teacher says it is a symbol of man's intellect, the ability to separate the wheat from the chafe, truth from lies. The ability to make decisions and think sharply."

"That makes sense," Guinevere said, "but there must be more than that."

"So what do you think it symbolizes?" Arthur said. It was not a condescending question. He genuinely wanted to hear her opinion.

"Well," Guinevere said and furrowed her brow in thought. "In the story when Merlin puts the sword in the stone he says it represents the wound to the land, so that part is obvious. The question then, is what does it represent once it is drawn and the wound is allowed to heal." She absentmindedly played with her crucifix as she thought. I saw her eyes widen as pieces of her thoughts came together.

"A sword is shaped like a cross," she finally said. "The way this sword stands in the stone is just like Christ's cross on the hill of Gethsemane. Christ had to die there and be removed from the cross in order to be resurrected. Pulling the sword from the stone is like taking Christ from the cross. Only then can Britain be born again." She smiled at this reasoning.

"Or," Morgan said with a mischievous grin, "it is like the Lady Vivienne teaches. She says that the sword is a symbol of the skyfather and the stone is the great Earth Mother of us all. They are copulating in order to give birth to a new Britain. No one can draw the sword because we all know new life cannot be made if it is pulled out too soon."

Morgan locked wicked eyes on Arthur as she spoke. Guinevere blushed to the very ends of her long hair, and I'm sure I did as well. I had never heard any woman speak so brashly of sexual matters.

I think that was the first I was really consciously aware that, in addition to the various petty kings and their claims to the land, there were two other Britains at war in the minds of her people. Most of the common folk still worshipped the old gods, primarily the Goddess in all of her many forms. Avalon was the spiritual center of the traditional beliefs, but there were shrines all over the country. Every village had a wise woman who administered healing and served as a midwife.

Yet in the last few centuries the new religion of Christianity had grown dramatically. Most of the adherents of the old ways saw Christianity as a variation on the things they had always believed. Christ was a dying and resurrected god like so many other deities of the harvest and the hunt. Britain was used to regional differences in the way the god and goddess were viewed. But increasingly, believers of the Christ preached that theirs was the only true religion, and that any other way was wrong. This view was gaining great popularity, and I knew that there were churches being built and thousands of Christians in Britain.

In Ector's village both beliefs existed together. My mother offered prayers to the Christ, and still made offerings to the Goddess. We really didn't give much thought to the differences. There was room for many beliefs, I thought, but I had heard that some of the more zealous Christians were actually killing those they thought were heathens and disbelievers. If this was true, then the fanatical Christians coming into our country were as dangerous to our way of life as the Saxons, and much more insidious.

Hopefully, this Father Emrys of which Guinevere spoke was not one of those priests who advocated the destruction of the old ways. We did not need religion as one more sword to wound and divide us. It was two more factions the new High King, whoever he may be, would need to unite.

Our discomfort, both sexual and metaphysical, was interrupted by loud shouts of laughter and the sudden thrumming sound of horse hooves breaking into the clearing. We looked up in time to see two young riders leaning into their mounts, urging them at a breakneck pace directly toward the Shrine. The whooping laughter came from the one in the lead. Sure they were going to plunge directly into our midst I reached out to grab Guinevere to whisk her out of harms way. Just when I thought it was too late the lead rider pulled back on the reins and brought his horse to a stop. While it was not the most graceful move I could tell he was not a complete stranger to horses either.

"I win!" he shouted and pumped his arms into the air in triumph. He slid out of his saddle as the second rider came to a halt behind him. He ran and grabbed his companion and pulled him off of his horse and onto the ground. They wrestled for a moment, raising a cloud of dust, until the first rider sat astride the second, pinning his arms to the ground.

"Who's the best rider?" the winner of the race said.

"You are," said the pinned youth.

"Who has the fastest horse?"

"You do."

"Who has to groom them both now?"

"I never agreed..."

"That's right," said the victor as he stood up. "You do." He turned to look at the Shrine and a smile lit up his face.

He was our age, or near enough. Broadly built, muscular like Owain though perhaps a head taller. His hair was a great unruly shock of deep auburn, with random braids dangling in its midst. His jaws carried the first thin blush of facial hair, which looked incongruous on his wide, smiling, incredibly boyish face.

"So that's Excalibur is it?" he said. "Well then..."

He entered the Shrine and walked straight to the sword. He spat into his hands, rubbed them together, and grabbed Excalibur by the hilt. He pulled with all of his considerable might, and through my shock I noted his own look of surprise when the sword didn't budge. After a few seconds exertion he released the sword, looked at his palm for a second, and then shrugged. A moment later he was laughing again.

I was astonished that anyone my age would have the impudence to even touch Excalibur, let alone with his complete lack of ceremony or shame. I saw that Guinevere shared my disapproval. Arthur, on the other hand, seemed oddly amused.

"Well," the newcomer said while wiping his hands on his trousers, "that settles that. That sword isn't meant for me any more than it was meant for Father, no matter what Mother says." He turned to Morgan then and if anything his smile grew wider.

"Hello, Auntie Morgan," he said, then swept her up in a bear hug, swinging her around several times until she was laughing as well.

"Gawaine," she yelled with glee.

It came together for me then. I should have recognized the name of Gorlois and Igraine's youngest daughter Morgan. She was only three or four when she was placed in the care of the ladies of Avalon, shortly after Uther's army killed Gorlois. I'm certain Ector must have known who our young guide was. If she were this Gawaine's aunt, then he would have to be the son of Morgan's older sister, Morguase.

The son of King Lot of Orkney.

"You great oaf," Morgan gasped, "put me down!"

"Yes, m'am," Gawaine said with mock contrition and set her on her feet. "Wouldn't want to shatter the old woman's bones. What are you now, forty? Fifty?"

"Enough older than you to still kick your scrawny behind," she said. She put her hands on her hips and studied him. "Though not so scrawny anymore, are you? You've grown since I saw you last."

"I should hope so. I was ten years old then," Gawaine said. "I'm not the only one who has filled out I see." Morgan slapped away the hand that had reached out to tweak her breast, though I sensed no true anger.

"So then this must be Agravaine," Morgan said, gesturing to the second rider, who had remained silent since lifting himself off the ground.

In the clamor of Gawaine's attempt at the sword I had forgotten he was there. He went stiff as Morgan embraced him, not even attempting to hug her in return. Agravaine was a study in contrasts when compared to his brother. Where Gawaine was husky Agravaine was thin. His muscles were whipcord tight, but he had no real mass behind them. His hair was black like Morgan's, and trimmed short. Gawaine's face was round and made for laughter. His brother wore a sere countenance on his thin, hawk-like face.

"Where is the rest of your delegation?" Morgan asked.

"Somewhere on the trail just off the Roman road," Gawaine said. "We decided we couldn't wait for them."

"Is your mother with you," Morgan asked. There was the slightest note of distaste in her tone.

"No," Gawaine said, his smile growing wider. "She and Father stayed in Orkney. They will be here later in the summer for the festival. I'm sure Father will try his luck pulling the sword again. He'd have much more luck pulling his own rod than in budging that thing. I don't know why he doesn't just give it up. He 's too old to be a High King now anyway."

"They let you and Agravaine come ahead on your own?"

"Not exactly alone," Agravaine ventured. "There are nearly forty people in our train."

"Neither of them saw much point in going to Benwick," Gawaine chimed in. Stormcrow talked Mother into letting us go, though Agravaine cried because he didn't want to be away from her."

"I did not."

"Stormcrow?" Arthur asked.

"Yeah," Gawaine said. "He's this painted up old druid who comes around and teaches us hunting and woodcraft and stuff." I saw Guinevere make the sign of the cross again at the mention of a druid. "Who are you?"

"Arthur, foster son of Ector. This is Bedivere and Guinevere, the daughter of King Leodegrance." Gawaine shook hands with both of us then bowed his head to Guinevere.

"You're quite the young beauty," he said. Guinevere's blush

returned. "I can see you'll be a heartbreaker some day. Which of these boys do you have your sights set on?" I thought she was going to melt into the ground with embarrassment.

"Gawaine," Morgan said, reprobation in her voice.

"So," Gawaine said, "anything to eat around here? I'm starving. Then maybe you can introduce me to some of the more attractive acolytes."

CHAPTER SEVEN

Writing this history has proven more difficult than I imagined, and when it was first suggested I couldn't imagine it at all. It's not the actual writing, though my hand does cramp around the quill at times. I've been surprised at how easily I've found the words I needed (though my host has added some of his own, more flowery touches to some of the descriptive passages). I credit this ease with how vivid and powerful some of my memories are.

And that is where the difficulty lies. It has become clear to me how many things I have forgotten as I compose this. Some people are vague outlines in my memory, others I'm sure have simply disappeared. Was Ivor really the name of Uriens' man? I think so, and for the purposes of recalling these events the name suffices, but I wouldn't swear to it.

But some things are as clear as if I had experienced them this morning.

Gawaine's laugh resounds in my head, as loud and rowdy as the first time I heard it. Over the years it only became more boisterous. I can still see the astonishing blue depths of Morgan's eyes, like staring into the unfathomable depths of the sea or the sky, knowing that so much more exists beyond what you can see. Guinevere, who was shy and beautiful and more insightfully intelligent than the rest of us combined.

And of course, Arthur, standing in our center, giving us form and purpose without even realizing it.

There have been times when my hand pauses over the parchment simply because I am overcome with emotion. We never know when we will encounter those who will accompany us on life's journey. To have met so many of them in a single day is remarkable.

But that first day at the Shrine was not the only remarkable day that long summer.

Morgan went with Gawaine and Agravaine to greet the rest of Lot's delegation. Arthur and I rejoined Ector and were immediately given the task of helping the acolytes set up the numerous tables and benches needed for the evening's feast. Guinevere tagged along, determined not to be left out of the proceedings. She quickly gave up trying to lift the tables, all of which weighed more than she did. She helped the younger acolytes decorate the clearing with flowers and colorful ribbons, though she did stay as near to Arthur and I as her duties allowed.

"I think someone has a crush on you," Arthur said while we wrestled a bench into position.

"What?"

"Guinevere," Arthur teased. "You haven't noticed the way she has looked at you all afternoon?"

"She's a child," I protested.

"For now, maybe," Arthur said. "She'll be marriageable in a couple of years. Don't rule anything out." I rolled my eyes, uncomfortable with the whole idea, not just of Guinevere but of marriage and women in general. Yet when I glanced up I saw her looking at me, a knowing smile on her face.

By the time the acolytes summoned everyone for dinner I was more than ready to sit down and eat. Apparently the unspoken tradition at Avalon for gatherings such as this was for each of the various parties to be seated with their own people. At Ector's suggestion, the Lady Vivienne had arranged for all four of the delegations present to be intermingled. I saw the echo of Arthur's idea at the springhouse and wondered if that was what inspired Ector.

I got my first look at Lady Vivienne at the head table. She was tall and thin. Her hair was long and worn in a plait down the middle of her back. Though it was white as a summer cloud she seemed ageless to me. She moved with the same lithe grace and energy as her young acolytes.

Ector, Uriens, Leodegrance and their closest retainers were seated with her. A seating arrangement I am now sure was no accident placed Arthur and I with the other young people we had met. Owain, Gawaine, and Agravaine joined us at a small round table near the head dais. Kay and Eiddelig were supposed to be there, but declined to sit with "the kids" and went to join a group of the fighting men. Guinevere carried a chair from her assigned place next to her father and sat between Arthur and me.

Acolytes and servants meandered around the tables, serving drinks. Trenchers of food were being prepared though not yet served when Lady Vivienne stood.

I had never seen anything like it, though in years to come Arthur would consistently have the same effect whenever he wished to speak. She did not yell out for our attention. No bells were rung. No one banged on the table to call us to order. She simply stood there. But something drew our attention. Her simple presence was a calm center in the hubbub. Voices became quieter and gradually came to a stop. Soon all eyes were fixed on her.

"Thank you for coming to Avalon," she said. Her voice was low, yet seemed to carry. Her words were clear in the evening air. Later, Owain would confide to me that he believed she was speaking directly into our minds, a power he said all the witches of Avalon possessed. Owain was always one of the more superstitious of our number.

"We are honored," she continued, "to have so many of you here this early in the summer. Any peaceful gathering of the people of Britain is a reason for celebration. This is a small sample of the numbers who will arrive here later for the festival of the sword, and we are pleased that so many of you will be staying with us until that time. This a rare opportunity for all of us to get to know each other better, to live together here for a time, as a community, as we must all live together as a people in this land.

"But those are issues for the days ahead. Tonight we celebrate. Tonight we share food and communion. Tonight we share our stories with one another. We thank the Goddess and the God, the Christ and all of the other names we use to invoke that which is larger than ourselves, and to bless this meal and look favorably on this union."

Vivienne paused here, but it was clear she was not finished.

"But, before we eat..." she said with a twinkle in her eyes. There was a collective groan from the crowd, the first sound uttered since she had begun, followed immediately by good-natured laughter.

"I know, I know," Vivienne laughed, "but my sisters have worked hard to prepare entertainment for this special occasion. Please, give them your attention."

A drumbeat echoed through the clearing. Strings and flutes soon joined it, as did the beat of other percussions. A group of musicians glided into the open area directly in front of the Shrine. As the music swelled I saw a small fleet of the swan boats coming to shore from the island. They were full of the acolytes of Avalon, all clad in the same white dresses and wearing wreathes of flowers on their heads.

The boats came to ground on the shore and the women flowed out of them, dancing around either side of the Shrine and then rejoining in the clear space in front of it. The dance they performed, and the music we heard, was perhaps the most magical thing I ever saw at that lake until many, many years later.

To this day I don't know how to describe what I saw. They danced, but it was more than that. A story unfolded, told without words. Morgan, who was a featured dancer, told us later that it was a recreation of one of the stories of Queen Mebh and her flirtation with the god of the forest and the hunt. I know I didn't understand the subtleties, or follow the whole narrative, but my attention was captivated. Part of it was simply watching that many beautiful young women. Their movements were lithe and graceful, sensual and arousing.

But there was more to it than that. As I watched them weave in and around each other with ever increasing speed and complexity I found myself wondering; what must it be like to be able to move with that sort of dexterity and precision? The only comparison I was able to make in my own life was the feeling I had on horseback. I had trained Butter to a level of agility beyond that of most of the other horses. We became one when I was riding; my thoughts were his actions. We moved with speed, power, and agility. If a horse can be said to dance, then Butter did when under my control. But we were alone whenever we did this. What would it be like to maneuver like these dancers did, with so many others around? Would it be possible to train an entire cavalry to this level of proficiency? And if so, to what end? The acolytes' dance was meant as entertainment, to tell a story. What would be the purpose of training horses to a similar dance, beyond the ability to simply prove you could?

I was still envisioning herds of horses in synchronized movement when the dancers came to a moment of complete stillness and the music echoed until there was no sound left. The crowd erupted into loud applause and cheers while the ladies of Avalon curtsied and bowed.

Gawaine whistled shrilly and cried for more, though I'm sure he was more interested in watching supple young females in motion than in the dance itself. Agravaine applauded politely.

Arthur cheered and clapped as fervently as the rest of the audience. He caught Morgan's eye and I saw her give him a wink.

"So," Arthur said as I joined the ovation, "what did you think?"

"It was really good," I said. "The girls are really talented." It was a poor response, but under the circumstances I couldn't very well admit I had been thinking about horses.

Food was served soon thereafter and we all tucked in. I have no memory of what we ate. It blends together with all the other meals I had at Avalon over the years, but I have no doubt it was wonderful. The women there worked magic in their kitchens.

Morgan joined us, sitting by Arthur's side. Her dress clung provocatively to her sweat-sheened body. Her hair was loose and long, a pitch-black waterfall that reached the small of her back. She wore makeup to enhance her role in the dance. Dark black kohl outlined her eyes, making the pools of blue even more startling.

"That was wonderful," Arthur said to her and he started another round of applause at our table. "How long have you rehearsed for that?"

"We dance all the time at Avalon," she replied. "Most of the dances are oft-told stories and the steps are traditional. From the time we first arrive here as young girls we become a part of the ongoing dance. We don't learn it. We live it."

"You were all beautiful," Guinevere said.

"Especially that redhead with the big..."

Morgan stopped Gawaine from finishing his sentence by

clapping her hand over his mouth.

"I've never seen anything like it," Guinevere said. "I wish I could do that."

"Maybe I could teach you some moves sometime," Morgan said.

"I would like that," Guinevere replied. Happy with the offer she went back to her food. I'm pretty sure I wasn't meant to hear the offer Morgan made to Arthur then.

"There are some moves I would like to teach you sometime as well," she said.

Dinner eventually concluded but the evening's activities continued. People wandered off and reconvened in small groups. There was music, and storytelling. Wine and ale flowed freely, as did conversation. I think, because of the seating arrangements at dinner there was more interaction among the members of the various factions present. Though it was a warm summer night torches and campfires were lit. The heat wasn't needed, but there is something about the light of a fire that breeds companionship.

My table companions and I retired to a secluded spot near Ector's camp. Owain got our fire going while Gawaine broke out the ale skin. I don't remember what we talked about. The conversations of the young I suppose, trying to establish our identities and expounding on our understanding of the way the world works, with all the arrogance of the inexperienced.

Morgan sat close to Arthur, and moved gradually closer as the evening wore on. Looks passed between them that I now recognize as attraction and lust. At the time I knew something was happening between them, but my inexperience with women and the ways of sex was so complete that I really didn't figure it out.

Guinevere sat close to me, and like Morgan she moved closer as time passed. In her case I don't believe the movement was as calculated, or even that Guinevere had anything in mind beyond being near to me. Still, I was uncomfortable with her proximity. I never questioned the appropriateness of Guinevere's unescorted company. I suppose it was testament to Leodegrance's trust in us, though in retrospect I suspect some chaperone was within eyesight of her at all times. I do know that before the hour was too late someone came to escort her back to her father's camp. She bid us all goodnight.

"May I ride with you tomorrow?" she asked me before leaving. The trip to Benwick was scheduled to continue then and Leodegrance's entire group was going. I assumed she meant to accompany me on the road.

"Uh," I stammered, "I guess so." Guinevere beamed and skipped off to her own bower.

"Someone has a crush on Bedivere," Gawaine teased when she was well out of earshot.

"No she doesn't," I defended, though I knew better. I felt awkward by the obviousness of it. The most desirable young acolyte at Avalon was leaning into Arthur with obvious invitation in her eyes. I had no doubt Gawaine could wander off and find some sort of female companionship. It was just my luck to be the object of a child's first crush.

"Yes she does," Morgan said. "Believe me, as a woman, thirteen is not too young to be attracted to a man. Look closely at how wide and moist her eyes are whenever she looks at you."

"I'm sure that's not all that's wide and moist," Gawaine said, taking the profane path as always.

"That's enough," Arthur said. "Crush or not, she's young and not a fit target for barracks humor."

"Sorry," Gawaine said and acknowledged the reproach with a nod.

I stood up, more embarrassed than angry.

"I'm going to take a walk," I said.

"Come on," Gawaine said. "I'm said I was sorry. I didn't mean anything. My mouth sometimes says things my brain hasn't heard."

"It's all right," I said. "No harm done, as long as Guinevere didn't hear you. I just need to stretch my legs."

"He always checks his horse before retiring," Arthur confirmed, giving me the excuse I needed.

"Probably needs to piss like one after all this ale," Gawaine laughed. He was genuinely puzzled at the looks of reprobation the others gave him. I didn't let him see my smile as I walked away. In spite of his unruly behavior I liked Gawaine. He was blunt as a hammer, but as honest a man as I ever met. No one I have ever known took more actual joy from life.

I did visit the latrines before the stables; Gawaine's assumptions were correct in that after all. I made sure Butter was settled in and well cared for and gave him an apple I had pocketed at dinner. I realized as I walked back to our campfire that I was tired. It had been a very long day.

Owain and Agravaine sat in silence at the fire. No one else was there.

"What happened to Arthur?" I asked, though I had my suspicions.

"He and Morgan took a walk together," Owain said with a knowing smile.

"I think," Agravaine added, " that my brother went to look for that redhead he was so enamored of. Though I believe he may be too drunk to do anything if he finds her."

"And," Owain said as he stood and wiped off the seat of his pants, "I think I need to sleep. It was a good day." With that he bade us both goodnight and wandered off into the dark.

I sat down. Agravaine poked at the fire with a stick, but said nothing. What followed was a long, uncomfortable silence that set the tone of my relationship with Agravaine for the rest of our lives.

Poor, aggravating Agravaine. I never warmed up to him. I don't know if anyone did. He was simply one of the most unlikable people I ever knew. I don't know if it was because he had suffered as the most frequent target of Gawaine's jests, or simply because he had grown up in the shadow of his overly ebullient brother. I think he was just one of those people, born with a permanent burr up his butt. Not only would he never be happy, he didn't want anyone else to be either.

"Well, " I said after much too long a time, "I need to get some sleep. Tomorrow will be the first of several long days of riding before we get to the boats and the shore. Good night." Agravaine nodded but did not speak as I stood.

I went to my tent. Kay and Eiddelig both were snoring on the ground next to their dying fire. They cradled empty wineskins like lovers. Tomorrow was going to be a long, difficult day in the saddle for both of them.

I shucked off my boots and curled up in my bedroll. I was asleep quickly and didn't know Arthur had returned until I woke to find him there the following morning. A smile painted his sleeping face. Leaves and twigs were entangled in his hair. He smelled of dirt, crushed fresh grass, and sweat. There lingered about him a scent of something I did not recognize then, but which every man who knows the charms of women becomes acquainted with.

CHAPTER EIGHT

I have wondered about that first meeting between Arthur and Morgan many times over the years. Ector knew he was fostering Uther's son, had known from the day Merlin showed up on his doorstep with the newborn babe. He also knew that Arthur's mother Igraine had two daughters to Gorlois before Arthur was conceived. The older, Morgause, was quickly married off to King Lot and went north where she birthed Gawaine and Agravaine. The younger was of course Morgan, sent to the island of Avalon on the death of her mother when she was still a child. Ector had to know who Morgan was.

So why had he been so careless in allowing them to come together as he did? Did he simply believe that, given the number of young available women there, the chances of Arthur going to his half-sister's bed were too slim to take into account? If Ector had made some special effort to keep them apart it might have looked suspicious I suppose. Maybe he counted on Arthur's naiveté and honor to keep his pants on. Even Merlin had to have known the potential for disaster that lay in their union.

Whatever Ector's motivations, I now know there was a larger plan in motion, even then. I don't know how Ector, simple man that he was, was convinced to facilitate the union.

I still don't claim to fully understand what Merlin was attempting, or even that I fully approve. How did he ever think he could control events and take everything into consideration? I sit here in my small room attempting to simply recount events that have already happened and they scatter before me like leaves on a wind. I saw too much of the fallout and what went wrong to ever believe Merlin could foresee the outcome. He was always behind the scenes, always trying to create a tapestry of mystical events, always just shy of understanding normal human hearts until much too late.

I have been made privy to much that is private and unknown to the world at large. I know why Morgan came to Arthur that night. I know the answer to the questions countless Britons have asked. Through Arthur I came to know Morgan, and as I have said, she loved him, as a sister, as her lover, and as the sacred High King of the land. But those answers came to me later, and as much as I want to recount them here, those events happened well after my first trip to Avalon.

That morning, after Arthur returned to our tent, I only knew he had crossed a threshold into true manhood I had yet to reach. I didn't know the answer to that simple mystery. I didn't have an inkling that there were larger mysteries at work

I didn't know then that Morgan was Arthur's half-sister. I didn't know then that she knew exactly who he was.

Arthur was groggy, tired and exceedingly happy as we packed

up Ector's camp and prepared to continue our trip to Benwick. I looked at him with envious eyes. He seemed removed from me somehow. He possessed knowledge I did not. It was the first time in our lives I felt separated from him by a gap I didn't understand. As the years went by I felt that gap widen many times.

I know now that friendships change, and that none of us remain in stagnant relationship with anyone in our lives. The core of our bond remained, the love we shared. But his tryst with Morgan was my first step in sharing his affection with the world and losing my privileged place with him. I am ashamed to admit how often I felt jealous of the time he was required to spend with so many others as his role and his responsibilities grew. It sounds self-indulgent but he was my friend first and there were many times when I still needed him. Yet for most of the rest of our lives someone else's needs always seemed to come first.

It is difficult growing in the shadow of someone who would one day be a legend. Now, everyone has a piece of him in the form of the stories that are told. My consolation after all this time is that while everyone has the legends I am one of the few who has memories of the real man.

Breakfast consisted of leftovers from the previous nights feast. Special provisions for the road had been packed. The acolytes gave them to us to store in our saddlebags as we mounted up. As a gray-haired matron handed one to me I happened to look toward the edge of the forest. Arthur and Morgan stood together in the shade of a giant oak, embraced as though they were but a single person. I'm afraid I would have continued to stare if a familiar greeting hadn't drawn my attention.

"Good morning, Bedivere," Guinevere chirped. I turned back quickly, guiltily, and hoped she did not see what I was looking at. "Are you as excited as I am?" she said as she sidled her mare up next to Butter.

"About the trip?" I said, though that was obvious.

"Of course, silly," she laughed. She was dressed for riding and presented a very different picture from the well-dressed princess from the night before. Her hair was pulled back in a long braid. Gone was the frilly dinner gown. She looked boyish in her leather riding pants, high boots and a white linen tunic.

Leodegrance's party lined up with ours as we prepared to leave. Riders and wagons and those who walked all gathered near the path that led away from the lake and into the woods. A small detachment came from Uriens, one single wagon and an even dozen men. Owain waved as he walked by. A slightly larger group came from the Orkney camp. Gawaine and Agravaine rode by, racing to be the first along the path.

"Good morning, Guinevere," Arthur said when he finally joined us. He was still smiling, but as the entourage came together his distraction disappeared. Leodegrance had given Ector free rein to organize our departure. Arthur paid close attention.

Finally, we were ready to leave. Ector gave the train a once-over, then waved his arm in the air and began to move forward. Very slowly, a unit at a time, we began our journey through the forest on the path that led back to the Roman road. Lady Vivienne stood at the Shrine surrounded by priestesses and acolytes. They sang as they waved their farewells.

The forest path was well traveled, but still slow going for the number of people and wagons we had. It was midday before we reached the paved thoroughfare. From there our speed increased, though we were still limited by those who walked.

The day was sunny, warm and pleasant. Though Ector assigned outriders to precede the main body there was not really any fear of attack. We were traveling through friendly lands and we were too large a group for petty bandits to harass. Only a large group of armed men would pose a serious threat. We would already have been aware of any Saxon incursions between Avalon and the coast. Our progress was leisurely and enjoyable, allowing for much sightseeing, contemplation and conversation. Guinevere rode next to me most of that first day.

"I've never been this far from home," she said as we rode through heather covered fields. "I've already seen so much more than I ever dreamed. Last night was so wonderful. I wish I could see the island of Avalon itself. It must be even more astonishing there."

"Maybe someday you will," I said.

"I doubt it," she replied with a down-turned smile. "They are very careful with visitors, I hear. There are mysteries that are only shared with adherents of the old religion and taught to the acolytes."

"No offense, but does that frighten you? What I mean is, I don't know very much about either the old ways or the Christians. I know some followers of the Christ think the old ways are somehow evil."

"Some, I guess. There have been priests at home who said that, but my father usually doesn't allow them to stay long. He says there are still too many followers of the old ways for them to be completely wrong. Father Emrys says that being Christian is a new way of looking at the old mysteries, but down deep they are all the same. I don't know enough about it, but that makes sense to me, even though the Church would probably disagree."

"But aren't there consequences to disagreeing with the Church?"

"Well... the Church says if you believe in anything it doesn't approve of you will spend eternity in Hell. But they also say Jesus and God are loving and forgiving. I can't believe in a god that loves you but will send you to Hell for small infractions of his will. That would be like following a king who doesn't want the best for all of his people. One who would punish and torture anyone who questioned his decisions. What about all of the people who lived before Jesus? What about everyone in other lands who lived and died without ever knowing about Christ? Would a loving god punish them for their ignorance?"

"It all sounds too complicated for me," I said.

"Exactly," Guinevere replied. "Father Emrys says that whatever God is, it's big enough to have it all figured out in a way that includes everybody."

Father Emrys didn't sound like any Christian priest I had ever heard of.

"I like talking to you," Guinevere said. "It feels like I've known you my whole life." At our tender ages neither of us knew just how long a whole life can be, or ultimately, how short.

The details of traveling, much like traveling itself, are tedious. I was to spend much of my life in places between destinations and there is very little to relate of significance. The four days we spent getting to the coast are more vivid to me than most of my sojourns simply because it was the first time.

Guinevere continued to be my regular riding companion when I was not engaged in other duties. I was constantly impressed with how thoughtful and insightful she was. Father Emrys had done a good job training her critical thinking skills. She was well versed in the classics and in history. There were times when she and Arthur got lost in discussion and debate over some old text they had both read which I had not. I couldn't participate, but still enjoyed the flow of conversation as they both made points and defended their own thoughts. I began to see that their discourse was much the same as being trained to fight; it was sparring, only with words. They would strike out, looking for a weakness in the others defenses, or be raised in defense of their own position. There were times when it became heated, though Arthur was always the more restrained of the two. He often sought refuge in pure reason while Guinevere argued from a place of passion. Even then I saw the balance they provided for each other as they unknowingly practiced the skills of statecraft.

If my first view of the lake at Avalon impressed me it had done nothing to prepare me for my first encounter with the ocean. I had heard it described, but for those of us who had spent their entire lives landlocked the immensity of it simply could not be imagined. We could smell it on the breeze long before it came into sight. Next came the crashing sound of the breakers and the squalls of sea birds.

"Come on!" Guinevere cried as her excitement finally got the best of her. She urged her mare into a gallop and surged forward to the top of the rise that overlooked the ocean. Arthur and I caught up a second later. All three of us reined to a halt, speechless.

The water stretched out before us, coming to an end only where it met the sky. I had seen the far horizon from hilltops of course, but this was different. Maybe it was just because I was raised inland and took it for granted, but it was always easy to imagine another field or hill just beyond the last one you could see. Here it looked as if the world simply came to an end. I knew better, of course. History told me ships had sailed the ocean for centuries and as far as I knew none had actually fallen off the edge. I knew the continent was really not very far away from where we stood, much closer than the distance we had already covered if the accounts were to be believed.

"What must it be like to be out in the middle of that?" Guinevere said. The look of awe on her face mirrored what I felt. "I hear there are places on the ocean where you can't see land at all. It must be terribly lonely to sit there, surrounded by the entire world but unable to touch it."

"We're about to find out," Arthur said and pointed to the beach. In our wonderment at the sea we had not paid attention to the ships docked at the busy port below. The area bustled with preparations. A large group of other travelers had already arrived; King Mark's entourage if I recognized the Roman eagle banner he flew correctly.

The rest of our party caught up with us. I expected Gawaine to give loud voice to the wonder the rest of us felt, but he was unmoved by the spectacle of the sea. I had forgotten that his home in the Orkneys sat along a windswept rocky coast. These waves must have seemed tame to his eyes.

We rode down to the port. Ector and Leodegrance went forward to meet with the dock master and confirm our arrangements to sail. When they returned the next few hours were taken up with organizing all of our belongings and preparing them for transport. The wagons, and to my disappointment, all of our horses, would be cared for here until our return. King Ban had made traveling arrangements for us on the continent. It wasn't until years later that I would experience the joys of transporting frightened animals across the sea firsthand.

I said goodbye to Butter at the stables and then rejoined Arthur as he finished packing Kay's gear. Once that was done we were free to roam and explore. It would be several hours before everything was loaded onto the ships, and we weren't scheduled to actually set sail until the morning tide. We sought out Gawaine and Agravaine to join us, and it wasn't long before Owain found us as well. Guinevere, with a chaperone trailing not far behind, met us at the docks. The bonds were already being formed.

We were surrounded by the noisy hustle and bustle of dock life. None of us, even the Orkney brothers, had ever seen anything quite like this before. The docks were a small community. Most of the activity was based around the comings and goings of the ships of course, but I was surprised to see so many other businesses. Mixed in with the shops dedicated to seafaring endeavors we saw vendors selling food and other wares, a blacksmith's shop, and of course, a tavern. Most of the people we saw were of common British stock, but there were a few more exotic visitors as well. I saw swarthy Mediterranean complexions, not all that uncommon since Rome had come to Britain, I suppose, but unusual enough in my experience. There was a group of Christian mendicants asking for alms. I saw one man whose skin was the color of coal dressed in colorful silks and carrying a large curved sword.

We were wide-eyed and incredulous. In less than an hour we all saw and experienced a wider range of what the world had to offer than any of us had ever seen.

Late in the afternoon our attention was drawn by the sound of music.

"Listen," Guinevere said. She actually grabbed my hand to stop me. I felt the blush rise up my neck when I saw Gawaine had noticed. I ignored his annoying smile and tried to focus on the song.

Unlike the complicated instrumentation we heard the night of the dance in Avalon this was a simple melody played on a sweet-sounding string instrument. The tune was lively, but a melancholy air seemed to underscore the whole. We were drawn to discover the source.

Before we spotted the musician he began to sing. I recognized the ballad of Culwch and Olwen, a traditional song everyone knows. I had heard it performed by traveling bards many times at home but I had never heard it rendered with as much passion. The voice belonged to a young man, but it was rich and full, powerful without needing to be loud. I believe we were all captivated by the performer's magic before we ever saw him. Once we did find him the spell was complete.

He sat on top of a pallet laden with crates and traveling trunks. A group of people formed a circle around him, as enthralled by the music as we were. At first it didn't appear to me as though he could possibly be real. He was simply too beautiful for that. And yes, I describe this youth as beautiful, for there are no male equivalents to that word that could do him justice. Arthur was handsome. Gawaine was boyish. In later years my own face was described not unkindly as rugged. This young man was beautiful, like someone from the Otherworld or like what angels have been described to look like. His hair was exceedingly pale golden blonde and fell about his shoulders in ringlets. His eyes were as dark as Morgan's hair. He wore a bright wine-colored silk tunic, tied around his waist with vibrant scarves. The full sleeves were rolled up on his arms and bound in place with yellow ribbons. His fingers were long and nimble on the strings. He looked strong, but somehow fey.

The instrument he played was unfamiliar to me at the time. I discovered later it was Welsh in origin and called a *crwth*. It had a box-shaped body with six catgut strings stretched along a short neck.

He poured his heart into the song in a way I had never heard. Guinevere clutched my hand ever more tightly as the tale of tragic love unfolded. I don't think anyone in the audience was exactly sure when he finished. The images he conjured and the music he made lingered in our minds even after he was through. Eventually someone began to applaud, and the spell was broken. We all joined in then. The singer nodded his thanks and began to gather the coins that were being tossed into his open instrument case.

Guinevere pulled me in her wake as she ran forward to speak to the young man.

"That was beautiful," she said. "I've never heard anything so beautiful."

"Thank you, my lady," the young man said. He took her small hand and kissed it. "Your praise is all the payment I need."

"That and the coins you've collected," Agravaine sneered.

"These?" the singer said as he lifted his cloth purse, now full. He laughed. "I plan on giving these to the children along the docks. I have no need of coin but I can't seem to stop people from giving it to me when I play."

"Do you live here?" Arthur asked.

"No, I just arrived last evening. I'm traveling to Benwick tomorrow."

"We're all going to Benwick as well," Arthur said. He shook hands with the musician and introduced all of us. "You must be part of King Mark's entourage."

"Mark is my uncle," the musician said with a wide smile. "My name is Tristan."

"Oh," Guinevere said, "Father has mentioned you. He was friends with your father Meliodos once." Guinevere suddenly blushed and clapped a hand over her mouth. I remembered then, as did she I assume, that both Tristan's father and mother had died when he was but a babe.

"I'm sorry," she said. "I didn't mean..."

"It's okay, my lady," Tristan said. "I don't remember him. My only sorrow is that I have no memory, so any story about or mention of my parents is welcome. In the meantime Mark has been as good a father to me as I could have asked for.

"And," he added, "I have heard of all of you as well."

"How?" Owain asked.

"You're the sons, and daughter, of many of the kings of Uther's time. Taliesin has mentioned you all."

"Taliesin?" Arthur asked.

"A traveling bard. He is my music and history teacher. He said I would probably meet some of you on this trip to Benwick, but I expected something more formal than this random encounter."

"It does seem strange," Arthur said.

"Or destined," Tristan laughed. "Perhaps we are at the beginning of a great adventure. They all start with strange encounters."

Tristan swore to me for years, whenever we discussed our first meeting, that that was exactly what he said. He swears it still. But then he has a flair for the dramatic and is a liar in the way the best storytellers are. I don't really believe him, but my memory doesn't hold what was actually said.

I don't suppose there was any one of our Companions I understood less than Tristan. We were so very different. But unlike

Owain or Agravaine whom I never warmed up to, it was impossible not to love Tristan. I suppose it was because he gave his own so readily. While the rest of the world struggled to decide if their allegiance was to the old gods or the Christ, Tristan was wholeheartedly seduced by the god of love. More than anyone other than Gawaine, Tristan drank fully from the cup of life, and took more joy from simple pleasures. Unlike Gawaine, Tristan was a more complex soul. Life brought him great delight, but its sadness genuinely hurt him. I'm told his name means "born in sorrow" and if he wore his joys on his sleeve, he also carried life's burdens on his shoulders. There was a wide stream of melancholy that wound its way through his life, and I believe that much of his profligacy was an attempt to distract him from his pain.

I saw no evidence of Tristan's sorrow that first afternoon as he took on the role of guide. Not only had he been on the docks longer than the rest of us and knew his way around, but he had also spent much of his life on and around boats. Cornwall sticks out into the ocean like a large thumb. Many of its villages lie along the coast and make their living from the sea. It also made them the frequent target of Irish raiders. Many attempts had been made at treaties with the Irish, but so far none had come to lasting fruition.

Tristan pointed out the various types of ships while we walked. Guinevere was nervous about her first trip on the sea, and truth be told, so was I.

"How do they know where they're going?" she asked. "There are no landmarks, nothing to judge where you are or where you have been. Why don't they get lost?"

"These ships make the trip across the Channel all the time," Tristan said. "They know the route."

"They know their position by using the position of the sun and the stars," Gawaine added.

"But what if the boat sinks?" Guinevere said.

"It won't," Tristan assured her. "We're not traveling in stormy weather."

"These waves are puny," Gawaine said. "The ocean back home is a wild horse, bucking and whirling, but the men of Orkney sail it with ease. They would look at this sea like it was a warm bath."

"What about the Saxons?" Owain asked.

"There are no reports of Saxon raiders anywhere along our route," Arthur said. "Ector says they have been quiet along the southern shore for quite some time. I don't think this trip would have been planned if there was a serious threat."

"And there are armed men on board," Tristan said. "The ships are always wary of raiders and pirates and have taken measures to protect them selves. This trip involves a great number of boats. No small group of raiders would dare attempt to attack us."

"I'd like to see them try," Gawaine said. "I'd send a boatload to the sea floor all by myself."

The banter and conversation continued throughout the rest of the afternoon. We toured the docks, walked in the sand along the edge of the ocean, threw rocks into the water, and later during an impromptu snack bought from dockside vendors, I ate a raw oyster for the first and last time in my life. Tristan continued to regale us with unlikely tales. His energy and enthusiasm were infectious and I remember few other days in my life filled with as much laughter.

But eventually the day came to an end and we all returned to our camps.

We boarded the boats early the next morning. Unlike the camaraderie we had enjoyed on the road, our passage across the Channel would be shared with only our own groups. It took three ships to ferry all the members of Ector's entourage and two each for Leodegrance and Mark. The men of Lot's group were few enough so that only one ship was needed, even with the addition of Uriens' dozen to their number.

As the tide came in oars slipped into the water and pulled in unison to move us away from the dock. We were lucky to have a steady wind with us that morning, so once we were far enough from shore the oars were shipped and the sails unfurled. They billowed out and we drifted forward. Within a very short span of time we were moving swiftly away from the coast of Britain.

Arthur, Kay and I stood at the railing and watched the land recede and the water churn beneath us. The motion was strange and at first my legs wobbled beneath me with every pitch and yaw of the deck. But, much like riding a horse, I soon found my rhythm and ceased to even notice the constant movement. There are those who become seasick when traveling by boat. It afflicts some people once and then they get over it. Others are never able to ride across the waves and keep their dinner down. I was told both Guinevere and

Owain suffered this affliction, and I witnessed poor Kay turn green and lose his breakfast over the starboard rail–a scene he made us swear never to relate, though I think enough years have passed that Kay would forgive me for breaking that vow in this account.

For myself, the trip was uneventful. I've never understood those who are drawn to the sea and love to travel upon it. At first the novelty of not seeing land intrigued me, but that very soon wore off and the unchanging landscape of waves around us ceased to be anything for me but boring. Perhaps if I had been in control of the boat, actually sailing it instead of being little more than human cargo I would have a different feeling about it. Give me a horse to ride through a changing landscape with trees and rocks and mountains and valleys any day over the visual monotony of the sea.

Luckily, the voyage across the Channel to the continent is a short one, though I'm sure it can be argued that this proximity is part of what allowed the invaders such easy access to our land. Within hours of our departure we docked on the shores of little Brittany and I set foot on the land where I would leave so much behind.

CHAPTER NINE

The small room in which I write is cold this morning. The temperature dropped last night, not enough to leave frost on the grass, but I suppose that will come soon enough. I knew the change in weather was coming; the ache in my arm always lets me know. It is not yet that late in the season. We will still have warm days, even hot ones before the leaves fall. But I have noticed darkness coming earlier each evening, sometimes bringing my task to a close sooner than I am ready. Still I am loath to use the lamps or candles yet. They are precious commodities I don't wish to waste. The long dark hours of winter still lie before us.

The day I first saw the continent was hot and bright. The breeze off the sea was welcome, but the blinding light reflected from it was not. Even shading my eyes with my hands did not help for the light came both from above and below. The shore was a vague image to me until we came very close. A party of men, wagons and horses waited there for us on a sandy beach ringed with tall rocky cliffs. They flew the flag of Benwick.

"I would hate to be a party of raiders attempting to land here,"

Arthur said from the railing where we stood.

"Why?"

"Those cliffs are steep and could hide hundreds of men," he said. "Place a few fortifications on the hillside, arm it with catapults and ballista, and no ship could get close. Then there's all of that open beach for troops to cover, with no retreat except the ocean."

"A shield wall would still have to face them though."

"Yes, but what if there were archers on the hillside? How many could be picked off before they even had a chance to form their lines?"

"Men on horseback could harry them mercilessly as well."

"Good point," Arthur conceded. "Too bad we're not defending this stretch of land from the Saxons."

Unlike our point of departure, there was no dock here. We had to ferry men and equipment to the shore in smaller boats. It was a time-consuming process that took many trips. Arthur, Kay and I were among the first passengers on Ector's craft. Rowers took us right up to the beach, but we still got our feet wet as we waded onto shore.

The envoy of King Ban greeted us. Their leader was a tall man, but I have no other real memory of him. I don't recall ever seeing him after our trip to Benwick, though I must have at some point. Ector greeted him as though he knew him.

Leodegrance, in a second boat right behind us, landed before introductions could be made. Kay helped him from the boat; it had come to my attention while we traveled that Leodegrance was frailer than he liked to let on. Arthur and I moved to help Guinevere and try to keep her from stepping into the surf, but before we could move a young man from Ban's party rushed forward and lifted her out of the boat. She squealed in delight at being swept up into his arms and continued to laugh as he carried her across the threshold of the sea. I thought him bold to touch her in so casual a manner, but even then I knew it was the same thing I had stepped forward to do. Still, I had come to know her in the past few days and this brash youth had never met her before.

It was the first time I felt jealousy toward this man. It was not to be the last.

"Thank you," Guinevere said, "but you can put me down now." He lowered her dainty feet to the ground, and then treated her to an innocent smile.

He was handsome with more than a trace of the old Roman look about him. He had an angular face with dark blue eyes. His hair was black, cut short with just a hint of curl.

"At your service, milady," he said, and swept into a low bow.

"And who might I say is in my service?" she asked. There was playfulness in her voice.

"You can tell everyone that Lancelot, son of King Ban of Benwick, is your humble servant," he said, and bowed again.

Arthur and Kay laughed and introduced themselves.

Was I the only one not charmed by Lancelot? He seemed arrogant to me, and presumptuous. I now realize that he simply carried himself with the same self-assurance that Arthur did. But I had always known Arthur and took his confidence for granted. Lancelot just simply rubbed me the wrong way.

I also realize now that I was envious of him. I remained partly so throughout our lives, even as I got to know him better and saw how alike we were in many ways. We shared a love of horses that would translate into one of Arthur's greatest strengths. I could not have been as successful as Marshall of Arthur's cavalry without him. We worked together, and fought at each other's sides. We both played our roles in the forging of Camelot and a united Britain.

But I could never understand why everyone seemed to love him so. It may sound petty of me, but it galls me when the storytellers refer to him as Arthur's closest friend, and to the tragedy of their love triangle with Guinevere. I believe he loved Arthur, and I believe he loved Guinevere, and he claimed to love the Christian God. But in the end he didn't love any of them enough to make a choice. He loved himself too much to deny any of them, and as a result betrayed them all.

But I get ahead of my story, though the basic outline of many of the events that followed seem to be known by everyone.

The unloading of the ships and transference of the cargo to the waiting wagons took the rest of the day. We were all kept busy with various duties. It wasn't long before my eyes were drawn to the horses the men of Benwick rode.

I fell in love that day, and I now realize that was the true beginning of Arthur's cavalry. It was also the bond I shared with Lancelot. We were from different continents and of different temperaments, but our shared love of horses was a bridge where we could meet. It was a narrow bridge, perhaps the width a sword's edge, but it was there. My fondest recollections of Lancelot are infused with the scent of horses and the remembered feel of riding.

He saw my interest immediately.

"Would you like a closer look?" he asked. I nodded and we approached the herd. Warok was already there, inspecting the mounts and taking stock of the needs of Ector's men. I spoke a greeting, but he didn't hear me. I assume he was as enthused by the animals as I was.

"They're beautiful!" I said. Like our own arrangement at home the horses here were separated in two groups–the working class animals that pulled the wagons and carried the loads, and the warhorses. But there was a bigger difference between them than I had ever seen, though that perhaps speaks more to my lack of worldliness than to the uniqueness of the Benwick herd.

"Thank you," Lancelot said. He rubbed the forehead of a black charger with true affection. "They descend from Arabian stock." I had heard of Arabian horses, but had never seen one.

"They're smaller than our horses back home," I said. "Are they strong enough to pull wagons and carried armored men?"

"We have different stocks for each task. Look over where the wagons are. Those are dray horses, bigger and stronger than these. They can pull a wagon with ease, but are not known for their speed and maneuverability.

"These, on the other hand," he continued, referring to the Arabians, "are for our cavalry. They can carry an armored man, as long as it is light armor. What they lack in size and power they more than

151

make up for in speed.

"Would you like to take a ride?" he asked with light in his eyes.

There was nothing I wanted more. I sought out Warok to make sure there were no other duties I had to attend to first. He saw my excitement and gave me permission to go.

"We need an assessment of their abilities," Warok said. "You're the best man for the job. Go and see what these little things can do."

In short order Lancelot and I were in the saddle and riding along the edge of the surf. My mount was chestnut in color, with a light, lacy whiteness along the belly and lower legs. He felt strange beneath me in comparison to Butter. But in spite of my unfamiliarity, he was well trained and responded quickly to the reins and, more importantly, to the subtle commands I gave through my legs and the shifts in my weight.

We started at an easy walk. We left the beach and followed a well-used trail up over the steep hill to the fields beyond. Once there the horses began a trot and then moved up to a canter. My mount was agile and noticeably faster than Butter. As we rode I could sense his desire to run, a barely contained energy coursing through his body.

"Go ahead!" Lancelot yelled. "Let him go. Race me to that distant line of trees." With that he sped ahead. Smiling at the challenge I urged my own mount forward. It launched into a gallop with a quickness I had never before experienced, and soon I was traveling over the field faster than I had ever moved before. It was exhilarating, the wind against my face and the feel of power between my legs. But throughout our race I still felt completely in control of the horse. This was no wild dash across the meadow, but a focused act of will between horse and rider.

I caught up with Lancelot easily and paced him. Just when I thought I was about to pull ahead I saw that he was toying with me. He dropped behind my horse and before I had even realized what he had done he was riding along my other side. He easily pulled ahead and pranced his mount to the side in front of me, then fell back to my side again. I tried to speed up, but he simply fell back and did the same stunt again. It is an old cliché, but he was riding circles around me.

A row of low bushes stood ahead of us. Lancelot drove his horse straight at them at an uncanny speed. I knew, at this pace, Butter would never have been able to stop in time and would simply crash right through them. Lancelot's mount didn't stop either. To my surprise he leapt completely over the low hedge and landed gracefully on the other side. A moment later my mount did the same thing, and in that moment I was flying.

But the race was not yet over. Now I had a better sense of what my horse could do. I had to stop thinking of Butter and the limitations of movement his larger size demanded.

Lancelot's actions reminded me of the dancers I had seen at Avalon, and the thoughts I had that night came back to me. I pulled alongside my rival and smiled. Secure in his superior horsemanship he returned the grin. It faded quickly as I dropped back and then charged up on his other side and then in front of him, using the same stunt he pulled on me. I dropped back alongside him again and winked. He acknowledged my achievement and took it as a challenge. His horse leapt forward again.

We continued in this fashion for the length of the field, each of us making new uses of the horses' natural skill and reacting to each other's feats. We wove around each other in complex patterns and I wondered what we could do if we added a third rider, and a fourth, or eventually a whole fighting unit. How could this added dexterity be used in a practical way?

We reined in at the edge of the forest. Lancelot beat me there, winning the race. He was the better horseman, though at the time I believe part of it was his familiarity with his steed. We dismounted and led the horses into the shade where we found a small stream. I needed a cool drink as much as the horses did.

"You ride well," Lancelot said. I wasn't sure if it was meant as a genuine compliment or an expression of surprise. I tried to take it as the former.

"Give me time to familiarize myself with this horse and I will ride better," I said. "Do you have much opportunity to use these horses in battle?"

"Not really," he admitted. "The Saxons don't seem to be as interested in our land as in yours. They pass through here on occasion to access the Channel, but rarely in force. We are too small a kingdom to attempt to stop a large invasion force, and too large a country to notice every small war band that moves through quietly in the night."

"Your cavalry would be excellent at chasing down a defeated enemy, or harrying an already broken line, but they probably don't have the weight or power to break a shield wall." I spoke as though I was an veteran warrior instead of an untried youth who had only studied tactics and heard stories from those far more experienced than I. Shield walls were usually the provinces of men, though occasionally horses were used to break one. Our large warhorses were simply a heavy hammer slamming against the shields, using speed and weight to crush an enemy that men can't break through. The problem with this tactic is the cost. Far too many horses are killed on the spear points of the front line. The sad truth is that a warhorse is more expensive to train and maintain than a soldier is. An army can more easily afford to lose countless men on the shield wall than to spend horses.

"That's true," Lancelot conceded. "We rarely have need of those tactics here, though. Like I said, no large army of invaders has ever stretched a shield wall across our land. King Hoel has our southern border covered. We use our cavalry mostly to chase down bandits and in the occasional skirmish."

"You're lucky then," I said, as though I had been fighting Saxons my whole life.

"Except for Ysbaddon to the east at Mont St. Michael we really haven't had a regular threat for years."

"Ysbaddon?" I asked. "Isn't that the name of the giant in Culwych and Olwen?" The name was familiar to me, and to anyone who had heard the ballad. It was fresh in my mind from Tristan's performance.

"Yes," Lancelot laughed. "It is said he took the name because he *is* a giant. I've never seen him, so I don't know."

"How much of a threat is he?"

"Not much. The castle of Mont St. Michael lay empty until five years ago. Ysbaddon is the rightful king of that small plot of ground, though he had been missing and presumed dead for a long time. He moved back in with a small army, though might be better to describe them as a gang of bandits. They terrorize the small population of the land he claims is his. There is an occasional raid wherein they steal cattle from some poor farmer and then run away. Some lives have been lost, but not enough to justify a response."

"Why not?"

"His fortress sits on a steep hill with a supply of fresh water inside. No army could break through his gates and a siege would last forever. We can't spare the men for the length of time it would take to break him."

"So you tolerate a neighbor who is dangerous to your people?"

"What should we do? Risk the lives of our men in a prolonged siege or battle to stop what is essentially a nuisance?"

I was pretty sure the farmers and all of the others who lived in the shadow of this "giant" would not think their loss of life and property a mere nuisance. But, I didn't know all of the details of the situation, so I reined in my idealism until I was better informed.

We took our time returning to the beach, allowing our horses to walk at their own pace. Our conversation continued with the focus returning to horses. I forgot about Ysbaddon, little knowing the role he was to play in the next two days, or the lifelong effect he was to have on me personally.

CHAPTER TEN

We were so foolish...so arrogant... so young. We had no real understanding of what we were getting into. It can be argued that we were successful. Our raid saved lives and ended the reign of a tyrant. It also bonded those of us who participated in ways that would last a lifetime. The core of the Round Table, not the physical object but the men who embodied it, was forged that night.

But the cost was high, and it could have been so much worse.

I'm getting ahead of myself again.

The remainder of the trip to Benwick was uneventful, and I have already spent too much of this account talking about traveling. The developing friendships among us began to slip into patterns that would accompany us for years. Owain and Agravaine were always present with the rest of us, but they were both quiet by nature, as was I. I barely recall their presence, and I daresay they would have said the same of me in their memories as well. They were quite the contrast to Gawaine and Tristan, whose laughter was frequent and heartfelt, as well as loud. They hit it off immediately and I think no one enjoyed the trip more than the two of them.

Guinevere continued to be my riding companion and engaged me in ongoing conversation. There were times I was hard pressed to keep up. To my consternation, Arthur's attention was taken up almost entirely by Lancelot. They talked and laughed for most of the trip and there seemed to be very little room in their banter for anyone else.

I think each of them saw a reflection of himself in the other. Both were charismatic. Both were natural leaders whose mere presence inspired loyalty. Even as young men they were both filled with self-assurance that few ever know. They were, in many ways, two of a kind. I recognized this immediately, and have spent a lifetime trying to understand how I could love one of them so much and be so judgmental of the other. Simple jealousy accounts for some of it, though I am embarrassed to admit it. But there is more than that. Arthur's circle was inclusive and made room for everyone. He was always the king, and everyone around him was enclosed in the circumference of his personality. Lancelot was the warrior. The circle around him was well protected and constantly defended. He let very few people, if anyone, get inside. For all their similarities, only Arthur remained true to his ideals.

Benwick was in an uproar when we arrived. Ector, Leodegrance and Mark were immediately summoned to King Ban's presence while the rest of us unloaded our baggage and got settled in. Rumors flew wild as we established our camp, but no one really seemed to know what was happening. In the course of a few hours I heard everything from an attack by a Saxon army to the return of the Romans. One wide-eyed stable boy told me with all sincerity that a nest of dragons had awakened to our south and were even now flying here to burn Benwick to the ground.

It wasn't until dinner that we heard the real story. A feast had been planned for our arrival, and although there was plenty of food available our official welcome had been delayed. None of the higher-ranking members of the kingdom of Benwick or of our entourage were present.

Our small group of friends had met at the great hall for dinner. Guinevere and her maid had joined us, as had Kay, though Eiddelig was nowhere to be found. We sat at a long table, eating our fill and doing our share of speculation when Lancelot joined us. As the son of King Ban and eventual heir of Benwick he had been allowed into the meeting in the throne room and heard firsthand what had taken place.

"It's terrible news," he said as he sat next to Arthur.

"What happened?" Arthur asked.

"Ysbaddon," Lancelot said, and then gave the others the same information he had shared with me about the giant of Mont St. Michael.

"King Hoel was traveling from his kingdom to the south to join the meeting here," Lancelot explained. "He was traveling light, with his family and just a few men at arms. That part of the kingdom is peaceful. There has not been an incident there, not even an occurrence of bandits, in many years. He has made the trip a hundred times with no problems."

"But not this time," Arthur said.

"No. His train was set upon by a group of armed men, led by

Ysbaddon himself. He has never strayed so far into our lands before. Hoel's men were struck down almost before they knew they were being attacked. Ysbaddon killed the horses that pulled the king's carriage with an ax, and then ripped the door right off. He pulled Hoel out and struck him in the head. Ysbaddon simply threw Hoel into a ditch along the side of the road and left him there."

"He's not dead, then?" Kay asked.

"No, though he does have a head wound. He will heal. One of his men also survived the attack, although he was wounded as well. He found King Hoel and carried him here on horseback."

"You said he was traveling with his family," Guinevere said. "What happened to them?"

A dark cloud passed over Lancelot's face.

"The surviving man at arms said that Queen Eigyr was killed trying to protect her children. A detachment has been sent to collect the bodies of the Queen and the fallen soldiers."

"What about the children?" Guinevere asked.

"They are gone," Lancelot answered.

"Gone?" Tristan said. I could see tears in his eyes, though of grief or fury I could not tell.

"Ysbaddon took them," Lancelot said. "He has petitioned Hoel for the hand of his eldest daughter Helena in the past. Hoel has never dignified him with a response. It's assumed he has kidnapped her to be his wife."

"But there are other children as well?" Arthur said.

"There is the boy, Kahedrin," Lancelot said. "He is but nine or ten. And there is the baby, of course."

"Baby?" Guinevere cried.

"Yseult. She's not much more than a year old. Father believes, if they are still alive, Ysbaddon keeps them for either ransom, or insurance against retaliation."

"He's a monster," Tristan said.

"What's being done?" Arthur asked.

"Talking, mostly," Lancelot said. "There is no common agreement as to what action should be taken."

"Why is there even a debate?" Gawaine stood suddenly, knocking his chair over with a crash. "We should take our armies and crush this villain! The sooner the better."

"But what if he kills the children?" Guinevere said. "We can't risk that."

"And," I added, "his fortress may be impregnable." I related what Lancelot had said about Ysbaddon's defenses and the impossibility of a direct assault or the likelihood of a prolonged siege.

"So he just gets away with this?" Owain said.

"He can't stay in his castle forever," Lancelot said. "Eventually he or his men will come out. We can arrest him then."

"And until then he's allowed to rape King Hoel's daughter?" Guinevere asked. We were all taken aback by her outburst. Rape wasn't a topic anyone discussed, and especially not thirteen-year-old virgins.

"Don't look so surprised," she said. "You all know full well that is what is happening even now. He has asked for Helena's hand. He was refused so he has taken her for himself."

"His plan makes sense," Agravaine said. "He will marry her within his own kingdom, with or without Hoel's blessing. The marriage will be official and Ysbaddon will be legal heir to Hoel's kingdom. Once he has defiled Helena she will be spoiled goods and unmarriageable to anyone else. Hoel will have to acquiesce. He may have already killed the others."

"Why would he do that?" I asked, appalled at how quickly Agravaine grasped the situation. It said something about the turn of his mind that I did not like.

"Because they are heirs also, and stand in his way."

"I don't think he will have killed them yet," Arthur said. "Right now, they give him additional bargaining power. He will keep them safe as insurance of Hoel's assent to the marriage.

"I assume," he asked Lancelot, "that this is the very debate going on in your father's chambers."

"It is," Lancelot said. "There seem to be no good options."

"Killing the bastard seems the best option to me," Gawaine spat.

"Aye, to me as well," Tristan added.

"There's no way we can take troops to Mont St. Michael with any hope of success," Lancelot said again.

"And so the talk goes round in circles," Guinevere cried out. She stood and gathered her skirts around her. "And while the men talk Helena is ravished. Father Emrys has told me time and again that the responsibility of a true king is protecting the land, and protecting its people, especially the weakest among them."

"My teacher, Father Ambrosius, says the same thing," Lancelot said. "He has volunteered to go alone as an ambassador and to check on the safety of the children, but I doubt he will be able to do much else except become another captive."

"So every one of our elders and our teachers give voice to doing the right thing, but when the time comes it's all about the difficulties, and the politics," Guinevere said. "What if it were me laying under that monster at this very instant? Would you all stand here debating whether it was just to attempt to rescue me? No wonder Britain is falling apart if something as simple as this takes hours of debate. No wonder we have no High King. There isn't a man alive deserving of the title."

She broke into tears then and rushed from the room, her maid quick on her heels. We were stunned, and I think, to a man, ashamed.

"She's right," Arthur finally said.

"I've been saying that all along," Gawaine grumbled. "But there is a truth to the situation that can't be ignored. If the castle can't be breached by force of arms, then that is the military reality of it. The girl can't be expected to understand that."

"Lancelot," Arthur said. "Have you ever been inside Mont St. Michael?"

"Once, years ago," Lancelot answered. "Father surveyed the area when it looked as though no heir was alive to claim it. Then Ysbaddon came. It was run down then, but still a fortress."

"Could you remember the layout?"

"I think so," Lancelot said. "Father was always quizzing me on defenses and strategy. I remember him asking me lots of questions when we were there."

"Walk with me," Arthur said as he stood up from the table. "I have some questions of my own."

"Do you have a plan?" I asked. "Ector would listen, I'm sure."

"No, Bedivere, I don't have a plan. Not yet. But Guinevere is right. Something must be done." With that, he and Lancelot walked away, heads together in deep discussion.

The rest of us dispersed and went about our respective duties. Since the horses belonged to Benwick and were taken care of by the locals I was at a bit of a loss as to what to do. I spent some time cleaning Eiddelig's mail, though that was an unnecessary task. I was restless and cranky. Truth be told, I felt left out of Arthur's planning and replaced by Lancelot. Not that I had anything to contribute in terms of knowledge of Mont St. Michael, but it would have been nice to be included in whatever was going on.

Ector and the other senior members had been given rooms in the castle of Benwick, but the soldiers had set up our usual arrangement of tents in an adjoining field. It was just dark and I was considering going to sleep when Arthur returned to camp. He stuck his head in our tent and whispered to me in a low voice.

"Grab your gear and come with me to the stables. Your sword and buckler and your knife. A mail shirt and leather greaves, but nothing heavier. Your darkest cloak. Hurry. We have miles to ride before dawn."

Unsure of our plan I nonetheless did as Arthur asked and

followed him out into the darkness. Kay stood next to the tent wearing a mask of disapproval and fear of being caught. Arthur motioned me to silence with a finger to his lips and then we crept through the night to the stables.

Lancelot was already there, equipping the horses. Arthur bade me help him as quietly and quickly as possible. By the time we were finished the others had arrived.

A lamp with the wick turned low stood on top of an overturned barrel. Eight of us stood around the light, clad in heavy shadows; there was Arthur, Kay and myself, Gawaine and Agravaine, Owain, Tristan, and Lancelot. We had all been summoned, and while I thought I knew in general what was about to take place I couldn't conceive of what really lay before us. We all stood in silence, waiting for Arthur, our acknowledged leader even then, to speak.

"We're going to rescue King Hoel's children," he said. If there was any doubt as to our ability to accomplish this it was not present in Arthur's voice.

"About bloody time," Gawaine said.

"How?" Owain asked.

"After I spoke with Lancelot about the layout of Mont St. Michael we realized the castle itself cannot hold very many troops," Arthur said. "They have to be billeted in the surrounding courtyard and outbuildings. If we can get into the castle itself we should encounter very little resistance."

"We still can't get through the gate and into the courtyard," Kay said, "let alone sneak past the troops you say are there."

"That would be true," Arthur said, "but we had a bit of luck fall into our laps this evening. Lancelot remembered a bolthole in the main castle. King Ban pointed it out to him when they were surveying the fortress. It is a narrow tunnel carved through the ground under the hillside leading out. It was designed to allow for the escape of a few individuals in the event of a siege."

"Parts of it had collapsed when I was there," Lancelot said.

"You can be sure Ysbaddon has made it usable," Arthur continued.

"Won't it be guarded?" Agravaine asked.

"I assume," Arthur said. "But our luck continued. After leaving me Lancelot ran into Father Ambrosius, who was getting ready to leave for Mont St. Michael. His instructions are to ascertain the health of Hoel's children and to see what Ysbaddon's plans are. He is to hold the promise of marriage to Helena as a prize for her safety."

"That's terrible!" Tristan said.

"And a lie," Arthur said. "Hoel has no intention of giving Helena to him. It's a ruse to keep her safe until her rescue can be managed."

"So why don't we wait and see if it works?" Kay asked.

"Ambrosius doesn't believe it will," Lancelot said. "He believes Helena has already suffered that monsters' attention. He will never allow her or the others to leave his castle until Hoel has signed the documents making him legal heir."

"Ambrosius will be let in," Arthur said. "Ysbaddon dare not completely offend the Church if he wants a legal wedding. He won't give Ambrosius any satisfaction, but he will not harm him."

"And in the meantime," Lancelot added, "we have a man inside the castle who now knows the location of the bolthole. It will be open for us when we arrive."

"We go in," Arthur said, "quietly, and if at all possible we spirit the children away without confrontation. I don't think that is likely. There will be guards, and Ysbaddon himself. If we have to fight, we must be prepared to do so. We have all trained for this. We are warriors, even though we have not been tried. With surprise on our side, and the assumption of just a few weary guards in the middle of the night, we should be successful."

"I should try to stop you," Kay said. "Ector would never approve."

"Which is why we're not telling anyone," Arthur said. "Kay, we need you. *I* need you. You have the most training and are the most skilled among us." Kay stood for a moment, considering. He was cautious by nature, more afraid of getting into trouble than of fighting Ysbaddon. Arthur was canny in appealing to his sense of self-importance. Eventually, Kay nodded his assent.

"But," he said, "if I decide it's too dangerous we're all coming home."

"Good," Arthur said. "Any questions?" No one spoke. "Then saddle up. We have a long way to go."

"You're all crazy!" Agravaine suddenly shouted. "We can't rush off without telling anyone! We don't have any authority. We certainly don't have any experience!"

"Shut up Agravaine," Gawaine growled.

"We've all been trained," Agravaine continued, "but who here has actually fought a real man in combat? Have any of you killed anyone before? We may have to before the night is over. Not only could we all get killed, which I think is pretty likely, but we could also get Hoel's children killed. What if we fail?"

"What if no one tries?" Arthur said.

"Why not tell your plan to someone and let King Ban send experienced warriors?" Agravaine said.

"Because he is still bound by the politics of the situation," Lancelot answered. "His hands are tied."

"Come on," Gawaine snarled. "This is the kind of thing Father would have leapt at in his youth. Think how proud he will be. Imagine the acclaim when we ride back with the rescued hostages."

"It's not our responsibility," Agravaine said. "Hoel is not our king. This isn't even our country. Do you have any idea how much trouble we'll be in if we fail, or even if we don't, assuming we survive."

"Coward," Gawaine said.

"I can't force you to come with us," Arthur said. "I wish you would change your mind. We need all the help we can get. But if you don't come with us, I will ask you to keep our secret until we have had a chance to make our attempt."

"No," Agravaine said. "I won't. I'm going to find Ector, or King Mark, or someone, and tell them what you're doing. They'll put a stop to this nonsense."

Agravaine turned to leave but didn't take even one step before Gawaine's large fist slammed into the side of his head. Agravaine dropped to the stable floor like a sack of grain.

"Gawaine!" Arthur shouted. "That wasn't necessary."

"Yeah, I think it was," Gawaine grinned. "Had to save the mission somehow. Agravaine is bull-headed. If he said he was going to tell someone then that is what he was going to do. Now get the horses ready while I make sure he isn't going anywhere until we're well away from here."

Gawaine tied Agravaine to a post inside one of the stalls. Agravaine struggled, but it was obvious he was more than a little dazed from his brother's assault. Gawaine shoved a rag into his brother's mouth and bound it there with a strip of cloth. None of us were comfortable with this, but we were determined to carry out Arthur's plan. We would be stopped cold if Agravaine told anyone.

"There, done. Don't struggle and someone will find you come morning." Gawaine tapped Agravaine on top of his head playfully. He turned to the rest of us and said, "Let's go."

We led our horses out of the stable, quietly closing the doors behind us. We were well out of earshot of the camp before we mounted. Arthur paused to take stock of us.

"Seven warriors," he said. "Hopefully it will be enough. Follow Lancelot. He knows the way. When we get to Mont St. Michael we will look for the signs Father Ambrosius has left for us. I know that I'm asking a lot of you. Agravaine is right; this will be dangerous. But I believe it is the right thing to do. Thank all of you for coming along."

"Let's go," Gawaine said. That was the final urge we needed. Arthur spurred his horse into motion, and as one, the rest of us followed.

Our trip to Mont St. Michael is a blur. It was a clear, warm night, and under other circumstances I would have thoroughly enjoyed riding such a fine horse under the light of a bright three quarter moon. As it was I was too full of conflicting emotions to appreciate the beauty of the night. There was excitement and anticipation, of course, but that was leavened by an equal amount of fear and anxiety. Agravaine was right in much of what he said. We were going against the wishes of our elders and the King of Benwick. Even if we were successful chances were we would be severely reprimanded and punished. The cost of failure would be even higher.

But my fear of punishment was secondary to my fear of the possibility of battle. This was what we had been trained for. We were all warriors, at least in theory. Each of us knew that our training with sword and shield would someday be put to the test in actual combat. We were mentally prepared, as much as anyone can be, to not only face our own deaths, but to deal the same to our enemies. Make no mistake, for all of the beautiful ballads about the glories of war and the chivalry of Arthur's Companions, we were warriors, soldiers, and in far too many cases, killers. The blood spilled by each of us in the years to follow would fill the Channel, and while I believe our cause was justified, the killing never came easily or lightly, and the fear never completely disappeared.

That night, we were boys off on our first battle, wet behind the ears and too damn foolish to realize what we really faced. We rode into danger the way we believed men were supposed to do. I gripped my reins far too tightly and swallowed my terror, ashamed to be feeling it at all. In my naivety I thought I was the only one of us who was frightened, and I couldn't let my companions know for fear of letting them down. Since that night I have discovered that each of us carried our own share of fright, and each of us bottled it up for the same reasons.

All except for Lancelot. I don't know if he felt fear the way most men do. I've never heard him admit to it. For him, battle was a matter of calculation. While he never reveled in it, he was coldly efficient.

We rode for three hours in silence, wrapped in our own thoughts. I reckoned it was just past midnight when Lancelot informed us we had crossed into Ysbaddon's land. It was another hour before he bade us halt. We dismounted and followed him on foot to the top of a small rise. Lying in the grass we were able to see the castle of Mont St. Michael.

It stood illuminated by the moon on top of a steep hillside. A small settlement, less than twenty buildings, sat at the foot of the hill. The only road that led directly to the castle ran through this village and ended at a large gate set in the castle wall. I could tell from the construction that there had to be a large inner courtyard just inside that gate. From here it looked as though there was no other way inside.

"There it is," Lancelot whispered.

"Now what?" Owain asked. Arthur motioned for us to return down the rise to where we had left the horses. We crawled until we were well out of sight of the castle, though the chances of anyone seeing us at this distance were slim.

"The outside entrance of the bolthole is on the far side of the hill," Arthur said. "It's hidden among an outcropping of rocks and covered by bushes. If Father Ambrosius was successful there will be a small lantern set there for us to see."

"And if not?" Kay asked.

"We spend some time looking, and if we can't find it on our own we go home," Arthur said.

We rode around to the other side of the castle, staying behind hills and trees the whole way. We watered the horses and then tied them loosely in a stand of birch trees. We gave them oats in their feedbags and then made our own preparations. Arthur reminded us of the usage of hand signals, and then quietly, we slipped off through the trees toward the back side of Mont St. Michael.

The moon had progressed far enough so that we were in the shadow of the fortress and the rise. We had not covered very much ground when Tristan threw up a hand to halt our progress. He pointed to a spot around the hillside to our left.

"There," he whispered. I looked in the direction he pointed and saw, very clearly, a flicker of light. I hoped no one else was out and about, for if they were our plans were dead. The light would be obvious to anyone with eyes and any of Ysbaddon's soldiers or guards would be bound to investigate.

"Father Ambrosius did it," Lancelot said. "We're in."

"We still need to be cautious," Arthur advised. "This looks good, but until we know for certain that's Ambrosius waiting for us up there and not Ysbaddon be ready for battle."

He motioned us forward. I took a deep breath to settle my racing heart and drew my sword. It felt heavy in my hand, and the small buckler on my left arm felt like scant protection. We crept through the darkness. Every footstep sounded too loud in my ears. Each breath was a windstorm bound to alert our enemies. I thought of my mother and Lucan, safe at home and wondered if I would ever see them again. I wondered if my father had ever felt like this when he rode into battle at Uther's side.

I thought of Guinevere, and of her horror of this situation. I thought of Hoel's daughter, Helena, who had been at the mercy of Ysbaddon for well over a day now. I thought of Kahedrin and the baby Yseult, who saw their mother die and believed their father to be dead as well. Whatever fear I felt was nothing to the terror these innocents had experienced, and the more I thought about it the angrier I became, until eventually my indignation replaced most of my fear.

We were within fifty yards of the light when I heard the cry of a nightbird from near the light. To my ears it was a bird and didn't arrest my attention. Lancelot however, threw up a hand for us to halt.

"That's Ambrosius," he whispered. "That's the signal we agreed upon." Lancelot attempted to make an answering call, but no one would have mistaken it for an actual animal. He looked back at us and shrugged.

"I was never very good at that," he said. "But Ambrosius will recognize me anyway."

Suddenly from my right there was a shrill whistle that sounded exactly like the cry that had greeted us. If I hadn't seen Tristan finishing the call I would have believed it was an actual bird. Immediately there was a response from Ambrosius. Tristan smiled.

"Taliesin taught me to do that as part of my voice training," he said.

We walked toward the light feeling more secure in our safety. We climbed a small rise to a cluster of foliage. A narrow footpath led into the thicket, covered over in such a way that it would have been invisible to anyone not looking for it. Arthur pushed aside some bushes and stepped through. We followed.

The bolthole was a narrow crevice in the side of the hill. It looked like it had been a natural passage at one time, but had been widened by human hands. If Ysbaddon was truly a giant I'm not sure how he planned on fitting through here.

A man stood by the entrance, clad in a hooded robe that obscured his features. His anonymity was further hidden by the deep shadows thrown by the oil lamp he held. A gold crucifix sparkled on his chest.

"Father Ambrosius," Lancelot greeted. "You succeeded. Are Hoel's children okay?"

"The boy and the baby are scared, but unharmed," Ambrosius said. His voice was a low whisper. "Helena lives, though I'm not sure she wants to. She has been... damaged."

"He has raped her then?" Arthur asked. Ambrosius nodded.

"Then we find him and kill him before we leave," Gawaine said.

"Getting the children out safely is still our priority," Arthur cautioned. "Especially Helena. We can't risk alerting Ysbaddon or the guards. This mission will be truly successful if we are able to leave without ever drawing our swords. Do you know where they are being held?"

"Not exactly," Ambrosius said. "Ysbaddon allowed me to see them in the throne room, and then spirited them away. They have to be on the second or third floors. There will be guards, though I hope the little extra I slipped into their wine will insure they are sleeping. Helena will probably have a nurse. You must hurry. Ysbaddon has commanded me, on pain of death, to perform a marriage in the morning. If I have to do this it will be a legally binding union and Ysbaddon will have claim to Hoel's lands.

"The passage here leads into the kitchens," he continued. "They are empty at this time of night. From there you can access the steps to the upper floors. I will lead you there."

"We need to search as quickly as we can," Arthur said. "When we get there we will search both floors. Two groups. Kay, you take Bedivere and Tristan to the third floor. Lancelot and Gawaine will go with me to the second. If anyone finds any of the children don't wait for the rest of us. Bring them back here and take them out and ride for Benwick. They are our priority. Owain, you stay here with Father Ambrosius and guard our exit.

"Are we ready?" he asked. We all nodded, and then followed Ambrosius' dim light into the passage.

I wondered about the wisdom of splitting our small force, but Arthur's desire to search the castle more quickly made sense. I think I was more disappointed that I was not included in Arthur's group than anything else. Once again I felt as though he had chosen Lancelot over me. I bristled slightly at having to follow Kay as well.

The passage smelled of must and dirt. Old timbers of questionable strength held the earth above our heads. Ambrosius lit small lamps along the way to illuminate the passage in the event of a rapid retreat. It came to an end at a large wooden door.

"The kitchens lie on the other side," Ambrosius said. "I had to move some crates which hid this doorway. If anyone has come into the kitchens it would be obvious. I believe they would have followed the passage by now, but there is still the possibility of someone on the other side. Be ready."

Our swords were already out. As Ambrosius opened the door I felt a surge of fear and excitement and energy. There was no turning back now.

No one waited for us on the other side. We filed out of the passageway and broke into our two groups. Owain took up position by the door. Ambrosius pointed to the entrance to the kitchen. I could see stairs just beyond. We were in full combat mode now. No one spoke. Arthur signaled us to move forward and we crept, quickly and quietly toward the stairs. We went up one floor and Ambrosius indicated we needed to go one higher since the kitchens were in the basement. He waited there while we ascended. At the second floor Arthur's team split off and left us. He silently mouthed "Good luck," and then the three of them disappeared into the hallway. Kay signaled Tristan and I to keep moving upwards.

We came out of the stairwell into a long hallway. Small candles in wall sconces gave off weak, flickering light. A bright torch lit the t-juncture of an adjoining hallway at the far end. Three wooden doors were set on each side of the passage. We didn't have to wonder how we were going to search them without raising an alarm, for two guards were sitting on the floor in front the third door on the right. We could hear them snoring; whatever Father Ambrosius slipped into their drinks had worked its magic.

Kay turned and gave us orders with hand signals. He pointed to me as he sheathed his sword and drew his dagger. His meaning was clear, so I did the same.

We crept forward as silently as possible. Kay and I paused on either side of the sleeping guards while Tristan slipped farther down the hallway to check the area beyond our sight. He leaned back against the wall and cautiously peered around the corner, looked both directions, and then gave us the all clear sign.

Kay looked me in the eyes and nodded. The blood thundered in my ears as I leaned forward, placed my left hand over the guard's mouth and drew my knife across his throat. He was dead before he ever came fully awake. In that moment I became, for the first time, truly a soldier.

Those who have never been in battle may read this and cringe. It is a far cry from the deeds of valor in the songs. But there is a difference between battles and ballads. Was our calculated murder of these two guards just? Perhaps not, but while standing there in Ysbaddon's fortress we had no time to make that judgment. They were soldiers in the employ of our enemy. They may have been the very men who had attacked and killed Hoel's party, or they may have been innocents who had simply drawn the short straw for guard duty. We could not wake them and ask, or challenge them to fair combat without rousing the entire castle. There is no fairness in war. If their deaths were unjust then I am guilty of countless injustices in battle over the course of my life, and so is every man who has ever raised arms. All I knew standing in that hallway with the blood of a dead man on my hands was that we had a mission to accomplish and that our cause was just.

Kay and I wiped our blades on our victim's clothing, sheathed the knives and drew our swords. Kay motioned for Tristan to keep watch and then opened the door.

We were greeted by a gasp as a woman leapt up from a chair next to the bed and retreated to the window.

"Please," she said. "It's not my fault. I was checking the other children and found her like this when I returned."

"Shh," Kay said. "We're not here to harm you. We're here to take Helena and the other children to safety. Please don't raise an alarm or I'll be forced to restrain you. Do you understand?" She nodded. "Now what has happened here?" Kay asked.

"He hurt her so badly," the woman sobbed. "You know... inside. She was in pain and despondent when he left. She wailed and wept, and no matter what I did I could not get the bleeding to stop. I gave her a drink to help her sleep and then went to check on the others. I guess she broke the lamp to get the glass. She... she was like this when

I returned."

We looked at the bed more closely. The nurse had pulled the covers over Helena's head, but we could see that they were soaked in blood. Kay carefully drew the covering back.

Helena was dead by her own hand, though I think she may have died anyway. She had cut her wrists with a shard of glass. Her left eye was swollen shut where someone had hit her. Her throat and breasts were covered in bruises and bite marks. The area between her legs was covered in blood and other wetness. I think her hip may have been dislocated. I felt my gorge rise with my anger.

"Ysbaddon did this?" Kay asked. The woman nodded as he wrapped Helena's body in the coverlet and gently lifted her from the bed.

"Where are the other children?" I asked. She pointed to another door in the room. I went to the hallway and signaled for Tristan to join us. He came into the room and together we went to the second doorway. It opened into a smaller adjoining room, filled with darkness.

"Stay back," said a trembling young voice from inside. "Stay back or I'll kill you." I lifted a lamp to illuminate the room. A boy, Kahedrin I assumed, stood in front of a small bed on which lay a baby. His face was swollen and wet from tears, but set in determination. His fists were doubled up and thrust forward.

"Shh," Tristan said. He sheathed his sword and knelt before the boy. "We're not here to harm you. We're here to take you home. Your father sent us."

"He's dead," the boy said, but I saw him falter as a look of hope crossed his face.

"He survived the attack," Tristan said. "He sent us to find you. My name is Tristan. Is that Yseult behind you?" Kahedrin wiped an arm across his face and nodded.

"Where's Helena?" he asked. I turned to Kay and with my eyes told him to take Helena's body back to Ambrosius before the child could see her. Kay nodded and left the room.

"My friend Kay has her," Tristan said. "Will you let me take you and Yseult to safety?" Kahedrin nodded, then lunged forward into Tristan's arms. Tristan held the boy for a moment and allowed him to weep. He then stood and went to the bed. He gently picked Yseult up and snuggled her against his chest. He took Kahedrin's hand with his free one and led them from the room.

"Come with us," I said to the nurse. She silently agreed.

I checked the hallway before we left the chamber. Kay was just entering the stairwell and the way looked clear. The nurse went first, followed by Tristan with the baby and the boy in tow. I brought up the rear.

Our escape was not to be that easy. We were almost to the stairs when a great roaring voice screamed at us from the other end of the hallway.

"HALT!"

I turned to see a man at the t-junction of the hall. This could only be Ysbaddon. He may not have been a giant in the mythical sense of the word, but he was the largest man I ever saw in all of the years of my life. He towered over us, nearly seven feet tall and broad across the shoulders and chest. It seemed the tufts of his thick hair brushed the ceiling as he strode toward us. He wore only a nightshirt and trousers, but he carried an ax. He howled his rage and charged.

"Run!" I said to the others and turned to face the giant of Mont St. Michael.

I have to say, at first I did well against him, in spite of his size and experience. I was smaller, quicker and far more agile than my opponent. At least twice his attacks were stopped by his ax scraping across the stone walls of the narrow hallway. I parried a slash with my buckler and felt my left arm go numb from the blow. I turned three attacks away with my sword and scored a long bloody stripe down his thigh. Ysbaddon staggered backward and clutched the wound. I stepped forward to press my momentary advantage.

That was when I heard Lancelot cry my name from the top of the stairs behind me.

I don't blame him for what happened next. Not really. I shouldn't have let his cry distract me. If anything I should have used it to my advantage. Ysbaddon looked up to see my companions as well. In that moment I should have lunged in and ended it. Instead I glanced behind me and for just an instant dropped my guard. It was enough. Ysbaddon recovered before I did and swung his ax with all of his incredible might.

I felt a tug at my right arm and turned in time to see my sword go flying away. Stupidly I tried to grab it from mid air. It was then I saw the bloody stump at the end of my arm and my hand still stubbornly clutching my sword as it clattered to the floor.

The next moments are a blur. I remember seeing Gawaine slam bodily into Ysbaddon and Lancelot rushing into the fray with his sword drawn as I dropped to my knees in a spray of my own blood. Arthur was next to me in a heartbeat, wrapping a leather thong around my arm to stop the bleeding and screaming for someone to get the torch.

I remember nothing more until the following day.

CHAPTER ELEVEN

I wrote nothing yesterday. A storm buffeted the land for hours. A heavy curtain of rain swept in from the horizon and stayed until well after sunset, though the cloud cover made it difficult to tell exactly when that was. Wind tore limbs from trees and thatch and shingles from roofs. We were confined to the dim rooms of the castle all day and our moods were as dark as the sky. When we awoke this morning frost covered the ground and I could see my breath in the still air of my bedroom. This is the first real blast of the bad weather that will keep us trapped inside for all the winter months.

I knew it was coming. My stump has ached for days.

Two days ago I had some of the younger men help move my writing table and chair into my bedchambers here in the castle. I have my own fireplace, which I'm sure will be useful as the days and nights go by. I get much colder than I used to. A stock of candles and lamp oil has been laid in as well. Perhaps I am over preparing but it feels like this winter will be a bad one.

I miss the small cottage where I wrote already. Nothing clears my head and prepares me for this task like a morning walk or ride.

Today is clear and I have a good view from my window. It still surprises me just how far I can see from this third floor chamber on Mont St. Michael.

Yes, I am currently in residence at the very site where I lost my right hand. How Tristan came into rightful possession of this land is a later part of my tale, but suffice to say I was surprised to find myself here in my dotage. When I first arrived it brought back all of the memories of that awful night, and I was not sure I would ever be able to sleep here. But that was a lifetime ago and one would never recognize this castle as the dreary haunt of a monster. Years under the guidance of a beautiful woman's hand have transformed this fortress into a home.

It was difficult to relive that tragic moment in my life. I paused many times while writing to reflect and remember. There are details that are, I'm sure, inaccurate, colored and changed by time and failing recall. All of what happened immediately after Ysbaddon hacked off my hand I know only from the stories told to me. I mercifully passed out from blood loss and shock.

Arthur saved my life that night. He tied a leather thong around my arm to slow the bleeding. It must have taken tremendous courage for him to grab the torch from its wall sconce and cauterize my injury. The burn was terrible and I fought infection and pain for weeks, but he successfully sealed the wound and kept me from bleeding to death. The scar tissue that surrounds my stump is the result of Arthur's quick thinking more than the giant's blade.

Gawaine and Lancelot engaged Ysbaddon while Arthur tended

to me. Gawaine's sudden charge succeeded in taking the giant off guard and knocked him backward down the hall. Lancelot was quick to press this advantage and, according to Gawaine, struck off Ysbaddon's head with a single mighty swipe of his sword. I have fought in enough battles to know just how hard it is to fully decapitate a man with one blow. Ysbaddon's neck was twice the thickness of any normal man, and Gawaine was given to much exaggeration. Whatever the truth of that fight, Lancelot did indeed kill the giant of Mont St. Michael, so that part of the legend is true.

While this was happening Kay and Tristan rushed back to the kitchens with their charges. They were greeted there by Owain and Father Ambrosius and taken out through the bolthole, successfully making their escape. Morning was just beginning to appear on the eastern horizon when they stepped out of the passage. The mounted cavalry of Benwick greeted them immediately.

Agravaine had managed to free himself only a couple of hours after we had left, and true to his word went immediately to Ector and told him what we were doing. It took quite a bit of time for the rest of Benwick to be alerted and a mounted force readied to ride, but ride they did. I think it's safe to say Agravaine saved the rest of us that day.

Our battle in the hallway had roused the rest of the castle and armed men confronted us as Arthur carried me toward the bolthole exit. The sight of their king's head being carried by Lancelot gave them pause. Leaderless and fearful of reprisal from Benwick, they were unsure of what to do with us. They held us at sword point and debated our fate and their own disposition until a messenger informed them that an army was at their gate demanding their surrender and the safe return of their hostages. This demand was given even more weight by the force of soldiers who suddenly poured into the castle from the secret entrance in the kitchens. They surrendered quickly and we returned with haste to Benwick.

The next few days are a blur of pain and fever to me. Father Ambrosius ministered my wound and prepared concoctions for me to drink to ease the pain. I remember dreams and visions and agony. I know Arthur was at my bedside frequently, as were Kay and Ector. I am told that Guinevere refused to leave my room except to sleep, and remember her wiping a cool cloth across my brow. But I recall other things that made no sense to me at the time. I saw my mother and Lucan. I saw Lailoken hovering over me and fussing with my wound. Many times, in later years during my odd friendship with Nimué, she would press me for details of what I saw in my dreams, convinced that I had had visions that she could interpret to our benefit. I've never had a vision, so far as I know, and truly believe that most of what I remember seeing was simply a nightmare confusion of reality and my own pain and drug induced imagination.

My first real conscious memory, not clouded by delirium, is waking up on a warm afternoon in a large, comfortable feather bed. My fever had broken and I had slept soundly for hours. At first I wondered where I was and was even more confused to feel a small warm hand clasped in mine.

In my left hand.

I squeezed the hand gently and felt it respond.

"Bedivere?" I recognized the voice and was pleased when Guinevere stood up and moved into my vision, holding my hand tightly to her breast.

"Are you alright?" she asked. "Are you awake? Do you know me?" Her face was swollen from tears. Dark circles underlined her eyes. She looked tired and worried and relieved and beautiful.

I tried to respond, but my voice was hoarse and dry. Guinevere held a small cup of water to my lips and cautioned me to drink slowly.

"Are you alright?" she asked again when I had finished.

"I think so," I croaked.

"Let me get someone to check on you," she said. She let go of my hand and turned to leave the room. Before going a step she turned back to me. There was a bare moment of hesitation before she leaned forward and kissed me on the cheek. Her face was flushed when she rose back up, and then she quickly turned and ran from the room.

I realized I was ravenous and hoped someone brought food to go with the water. I felt pain and a dreadful itch in my right hand and flexed it to restore circulation. I reached to scratch my itchy palm and sat in horrified silence when I saw the bandaged stump at the end of my right arm. At first I thought I was dreaming again, another nightmare. This couldn't be my arm. I could feel my hand, flex my fingers. My palm itched from a thousand insect bites. But whatever I felt in that empty extremity was false. My hand, my sword hand, my good right hand, was simply gone.

Guinevere and Arthur stepped into the room then, followed by a nurse with fresh bandages. I turned to them as the reality of my injury washed over me. They saw my terror and my grief and did for me a kindness I can never fully repay. Arthur and Guinevere both climbed into the large bed at my sides and held me while I wept.

I woke again hours later, well after dark. Arthur was still there, sitting in a chair at my bedside. He looked tired.

"Where's Guinevere?" I asked. He looked up at me, and though he smiled I saw grief etched on his face.

"Gone," he said. "To bed. Leodegrance nearly had to have someone carry her away." I nodded and then motioned to the water pitcher. Arthur poured a cup and held it out to me. Of course, I reached for it with my right hand. The newly bandaged stump rose out of my coverlet and hovered between us like an accusation.

"Oh my God, Bedivere." Tears coursed down Arthur's face. "I am so sorry. Can you ever forgive me?"

"For what?" I said. "You didn't do this."

"It was my dim-witted plan," he said. "You should never have had to face Ysbaddon alone. I was so stupid to think we could just walk into his castle and escape unscathed."

"Did we save the other children?"

"Yes," Arthur answered. "The baby is with a wet nurse and Kahedrin is following Tristan around like a puppy."

"And Ysbaddon?"

"Dead. His power broken and his land ceded to Hoel."

"Then your plan was a success," I said.

"But your hand..."

"It was war, Arthur," I said. My voice hitched in spite of my intended bravado. "This, and worse, is the chance we take anytime we go into battle. You know that. I knew that. If my hand was the only casualty then we bought Yseult and Kahedrin's lives at small cost."

"You're more gracious than I deserve."

I shrugged. I believed this meant the end of my military career. I knew it would change the way I rode and controlled horses. At the time I had no concept of what my life would be like from that point on. Everything I expected for my future had been chopped away with my hand. It was too big to think about at the time.

"How much trouble are we in?" I asked.

"Some. Not much. I have extra duties to attend to. So do the others. But, I guess, we were successful. Hoel has heaped praise on us and promised us great rewards and undying loyalty. I think our actions have cemented his continued support for Britain, though that wasn't really in question anyway. I think Ector believes what happened to you is punishment enough for all of us."

"Eiddelig will need a new squire," I said.

"So will Kay," Arthur smiled. "We've all been officially knighted, at Hoel's insistence. You as well."

"I'm afraid I won't be much of a knight now."

"You will always be needed."

We spent another few days at Benwick while I gathered my strength. The original purpose of our trip, the meeting of representatives of Britain with our continental allies, took place during that time. The entire summit was colored by the events at Mont St. Michael. My fever came and went, as did the infection. The pain gradually lessened. Father Ambrosius, who had ministered to me in the first few days, had been called away, so I wasn't able to thank him. In this time I began the grueling process of learning to do everything with my left hand. I lost track of how many times I reached for a cup or tried to scratch my nose with a hand I could still feel but wasn't actually there. I have spent decades since then being, for all intents and purposes, left-handed, and it still happens.

I was probably not really ready to travel when we left Benwick, but the Festival of the Sword was due to take place at Avalon. We would already be hard-pressed to make it back in time. King Ban offered to house me until I was well, but I refused. I wanted to go home, even though the trip was very hard on me.

I sat in one of the wagons as we prepared to leave, angry and frustrated at my inability to ride. Guinevere rode with me, forsaking a horse as well in order to keep me company. I was in a black mood, and felt nauseous and feverish. I'm sure I was not very good company, but Guinevere maintained her grace in the presence of my disposition. My attitude was not helped when Arthur, accompanied by Lancelot, rode up next to our wagon. They were checking to see if we were ready to leave, but their presence was a bitter reminder of my new limitations.

"I've been instructed to inform you of a gift," Lancelot said to me. "It is a gift for all of you, from the kingdom of Benwick, in acknowledgement of the treaties signed here and as a pledge of support to the kingdoms of Britain. But I thought you in particular should be made aware, since you will be more directly involved than most others."

In spite of myself my interest was piqued. I couldn't imagine what gift would involve me.

"Benwick has pledged threescore of our Arabian horses," Lancelot said. "They will be transported back to Britain with you."

"But I can't even ride," I protested. I was pleased, but also further frustrated.

"Not now," Lancelot said. "But you will again. I've never seen a better natural horseman, and Warok agrees. You will be back in the saddle before you know it. In the meantime, I think your ideas about new strategies for the cavalry are sound and need to be developed. Our Arabian stock will add speed to your warhorses. I'm curious what you will do with them given time."

I realize that Lancelot was trying to lift my spirits, and in the end he was right, but at that moment all I heard were platitudes. I thanked him, but I'm afraid there was no genuine gratitude in my voice. Still, though I was determined to wallow in self-pity, my mind immediately began to imagine new possibilities for the horses.

We said our farewells and left Benwick behind.

CHAPTER TWELVE

The trip back to Avalon was a nightmare. I was not well enough to travel. I spent the entire time on the boat with my head over a bucket, emptying the meager contents of my stomach. It was quite the contrast to my stalwart experience on the original trip. My fever returned causing me to suffer chills in spite of the warm summer weather. The infection in my stump, after seeming to have mostly cleared, worsened. My head ached and every bump of the wagon on the road was torture.

When we finally arrived I was immediately sent across the lake and onto the island of Avalon itself. I have vague memories of seeing many people camped in the clearing by the Shrine of the Sword. The festival was under way, but I do not know if there had yet been any attempts to draw the Sword. My understanding was that traditionally no one would try his hand until everyone was present and all other business had been concluded. I have to say, at the time, I couldn't have given less thought to it.

Morgan cradled my head in her lap as we crossed the lake in one of the swan boats. She made me chew on some extract from willow bark, to ease my pain and reduce my fever, she said. The slight waves conspired to make me nauseous again, but I think my body was simply too exhausted to respond.

I was carried to a well-lit room within the halls of Avalon and made comfortable in a large bed. Morgan stayed at my side and ran cooling cloths across my brow and under my arms while other young maidens brought pitchers of hot water, and rolls of clean linen. They stopped moving when the Lady Vivienne herself entered the room.

She came to me and felt my forehead with the back of her hand. Her long fingers felt cool against my skin. She took a steaming mug from a tray proffered her by an acolyte. Morgan lifted my head while Vivienne held the cup to my lips.

"Drink this," she said in the gentlest of voices. "It is bitter, I know. I'm sorry. But it will help with the pain and help you to sleep."

Bitter is not the appropriate word to describe the foul concoction she offered, but I drank it down to the silty remains at the bottom of the cup. Sweat broke out on my body before I had finished, and it may have been my imagination, but I swear the pain in my arm began to subside immediately. Morgan allowed my head to fall back into the pillow and before I was still I could feel my eyes begin to close.

"Morgan," I heard Vivienne say just before I slipped into unconsciousness, "bring me the sharp knife with the small blade. I'm going to have to cut away some of the rotten flesh."

I woke the next day feeling better than at any point since my encounter with Ysbaddon. There was pain in my stump, but it was far less than I had been experiencing. I looked to see clean bandages, and for the first time they weren't crusted in blood and pus. Instead of the rotting smell that had been accompanying me there was a strong medicinal scent, not pleasant exactly, but clean and healthy. My fever seemed to have broken completely, and though it returned in the next few days it was never again the inferno it had been.

An acolyte had been stationed just outside of my room, and I had barely taken stock of my surroundings before she came in to check on me and give me a hot medicated drink. I felt well enough to protest as soon as I realized the drug was making me sleepy again. When I once more came awake it was afternoon. This time I was allowed to get up to use the chamber pot on my own. My head swam, but it felt good to move unaccompanied. I was given broth and bread, and then another dose of medicine and back to the land of dreams.

Time was muddy to me, but I believe I was in that room at Avalon for about a week. My routine each day was much the same as I just described. I was anxious for news from the outside world, and if anyone had tried to draw the Sword yet. The acolytes assured me that nothing but talking and arguing had yet taken place. Only two events that occurred that week, other than my seemingly miraculous recovery, bear recounting.

The first took place on my third or fourth day there, my first when I felt fully in control of my faculties. I was healing well, and very quickly. Whether this was due entirely to the expert care and medicine I was being given, or if there was a subtler magic at work I cannot say. Whatever the case, I was well enough to have started to feel bored and restless in my confinement. I missed Arthur and the rest of my friends, and while I had had messages from them, none had been allowed to come to the island to see me. Aside from the traditions of Avalon, they were all being kept very busy by the demands of the Festival. To say I was glad to see Morgan walk into my room with a basin of water and washcloths on a tray is an understatement.

"Hello, Bedivere," she said as she set the tray down on a small table near my bed. "You look much better than the last time I saw you. Of course you were unconscious then."

"Hello, Morgan," I replied. She placed a hand on my forehead and held it there for a moment. She smiled as she removed her hand and turned to the washbasin.

"What are you doing here?" I asked, trying to inject a playful note into my voice. I dreaded seeing her pity. "Wouldn't you rather be with Arthur?"

"It's my turn," she said with a ready smile, and I saw no trace of pity on her face. "And," she continued with a cocked eyebrow and glow of mischief, "who's to say I haven't been with Arthur?"

"True," I answered as she soaked a cloth in the basin and then wrung it out. "I've been a little out of touch up here. What can you tell me about what's going on out in the real world?"

"Not very much, really," she said. "A lot of talking during the day. A lot of drinking during the night."

"Has anyone tried to draw the Sword?"

"No, not officially at least. Some kids tried their hand. Various people with no claim at all. That always happens. People like to dream, and for most it's enough to be able to tell the folks back home they made the attempt. But none of the petty kings have tried. That's usually a big and very tense ceremony at the end of the Festival. That's several days off, at least. It depends on how quickly all of the other issues are resolved. Now lay back."

She wiped the cloth across my face and rubbed behind my ears. I realized that this was not an attempt to reduce my fever. She was bathing me! I'm sure, after days of feverish sweat, I needed it, but this was unexpected. I laid still and hoped the flush in my face was not too noticeable.

"Do you think anyone will succeed?" I asked, trying to distract myself as she wiped the cloth down my neck.

"Not this year," she said with a knowing smile on her face.

"Why not?"

"It's the same old men who have been trying for years," she said, and pulled the covers back from my bare chest. "I don't know why Uriens still thinks he can be High King when he has failed to draw the Sword every time he has ever tried. Given his health and his belief system, he is less qualified now than ever. The same is true for all of them. King Mark tries every year, but he has no real desire to rule anywhere other than Cornwall. He at least recognizes his limitations. Malaguin showed up while you were away and has been nothing but an irritant to everyone here. That man would be an absolute disaster as High King. He is trifling, and small, and I think evil. He has been a blight to Britain his entire life, and his son seems determined to follow in his path. I daresay no one would follow him if he drew the Sword, and the Goddess and the Christ showed up in person to give their blessing."

I laughed in genuine amusement, but also to cover my discomfort as Morgan drew the covers lower and began to wash my stomach.

"What about Lot?" I asked.

"Don't get me started on Lot," Morgan said. "He's my brother-in-law. I know too much about him to be objective. The sad part, if everything I've heard is true, is there was a time when he may have been the best successor to Uther. He was loyal then, and a great warrior. He seems he governs Orkney fairly and well. I think he may have been a great man once."

"What happened?"

"My sister," Morgan scoffed. "Instead of staying here in the south and trying to unite the kingdom in the wake of Uther's death he took Morgause as his wife and retreated to the ends of the earth. Other than the annual Festival he has remained sequestered there, year after year, hearing nothing but her poisonous rants."

"You don't like her very much?"

"To be fair, I don't really know her," Morgan said. "I was very young when my father died. I barely remember our home at Tintagel, and my father not at all. My mother Igraine had been an acolyte here when she was young, before Gorlois claimed her. She seemed to believe I had some talent or gift for the life of a priestess of the Goddess, so I was sent here."

"Morgause didn't have that gift?"

"The only gift Morgause has," Morgan laughed, "is the one between her legs. She has been pregnant nonstop since she was fourteen years old."

"She has, what? Four sons?"

"That survived, yes. There are quite a few years between Agravaine and Gaheris. She has had many miscarriages and other children who did not live to see their first birthday. A healthy child can be difficult for any woman. It has to be much harder in the cold wastes of the Orkneys. But, she keeps trying, bound to give birth to the future High King or die trying."

"What do you mean?"

"Morgause is a bitter woman. She blames Uther for our father's death and has never forgiven him, or any of those she believes were his allies. She resents losing the kingdom of Cornwall, and feels she was given to Lot as chattel. There is no love there, no matter how often she carries his seed.

"She makes Lot come here every year to act out the farce of drawing the Sword, but I can tell he is content to hide in his cold castle and no longer wishes to husband the land of Britain. Morgause wants to be High Queen. It takes more than simply giving birth to be the sacred Queen of the land and the Goddess's vessel on earth. She hasn't been consecrated and prepared her entire life. Her wedding to Lot was not the *Hieros Gamos*."

I had no idea what she was talking about. I didn't know what she meant by sacred queen or *Hieros Gamos*, but the phrases jumped out at me and stuck in my memory. By the following spring I knew about both, though I still don't claim to understand.

"If she can't be High Queen," Morgan continued, "then she is determined to be the Queen Mother. She still believes our father was destined to be High King, and that the blood of his destiny runs in her veins. She just knows that one of her sons will wield Excalibur. Gawaine in particular, has heard that litany his entire life."

"But he failed to draw the Sword," I said.

"To his relief, I'm sure. Gawaine is a follower, and will be one of the rocks the High King will build his kingdom on, but he will never be King."

Morgan had continued to wash my lower stomach while we talked, and though our topic could in no way be considered erotic, the feel of her hands on my skin and the view of her lovely body had had the predictable effect on my lower regions; an embarrassing effect that tented the covers in a very noticeable fashion.

"I see you truly are getting better," Morgan smirked. To my relief, and a little bit to my disappointment, she dropped the washcloth back in the basin. "Let's take a look at that arm."

She sat on the edge of my bed, disconcertingly close to my hardness, and began to tenderly unwrap the bandages from around my stump. I was more embarrassed by this naked exposure than by my errant manhood, which subsided along with the bindings.

"It looks good," she said. "There is new skin instead of wounds. It will no doubt continue to be sensitive, but I believe your healing is nearly complete."

Where she saw healing all I could see was emptiness, at the end of my arm and in my future.

"Do you have any idea," she said, "of how highly Arthur speaks of you? He loves you as his brother, and he feels so terrible about this. He believes he failed you somehow, that you were under his protection and he allowed this to happen."

"That's not true," I protested.

"Still, your wound is his wound. In very different ways, of course, but he will carry remorse for this until the day he dies..."

Morgan's eyes glazed for a moment and she spoke in a whisper.

"Until Excalibur is carried back to Avalon and Arthur and I are reunited."

She shook her head and then continued in a more normal tone of voice, seemingly unaware of what she had just said.

"He will need you at his side, Bedivere."

"I won't be much good as half a man."

"Nonsense. Some souls are bound together long before our births. It is your friendship, and your mind, and most importantly, the love you bear for each other that will best serve him in the years to come."

"Now you sound like Lailoken," I said, and in my mind at least, I was referring to her strange pronouncement as much as to her sentiment.

"I'll take that as a compliment," she said with a wink. She gathered the clean bandages. Before she applied the liniment and wrapped the cloth around my arm she washed the new flesh gently.

Her fingers ran over my stump, lightly, reverently. She brought it up to her full lips and kissed it. It was more personal and intimate than anything else she could have done.

She stood and gathered her things and then turned to leave the room. She paused at the door and turned back to me.

"I think you are nearly ready to go back to the shore," she said. "In a day or two. I'll speak to Lady Vivienne and make arrangements if that's alright with you." I nodded my eager assent.

"And," she said with a wicked gleam in her eye, "perhaps I can find someone, one of the acolytes maybe, who can come back later and take care of your other needs."

She was gone before I had time to blush.

The second event of note took place on my last night there, and quite honestly I am uncomfortable relating it. My hosts however, howled with laughter when I broached the subject with them and assured me my story needed just this sort of thing.

I woke from a light doze to the sound of someone moving in my room. I opened my eyes just wide enough to ascertain that it was an acolyte, bringing fresh water or emptying the chamber pot. Satisfied with this explanation I closed my eyes again. I was surprised to suddenly feel a warm and completely naked body slide under the covers next me.

"What?" I said, startled by the intrusion. My protest was cut short by warm wet lips pressed against my own. My brain didn't know what was going on, but my body responded. When the kiss ended my bed partner raised her head and laughed at the look on my face. Bright red curls framed her face. She looked familiar, but in my confusion I could not place her.

"So Gawaine tells me you went toe-to-toe with a giant," she said, and I then recognized her as the acolyte my boisterous friend had bedded on our previous visit.

"I'm afraid I came out on the worst end of that encounter," I said and lifted my stump for emphasis.

"Nonsense," she said. "It's a battle wound. Gawaine says you are a hero and deserve a hero's reward. Morgan says you need the same thing."

"And what reward would that be?" I truly wasn't trying to be clever. I was far too naïve for that, and the real answer to that question, even with a naked woman draped over me, really didn't occur to me.

That night I claimed my reward many times over, with the fervor and quickness that are the provinces of the young. It might seem that I am being chivalrous by not naming my paramour of the moment, but the truth is, if I ever knew that girl's name it has long since escaped me.

There is a third event that took place that week, though strictly speaking it did not happen to me.

It was the morning I was to leave the island and go back to the shore. Lady Vivienne came to check on my arm and give her blessings. Though I still had a long way to go I was as healed as I was going to get lying in bed. It was time for me to return to Ector and see what my new life held in store for me. I hoped to continue in some fashion with the horses, but I believed my days as a warrior were over.

Vivienne brought me clean, new clothes, and an odd contraption for my stump. A tooled leather cup had been fashioned to fit over the raw end of my arm. The soft padding inside would provide some measure of protection for me from minor bumps and accidents, and while no one said so, it also served to hide the ugly lump of mottled flesh at the end of my arm from anyone's sight. If I were not fresh from a night of sensual awakening and secure in my newfound manhood I may have been mortified to wear it.

But then, Morgan had known that.

Someone came and whispered a message to Lady Vivienne, who excused herself abruptly and left. I was walking out of my room when a great commotion erupted in the hallways of Avalon. The acolytes were running around and raising quite a fuss, and I was unable to get much sense of what was happening in the din of their chatter. Finally I saw my red-haired companion running toward the exit to the main grounds. I stopped her with a gentle hand.

"What's going on?" I asked. "What's all the fuss?"

"Haven't you heard?' she said, barely able to contain her excitement.

"Heard what?"

"Someone has drawn the Sword!" she exclaimed. "Excalibur has been claimed!"

"By who?" I asked. I'm sure I looked as excited and incredulous as any of the young women flitting about me.

"They say it was Sir Ector's son."

"Kay?" I said, unable to believe it.

"No, the other one, the foster son."

"Arthur," I said.

CHAPTER THIRTEEN

There are so many stories about the day Arthur drew Excalibur. I've heard that he had lost Kay's sword, and as his squire had to find him another, so took the Sword from the stone. Aside from the fact Arthur was no longer Kay's squire, how stupid would he have had to be to choose that one? It's an absurd piece of fiction. I've heard that lightning flashed and thunder rumbled. Also not true. The day was as clear as an afternoon in early August can be, and while I may not have been there when it happened I was certainly close enough that I would have heard thunder if there was any. Some say a golden crown immediately appeared on his brow, and everyone present went down on their knees in recognition of the new High King. If only it had been that easy.

I heard the story straight from Arthur later that day. Only four other people actually saw what happened, and only one of them kneeled, and then only as an afterthought.

The excitement on Avalon was palpable. Lady Vivienne had already departed in one of the swan boats to join the hastily convened council of the petty kings. I found room in a small boat and spent the short trip across the lake wishing we could move faster. We ran ashore near the Shrine. The first thing I saw was the stone and the empty fissure where the Sword had been.

I saw Vivienne standing in the main pavilion as I stepped out of the boat, exuding calm in the middle of a storm of shouting invective. A swarthy dark-haired man was screaming directly in her face. I did not recognize him but later discovered this was Malaguin. Ector was there, as was Leodegrance, Uriens and Mark. I saw an older man with a heavyset but beautiful auburn-haired woman at his side; from the descriptions I had been given I assumed it was Lot and Morgause. There were also several of the priestesses of Avalon and a few hooded monks in attendance.

I did not see Arthur. Knowing I would not be welcome in the pavilion I ran toward Ector's camp. I was surrounded by the beehive noise of excited conversation. Arthur's name was on every pair of lips. Questions were shouted in my direction, but I knew less than anyone here.

A large crowd had gathered at Ector's tent. I pushed my way through them, overly cautious of my injured arm, but feeling the pain of casual contact nonetheless. Morvawr and Turmyr, Ector's men-at-arms, stood guard at the entrance, keeping the mob at bay with seething stares. I was allowed through to the jeering complaints of the assembly.

"Arthur!" I called as I stepped into the tent. He sat on a field chair with his head in his hands. Kay stood next to him, a protective hand on his shoulder.

"Bedivere!" Arthur exclaimed. He jumped to his feet and pulled me into a tight embrace. "How are you? Is your arm okay?"

"Yes, yes," I said, impatient to find out what had happened. I was already growing tired of my disfigurement being a topic of conversation. "What's going on? They're saying you pulled Excalibur from the stone."

He sighed and sat back down.

"So it's true then?" I asked.

"Yes," he said. "It's true. I don't know how it could have happened, but it's true."

"How? Where is it?"

"I gave it to Lady Vivienne to hold in trust until this is sorted out. I don't know what comes next."

"How did this happen? Why did you do it?"

"Sit down," he said. I pulled another field chair next to his and did as he bid. He stared for a moment, gathering his thoughts.

"I was with Morgan," he finally said. "We were running an errand for Ector. We were near the Shrine when Guinevere called to me. We stopped so that she could ask Morgan about your health. While we were talking Maleagant approached us."

"Maleagant?" I asked.

"King Malaguin Bagdemagus' son," Arthur explained. "He had been drinking, which is the state he has been in since we first met him."

"He's a foul piece of shit is what he is," Kay added.

"He bulled his way into our conversation," Arthur continued.

"He said some very crass and vulgar things, worse than you will hear in barracks talk. I asked him to stop, because of Morgan and Guinevere, but he would not. He started shouting at us. He called Morgan several choice words..."

"A whore and a cunt," Kay elaborated.

"I told him to leave," Arthur said, "and I was not gentle in my command. He began laughing at us, and shouting his insults. This drew Gawaine's attention, and he was on his way to join us when it happened."

"What?" I asked.

"Maleagant drew his sword," Arthur said. "He grabbed Guinevere by the arm and pulled her against his body."

"Tell him what he said," Kay implored.

"It doesn't matter," Arthur said.

"He said he would make sure that Guinevere was broken in before the Festival was done," Kay said. "He said he would make her his whore."

"Enough, Kay," Arthur said. "Gawaine wasn't quite there yet, and I was stupidly unarmed."

"So you reached for the nearest sword," I said.

"So I reached for the nearest sword," Arthur confirmed. "I wasn't thinking. This... man was threatening Guinevere and Morgan. I reacted to protect them. Before I even realized what I had done Excalibur was in my hand."

"How did it feel?"

"I don't know."

"Yes you do," Kay said.

"It felt right," Arthur said. "Is that arrogant? The blade slid out of the stone with no resistance whatsoever, easier than my regular sword out of its sheath. It was light, and easy to hold, like the grip had been made from a mold of my hand. It felt like discovering a piece of myself that was missing.

"Oh, Bedivere, I didn't mean..."

"I know," I said. "What happened then?"

"Everything stopped. Guinevere was the first to realize what had happened. She gasped and said, 'Excalibur.' Morgan seemed to glow with pride, but not surprise."

"Maleagant?"

"Sobered up pretty quickly," Kay laughed.

"He let go of Guinevere and ran," Arthur said. "I stood there, feeling stupid. My first thought, believe it or not, was to put the thing back in the stone and hope no one noticed. But Gawaine made sure that couldn't happen."

"How?"

"He yelled a colorful expletive..."

"'Holy shit' was what I heard from across the clearing," Kay said.

"And then ran forward and picked me up in a giant bear hug," Arthur said. "He was whooping, and laughing, and yelling for all the world to come see the new High King of Britain. He got a sudden, serious look on his face and set me down, and then he dropped to one knee before me."

"What did you do?"

"I told the big goof to stand up," Arthur said.

"That's when chaos erupted," Kay said. "Suddenly everyone was running toward the Shrine, and there stood the Wart with Excalibur in one hand and a stupid look on his face."

"Ector managed to get me here and station a guard before things got too out of hand," Arthur said. "A little later Lady Vivienne arrived to hear my story. That's when I gave her the Sword. Whatever happens, it's too valuable to leave here until this is all straightened out."

"Now what?" I asked.

"I don't know." Arthur stood and began to pace the small boundaries of the tent. "I've been confined here. Vivienne called a meeting of the petty kings and I've heard nothing but shouting from over there ever since. I don't know what this means, or what they're trying to decide. I mean, who am I to have drawn Excalibur after everyone else has failed for all these years? I'm a foundling, the foster son of someone who has never laid claim to the title of king. I have no lands, no army, no claim to anything. I can't be the heir to the title of High King. I don't even know who my real father is."

I was beginning to believe I knew the answer to that question, but I held my tongue. Although it all seemed to fit, I was not in possession of the facts, and truth be told, it was all too big and unlikely for my head to grasp in that moment.

I didn't have time to think on it too closely, though. The tent flap opened and Ector stepped inside. He greeted me with affection and said something about being glad I was feeling better, but his attention was obviously on something more important.

"Arthur," he said, "it is time. The council of the petty kings has summoned you. There is much debate and dissension over what has occurred. We need to settle this quickly."

"I don't want the Sword," Arthur said. "I'm not qualified."

"There is much you do not know, son of my heart." Ector embraced Arthur and then stood back from him. "There are many plans that are coming to fruition, sooner than we had planned, but the time it seems has come. Be prepared Arthur. You are at the center of a great moment, and many things are about to be revealed. Stand strong.

"As for me," Ector continued, "as far as I am concerned the prophecy has been fulfilled. I will always love you like a son, but from this moment forward, know that I acknowledge you as my king."

"I don't understand," Arthur protested.

"You will, lad." Ector wrapped a protective arm around Arthur's shoulders and turned him toward the exit. "Now come along. You have a kingdom to claim. Kay, help me guard him as we walk."

"What about Bedivere?" Arthur asked.

"He's to come along as well," Ector said. "He's your right hand man isn't he?"

I felt pride at the intent of those words, but flinched at their unintentional reference. I hoped to serve Arthur in whatever way I could, given my new limitations, but feared I would end up as ineffective as the emptiness at the end of my arm.

Kay and I followed Ector and Arthur out of the tent and were immediately buffeted by the questions, shouts and cheers of the clamoring crowd. Morvawr and Turmyr closed ranks around us and provided a guard as we made our way to the pavilion.

"Bedivere," Kay said to me amidst the tumult. His face carried a more serious and determined look than I had ever seen him wear.

"Yes?"

"Are you ready for this?"

"I guess."

"Don't guess. Know."

I felt a rush of anger. Who was Kay to tell me what to do, especially now? He didn't know what I had lost, or how adrift I felt. Everything I thought I was going to be was in question. An uncharacteristic envy of Arthur washed over me. Here he was, possibly about to be elevated to the role of High King, and I couldn't tie my own laces without help. What possible role could a cripple have in a land of warriors? To Kay's credit, he saw my reaction and softened his speech.

"Look, Bedivere, I know this is sudden, for all of us. Everything that has happened this summer has changed all of our lives. All I'm saying is, Arthur needs us, now more than ever before. I don't know what lies before him, before all of us. But you and I are his family, his closest companions. I never thought I would hear myself say this about my annoying little brother, but he has always been the best among us. Whatever happens I plan on supporting him and doing everything in my power to stand by him. But if there is anyone he needs more than me, it is you, and you know it."

Kay surprised me. This one speech showed more depth than I

had ever seen from him before. I knew he was right. It was time to step up out of my self-pity and find my place. I was not dead, and it didn't look like I was going to be any time soon. I looked at Arthur and saw my future. Where he went, I would be by his side.

We entered the pavilion amidst curious silence. Everyone stared at Arthur as he was led to the main dais where he was given a seat next to the Lady Vivienne. I looked around and saw all of the petty kings arrayed throughout the enclosure. Gawaine and Agravaine stood close to King Lot and Queen Morgause, and Tristan was seated at Mark's side. As the heirs of their respective kingdoms with claim to the throne themselves what happened here concerned them as well. Guinevere sat by her father, taking in everything, a look of excited concentration on her face.

Excalibur stood gleaming on the main dais, propped up by and iron brace.

"Lady of the Lake," Ector said in loud, formal tones. "Priestesses and acolytes of Avalon. Kings and citizens of the kingdoms of our land. The rightful High King of all Britain has drawn Excalibur from the stone where Merlin placed it so many years ago. The wizard's prophecy has been fulfilled. It is my pleasure to present to this august assemblage, your new sovereign, King Arthur."

Ector went to one knee in acknowledgment of his obeisance to his proclamation. I had time to see the pained expression on Arthur's face before I, along with Kay, Morvawr, Turmyr, and all of the members of Ector's household in attendance in the crowd, followed his example.

"This is completely absurd!" screamed a voice. "He's a boy! More than likely a bastard. His claim is a joke on all of us!"

"Malaguin!" Vivienne said. "You will have your turn to speak. We are here to determine the fate of Britain, and everyone will have a voice. Sit down and hold your tongue."

"Who are you to tell me to shut up?" Malaguin persisted.

"I see where Maleagant gets his charm," Arthur said. He bid all of us to stand. Kay and I immediately went to his side as he continued. "You are right, Malaguin. I may have no claim. This is as much of a surprise to me as it is to you. But for years everyone here has come to this spot and tried to draw the Sword, including you. If you had been successful you would have claimed the title of High King immediately and expected everyone to follow you. That speaks of at least a token belief in the prophecy. In honor of that, I believe you are bound to at least listen to what is said and decided here. I yet claim no authority to enforce your cooperation, but I do demand that you speak with more respect for Lady Vivienne, and if you do not I'm sure I will be joined in implementing that request by most everyone here, authority or not."

I was not the only one stunned by Arthur's composure. I saw a grin on Kay's face that mirrored the one on his father's. There was complete silence in the clearing as Arthur and Malaguin each took the measure of the other.

"Sit down and shut up, Malaguin," King Lot said. "You are not the only one here who doubts the veracity of this whelp's claims, but we will not turn this into a tavern brawl."

"For once I agree with Lot," Uriens said.

"I will not!" Malaguin shouted. I think if Lot and Uriens had kept quiet Malaguin would have been more tractable, at least for a little while. But his lifelong dislike for these two men, combined with his own foul temper and misplaced pride, prevented him from backing down.

I cannot begin to remember everything that was said in the next few moments, mainly because the pavilion erupted into a cacophony. Following Malaguin's lead, everyone began to talk, and then to shout. Insults and challenges were hurled, overriding the pleas for calm and decorum from the dais. I genuinely believe violence may have erupted if not for what occurred next. I happened to be looking down the length of the main table and saw one of the hooded priests stand. He drew his hood back from his face and I was surprised to see I recognized him. Before my shock registered though he yelled out in the loudest, most commanding voice I had ever heard.

"ENOUGH!"

Silence followed instantly and every head turned to see the imposing presence of the tall gray-bearded man I had known as Arthur's teacher since childhood.

"Lailoken?" Arthur said.

"Merlin," the Lady Vivienne corrected.

CHAPTER FOURTEEN

I don't suppose I have been very canny in hiding Lailoken's true identity in the course of this narrative. Now it is common knowledge that Merlin came to Arthur in his youth to teach the art of kingship. The name Lailoken is not even known by most, and why should it be? It was never his real name, but an identity he wore while in our presence that he stripped off like a cloak when he went to other places.

What is not as well known are the many other identities Merlin wore in the years he was thought to be absent. Arthur and I were not the only young men in the pavilion to be surprised that day. Owain saw his teacher Myrddyn while Guinevere saw Father Emrys. Gawaine and Agravaine were surprised to see their druid Stormcrow and Tristan delighted by the presence of Taliesin. We later discovered that it was Merlin under the dark hood of Father Ambrosious who led us into Mont St. Michael.

It is said that, among his many wondrous powers, Merlin is a shapeshifter. How else could he come and go unnoticed as easily as he did? Ector always knew who Lailoken was, but Merlin certainly would not have been welcome in Lot's kingdom. Morgause would rather have seen him dead than allow him to teach her sons. I don't know how much magic he used to help with his disguises, but he did once confide some of his secrets to me, years later. He said that most people only see what they want to see. A change of clothing and hair color, a few extra fake warts, and a limp and people will not recognize someone they have known for many years. Add a measure of circumspect avoidance to the mix and Morgause, Lot, and many, many others never saw the great magician Merlin, only simple teachers and priests.

Why the deception? Because Merlin had given up on Uther's generation. He had grown tired of his ceaseless work to unite Britain being undermined by old feuds and trifling egos. He had come close to placing Uther on the throne, only to see the work undone by Gorlois' defection, and the rapid dissolution of the union after his unfortunate death. Merlin had decided on another plan, one with Uther's heir at its center. But, while Arthur was central to the plan, Merlin had discovered that no one man could unite Britain on his own. The new High King would need loyal companions, and no matter how strong or effective a leader he may be that sort of loyalty could only grow in soil that had been prepared. Merlin went to the sons and heirs of each of the petty kings, and from the beginning taught them to value the idea of a unified Britain. He tried to instill the belief that no one of the smaller kingdoms was safe from foreign invasion by itself, and that the only hope for survival was to embrace the concept of the High King as symbolized by Excalibur. By the time Arthur drew the sword the next generation of the kings of Britain were ready to follow him.

That truth determined the course of the council.

Merlin's abrupt appearance caused a sudden stunned silence in the clearing. I thought the chaos would return immediately but to everyone's relief that did not happen. Whatever old grudges still remained, respect for Merlin's presence, or perhaps fear of his power, was enough to make the petty kings a little more civil.

"I see nothing has changed in the years of my absence." Merlin 's voice echoed through the clearing, resonant and commanding. "You all still enjoy squabbling over Britain like a pack of dogs over an old bone. I am not surprised the Goddess would not give the Sword to any of your hands these many years. Why haven't you invited the Saxons to join the party like Vortigern did? Do you care so little for this land? Do you really believe that each of you defending your own little turret will keep our enemies out of the castle? Nearly twenty years I am gone and here you are, older but no wiser, the same old faces with the same old feuds. Each of you is the spoke of a great wheel with no axle to turn around. No wonder you haven't covered any new ground.

"The time comes soon when the Saxons will land on our shores like flies on the carcass of a dead beast. They will feed on your crops, and sleep in your beds with your daughters in their arms and you old men will crouch in the last unoccupied cave in Britain and blame each others ancestors for your misery.

"It is time to stop scratching the itch of your old wounds and look to the future. It is time to share your strengths and stand side by side instead of being afraid to turn your back on each other. It is time to set aside your differences and embrace what unites us. The prophecy has been fulfilled. It is time to pledge allegiance to the new High King. It is time to declare your support for he whom the god and goddess have chosen to wield Excalibur. It is time to recognize Arthur Pendragon, son and only heir of Uther Pendragon and Queen Igraine of Cornwall."

An audible gasp surged through the assembly. I had started to believe this was the truth of Arthur's parentage, but to have it confirmed so bluntly still came as a surprise. Like so many others I turned to look at my friend and saw by the expression on his face that no one there was more surprised than he. In fact, the only faces I saw that did not look astonished were Merlin, Ector, Vivienne, and oddly enough, Morgan.

And when I looked at her the implications hit me fully. Morgan was Arthur's half sister! As the truth of this exploded in my mind I saw Arthur make eye contact with her and knew he was thinking the same thing. How many people here knew of his dalliance with her? Had she known who he was, and if so, what sick game was she playing? Before I had a chance to formulate all of the questions running through my mind Merlin spoke again.

"Arthur," he said, "I know this is a surprise to you more than anyone here. Forgive me for not telling you for all these years. I judged it was best to keep you hidden. The heir of Uther would have been, unfortunately, the target of misdeeds by some of the men who sit here now. That is but one of the reasons these men are not fit to rule."

"I forgive you," Arthur said. "But I don't understand. How is it possible that I am Uther's son?"

"That's a good question," Morguase said.

"Woman," Lot chided. "Mind your tongue. I wish to hear the story as well, but you are out of place."

"I will not mind my tongue while this charlatan tries to put an unknown bastard on the throne of Britain," Morguase said. "If this boy is Uther's son I want some proof, and even then he is the spawn of Uther's rape of my mother and has no claim."

"Well, Merlin?" Malaguin sneered. "Convince us."

"Whatever you may believe of your mother, Morguase," Merlin said, "she was never raped by Uther. Igraine was given to Gorlois in marriage when she was very young and never truly loved him. It's a story I'm sure you can relate to."

"Careful, wizard," Lot warned.

"She suffered under both his selfish desires and his indifference," Merlin continued. "She gave birth to you and then to Morgan, but there was no love involved in the process. Think back Morguase. Did your father ever give you reason to believe he wasn't disappointed you were a girl?"

"You bastard!" Morguase cried.

"True, I have no father," Merlin said. "But that is not true of Arthur. For you see, Igraine met Uther, and found all the love she had long been denied. The Goddess placed her in Uther's path for purposes beyond our ken. She may have been married to Gorlois in the Church, but never in her heart."

"Then Arthur is illegitimate!" Morgause accused. "She was

legally wed to my father, whether her heart was in it or not."

"She was wed to Uther when Arthur was conceived," Merlin asserted.

"Impossible," Morgause said. "How? Uther snuck into Tintagel, with your help I might add, and raped my mother while his men had Gorlois killed. I will certainly not believe she married her rapist simply because you claim so."

"Morgause," Vivienne interjected. "Please stop calling it rape. You were not present, and too young to understand what took place that night."

"You should side with me, Vivienne!" Morgause said. "Igraine was your sister! How can you support this?"

This was information I did not know. How close were the ties between Arthur and Avalon? The young remain unaware of the full history of those who precede them. We are all born in the middle or the end of someone else's story.

"Because I knew Igraine better than you. Because I know more about what happened that night."

"Then please share with the rest of us," Malaguin said.

"Gorlois was mad with jealousy," Vivienne said. "And perhaps that is the one thing in his actions that is justified. Igraine did love Uther, and Gorlois saw it. He was not jealous of that love. He knew nothing of love. But Igraine was his property. Don't you remember the fighting, Morgause? The screaming and the threats your father heaped upon your mother? The bruises?"

Morgause did not respond.

"Morgan was much younger than you," Vivienne continued, "but she knows that she feared Gorlois. And well she should have. Gorlois had promised to lock Igraine and her daughters in Tintagel and never let them go. He promised he would kill all of you before he allowed Uther to look on her again. Igraine wrote to me of this. She believed Gorlois would follow through on his threat, whether Uther did anything or not.

"Igraine was raised here on Avalon," Vivienne explained to the crowd. "She was an acolyte, but her gifts were not those of a priestess. While I was raised to be the Lady of the Lake my little sister went out into the world. Does that sound familiar, Morgause. You and Morgan have fallen into the same roles. You have been luckier than your mother, because as near as I can tell, Lot is good to you, in his way. But I believed Igraine's life was in danger and could not allow that to happen.

"I sent Merlin to Tintagel to spirit her away. He did so, with Uther's help. Morgan was brought here as well, and you would have been if you hadn't already made your way into Lot's bed without telling anyone where you were. Uther didn't touch your mother that night except to lift her onto a horse. We were all surprised at the news of Gorlois' death that same night."

"At the hands of Uther's men!" Morgause retorted. "How convenient. Don't try to convince me that assassination was not part of the plan."

"It was not," Merlin said. "Uther's forces were camped, planning an expedition against the Saxons; the very same Saxons who would kill him a few days later. Gorlois attacked Uther's men that night, the first in a planned series of strikes designed to kill Uther and bring Gorlois to the throne. It was a betrayal of the council of kings. You were given to Lot as payment for staying out of the fight. When Gorlois lost not only that skirmish but his life as well, Lot took you and his army and returned to Orkney. The union was broken."

"Are you accusing me of cowardice, Merlin?" King Lot asked.

"No, not really," Merlin said. "I suppose prudence might be a better word. You knew Gorlois' betrayal would split the union, and none of you stood a chance against the Saxons alone. Since you had not backed the winner you did what a smart king of a small distant kingdom should have done. You cut your losses and returned home. As did Uriens, and Malaguin. Mark didn't have the luxury to leave. Someone had to take control of Cornwall before it all fell into enemy hands."

"Usurper!" Morgause spat. "Cornwall belonged to my father. Mark sits on a throne that should belong to my sons."

"Could you have defended it?" King Mark asked. "You were on your way to your throne in the north while I and my armies bled and died to secure Cornwall. If not for this usurper Cornwall would be Saxon or Irish by now."

"He speaks true," Uriens said. "We all left to see to our own lands. If the Saxons could not be stopped there, which seemed likely with the union broken, then they would have broken through to threaten all of us."

"And Uther died defeating that threat," Merlin said. "And all of you knew years of relative peace thanks to his sacrifice."

"None of this explains Arthur's heritage," Leodegrance spoke up. "I wish to believe he is the High King, but I need to be convinced that he is Uther and Igraine's legitimate heir."

"Igraine was brought here, to Avalon," Vivienne resumed the tale. "She was here less than a day before we heard of Gorlois' treachery and death. She was a widow."

"And she celebrated by rutting with Uther?" Morgause said. "Maybe not as vile as rape, but Arthur is still a bastard by law."

"No, Morgause, he is not," Vivienne said. "Uther and Igraine were both followers of the Goddess and the old ways. They were married here, in the eyes of the Goddess and the God, in the ceremony of the sacred wedding."

"You expect us to believe that?" Morgause asked.

"I swear it as high priestess and Lady of the Lake of Avalon," Vivienne said. "For anyone who knows either me or the traditions we keep here that should be enough, but if not there were many witnesses who are still in service here. Many of them stand in this crowd right now as we speak. As Igraine's sister and confidant I also swear that Igraine went to her second marriage bed untouched by Uther until that night. Arthur was conceived the day they were married."

"How can you be so sure of that?" Malaguin asked.

"Because he rode from here the next day and died before he ever returned, you fool," Merlin said.

"Igraine died in childbirth nine months later," Vivienne said. "In my arms as we both held her new son. Arthur."

"Why wasn't I raised here then?" Arthur asked. "I would have been safe here, wouldn't I? Why make me believe I was an orphan?"

"Avalon is no place for a growing boy," Vivienne said. "And no, if Uther's enemies found you we could not guarantee your safety."

"Anonymity was your only shield," Merlin said. "Ector knew, of course, but he is a rare sort of man. Completely trustworthy once he has given his word. We couldn't tell you, because what boy could help but announce he was the High King's son? Even if most thought it was just the fantasy of a bastard child, all it would take would be the wrong word to suspicious ears. I also believed that you needed to be raised in the real world. Avalon is wonderful for priestesses and those with the gift, but not a place for the future king to learn the ways of man's society.

"But," Merlin continued to the crowd, "this goes on too long. For those who still doubt, we can produce witnesses to the wedding of Igraine and Uther, and Avalon is not without its written records as well. All of that is in the past, and it is the future we must face. Uther's heir has drawn Excalibur. By the grace of the Goddess Britain has a High King. It is now up to those assembled here to decide whether this is a future they will embrace, or if they will continue to follow old and broken ways. I, Merlin, have been and will remain as Arthur's counselor and advisor. Who else will stand beside the new King?"

"Arthur has the blessing of Avalon," Lady Vivienne said. "It is the will of the Goddess and of the God that he husband the land of

Britain."

"I have already made my decision known," Ector said. "My lands, my holdings, and my army are at the command of King Arthur. I have acted as his father for his entire life, and all I ask is that he allow me to continue to do so, now that he knows who his true father is."

"I will always count you as the only father I have known," Arthur said.

Leodegrance stood and took a moment to gather his thoughts.

"I knew Uther," he said, "and though he was arrogant and at times bull-headed, I did believe he was the best man to unite Britain. A united kingdom is a dream I have spent much of my life believing in. Arthur is young, but I believe with the right advisors and people around him he can grow into his role. My daughter has convinced me of his worth. His actions in Benwick, while perhaps rash, were well intentioned and in the end, cut through to the heart of a matter we old men could only talk to death.

"I believe Uther and Igraine were married here," Leodegrance said. "And though I could wish the wedding had taken place in the Christian Church, I realize their beliefs and customs are valid for the purposes of establishing Arthur's legitimacy."

"Our gods are the same, Leodegrance," Merlin said. I could tell from his voice this was a resumption of an old and well-loved discussion between the two men.

"Yes." Leodegrance smiled. "So you've told me. Our lord Jesus is the same as your gods of the harvest and the hunt who die and resurrect. You'll pardon me if I maintain that there are significant differences still. I do look forward to continuing our debates on the topic. It has been much too long. But that is for later. Like I said, I recognize Arthur's claim as legitimate. So I too, declare my allegiance to the new High King. My lands, my holdings, and my army are his to do with as he sees fit."

With this pronouncement Leodegrance kneeled before Arthur. Guinevere came to her father's side and joined him in his obeisance. A moment later all of the members of his party spread throughout the crowd did the same.

"Thank you, Leodegrance," Arthur said. "Please rise and know that I will value your experience and counsel. Anyone who has raised a daughter of such wit and intelligence has much to teach me as well." Guinevere blushed, and looked away from Arthur. She caught my eye and raised her eyebrows. I didn't need the gifts of Avalon to read her mind. Her expression told of mixed disbelief, excitement and pride.

"Sure," Malaguin said. "The two men who have the most to gain and have nothing to lose are the first to declare for this upstart. Ector's reasons are clear enough. He stands to gain substantially if his son becomes the High King. But what's in it for you, Leodegrance? Wait a moment... I think I understand. Arthur attacked my son for speaking to your daughter. You already have a royal marriage in mind, don't you?"

From the look on Leodegrance's face, this was the first the thought had crossed his mind. Guinevere was stunned and turned red. I think I was the only one to see the stolen glance between Arthur and Morgan.

And why did I feel anger at the suggestion?

"Don't deny it," Malaguin said. "This is part of this whole charade. This has been planned. This is why you have repeatedly ignored my requests for an arrangement between your daughter and my Maleagant."

"I have ignored those requests," Leodegrance said with more steel in his voice than I would have imagined possible, "because I remember what sort of man you have always been, and how you have always treated the women in your life. If Maleagant is anything like his father I want him nowhere near Guinevere."

"Insult me, will you?" Malaguin stood and reached for his sword. I saw Merlin begin to speak, but Arthur's voice rang out."

"Sit down Malaguin," he said. "There will be no violence here. Not today, not ever. This is sacred ground, and if you have no respect for that, then leave here. I did not allow your son to molest Guinevere; I will not allow you to attack her father. I may not be king here yet, but I don't think I'm mistaken in believing you have enough enemies here that I would be supported in seeing you thrown in chains if you are stupid enough to keep that sword in your hands."

Malaguin glared at Arthur. A deadly duel of wills played out between their eyes. Malaguin broke his stare and surveyed the crowd, seeing the truth of Arthur's words. With a look of malice and disgust he sheathed his sword.

"You have made an enemy here today, boy," Malaguin spat.

"You may wish to reconsider," Arthur said. "We all, including you, have enough enemies in the Saxons all around us. Do you really wish to have more here at home? If you answer yes to that question, then I know I am in good company and I pity the people of your kingdom."

Arthur turned away from Malaguin. He didn't see the look of pure hate that Malaguin wore as he stood and left the pavilion, followed by his son and all of his retainers.

I don't know how else Arthur could have handled that situation. Everything I had ever heard about Malaguin tells me nothing any of us could have said would have appeased him. But Arthur did indeed make an enemy that day, and we would all suffer because of it.

"Now that that thorn has been pulled," Merlin said, "perhaps we can resume our business here."

"My suggestion," Vivienne said, "is that we all break for dinner and reflection. There has been much to take in this afternoon, much which changes all of our lives. While I believe we must all rally behind Arthur and give him our support I understand that this is not a decision to be made rashly. Let us all fill our bellies and reflect on everything that has been said, and look to the future as well. We will meet here again in the morning after breakfast. Decisions will be made then."

"No amount of food or reflection will change our decision," Morgause said. "We will never support Arthur."

"Be quiet, Morgause," Lot said. "Don't presume to speak for me."

"You can't seriously..." Morgause began.

"No," Lot interrupted. "Mind your place, and remember who is your husband and your king. This is my decision, based on what is good for Orkney and good for my sons."

"And what about your sons?" Gawaine piped up. "Do we have any say in this decision?"

"I will hear you," Lot said. "But I am still your father and your king. The final decision is mine."

"I respect you as my father," Gawaine said. "But I am old enough to make my own decisions for my life. And as for you being my king... well, I believe my loyalty to the new High King takes precedence." Gawaine turned to Arthur.

"So," he said, with his usual good humor in his voice, "it would seem that in addition to being my friend you are also my uncle." A look of surprise lit up Arthur's face as this notion caught him off guard. He smiled and began to respond, but Gawaine surprised us all yet again when he went down on one knee and kneeled before him.

"Knight me," he said. "I have seen what sort of man you are. From this day forward I pledge my allegiance to you."

"Gawaine!" Morgause shouted. "Don't you dare betray us like this!"

"Your mother is right, for once," Lot said. "Be careful what you do here."

"I am your man," Gawaine said to Arthur. "Now and forever. As heir to the kingdom of Orkney, I swear to be your vassal and make my lands your lands, for the good of a united Britain."

"Orkney is not your kingdom yet," Lot said. I could plainly see that he was angry, but there was another look on his face as well. Was it pride?

"Yet," Gawaine said. "Until that day it is still yours, father. Until that day I choose to stay here as one of Arthur's men."

"If you do this," Morgause spat, "Orkney will never be yours. You are not the only heir."

"Do you plan on passing the kingship to Agravaine?" Gawaine laughed. "Go ahead. We'll see how long he can hold it when I return to claim my right. Don't be foolish. Don't split the realm even further. This division among all of us is stupid. Our best chance to beat the Saxons, and the Irish, and the Northmen comes from working together, not fighting amongst our selves. Britain is one giant shield wall. We must overlap and protect each other. The moment one of us steps out of the wall the whole thing collapses. Support me in this. Support Arthur."

"I will never support that bastard," Morgause muttered.

"We will speak of this later," Lot said to Gawaine. "In private."

"We can speak all you want," Gawaine said, still on his knees in front of Arthur. "Right now, my wish is plain. King Arthur, make me your knight."

Arthur looked to Merlin, who nodded his approval.

"Lady Vivienne," Arthur said, "I gave Excalibur to you for safekeeping. It seems I have need of it."

Vivienne smiled and gestured to Morgan. Morgan stepped forward and lifted Excalibur from its iron stand. She turned to Arthur and knelt, offering the sword to his hand."

"King Arthur," she said. "In recognition of your sacred kingship of the land, and as a representative of the Goddess here on earth, the

Lady of the Lake gives Excalibur to its rightful bearer."

Arthur placed his hand on Excalibur's grip and lifted it from Morgan's hand.

"Thank you, Lady of the Lake," he said, though it seemed to me he addressed Morgan more so than Vivienne. He turned to face Gawaine.

"Don't do this," Morgause muttered. She was ignored.

"Gawaine," Arthur intoned. "First, let me say thank you for your offer and your loyalty. You have proven your worth to me, as a warrior and as a friend. I have already come to think of you as my ally and my companion. If this is your wish, then as my first act as High King, with the blessing of those around us, I will make this official.

"Do you, Gawaine, son of Lot, swear to uphold the laws of the kingdom?" Arthur said. "Do you swear loyalty to the rightful king of Britain and its people, to follow my lead as long as it is righteous, to be my sword in matters of war, to be my shield, to be my conscience? To follow me until the end of my days as long as my rule is just and fair? To serve the office and not the man?"

It was a speech I remembered all too well. I remembered the feel of a wooden stick upon my shoulders when I was a boy and the solemn promise I had made.

"I do so swear" Gawaine said. Arthur touched Excalibur to both of Gawaine's shoulders.

"Now rise, Sir Gawaine," Arthur said. "And welcome to my service."

Gawaine stood to the abrupt cheers of the crowd. My voice was loudest among them, though I admit to mixed feelings. Gawaine's gesture had more political impact, but I couldn't help but think it should have been me.

Even in the tumult Merlin noticed the look on my face. He spoke to me in a voice meant only for my ears.

"Don't think that either I or Arthur have forgotten," he said. "This is a very public display, and a necessary step to unite the kingdom. But you once made the same promise, and I was witness. Even though neither of you knew it then, Arthur was still High King of the land, and his actions were binding. Perhaps no one else will ever know, but be assured; you, Sir Bedivere, are the first knight of the realm. No one will ever replace you."

CHAPTER FIFTEEN

I may have been first knight of the realm, in Merlin's eyes, but that didn't give me access to Arthur that night after the council of the kings adjourned. He was quickly spirited away by Merlin, back to Ector's tent where he was placed under guard. A light dinner was served by the acolytes of Avalon, but while the momentous events of the day was the topic at everyone's table, the camaraderie of previous meals was gone. This was not as much of a sign of dissention as it might seem. Each of the petty kings had much to think about and discuss with their own retainers, so most took their meal within their own encampment. As much as I wanted to talk to Tristan and Gawaine, or even Owain and Agravaine, they simply were not to be found. Guinevere was likewise sequestered among her own people while her father conferred with Merlin, Ector, and Arthur.

I ate sparingly. It had only been a couple of days since I had been taking solid food again. Added to that was my frustration at the awkwardness with which I used my implements. It is amazing at how for granted we take doing something as simple as slicing a piece of food on our plate until the hand that holds the knife is gone.

I returned to Ector's site just in time to see Arthur and the others leaving the tent. This did not pass unnoticed by the camp, but the vast crowd that had gathered earlier in the day had dispersed. Still, guards surrounded Arthur. I saw that he wore Excalibur.

"Bedivere!" Arthur hailed. "Come, walk with me."

"Where are we going?"

"I'm being taken across the lake to Avalon," Arthur said. "I'm to meet with Vivienne and Lailoken... er, Merlin; I may never get used to calling him that. There is much I still need to know, about my parents and my heritage. Apparently there are mysteries the High King needs to be made aware of. Though I guess Avalon holds no mystery for you."

"I saw only my room and some hallways. They were beautiful, but I'm sure there are many wonders I didn't see."

"You're still in an elite crowd," Kay offered. "Most people never cross that lake. You're lucky. An entire island full of women... it's like something out of a dream."

"Unless you're unconscious for most of their attentions," I said.

"Most?" Kay teased. I felt the blush rise to my face at the memory of the red-haired acolyte. Kay jumped on my reaction. "Aha! I knew it! There's a story there I must hear."

I kept my silence through Kay's continued ribbing, and Arthur's admonitions for Kay to leave me alone. I was not going to tell them anything, but this resumption of our lifelong roles felt good. Arthur had apparently accepted his destiny, but with Kay and I his banter was the same as it always was

We reached the shore near the now empty Shrine. Morgan stood in one of the swan boats, and as I looked at her I once again wondered how much she had known about Arthur's identity. I was still uneasy in my knowledge of what had passed between them. As a knight of the true king, was it my duty to voice my concerns to Arthur? If I knew, was it possible the others did too? Gawaine surely suspected. Would Arthur's throne be forfeit if it became known he had engaged in incest, even unknowingly?

Arthur said his farewells to us and stepped into the boat. Merlin followed.

"We will be back before dawn," the wizard said. "Today went well, except for Malaguin."

"Did you expect better from him?" Ector asked.

"No," Merlin said. "I'm afraid someday we will have to deal with him, but for now he is not our concern. Oddly enough, in his tirades he offered a suggestion that may someday prove useful."

"Guinevere?"

"Exactly," Merlin said. "Our king will someday need a queen, one whom the people of Britain will love and embrace. I can think of no better match for Arthur than Guinevere."

"Lailoken!" Arthur protested, once again using the name he would always call Merlin in private. I saw the look that passed between him and Morgan, and I can't imagine Merlin missed it either.

"Easy, son," Merlin laughed. "You won't be marrying her today, or anytime soon. Maybe not at all, depending on what the kingdom needs. There is much you must learn before that step is taken, and much you must do. Consolidating your kingdom is the first step. Tomorrow will help decide the matter as we see where the other kings fall. I believe Mark is our man, but Uriens still concerns me."

"He is in no condition to rule, or to challenge us," Ector said.

"He is still full of his old pride," Merlin answered. "He won't simply bend the knee without asking for something."

"I'll deal with Uriens," Arthur said. Merlin raised a questioning eyebrow, but did not pursue the matter further.

"We'll see you in the morning," Merlin said. With that farewell he shoved the swan boat away from the shore and glided into the mist of the lake. We stood and watched as it slowly disappeared from our sight.

When we eventually left the shore I went to check on the horses. Butter was happy to see me. I brushed him down, but even that familiar task was made clumsy by my inexperienced left hand. By the time I was finished I was thoroughly discouraged and angry. I threw the brush against the railing of the corral as hard as I could. It was a weak and ineffectual action. I kicked a bucket of oats across the ground.

"What's wrong?" came a voice from behind me.

I spun around to see Kay standing just outside the corral. A circle of torches threw heavy shadows. He stood casually, but I saw that he held two swords.

Embarrassed to have been caught in my tantrum my anger flared further.

"What's wrong?" I yelled. "What do you think is wrong? I'm a cripple! I can't take care of my horse. I can't feed myself normally. I can't even tie my own bootlaces! I'm useless!"

"I can't, I can't, I can't," Kay mocked. "Are you going to wallow in your self-pity the rest of your life?"

"Shut up!" I screamed.

"No," Kay said. "Want to fight me about it?" He tossed one of the swords at me. Instinctively I reached for it with my right arm, but of course the sword hilt flew unhindered through the space where my hand should have been. I could feel my hand grasp at it, but my missing fingers lied.

"Pick it up," Kay said.

"I can't fight with my left hand!"

"You better," Kay said, and then stepped forward and took a swing at me with his sword. I ducked out of the way easily, but Kay persisted.

"Pick it up!" A backhanded swing cut near my stomach. I leapt out of reach.

"Stop it!" I cried.

"No," Kay said. "Defend yourself. If I were a Saxon do you think I'd take pity on you simply because you think you're a cripple? Just because you don't have a hand doesn't mean you won't have to fight someday. Pick it up!"

He whacked me across the thigh with the flat of his sword. It stung and left me with no doubt that there would be a bruise.

"There," he said. "If I were a Saxon you'd have lost a leg as well. What're you going to do about it?"

I was enraged. My leg ached, my stump felt tender, and my head screamed with the agony of anger. I reached down with my left hand and picked up the sword. It felt awkward and wrong, but I rushed headlong at Kay anyway, swinging wildly. He easily deflected my swing.

"That's it!" he said as I rounded on him and tried again. He parried this blow as well.

"Shut up!"

"That's good." Kay took a swing and I was able to deflect it. "I'm not used to fighting a left-handed opponent. It challenges me. All you need is practice, Bedivere. You can do this."

"Why should I?" I asked as I stepped back and prepared another attack.

"Because Arthur needs you."

"Arthur will have all the knights he needs. One cripple more or less won't make a difference." Kay swung again, his hardest attack yet. I felt the metal of my sword vibrate painfully in my palm.

"You still don't get it, do you?" he said. "It doesn't matter how many men Arthur commands, he will always need us. You and me."

"Why?"

"Because we're his family," Kay said. "From this day on, we're the only ones who will ever know him as a person instead of a king, and that's our job. To remind him he is a person. When he's sitting on a throne with the fate of all of Britain before him, I need to remind him of the time he fell in the hog wallow and came home stinking of shit. I need to remind him, whenever he's feeling too big for his britches that he's still my bothersome little brother who doesn't know nearly as much as he thinks he does. No one else will be able to do that. It's my role to be the obnoxious big brother who remembers all of the embarrassing things he did as a child. Not to put him down in front of others, but to keep him humble. I have faith in Arthur, but this is a large weight that has fallen on his shoulders. If we who have always loved don't help him carry it, no one else will either."

"And what can I offer him, like this?" I said as I parried another sword thrust.

"The same thing you always have," Kay said. "Your loyalty. But more than that, you are the one person he has always been completely himself with. You're his friend in ways I can't be. *You* are his confidante; you are the person he will talk to, about everything, the person he will ask for advice. No matter what Merlin or the others counsel, he will seek you out to discuss matters. You need to be the dependable one, as you always have been. You need to be caution to his more reckless impulses.

"Think of him like a horse," Kay suddenly laughed. "He's a good horse, with a good head on his shoulders, but every once in a while he decides to race off on his own. It's up to you to guide him, even if he's fighting against the bit."

"You're saying I should try to control Arthur?"

"Not control," Kay said. "Offer guidance. You know, a slight tug on the reins, subtle pressure with your legs. Give him his head, but keep him from jumping into a ravine. I know it's a stupid image, but whatever way you want to think of it. The simple truth is that we need to be prepared to give him the best of ourselves, and you can't do that as long as you think of yourself as a cripple."

Even as he said the words he feigned a thrust at my midsection and when I moved to avoid it he swept out his left leg and kicked mine out from under me. I fell onto my backside, but that was not the worst of it. I reached out to catch myself and rammed the leather cup over my stump hard into the ground. The calluses I have today had not yet developed, so the pain was incredible.

"How can I not think of myself as a cripple?" I said through clenched teeth as I stood.

"By getting good enough that I can't do that to you anymore."

I glared at him. At that moment I don't think I had ever hated anyone more. Still, his words rang true. Kay may have been blunt as a turnip, but he had a way of cutting to the heart of the matter. As angry as I was, I was still able to see what he was doing. In his own impertinent manner he was trying to lift me out of my mire.

"So," he said as he sheathed his sword. "I expect you to meet me here for sword practice in the morning before breakfast." He shot me a wink that I found maddening, and then turned and walked away.

I stood there, the sword's weight unfamiliar in my hand, still angry.

But Kay was right, and though I hated him for the way he did it, I loved him for doing it.

I met him bright and early the next morning with a sword in my hand and a much more determined attitude. Soon I was nursing new blisters on my left hand. I had no idea just how soon I was going to need my fighting skills.

We had just finished and were headed back to camp for breakfast when we saw Malaguin's group form up in preparation to leave. He had not brought a large company with him, and it was still early. I think if I had still been abed I wouldn't have noticed his passage. No one tried to stop him from leaving. I thought perhaps Merlin would appear to make one last effort to bring Malaguin to his senses, but the wizard did not show.

That was the first time I wondered, since Merlin had taken such great pains to be present in the life of so many of the Companions throughout their days, why he had not gone to Maleagant as well. If Merlin had taught Malaguin's son the same lessons he had brought to every other heir to the lands of Britain perhaps much hardship could have been avoided. Years later, right after the resolution of the affair of Guinevere's kidnapping, I asked Merlin about this.

"I did go to him," Merlin answered. "Some people just can't be reached. Maleagant had no interest in learning anything but the sword, and as harsh as this sounds, he didn't really have the wits to do much else. My attempts at becoming his teacher were met with disinterest at best and active malice at worst. I saw very quickly that that bad apple had not fallen far from the diseased tree which spawned it."

We don't like to believe these things of our children, but even the best child can be warped when presented with a steady diet of hatred by those who raise them. That was a truth that eventually caused the downfall of Camelot.

Kay and I stood and watched them go. Their passage brought a few more curious witnesses out of their tents, but very few seemed to care. If anything, there was an immediate lightening of the mood of the entire camp.

I ate a fairly large breakfast. My exertions with Kay that morning and the previous night had brought back my appetite with a vengeance. I could tell from how loose my trews and belt were how much weight I had lost during my convalescence. My arm ached as I spooned porridge into my mouth. Not only had I never used those muscles in my left arm before, but I had lost muscle mass all over my body since my injury. Weeks in bed instead of working had taken more of a toll on me than I realized.

The council reconvened under the pavilion shortly after the breakfast hour. With the exception of Malaguin and his people, everyone was in the same positions as the day before. Lot and Morgause still looked unhappy at the developments, but were at least present. Gawaine, Kay, and I were given an official placement as an honor guard on the main dais (no doubt a contributing factor to the frown on Morgause's face). Arthur appeared wearing Excalibur. Lady Vivienne spoke a blessing over the proceedings. A prayer from one of the priests followed. At the conclusion Arthur and everyone present, except the honor guard of course, took their seats.

Merlin opened with a reiteration of Arthur's claim, followed by a renewed plea for unification and the benefits it would bring everyone. It was a long and eloquent recitation, and no one attempted to interrupt him. The shock and immediacy of yesterday were gone.

Everyone had had time to reflect on the events and approached the new day with a calmer head. Malaguin's absence probably contributed to the peace as well. Queen Morgause was still obviously agitated, and she rolled her eyes several times as Arthur's royal lineage was recounted, but even she held her tongue and maintained the peace.

"Now," Merlin concluded, "we must make a decision, each and every one of us. Avalon, the center of the old religion, supports Arthur's claim to the throne of the High King. Ector and Leodegrance, followers of Uther and rulers of their vast holdings, have already pledged their loyalty and their support. The rest of you must decide where the future of Britain lies. Are we to continue as individual kingdoms, each of us vulnerable to foreign incursion and fearful of each other? Or, do we move forward as a united kingdom, supporting each other with troops, goods, and services in the name of a greater good?"

Silence greeted Merlin's question. I think he had made his point. The overt resistance to the notion of Arthur seemed to have vanished, and the wisdom of Merlin's vision was undeniable. But old ways die hard, and it is difficult for those used to being in control to bend the knee to someone else. I think the support for Arthur was present, at least among the people, but none of the kings wanted to be the first to capitulate.

Finally, the stillness was broken by the sound of chair legs scraping across the floor of the pavilion. We all turned to see King Mark of Cornwall stand.

While I had met him briefly on the trip to Benwick I didn't really spend any time with him. I was struck now by his presence. He was younger than any of the other petty kings. He couldn't have been more than in his early twenties when he fought at Uther's side, not that much older than Arthur and I were now. For him to have been able to rally troops to his cause and secure the disputed land of Cornwall in the wake of Gorlois' death said much about the man's ability as a commander and a king. Of, course, in the early days of that struggle Tristan's father Meliodos had been at Mark's side, but it was still a notable accomplishment. Everything I had ever heard about Mark was that Cornwall was ruled fairly and well. That wild coastal area of Britain was under constant siege from the Irish. Mark had fended them off tirelessly, and I had heard he had even opened peace negotiations with some of the Irish kings.

"Like everyone else here," he began, "I was taken by surprise when Excalibur was drawn. We all had certain expectations and hopes wrapped up in that sword. But every year when we came here and no one pulled it from the stone... well, I must confess I began to lose faith that anyone ever would. Now, I am told that a mere boy, one whom none of us even knew existed before yesterday, is the rightful heir of Uther and the new High King of Britain. In all truth, it's a little hard to swallow.

"But," Mark continued, "I have been convinced that Arthur is indeed who he is claimed to be. Merlin and Lady Vivienne have given convincing evidence. In addition, I knew Uther well, and many were the night we shared a campfire, drinks and stories. I see Uther in his son, the shape of his jaw and his nose. I knew Igraine as well, the obviously long-suffering wife of my former lord Gorlois. Arthur has her eyes and mouth. If he embodies half the qualities of his parents he will make a good king.

"I was in Benwick with him this summer. I am sad to say I really didn't pay much attention to him then. Why should I? He was a young man of another's household. If my nephew Tristan had not befriended him I don't think I would have noticed him at all. Not until he led an expedition to correct a mistake that older and wiser statesmen could do nothing but talk about. It was foolish and impulsive and it was absolutely the right thing to do.

"Last night I met with all of my advisors to discuss what decision we should make today. I was already leaning toward support, but it was Tristan who finally convinced me. He praised Arthur's qualities for most of the night. If it were simple youthful enthusiasm and loyalty to a new friend I would not have been swayed. But Tristan has proven to me time and again that he has an uncanny knack for seeing into the true heart of men. He believes in Arthur, and I believe in my nephew.

"So," Mark concluded, "after a much too lengthy explanation, I offer my full support to Arthur. I declare my allegiance to the new High King. My lands, my holdings, and my army are his to do with as he sees fit."

Mark dropped to one knee before the dais. Everyone in his entourage joined him.

"This is meaningless," I heard Morgause mutter. "He has no right to pledge my kingdom to anyone." Lot shushed her before she made a louder complaint.

"Welcome, King Mark," Arthur said, "and thank you for your support. Cornwall is the southwestern cornerstone of Britain, and you have kept it well for years. I ask that you continue to do so. As this new united kingdom grows we will see what benefits we have to offer each other. Please rise."

"I have one request, my king," Mark said as he stood.

"Name it," Arthur responded.

"Actually, it is more Tristan's request than mine," Mark said. Tristan stepped forward and knelt before Arthur.

"Make me your knight," Tristan said. "You will need someone who knows Cornwall, and someone who can act as your liaison with my uncle. I wish to be one of your companions and a member of your honor guard."

"I am honored by your request, Tristan," Arthur said, "but you are heir to Cornwall. Shouldn't you remain there?"

"I am heir only until my uncle produces a child of his own," Tristan said. "Even if Cornwall does someday fall to me, it is now a part of your kingdom. I wish to help you make the dream of a peaceful united Britain come true, and I believe I can do that best by your side."

"Then so be it," Arthur said. He spoke the same words to Tristan that he once spoke to me when we were children, and then touched him on each shoulder with Excalibur's gleaming blade. Tristan stood and took his place with Gawaine on the dais. Our circle was becoming complete, and no one was happier that our friends would be staying close than me.

Still, Kay and I had not been publicly knighted. The oversight wasn't intentional. Arthur simply took for granted that we were with him. We were of course, more than anyone, but at that age one wants to be acknowledged.

"Good," Merlin said as Mark resumed his seat. All eyes turned to Lot and Uriens. They were the last of the petty kings present, and between them represented the greatest portion of the north. They were also the oldest of the petty kings, with a history of both resisting change and hording personal power. They were the biggest challenge to overcome. If either of them actively challenged Arthur it could not only severely undermine everything that had been accomplished so far, it could, in the worst case, lead to war between the kingdoms.

Lot stood. His lanky frame swayed like a tree in the wind as he stroked his long mustaches. Morgause sat behind him; anger and impatience were clear in her demeanor. Lot took his time before speaking, gathering his words and not leaping blindly. I saw in those brief moments that Morgause was a force of nature, controlled only by the strong will of her husband. She was no doubt an influence on his thoughts and decisions, but when he spoke she listened.

"I believe Arthur is the son of Uther and Igraine," he finally said in a voice as deep and cold as the northern sea where he made his home. "For many of the same reasons Mark just mentioned. I am less convinced by the legitimacy of his birth or his claim. Still, he did draw Excalibur, and that is a covenant we all agreed to through our actions at this shrine every year.

"I am not ready to bend the knee to Arthur as High King just yet." I could feel the tension of the crowd as Lot spoke these words. Merlin scowled, and Morgause looked jubilant. Arthur simply listened calmly.

"However," Lot continued, "it seems my oldest son is. I may not believe in Arthur yet, but I do believe in my son. Gawaine was raised to be king. King of Orkney when I am dead and, we had hoped, High King. I still hope for both of those things. But he seems to think that following Arthur is his present path. I will not stand in his way. Nor will I stand in Arthur's

"Let me be clear," Lot said. I could see that Morgause was livid, but she held her tongue. "I will not oppose Arthur, or go to war to stake my claim. As much as I hate to admit it, I am too old and Orkney is too far away to wage war here. But I will not bend the knee to him either. My son may stay here if he wishes. I will return to my kingdom and rule there as I always have. I will defend my land from the Saxons, as I always have. I will not send troops or tribute to Arthur. If a temporary alliance benefits us both then so be it. We will continue to trade with the southern kingdoms as we always have. But as long as I live, Orkney will be an independent kingdom. What happens when I am gone is up to my sons to decide."

It wasn't the best we could have hoped for. I could see both Merlin and Ector scowling. Still, it was better than it could have been. Lot was not going to help us, but he wasn't going to fight us either. I hoped, if Arthur were successful with Gawaine at his side, in the long run Lot would come around.

Morgause would never be our ally. I knew that then, but I had no idea how insidious her influence would prove to be.

That left Uriens. I turned to look at the fat unhealthy king. His kingdom was in a shambles. His army was almost nonexistent. There was no heir apparent. Even if he wanted to challenge Arthur he would not stand a chance. Still, Uriens was the oldest of the petty kings, and had held out hope for the position of High King his entire life. He had ridden with Uther, and with Vortigern and Aurelianus before that. He was, at one time, the most serious contender for the title, and challenged Uther every step of the way. He was the most likely to hold on to old grudges. I had seen his way of dealing with problems when he had killed Owain's horse. Would his pride allow him to step aside for an unknown youth? If not he could not really stand against us, but I didn't think going to war against him was in the best interests of the kingdom either. Even if the outcome was in no doubt it would be time-consuming and costly, and open wounds that would take a long time to heal.

Uriens didn't stand. I wasn't sure he even could. His sallow bloated face was unreadable as we all waited for his pronouncement.

"I never believed Uther was up to the task of being High King," he said. "For years we have met here, admirable men who are kings in their own lands. Warriors all, yet not only did Excalibur not come to any of our hands, no one of us has been able unite this kingdom. I don't know if I have ever believed that goal was possible or necessary. Nothing I have heard here convinces me this untried boy is worthy. What does Arthur know about the needs of Gorre, or Orkney? I should follow Malaguin's example and go home."

"You're right, King Uriens," Arthur said. "I do not know enough about the needs of Gorre. But I am willing to learn. I am willing to listen to all of your concerns, and to take your advice as an experienced leader."

"Bah," Uriens scoffed. "I am not a king's advisor. I am a king. What benefit to me is there in bending the knee to you? What can you offer me that I don't already have?"

"The support of the armies of all of Britain," Arthur said. "Can you stand against the Saxons on your own? I don't mean small raiding parties. Someday their numbers will increase, and they will swarm over your land like ants on honey. Can you defeat them on your own? How many men can you field in your defense? How many trained horsemen do you have? I don't ask that you be my slave, Uriens. I ask that you join with me. Continue ruling Gorre as you see fit, but join your forces with ours to the benefit of all."

Uriens scowled. He knew Arthur was right about the state of his army, but pride still stood in his way. If only there was some way to make that pride work for us.

"King Uriens, I have a request." I was as surprised to hear my own voice as anyone else. My level of discomfort rose with every pair of eyes that settled on me.

"Control your man," Lot said to Arthur. "He is out of place."

"I value the counsel of all of my Companions," Arthur said. "Everyone in my circle has a right to his voice. Let him speak. Bedivere?"

"King Uriens," I continued, emboldened by Arthur's support, but still nervous. "We met earlier this summer after Arthur and I saved one of your men from a runaway horse. At that time you promised me a boon, with all of your camp and Ector's as witness. Do you remember?"

Uriens grunted his acknowledgment.

"I wish to claim it now."

"Be careful what you ask for," Uriens growled.

"My request is simple. I do not ask you to bend your knee to Arthur. I realize I have no right to make that sort of decision. But I do ask, as my promised reward from a just and honorable king, do not challenge Arthur. Go home if you must, but do not stand in our way."

Uriens glared at me. If he granted my request he would openly give up his last claim on the title of High King. If he refused it he would look dishonorable, and therefore unworthy of that title.

"I promise you a boon as well," Arthur offered. "Even if you do not support me, like Lot, I promise I will allow you to continue to rule your own kingdom without my interference. In addition, if Gorre comes under Saxon attack, all you have to do is ask and my armies will be there to support you. Even if you do not bend the knee to me, we cannot allow any portion of this land to be compromised."

Uriens continued to scowl as he weighed his options. Finally he spoke. I could tell the effort cost him. His voice sounded old and defeated as he let go of his life's ambition.

"Fine," he said. "I grant you your boon, Bedivere. I will not challenge Arthur for the title of High King. But I will not be his lackey.

I will return to Gorre and rule there until the end of my days. I will not offer my armies or my advice. Gorre has survived under my rule for decades now. It has a king. It doesn't need another one."

He motioned for his men. They lifted his litter and carried him away from the pavilion.

It was over. Although he had not won the full and enthusiastic support of all of the petty kings, Arthur had been confirmed as High King without bloodshed.

"With the blessing of all present," Merlin said, "we will begin to make preparations for a coronation. There are many treaties and documents to be signed, but I believe this council draws to an end."

"Not yet," Arthur said as he drew Excalibur. "There is one official duty I need to perform first. Kay, Bedivere... kneel before me."

I smiled and did as my king asked.

"The two of you have been with me always," he said as he stood before us. "I ask that you continue to be with me always. I know I do not have to ask for your oaths on this. I wish for you to be my knights, my companions. This is not an honor I bestow on you. You honor me by being the men you are."

Arthur once again spoke the words from that day by the pond, first to Kay, and then to me. When we stood again it was as knights of the new realm of the first true High King of Britain. Cheers erupted on all sides of the pavilion.

We didn't get a chance to celebrate.

A horse and rider burst into the clearing from the woodland road. With the commotion that was taking place in the pavilion we didn't even notice at first. Riders had been coming and going on errands of various sorts at all times during the festival. But then cries of anger and fear erupted as this rider plowed through the middle of the crowd. I turned my head to see what was happening in time to see the horse come to a stop next the Shrine and the rider fall from his seat to the ground.

"He's injured!" someone cried.

We pushed our way through the gathering. Merlin and Vivienne, as healers, led the way and knelt next to the fallen man. My eyes were drawn to the suffering horse. His flanks were covered in foam and his breathing was quick and shallow. His eyes were wide with fear and exhaustion. Whoever the rider was he had pushed his mount past all endurance. There was no saddle, and someone had improvised a bridle from torn strips of cloth. I stepped toward the horse, trying to calm him before his heart gave out and he simply dropped. As I came nearer to the animal I was sure I recognized it.

"Bedivere!" Arthur shouted. "It's Lucan!"

Lucan? My brother? He was supposed to be back at home, running Ector's household. I turned from the horse and saw Lucan cradled in Vivienne's arms. His right leg was bent at an unnatural angle. Old blood stained his clothes in crusty chunks, but fresh wetness ran from a deep wound in his thigh. He was shaking with exhaustion and shock.

I rushed to his side and knelt, taking his hand in mine. Ector had joined us by this time. Vivienne shouted orders to her acolytes to bring medical supplies as she cut off the clothes around the wound and attempted to staunch the bleeding.

"Lucan?" I said to my older brother, frightened of what he might say. My fears were justified. Lucan said the one word we all least wanted to hear.

"Saxons," he gasped.

CHAPTER SIXTEEN

The first snow of the season coats everything I can see from the fortress. It is not a heavy snow, an inch or two at most. From the heights of Mont St. Michael I can see a great sea of white for many miles. The early morning sun creates a blinding reflection and has already started to melt the accumulation on our roofs. My guess is that this will all thaw and we will see the ground again before another storm covers the land. Still, I sense that familiar feeling of wonder at the beauty of the pristine landscape and depression knowing that winter is full upon us. I'm glad I know that spring will return, because for now, it will only get worse.

We heard the basic story from Lucan quickly while Vivienne dressed his wounds. A large party of Saxons had poured into Ector's vale two days earlier. They attacked the homestead, killing anyone who offered resistance. Ector had left a token defense when we left, and perhaps we had been gone too long. But years of peace had lulled everyone. From Lucan's description, this was the largest raiding party anyone in our part of Britain had seen since Uther's time. It's possible the outcome would have been the same even if we had all been present. My brother fled, not out of cowardice, but because he recognized a lost cause.

Lucan saw our mother die.

He fought his way to the stables; he received his wound, a great gash in his leg, in the process. Once there he quickly mounted a horse. He hoped to find us, to find someone, and give warning before we all walked right back into an ambush. Somewhere along the Roman road he had passed out from blood loss and fallen from his mount. That's when he broke his leg. Somehow he managed to regain his seat and make it to Avalon.

I would say I can't imagine the pain he had suffered, but unfortunately I can.

Once we had heard the essentials of his tale, Lucan was carried to a tent where his leg could be set and his wound treated. I was stunned over the loss of my mother and my home, but the full reality of it did not sink in immediately.

"So now what, High King of Britain?" Lot stood off to the side of the crowd. His tone was demanding, but not derisive. He knew this was the first challenge of Arthur's kingship, and it came on the day he was confirmed. I think Lot, and many others as well, truly wanted to see what Arthur would do.

"Warok," Arthur called. Ector's horselord was there, of course, chomping at the bit to do something, if I may be so obvious in my description. Warok, like all of us, had certainly lost family to the Saxons.

"Yes?" he said.

"Have a full compliment of horses ready to go at a moment's notice," Arthur instructed.

"Rushing headlong into disaster?" Lot asked. "Like in Mont St. Michael?"

"I said ready," Arthur said. "Not that we were going yet. Though we should not waste too much time. We'll meet back at the pavilion immediately. Call all of the senior members of the kingdoms and the heads of their military. I want to decide what is our best course of action as quickly as possible, but I want to hear what our more experienced members say first. We need to get a force back there to ascertain what we're up against. Mounted men are the fastest, obviously, but if there are a lot of invaders we may need our infantry as well. They will not be able to get there as soon."

"Warok," I said. "Saddle the Arabians from Benwick first. None of our horses can match their speed. Have the rest of our warhorses ready to depart soon after. A group of us can go scout on the Arabians while the others catch up."

"Right," Warok said, and then signaled to several of the men closest to him and headed for the corrals. I was surprised that he didn't even think to question my decision or my authority to make it. Arthur nodded his approval at my suggestion.

"King Uriens!" Arthur called as he saw the obese ruler being carried toward us. "I know you have made your decision as regards my kingship, but it is my duty to inform you that Saxons have raided my homeland. Your kingdom is directly to the north of Ector's holdings, and my guess is that the invaders may move in that direction."

"Aye," Uriens said. "That seems likely."

"It would be in your interest, if not mine," Arthur said, "to alert your troops at home to the situation and to send your infantry south."

"None of my wagons or horses could be there inside of a week," he said. "It would take at least another day for my household infantry to be ready to leave, and two or three more to rouse the levy."

"We can send a messenger on one of the Arabians," I said. "Or two, one of ours and one of yours to convince your people the message is true."

"I'll go," Owain said. "As much as I hate the idea of getting on a horse again." Uriens nodded his approval.

"Good," Arthur said. "Owain, go to the corrals and find Kynon. Tell him of this arrangement but do not leave until you talk to me. We must make other plans before I will know what message to send. The rest of you, back to the pavilion. I'm calling a council of war."

I saw look of pride on the faces of Merlin and Ector. Even Lot and Uriens appeared to be impressed. That could change quickly before the day was over. Arthur still had a lot to prove.

Although there was certainly a sense of urgency to the proceedings nothing was rushed. Arthur listened to his advisors, each of the petty kings and the most experienced warriors. My plan to send mounted scouts as an advance cavalry was ratified. We were to ride as fast as we could to Ector's homestead. Lucan had made the trip in three days by nearly killing his mount. We would take longer than that, but not much. We would make much better time than on our original journey because we would be unencumbered by wagons and people walking along the trail. Still, by the time we arrived nearly a week would have passed since the raid. We were to approach cautiously; our primary goal was to ascertain if the Saxons had settled in the vale, or if they had moved on and if so, where. It was possible, though unlikely given their numbers, that they had already returned to their ships and departed. If we discovered a sufficiently small group we were to engage. If it was a large party we were to make camp and await the arrival of the warhorses and the infantry. They, unfortunately, would still be several days behind us. Until we knew the location and number of our enemy, more specific plans could not be made.

Owain and Kynon were sent on their way to Gorre. Since our assumption was that the invaders had sailed up the mouth of the river Glein– it ran south from Gorre to the sea and was the nearest access to our homestead– their instructions were to warn the kingdom of possible Saxon raiders. They were to gather the troops and march them south along the river as far as the border with Ector's land and then camp there until they received word from Arthur what to do next.

All around the festival site of Avalon people were preparing to leave. Warok chose the riders he wished to be part of the advance scouting party. The infantries of Ector, Leodegrance, and Mark prepared to make the long march in support of our cavalry. Messengers were sent to each of the kingdoms with word of the current events. Arthur even dispatched one to try and catch up with Malaguin so that he could be prepared as well.

Lot, true to his word, prepared to leave for Orkney to take care of his own kingdom, and spared no troops for our effort.

The council ended less than an hour after it had begun and everyone left to attend to their own preparations. After making sure everything was well in hand at the corrals I went to find my brother.

Lucan rested in a tent near Ector's. Morgan was just leaving it when I arrived.

"How is he?" I asked.

"Resting," she said. "He's still awake, but he won't be for long. I've given him a powerful sleep potion. His wounds will heal, though he will carry the scars all of his days. We did our best to set his broken leg, but I'm afraid it will never heal correctly. He will probably have at the very least a limp that will never go away.

"So he's your brother?"

"Yes."

"Then I have a favor to ask you. I've taken care of you, and now I have taken care of your brother. I know this is unnecessary, but I'm asking you, take care of my brother in the upcoming war."

Though the relationship between them was now common knowledge I was still surprised to hear Morgan speak of it so openly to me, given that she surely knew I was aware of the true nature of what had passed between them.

"Arthur is my brother as well," I replied. "And my king. It is my duty, and more than my duty, to watch over him and protect him from anything that may bring him harm."

"Does that include protecting him from me?"

"If necessary," I said. "Though I don't believe that will be required. Whatever passed between you was done in innocence of your true relationship. I have no desire to see that come to light."

"So you do know," Morgan mused. "I assumed, though Arthur swore he never spoke any details to you."

"He didn't," I said. "Arthur will protect your honor as well."

She laughed at that.

"Of course he will," she said. "He is that kind of man. But there are aspects of this whole thing you do not know, circumstances that Arthur is just now becoming aware of. He will need you at his side through all of what lies ahead. When you return to Avalon he and I will both need you to stand at our sides as the next part of Merlin's plan unfolds."

"What do you mean?"

"In time, Bedivere," she said. She embraced me and brushed her lips across my cheek. "There is much at stake here, and much you may never understand or approve of. But Arthur needs you. He must be the king of two realms. Merlin, Vivienne and I represent the spiritual kingdom. You are his primary connection to the physical realm. But those of us closest to him must be aware of his responsibilities to both. There are secrets and mysteries at work here, and you must be prepared to witness them, for Arthur's sake, and for the sake of the kingdom."

I had no idea what she was talking about. My head was not built for secrets and mysteries, and I had no desire to be part of any spiritual kingdom. But, if this were required of me by Arthur to fulfill

Merlin's plan, then I would do whatever was necessary. I nodded my understanding to Morgan.

"Thank you," she said. "Now go see to your brother before he is asleep."

I watched her walk away. I was curious about what I had just agreed to, but right then I had other, more immediate concerns. I lifted the tent flap and stepped inside its warm confines. Lucan lay on a cot, covered in thick blankets in spite of the heat of the day. I could see the outline of the splint that held his leg tightly bound under the covers. He opened his eyes as I entered. He looked groggy, but he was not yet asleep.

"Bedivere?" His voice was a mixture of exhaustion, pain, and grief. "Come closer." I went to his side and sat on the small stool I found there. I reached up and took his hand in mine. He started to speak, but then his eyes fixed on the leather cup that covered my stump.

"What happened?"

I briefly related the story of the giant of Mont St. Michael to him. Tears filled his eyes. My story was an extra sorrow on his already over-burdened soul.

"We make quite the pair, don't we?" he said. "You're missing a hand and I'll never walk straight again. How disappointed our mighty father must be."

"I don't think so, Lucan," I said. "We won our wounds in honest battle. He would understand."

"I–I'm sorry," he said. Tears dripped down his cheeks. "Sorry I couldn't save her. Sorry I couldn't save anyone."

"You were one man," I said, feeling the beginnings of my own tears. "Against a horde. You have nothing to be sorry about."

"I should have stayed. I should have fought more. I should have died like everyone else."

"You did the right thing. Someone had to carry the warning. To have come all this way as wounded as you were... that's the action of a warrior."

"Still... they're all dead, Bedivere. Everyone. Either dead or carried off into slavery. Our home is gone."

"We will get it back," I promised. "And make every last one of them pay for the lives they took."

"Our mother is gone. It won't bring her back. We can't bring any of them back." His eyes were drooping with much needed sleep.

"No. We can't. But we will honor their memory."

"There's nothing there anymore," he murmured. "Everyone is dead, and I no longer have a life."

"We'll find a way for you to serve," I said as his breathing leveled out and became deeper. "After all, Arthur is king now."

I felt his hand slip from mine as sleep finally claimed him. I pulled the covers up tight around his chin and then performed an unusual gesture, even though we were brothers. I leaned in and kissed his forehead. I paused at the tent flap and looked back at my only living blood relative and wondered what the future held for us, we the crippled brethren.

I could never have predicted that we would both be among the last men standing on the day that Arthur died.

I left the tent and headed toward the corrals. The advance scouts were preparing to leave. I hadn't ridden since my misfortune, but was anxious to get back in the saddle, especially on one of the Arabians. Even one-handed I knew I could control the animals better than most men. I would be unable to wield a sword at the same time, making me nearly useless in battle, but that was a concern for another day. I had seen other men in my life who were missing limbs. Some of them had fashioned a hook or other metal tool to the end of their stumps. I suppose that would allow me to keep the reins under the control of my right arm while I used a sword in my left. Not that I was anywhere near good enough to do that yet. A blade still felt awkward in my off hand. Two sessions of training with Kay were not enough to change that. Still it was a possibility to consider.

I was thinking about this option when I heard someone call my name. I turned to see Guinevere standing near Leodegrance's tent with her handmaid. She wore a worried expression and beckoned for me to come over. Even though we needed to get on our way, I couldn't ignore her.

"Are you going too?" she asked as I approached.

"Of course," I said. "My home has been destroyed. I must go."

"Oh Bedivere," she cried as she rushed into my arms in a tight embrace. "Please be careful. I couldn't stand to lose you. You don't know how worried I was when you were hurt. I couldn't bear it if something happened again."

"I'll be careful," I answered, "but Arthur needs me. I must be with him."

"Come back to me," she said. "Promise me."

"I promise," I said, though I knew how meaningless any promise like that is when war is involved.

Guinevere stood on her tiptoes and pressed her lips tightly against mine. I was surprised, but still, I responded and kissed her back. It wasn't a long kiss, or meant as a prelude to anything else. But it was sweet, and heartfelt, and the beginning of a relationship between us that I could never fully return.

She stepped back, cheeks the color of roses stained by the dew from her eyes. She said nothing more. Everything she wanted to tell me was in that kiss.

"I'll be back," I whispered, and then turned to go. It seemed that both Guinevere and Morgan were determined to confuse me on a day when I already had too much on my mind.

Outside the corral the horses were ready to go and most of the men were mounted, awaiting the order to leave. The Arabians sensed our mood and pulsed with their urgency to run. Our larger warhorses were in the corral, being saddled and readied for their own journey. I could see Warok, who was to lead the second wave of cavalry, moving among them, shouting orders and checking saddle bindings.

Arthur stood with a small group of his advisors. Leodegrance and Mark were there, offering last minute guidance. Ector and Kay were both climbing into their saddles, anxious to go home. When Arthur saw me he motioned for me to join them.

"Are you sure you're ready for this?" he asked when I arrived.

"Try to stop me from going," I said. I saw the "thank you" in his eyes. Arthur looked nervous, though I doubt any but those who knew him best would have noticed. A whinny drew my attention and I turned to see one of the younger boys leading a horse to my side. I immediately recognized it as the one I had ridden in Benwick.

"I'm going to have to find you a name," I said as I patted his head.

"Something more manly than Butter, I hope," Kay said from horseback.

"I know you can't see it, Kay," I said, "but I'm giving you a rude gesture with my right hand." I saw the look of surprise on Kay's face, and then heard him burst out in laughter as I swung up into my saddle. It was an awkward motion on my part. My sense of balance was off and I kept expecting to be able to grab things or brace myself in ways I could no longer manage. But, sitting on horseback, even with the reins clutched in my left hand, felt more natural and right than anything I had done in weeks.

Arthur mounted his own horse and turned to survey his cavalry. I knew most of the men from home, but there were a few from the other kingdoms. Tristan was there, sword at his side and a bow and linen sack of arrows attached to his saddle. His crwth was close at hand as well; I rarely saw him without it. Gawaine and, surprisingly, Agravaine sat astride their horses close by.

"Agravaine is going?" I asked Arthur.

"He volunteered," Arthur answered. "It seems he would rather stay here with me than to return home to Orkney as well."

"Morgause must be livid."

"I'm sure. Lot appeared to be grudgingly proud, however. If we can win over his sons I think Orkney will eventually join our union of kingdoms."

"You've already won over Gawaine. I'm not sure I trust Agravaine."

"He's young," Arthur said, and I smiled at the thought of him thinking of anyone as young. "And he has always followed the lead of his brother. He's trying to find himself. Merlin says he needs to feel valued for who he is, out from under the expectations of Lot and Morgause. I knighted him a few moments ago."

"That's a good first step," Merlin said as he rode up next to us.

"You're going with us?" I asked, unable to mask my surprise.

"Why not, Griflet?" Merlin asked, amused. "Are you afraid I'm too old to ride?"

"No, I just never thought..."

"Our kingdom has been attacked," Merlin said. "And this is the first test of the new High King. My place is at his side."

"Of course," I said. Arthur drew his sword and prepared to signal our departure.

"Arthur," I said, startled. "That's not Excalibur."

"It's not fully mine to use yet," Arthur said.

"But you drew it from the stone," I said. "It's the symbol of the High King."

"I haven't been crowned yet," Arthur said. "It's in Vivienne's care. Until I marry the land the sword still belongs to the Goddess."

"Marry the land?" I asked.

"I have explained it all to Arthur," Merlin said. "And when we return to Avalon I will attempt to explain it to you. This has all happened suddenly. We were not quite ready."

"For the Saxons?"

"For the Saxons, or for Arthur to draw the Sword."

"I thought that was planned."

"Oh, it was," Merlin, said. "We just didn't expect it to happen for another year or so. Arthur set things in motion by using Excalibur to protect Morgan and Guinevere. It was earlier than we had planned, but a clear sign from the Goddess that now was the time to crown the protector of the land. With this unexpected Saxon incursion, I suppose there couldn't have been a better time after all. The Goddess and the God know better than we."

As always, when deeper matters were discussed, I simply shrugged, unable to fully understand the machinations of the gods or those who served them.

"Are we ready then?" Arthur asked in a loud clear voice. He raised his sword above his head. Voices of assent called back.

"Let's ride!" Arthur pointed toward the trail with his blade and we began our journey. The cheers and well wishes of everyone at Avalon followed us into the woods. The reins felt unfamiliar in my left hand, but the feel of the horse beneath me, and the urgency to return home, were all the motivation I needed to begin learning how to ride again. We passed through the woods quickly and soon came to the Roman road. Our speed increased as soon as that paved highway was beneath us. A cool wind greeted us there, and I knew that before our journey was through we would have ridden out of summer and into fall.

We rode fast, alternating our horse's pace from walk to cantor to gallop and back again. We made good time, but none of us wanted to kill our mounts. On the first day, since we had started late, we rode well into the night. A clear sky and bright moon helped light our way. We made camp along the highway, sleeping in bedrolls on the ground without setting up tents. Within a few short hours, as the first shy hint of dawn peeked over the horizon, we were back on the road.

We ate provisions on the move. We watered our tiring horses at streams and springs, and took our own short breaks while they drank.

When we were stopped, as well as when the horses moved at a slow enough pace to allow conversation, Arthur was involved in constant discussion. None of us were sure what we would find. The Saxons could be ensconced in our old homes, or they may have returned to their boats and fled. The latter seemed unlikely; Ector's land was not that close to the coast after all. An attack that far inland was an indication of a larger, more organized invasion instead of a random raid. But until we were close enough to send in scouts we could not know. It paid to be prepared for anything.

It didn't escape me that we were riding into battle. This was different than our raid on Mont St. Michael. We were a complement of fifty-some mounted warriors. More cavalry and infantry followed in our wake. If the number of invaders were as large as we assumed then the possibility of warfare and widespread slaughter was likely. It was what we had trained for, of course, but the reality is something no one can really be prepared to experience. I had taken a life in Ysbaddon's fortress, but that easy killing was very different than the prospect of standing in a shield wall against an enemy determined to slaughter me. I was nervous, and frightened, and I was not alone. Each of us neophyte warriors carried some measure of uncertainty. On the trip to Mont St. Michael we were silent about our fears. But, that experience had bonded us. Kay admitted to his nerves, as did Eiddellig. Seeing Lucan, the most gentle of all of us from Ector's land, had unnerved them. It made the idea of invasion and warfare real for them. Tristan and I talked at length about what lay before us. I heard resignation and sadness in his voice. He was born to be a bard, but the fates had put a sword in his hand instead. He was in love with life yet the circumstances of our time had cast him in the role of dealer of death. Even Gawaine felt it. His speech was full of bravado, and I do think he was anxious to test his mettle in battle. But underneath his bluster there was a core of dread.

Arthur, most of all, felt the weight of the future on his shoulders. He carried his own anger and grief over the loss of our homes and families. He was troubled by his own anxieties about battle and warfare. Added to these burdens was the knowledge that his performance in the next few days would determine the course of his entire kingship. The concept of a united Britain rode on his young back, and any failure would be seen as his alone. Unlike the rest of us, he was under constant scrutiny by everyone present. He couldn't admit to his doubts as freely as the rest of us. I'm afraid I was as guilty as anyone of watching him to see how he was holding up. I like to think my motivations were more personal, but I know my hopes and fears for the future were tied up with his success as well.

We left the Roman road on the third day and began the cross-country portion of our journey. We made camp very late that day. We were on the borders of Ector's land, but still some distance from our home village. So far we had seen no sign of the invader. Our assumption was if the enemy was still present at all, he had set up camp in our homes. The Saxon menace was not limited to raids on our livestock and goods. In the bigger picture, they wanted our lands for their own. They wanted to settle here, bring their families, and farm our land. I didn't understand the complexities of their situation, and wondered why they didn't just stay in their own place instead of coming here. All I knew was that this was our home, and they were willing to kill all of us who were in their way. My mother was either dead or, worse yet, their slave. I didn't much care if the Saxons needed more land for their families.

When the horses were settled Arthur gathered us all together. It was a clear night, if a little cooler than we were used to. There were no fires permitted; we didn't know if we were being watched or not.

"The village is three to four miles away still," Arthur said for the benefit of those few among us who were strangers here. "Before we do anything else we need to know if the Saxons are still there. A small group of us who know the area well will go under cover of night and check out the village. The forest will provide shelter. We need to know their numbers and dispositions, if they have guards stationed and if so, where."

"My experience with the Saxons," Ector piped in, "is that they won't have any guards. They are lax and unorganized in any true military sense. That doesn't mean there won't be anyone awake to see or hear you."

"Do not engage anyone in combat unless you are spotted or attacked," Arthur said. "If that does happen try to end it as quickly and silently as possible. Scout around the whole perimeter of the village. See if there are others camped outside of the vale and if there are reserve troops who could easily come to help. Return here as soon as you can with your reports. If they are a small enough group we will hit them in the morning.

"I will be staying here," Arthur said. This surprised me. I assumed Arthur would go as a scout since he knew the countryside as well as any of us. A look passed between him and Merlin and I saw Arthur wasn't happy about this either. Then I understood; he was King now. It wasn't his place to put himself in danger on a simple scouting mission. He had a more important role to play.

There were a lot of volunteers for the mission; everyone was anxious to discover what had become of our homes. I daresay many of us continued to hold out hope that our loved ones were somehow still alive. In the end Arthur sent ten two-man groups. It was a significant portion of our entire force, but there was a lot of ground to cover. Some of the men from the other kingdoms were paired with those of us more familiar with the area so that they could see the actual layout of the village and surrounding area before any battle would be fought there. Tristan was my partner while Gawaine went with Eiddelig, and Agravaine with Kay.

Merlin created a map on a rolled up piece of parchment with quick strokes from a brush and jar of ink he kept in his saddlebag. We all knew the area well, so Merlin's lines were easily recognizable landmarks for us. We divided the area into different segments for each team to cover.

The area around Ector's vale was heavily forested. It was one of the things that had helped protect us over the years. It is difficult to move a large war band through the dense tree cover. A massed force of mounted men would be even more difficult. Arthur knew that, so our plan was to discover first what lay within our village. After that, if needed, we would bring the horses through the woods and surround the clearing where our homes stood. A mounted attack on the village would work because of the open space around it. If we were able to contain the area, none of the enemy would be able to outrun our horses and escape into the impenetrable forest.

After a quick bite of our rations we were on our way. My sword was belted on my right side and felt strange bouncing against that hip as I ran. I was still unsure of my ability to fight with my left hand if I really needed to, but I was determined to do my best.

We were blessed with another clear night, so my footsteps were sure on paths I had traversed since I was a child. Arthur and I had played on and explored every square foot of land within walking distance of our homes. Tristan followed closely, carrying his bow and trusting my knowledge of the area. When we needed to communicate we used hand signals.

We paused by the pond where Arthur had knighted me with a stick when we were boys. Somehow, seeing that clearing where we had played at being men and warriors made it all real for me. I had come full circle that summer. I left my home a boy, full of hope and expectation. I had no idea when I left that I would never return to the life I had always known. My stomach clenched as I truly realized that just a short distance away, at the end of a path my feet had trod a million times, were the ruined remains of my childhood. No matter what we found, or what the outcome of the battle that lay ahead, my old life was dead. It was as gone as my hand, and the sudden sense of emptiness and loss overwhelmed me.

Tristan, magician of the heart that he was, recognized immediately what I was feeling. He put a hand on my shoulder and drew me into an embrace. It was unexpected, but welcome. Without words he gave me strength, simply by acknowledging my grief.

After a moment I stepped back from him and drew my sword. It trembled slightly as I used it to point to the path that led home. I don't know if it was from emotion, or the fact that my left arm was not yet entirely used to its weight.

We were close enough now to use extreme caution. It was the middle of the night, and our chances of encountering a large group of armed opponents seemed slim. But the very darkness that covered us would offer protection to any posted guards as well.

We approached the end of the path that led into the clearing that surrounded the village. On my signal we crouched behind two large oaks that bordered the footpath. I cautiously leaned around the side and assumed a position that I knew would allow me to survey the remains of my home.

The clear night helped my vision, but it was still too dark to make out specific details. There were several campfires scattered around, most of them burning low or already embers. That indicated that someone was still camping here. I thought I saw several shapes that could be sleeping men near the glowing coals, but I could not be sure. Many of the houses, including my own, had been burned to the ground. Those fires were several days old now, so nothing remained but ash and a few burned timbers. The blacksmith shop still stood, as did the large horse barn and stables; the Saxons recognized the most useful structures. The granary had been raided and now stood empty of its meager supply of last year's grain. Ector's hall stood intact.

As dangerous as it was, we needed to get closer. I motioned for Tristan to follow me and stepped out from behind the tree. We crept down the embankment and entered the settlement. I felt exposed, and alone, even though I knew there were twenty of my companions scattered around, approaching the village from many different angles. Still, in the dark, I was a lone warrior. Even Tristan felt distant in his silence.

We slipped into the deep shadow of the horse stable. I walked slowly to the side entrance and with some difficulty due to my stump, lifted the wooden door latch and stepped inside. It was dark as pitch and silent. The horses were all gone. The Saxons were not much for riding, and had nothing in the way of a cavalry, but they recognized the value of horses. These would have been taken for their barter value. Some of them had probably ended up in our enemy's bellies. Most of the tack and tools were missing as well.

I had half expected to find sleeping Saxons, but the sounds of snoring and deep breathing were absent. In a few moments my eyes adjusted to the dark and my assumptions were confirmed. However many of the enemy remained, there weren't so many they had to use the barn. Most of them were sleeping in beds in the remaining houses. I guessed that limited their numbers to roughly equal our own. With horses, and the element of surprise, we had the advantage.

We exited the stable and walked through the village, rushing from one patch of darkness to the next. There were indeed men sleeping near some of the fires. As tempting as it was to slip up and slit their throats, we stayed clear of them. One shout of warning and not only would we be dead, but the entire mission would be at risk. We tried to peer in windows of the various homes, but most of our attempts were in vain. Thick coverings had been drawn against the cool of night.

Once we pulled up short when we saw movement around the corner of Ector's home. My heart, already beating at a cantor's pace, leapt into a gallop of it's own. Tristan drew his bow as I readied my sword. We both breathed a sigh of relief when I recognized Eiddelig and Agravaine. They signaled that all was well and that they were returning to camp via the way they came. I decided it was time we did the same. Short of going into every building we were not going to get an accurate count of our enemy. We had seen enough to make some educated guesses, and hopefully, with the information gathered by the other scout teams we would have a fairly accurate picture.

We made our way back to the barn quickly. Our trek back to camp would take at least another hour, and then we would have to debrief with the others. No matter what decision was made, we would all be riding into battle in the morning with little sleep. We stepped out of the barn's shadow and ran toward the path in the woods.

Two large men stepped out of the cover of the trees. We came to a sudden halt and I saw immediately that they were not our scouts. Their hair was long and matted and they wore mismatched pieces of leather armor. I had no idea why they were out there; whether they were guards making rounds, or if they had simply wandered off to relieve themselves. Whatever the reason, they were an immediate threat. They saw us outlined clearly in the moonlit open field and immediately drew the small axes that were tucked into their belts.

Before I could even assume a battle stance I heard two sharp twangs and watched as arrows from Tristan's bow took one Saxon in the throat and the second one directly in the forehead. They dropped to the ground, immediately and silently dead. I turned to see Tristan, another arrow already nocked and ready to fly.

The bow is not a weapon I was very familiar with, and given the limitations of my handicap I was never to use one. We used them for hunting, of course, but no one in Ector's vale gave much consideration to using them in warfare. They took a lifetime of practice to use effectively. I had heard tales of the magic the Welsh could weave with them. Apparently some of that magic had traveled south to Cornwall and fallen into Tristan's hands. Later, he told me his bow was named Failnot. Like his crwth, it was another stringed instrument he was deadly with. I have no doubt that his quick actions saved not only our lives, but also the fate of the mission. In another second the Saxon warriors would have shouted a warning and awakened the rest of the village.

We carefully walked to the bodies and checked to make sure there were no other Saxons about. Only then did I see Tristan's hands begin to shake on the bow. I realized then that these were the first men he had killed. I don't want to say that killing in battle ever became easy or offhand for me, but I do believe that each death weighed heavier on Tristan's soul than on any of the rest of us.

We dragged the bodies into the forest and hid them there. We didn't have the time or the inclination to give them a decent burial; either or both of these men may have raped or killed my mother. We did not, however, want their bodies discovered, so we rolled them into a shallow decline and covered them with branches and leaves. Anyone looking for them would eventually find them, but if all went well we would be back in the morning before anyone even knew they were missing.

After washing the blood off our hands in the pond, Tristan and I scurried through the woods and returned to camp to make our report. We had been the only scouts to encounter the enemy and as a result we were the last to arrive. Our report confirmed what all the rest had already said. In a dark and tired circle of men we made our final preparations for the battle ahead.

CHAPTER SEVENTEEN

The historians and the bards say that Arthur fought twelve great battles to rid the land of the Saxon invaders. I'm not sure how they arrived at that number. I remember countless skirmishes and battles that raged over the next fifteen years before we had our golden age of peace. Some stand out, mostly the battle of Badon Hill, the last and greatest encounter of the Saxon Wars of Arthur's early reign. But it's difficult for me to separate events into distinct battles.

It is generally accepted that the first battle took place at the river Glein. It certainly ended there, and was the last confrontation of the season before winter came. But there were days of fighting before we ever saw the Glein. Who is to say that those days were separate skirmishes or part of one large battle that ended on that muddy shore?

It began, with no equivocation, with our morning raid on Ector's village. That was the first battle that Arthur, as well as myself and the other new Companions of the King, participated in. Glein was still well in our future when we led our horses through the woods to surround the homestead in the early morning mist under cover of the darkness just before dawn.

The plan was simple. We were to wait until the Saxons were beginning to stir. We wanted them out in the open instead of holing up in the buildings where they would have cover. We discovered we need not have waited; say what you will about the Saxons, they were not cowards who looked for shelter in a battle. Once a number of them were in the open Arthur was to lead a mounted charge into the center of the village. My job was to lead a smaller reserve of horsemen and circle the perimeter, not allowing any of our foes to escape. I knew the primary reason I was given this task was because of my skills as a horseman, and Arthur had allowed me to choose the ten best riders and the fastest horses for the task. I also knew that I was not yet ready to fight from horseback with a sword in my off hand. Most of my team's job would be herding the enemy back into the village where they would have to face our main force. Among the men I chose were Eiddelig and Tristan. I had squired for Eiddelig long enough to know his skills with a horse were among the best we had. His knowledge of the area was also a consideration. I chose Tristan not for his equestrian prowess, but because he assured me his accuracy with Failnot was almost as good from horseback as on his feet. His arrows would find any of the Saxons who attempted to flee at too great a distance for us to catch.

We took our positions under the tree cover around the outskirts of town. I watched in silence as the sun slowly rose over the eastern hills. A sheet of light washed over the land, sparkling on the wet grass. The calls of morning birds and the steady dripping of dew through the leaves were the only sounds. Eventually I began to see movement in the village. Men trickled out of our homes, most to immediately relieve themselves against the houses. A few stirred at the ashes of last night's fires in preparation for cooking the morning meal. They were slow moving and sluggish with sleep, secure in their belief of safety. They had scoured the area days earlier and had relaxed their guard. It was the exact type of lax security and faith in their immunity they hoped to find in every village they raided.

There were maybe two score of them visible when I heard the hoof beats of Arthur's charge. Shaggy heads were lifted in alarm as forty plus mounted men descended on the village, blades shining in the morning sun. Arthur looked like a god out of one of Merlin's stories as he led the charge. Though awe-inspiring from my perspective it had to have been terrifying to the men on the ground. Before they had time to react the horses were among them and the slaughter had begun. I saw sprays of blood as metal blades cut through skulls and limbs. Men tried to dodge, but many were caught under the hooves of our chargers. Only one man in ten had the presence of mind to draw a weapon and try to attack the riders.

I rode out of the trees and looked to the left and right. My outriders were arrayed in a wide circle around the village. On my signal we began to ride widdershins around the perimeter.

Arthur's cavalry ran past the center of the village and then banked into a wide turn for a return engagement. Though this happened quickly it still gave a moment's respite to the Saxons. I saw more of them pour out of our houses, screaming in their own tongue, axes and swords drawn. We had underestimated their number. They formed a quick and sloppy wall of men to face the next charge. They were nowhere near as organized as the shield walls we were trained to employ. They were an almost naked group of men, standing without protection against a wall of moving horseflesh and steel. I wasn't sure if I was disdainful of their stupidity or admiring of their courage.

As our horses neared the Saxon line a swarm of small hand axes flew from our enemy directly into the midst of our charge. Horses and men screamed and went down. Our momentum was thrown into chaos, but not halted. I flinched as I heard the impact of horses and men and the bloody cacophony of battle. At that point there was no regrouping of our cavalry; it was a free-for-all in the streets of the village. Many of our men were still horsed, and chopped down at the Saxons who swarmed at their feet. Our horses were targets as much as our men. Others who had fallen fought hand to hand.

I lost track of Arthur in the confusion. I couldn't make out any individual in the chaos of running bodies, dancing horses, and flashing steel.

I felt fear in my stomach and chest. Part of me, the part that wished to live, wanted to run. Another part, a bigger part, wanted to ride into the midst of the melee and help my friends and family. I did neither. I had my orders and my role to play.

As the battle wore on I had my chance to participate. Very few Saxons would retreat from a foe. Most of them wanted a glorious death in battle to appease their strange gods. But when the battle was obviously lost many of them attempted to flee. Based on what we learned later, I believe they wanted to escape and rejoin the larger body of their company, or at least to warn others that there was a well-armed and trained army in the area. Whatever their motivations, several of them attempted to bolt into the forest. The first I noticed was when I heard Tristan shout my name from off to my right.

I turned in time to see two Saxons fall to his well-aimed arrows, one dead, the other crippled. But they were only two out of a group of five who were running towards the woods. I spurred my horse to give chase, and saw Eiddelig converging on them from the opposite side. He was closer and was going to reach them first. I yelled at him to wait for me, but he either did not hear me or chose to ignore my shout. I wrapped the reins around my right forearm, drew my sword and spurred my horse to a faster speed.

The Saxons heard our approach. They knew they would never reach the trees before we caught up with them, so turned to face us. I had closed the distance, but Eiddelig reached them first. I saw his sword rise as he prepared a killing stroke.

The lead Saxon, a large man covered in hair and jewelry, swung his ax over his head like he was attempting to split a log. The heavy blade slammed into the horse's skull and tore it nearly in half. The ax was ripped out of the man's hand as the horse plowed into him, crushing his chest. Eiddelig flew from his saddle and crashed into the earth with bone-crushing force. He screamed in agony and I heard the dry kindling snapping of his ribs. One of the other Saxons raised his sword and swept it down and Eiddelig screamed no more.

"No!" I cried as my horse drove in among them. I swung my

sword as hard as I could at the man who had just killed my friend. It sliced through his greasy hair and crushed his skull. Though my attack had succeeded, my grip was not what it should have been and as the dead man fell his weight pulled my sword from my hand. The other Saxon had grabbed the reins of my horse and pulled hard on my right arm. Already off balance I tumbled from my saddle and fell hard on the ground. Once again I instinctively reached out to brace my fall with my nonexistent right hand. The pain of the impact was inconceivable. My head swam and I fought nausea and shock.

I rolled over and stared at the face of the man I was sure would be my death. He screamed through a mouthful of rotted teeth as his ax rose into the air. It turned into a screech of agony as another of Tristan's arrows slammed into his chest and knocked him backward. In spite of my pain, my training and my desire to live took over. I reached out and grabbed the ax from the wounded man's hand and smashed it into his skull before he hit the ground.

The battle was pretty much over by that time. It was definitely over for me. I dropped the ax and crawled to Eiddelig's side. I had no doubt that he was dead even before I saw his crushed skull and empty eyes. I cradled his body and rocked. We were never close, as friends at least. He was older, and more often than not had treated me like a child. But I had known him my entire life. I had been his squire. I had cleaned his armor, and taken care of his horse and sharpened his sword, and been the butt of his pranks and now he was dead and would never be in my life again. He was the first close companion I lost in war. Obviously, he would not be the last.

I felt a hand on my shoulder. Tristan stood there, silent but supportive. He had dispatched the crippled Saxon with his knife; I had forgotten entirely about the wounded man. He helped me to my feet and together we draped Eiddelig over my horse's saddle.

Down in the village the battle was finished and the cleanup had begun. Our troops stood in readiness, swords still drawn in expectation of another threat. The battle rush is hard to let go of. The only Saxons I saw were on the ground. Some of the older men in our company had already begun the grisly task of giving the mercy stroke to the wounded.

As we approached I anxiously surveyed the crowd for Arthur. I didn't realize I had been holding my breath until I saw him. He stood, unscathed, with Merlin, Ector and Kay. They turned at the sound of our approach and grief clouded their eyes as they saw Eiddelig.

The rest of that day is a blur to me. My memory is overwhelmed with images and the emotions associated with them. Lucky though I was to have done so I had survived my first battle. Most of our men had. Eiddelig was one of only three casualties on our side, though there were several more wounds and broken bones of varying severity.

Four of the Saxons had escaped harm. We bound them together on fence rails where they could see their dead companions piled in a heap on the outskirts of town. They cursed us as we gathered kindling and lit our torches. The smoke and sickly-sweet smell of sizzling meat accompanied the bone-fire well into the night. Our treatment of our captives was cruel, but our sympathy for the men who had raped and killed our mothers and sisters and families was low. In later years

Arthur was well known for his justice and fairness. Those concepts are different in times of peace than they are during war. We saw what was left of our homes and our crops that day. What wasn't destroyed had been treated worse than we kept our pigsties. I don't know how the Saxons planned on settling in our country if they trashed the homes that were here. They had camped in our homes for less than a week and lived in filth the entire time.

If it had simply been the wanton destruction of our property I may have been more understanding in time. As a warrior, I too have destroyed crops and property to keep our enemy from having supplies or a place to rest. My actions have no doubt caused untold suffering for the innocents in our wake. But that is the sad truth of war, and I believe in the long run Arthur's campaigns brought more peace and relief than misery.

We found some of our families that day, still alive, though most of them wished they were not. Many of our women, nearly dead from a week of rape and abuse, were still inside our homes. Neither my mother nor Laudine were among them, and I'm not sorry to say I hoped they had died quickly instead of suffering the way the survivors had. Some of the men, mostly old, had been tortured, not for information but merely for sport. We found the scorched circle of bones where our people had been burned, and unlike our own fire I am not convinced all of them went to the flames after they had died.

We buried our fallen companions in a solemn ceremony near dusk. Merlin spoke and invoked the god and the goddess. Tristan sang and gave voice to the grief we felt for all we had lost. His tears were open and gave the rest of us permission to shed our own. Eiddelig had been Christian, but there were no priests among us to give him final rites. I hope his soul resides in whatever afterlife he believed in.

Arthur sent two riders back to find Warok and the rest of our men to apprise them of our situation. The rest of us began the task of cleaning up the village. It was to serve as our base of operations, and we all had the need to reclaim it as much as possible. Even so, I knew it would never be my home again.

Merlin spoke some of the language of our captives. Apparently they were Jutes instead of Saxons. I didn't know what that meant and didn't care. They were taken to one of the barns and held there overnight. I heard screams and what I'm sure were curses in their tongue, and by morning their bodies had joined their companions in the fire.

Gawaine had argued to let them go, not out of pity, but to warn any other invaders of the fate that awaited them. Arthur chose to keep our presence a secret for the time being, at least until the rest of our troops arrived and we had a better idea of what lay ahead of us.

The Jutes were remarkably resilient, and in the end only one of them told us anything of value. I think his fear of Merlin's magic was more effective than anything else.

The party that had attacked our home was a small part of a much larger force. Most of the raiders who had been involved in the initial assault had already departed to rejoin their compatriots. Many invaders had landed, and more were on their way. Their boats had crossed the channel and rowed into the mouth of the river Glein. They had come ashore at a wide spot in the river farther upstream and were still using that place to gather their troops and plan their movements. Our captured people were being taken there as slaves to be carried off and sold in distant lands.

The Glein had its origins north of our land, well into Uriens territory. Two more riders were sent to find Kynon and Owain. No boats could go that far upstream, but now we knew the location where we would most need Uriens troops. They were instructed to come south along the river until they were two days march from the Saxons landing point, and to wait there for further instructions from Arthur. They were cautioned to use scouts, preferably our horsemen, and not to engage the enemy until they were sure of our support.

Warok and our warhorses arrived in the afternoon of our second day home. Our infantry would be several more days at least. We didn't want to allow the Saxons any further raiding in our countryside, but without our full complement of soldiers we weren't yet ready for a full-scale battle. It was decided to use some of their own tactics against them. Scouts would go out and determine exactly where the enemy was located. We knew the place on the Glein they used as their staging area, but there had to be many of them scattered over our land, attacking the homesteads, farms and other small villages they encountered. We would send out small raiding parties to harass them and keep them off balance.

For the next several days I was part of a constant running battle. Groups of a dozen or so of us would travel to the places where our scouts had found the enemy. We would charge in on horseback, each of us dealing one or two blows with our swords, and then disappear back into the woods before they could mount any sort of resistance or response. The surprise attack worked every time. The forest terrain that prevented a traditional shield wall or an organized cavalry charge of any size actually aided our efforts by giving us a quick place to hide. We stumbled on the tactic of luring our enemy into well-laid traps as well. Tristan would step out of the woods in plain sight, dressed as a common woodsman, and drop two or three quick arrows into the midst of a Saxon raiding party. Once he was sure they were chasing him he would duck back into the trees. The enemy would find a group of armored fighting men where they expected a lone archer.

Gawaine in particular proved gifted at woodcraft and this style of fighting. He taught us how to attach leaves and branches to our cloaks so that we could blend into the forest and not be seen. He set many game traps that proved to be the end of several lone Saxons. He and Tristan were both gifted in making bird sounds so that I often lost track of where they were. I was surprised at Gawaine's proficiency, given the wild rocky shores he called home.

"I would ride out to the woods to hunt frequently," he told me once while we were hiding in a brush-covered ditch, waiting for the enemy to pass by. "And to avoid my parents," he laughed. "I would spend days living there. It's one of the few places I ever feel peaceful. I'm not a very religious sort, but the woods are the place I escape to. I call it my green chapel."

We did not decimate the Saxon numbers, but a lot of their blood was spilled. The heavy woods that covered Ector's land had never really had a name before, but by the end of that week it had been dubbed "The Savage Forest."

Not that we always attacked. Sometimes there were simply too many of our foe to confront. Twice we watched in impotent fury as a large group of them torched a homestead and killed its tenants.

I practiced with my sword technique every day, and our raids gave me plenty of practical experience. I was still not close to my previous level of proficiency, but I was motivated. Luck, or the gods, was apparently on my side during those days, for I should probably have died many times over.

Most of our encounters were similar enough that very few details stand out in my memory. One however deserves more attention, not only for what it would mean to my life, but also for the future of the entire kingdom.

It was late in the day and we had been trailing a group of Saxons for hours. The sign they left informed us they were a small party, and even if we weren't able to completely wipe them out we wanted to cause as much trouble for them as possible. There were about a dozen of us patrolling together, easily enough to deal with the size group we were following. But no matter what we did they continued to stay one step ahead of us. I don't know if they knew we were following and were being more cautious as a result, or if we were simply not being as efficient as we could have been. We were tired and hungry. All of us had been out for several days engaging in our raids. The bodily fatigue and the mental stress were taking their toll.

It was close enough to dusk that we were ready to call it quits and head back to the village. None of us wanted to sleep out in the woods for another night. The prospect of hot food and a relatively comfortable bed were proving to be more motivating than an encounter with yet another group of the enemy.

Rest proved to be many hours in our future.

"Is something burning?" Gawaine asked, calling our men to a halt with an upraised arm. I stopped and took a deep breath of the evening air. The crisp cleanness of early fall carried a taint of smoke and ash.

"Wind's from the west," Kay said. "I think there's a small family settlement that way."

"At least we know where the Saxons are now," Gawaine said as he spurred his horse into motion. I was riding Butter, who had arrived with Warok's cavalry, and we all followed at the fastest speed our horses could manage in the thick forest. We saw a column of smoke backlit by the setting sun rising over the crest of a small hill. Screams rode the wind to our ears before we reached the top.

We pulled our horses to a halt. Our short experience had taught us to take stock of a situation before charging in. No matter what the sign may have told us there could be far more of the enemy present than we had guessed. We could be rushing into a whole camp of them instead of the few we had been tracking.

Below us in a small clearing in the forest there was a small settlement. From the size of it I would have guessed the population to be thirty to forty people at most. They were all hunters and subsistence farmers and likely most of them would be related to each other as well. The houses were little more than huts with thatch roofs and mud filling the cracks between the timbers. Gardens filled small plots of ground nearby. A well sat in the center of the community.

It was all on fire. Saxons were running through the village, ransacking the huts with axes and torches. Bodies littered the ground and more people were being pulled from their homes and killed as we watched.

It wasn't the first time that week we had seen this, but this time we believed we could do something about it. There was less than twenty of the enemy. They outnumbered us, but we had our horses and surprise on our side. With a slight nod of my head we all drew our swords and thundered down the hill. It was too late to save most of the people of the settlement, but these Saxons would pay with their lives.

In the chaos of their own assault they didn't even know we were near until we were among them. My sword bit into the neck of a barbarian who was dragging a dead girl out of her home. My skills were still not what they should have been, but I no longer lost my grip when I killed someone. I urged Butter forward and ran down another barbarian who had just fled from a different home. He was covered in blood not his own when he went under our hooves.

It was over quickly. Our men hacked down their opponents all around me. Gawaine alone took out at least four men that I saw. He stood near the well and bellowed a battle cry that seemed to shake the earth, his sword a flashing instrument of death, reflecting the firelight and spraying the blood of his enemies.

I stopped Butter to take stock of the village. There were no Saxons near me, and those I could see were engaged with our troops. I was almost disappointed there was no one left for me to kill. Fires roared all around me and I knew we would not be able to bring them under control. Everything was too far gone for the few of us to have any hope of saving the village. I doubted if there were any survivors, though we would certainly look.

It was then I saw a large Saxon at the end of one of the lanes. He was carrying a massive ax in one hand and a severed head in the other. He kicked in the door of one of the huts and went inside. I immediately heard the wailing cry of an infant.

I kicked Butter into motion, hoping against hope that I would not be too late. The crying came to a sudden and unnatural stop as I reined Butter to a halt and slid from the saddle. A woman's scream followed.

"No, no, no!" I said out loud as I raced toward the door, but the woman's voice was silenced as swiftly as the baby's had been.

Fire in the thatch lit the interior of the hut as I stepped inside. The Saxon stood with his back to me, but I could tell he had drawn his loincloth to the side. He was lost in a blood frenzy of violence and rape. I don't think he ever knew I was there. My sword slashed across the back of his neck. I felt flesh and bone split under my blow and he toppled dead to the floor.

I looked around the hut. The head he carried had been dropped just inside the doorway. The tiny body of the baby I had heard was on the floor, head crushed in from having been thrown there. A woman lay beside it, her dress ripped off and her head twisted around nearly backward.

A girl of about three or four years old cowered in a corner of the burning hut. Tears streaked her dirty face, flowing from the largest, most soulful eyes I had ever seen. When I stepped forward to help her she whimpered and pressed farther back into the corner. How stupid was I then? She had just seen her family murdered, and I believe the Saxon had intended to rape this child before I arrived. I was just another strange man who had come into her home bearing a weapon.

I sheathed my sword and took off my helmet. I knelt down to be on her level, trying to remember how Tristan had won Kahedrin's trust at Mont St. Michael.

"It's all right now," I said in the softest, most gentle tones I was capable of. "That was the last of them here. Come with me. I'll make sure you're safe." I held out my hand.

There was a moment's hesitation, but then I saw a look of trust and relief slide over her tiny face. She leapt into my arms and clung to me. I lifted her as I stood up and felt her body shake as sobs wracked her body.

"Shh," I whispered. "It's all right. You're safe. We need to go before the fire spreads any farther." I felt her nod and I quickly left the hut, leaving my helmet behind since I didn't have another hand to carry it. We stepped out into the night, buffeted by the heat of the burning buildings. Butter had not fled, though I could see his mounting fright. I lifted the child onto my saddle and then climbed on behind her. She settled back against me, still crying. I wrapped the reins around my right forearm and wrapped my good arm around the child protectively. I felt her body tense as the rest of my party rode up to us.

"I'm going to take you someplace safe," I said. "These men are all my friends. They won't hurt you and they will help me protect you. We have to go now, okay?"

She turned to look up at me, brushing her matted red hair away from her swollen eyes.

"Okay," she said.

"My name is Bedivere," I said as Butter began to walk toward home. "What's your name?"

"Nimué," she answered.

We were a good three-hour ride away from Ector's village. Nimué grasped my arm as we rode and pulled it tighter around herself. She snuggled back into the safety of my chest and before we had traveled very far she had fallen asleep.

Though it was late when we arrived back home there was still a lot of activity. There was never a time when the entire village slept. With the help of one of the grooms I dismounted, being careful not to wake my riding companion. Now that we were back I had no idea what to do with Nimué. The men in camp were all warriors and would have little time and even less skill in taking care of a child. The few women here had all been the victims of the Saxon's depredations and were recovering from injuries, physical and mental. Nimué's sleeping head rested on my shoulder as I carried her to Ector's house. As the largest structure in the village it had become our center of operations. Arthur would be found there, and I didn't know who else to ask. This seemed to be a small matter, but it fell to him as much as anything else. The child in my arms was representative of everything we wished to preserve and protect. Some provision would have to be made.

Kay stood guard on the front portico where Arthur and I had been invited to join the adults in conversation for the first time only a few short months previously. How long ago that seemed. Out transition from naive boys to wounded men had happened much too quickly. I suppose that's true of anyone who is thrown into war.

"Survivor?" Kay asked when he saw the bundle I carried. He was more terse than usual. He was still mourning the loss of Eiddelig. I don't think I understood until he was gone that Eiddelig was to Kay what I had always been to Arthur; best friend and brother combined.

"The only one," I answered. "I don't know what to do with her."

Kay opened the door and motioned for me to enter.

The house was dark. Small candles lit the opening hallway, their flames flickering in the wind of my passage. I went to the central meeting room. If anyone were still up and about they would be there.

A small fire had been lit, more for light than warmth, though the nights were beginning to get chilly. The room was empty except for Merlin. He sat hunched over a pile of scrolls and other papers. A profusion of candles created a perimeter of light around his work. He absentmindedly chewed on a strand of his beard as he wrote.

He looked up as soon as the door opened. His friendly words of greeting stopped in his throat as he saw the still sleeping child in my arms. His eyes widened as he slowly stood. Though he was focused on Nimué his eyes stared into the distance at something I could not see. He looked alarmed and for the briefest moment he seemed to be a cornered animal who knew his fate was to die.

"What is this, Bedivere?" he finally asked.

"This is Nimué," I said. I told him the story of our encounter and how she was the only survivor of the raid.

"She has no family," I concluded. "I don't know what to do with her. I thought maybe you could help." I stepped forward and began to hand her to the magician, but to my surprise he took a quick step backward and held up a warding hand.

"No," he said. His voice took on that strange quality I had heard from both he and Morgan when they saw things the rest of us could not.

"If I take that child into my arms," he said, "I will never let her go until my death." Silence followed this pronouncement. I stepped away from him and held Nimué more tightly.

"She needs to go to Avalon," he finally said. "Only Vivienne can give this child what she needs."

"Vivienne isn't here," I countered. "And we can't spare anyone to take her back at the moment. We need someone to watch her now."

Merlin nodded, seeing the wisdom in my words. He stroked his beard and never took his eyes from the child. I watched as his face returned to its more normal countenance.

"You're right, of course," he said. "Find the women here. Give Nimué into their care."

"The women here are all recovering from their own traumas," I said.

"You'll see, very little will help them more than a needy child. Taking care of an innocent will remind them their suffering has not been in vain, and that they are still a valuable part of the world."

This time, I saw the wisdom in what he said. I turned to leave, anxious to relieve myself of my burden.

"Bedivere," Merlin called. I paused and turned to look at him. "Tell no one what you heard me say here. I know you do not truly understand these things, but I have seen my death today. It is a long time from now, and it is a good death, but no one, especially that child, should carry that knowledge. She will need friends in this life, but have very few. I count on you to always be one of them, no matter what happens."

What could I say? He spoke of things beyond me. I nodded my assent and left the room, giving very little thought to what I had promised.

I found the surviving women of our village staying together in one of the remaining houses. Merlin had been right in his assumptions. The moment I arrived with Nimué I saw smiles and the light of life among the women for the first time since we had rescued them. Nimué gave them hope for the future, something that had been forcefully taken away. I left the child there, assuming it was the last contact I would ever have with her in my world of men and warriors.

CHAPTER EIGHTEEN

Our skirmishes did not go unnoticed by the Saxons. In the course of that long week we stopped seeing small raiding parties. Their numbers grew as they became aware that there were hunters in the woods. It was obvious that they were looking for us. We couldn't be everywhere, so it was likely that some of their scouts had discovered we had reclaimed our village. The woods around the vale would protect us from a large-scale attack, but it did not pay for us to continue to send troops out. Even with the added force of Warok's cavalry we needed every man to protect the vale. A rider returned from Urien's land to inform us that his infantry was in position two days march up the river Glein. Our scouts informed us that our infantry would arrive in another day or two. Its ranks had swollen with the addition of men from Leodegrance's kingdom. He had sent a horse messenger home as soon as we had left Avalon. His troops were few in number, but still more than we had left after the destruction of our village. King Mark had also sent the infantrymen who were with him at Avalon, but Cornwall was too far away for any other help to arrive in time.

Fewer of the Saxons ventured forth from the Glein. Not that they were afraid, but they certainly became more cautious. It was obvious they were consolidating their forces. We had tipped our hand by letting them know there was organized resistance. They would not be content to be our targets for long. Our own scouts confirmed that they were amassing an army. While some of the boats stayed anchored in the river, others were seen to come and go, taking slaves and goods away, and bringing Saxon warriors back. In spite of the success of our attacks, a larger battle was on the horizon. Ector said he had rarely seen this type of troop buildup, even back when Uther's wars were at their height. This was nowhere near as large as his final battle had been, but it was a significant return to the Saxon threat of old.

It was obvious to everyone, Briton and Saxon alike, that a clash of our armies was inevitable. The invaders had chosen to make their stand at the Glein. The river was wide and deep where they were camped. Having it at their back prevented us from surrounding them. Their ships would be anchored there as well, giving them a possible avenue of escape. They had been there for weeks now, plenty of time to prepare defenses.

Once our infantry arrived Arthur took stock of our resources. He listened to what those of us who had been in the field told him about the disposition of our enemies and their defenses. Ector, Merlin, and many of the older veterans of Uther's war gave him insights into the usual combat tactics of our enemy and what we could expect from them.

Finally, a plan of battle was agreed upon. We sent a rider back to Uriens men to tell them to plan on converging on the Saxon camp in three days time. Tristan was given command of Mark's troops and sent ahead on a mission of their own. He was not the most experienced warrior among them, but he was the heir-apparent of Cornwall, so they followed him willingly. The rest of us sharpened swords and mended armor. The infantry drilled in shield wall formation while Warok and I put the cavalry through its paces.

We left the village early in the morning and made our slow progress through the vast woods. This would be the largest gathering of men I had yet seen, and certainly the largest battle. The Saxons knew we were coming. They had not yet conquered much of our land, but they showed no sign of running. I think they were surprised that we had fielded an army this large. Surely their intelligence on us was that we were still many small kingdoms who did not support each other. They had the misfortune of planning their invasion just as Arthur changed all that. Still, they did not know what we were capable of. Neither did we, really. Their leaders knew that if they could break us here there would be very little resistance anywhere else. Whatever had happened to unite us was new, and if this many men were here it was unlikely that there was a larger, more organized army waiting for them elsewhere.

We arrived at the edge of the forest that bordered the river plain along the Glein. My bowels clenched when I saw what awaited us. There were hundreds of Saxons lining the land. Their shield walls were already up, awaiting our arrival. Long pikes angled forward out of the ground in front of them like a hedgehog's quills. In my mind I could see my beloved horses impaled on them. The men carried axes and swords and long spears that would reach over the top of the shields to stab at the eyes and faces of our men. Closer to the river there were tents and other makeshift lodgings. Boats of various sizes bobbed in the river's currents.

When they saw us they began to yell; screams and taunts and insults in a language we didn't need to know to understand the intent. They beat their weapons against their shields and against the ground, raising tremendous tumult. The deep thrumming of war drums sounded somewhere in their midst, the resonant heartbeat of the great beast comprised of men that anxiously awaited our attack.

At that moment I wasn't sure anything could convince me to step out of the safety of the tree line and engage this fearsome assemblage.

Then Arthur spoke to me.

"There will be a parley," he said. "Before we clash we will speak to their chiefs under a flag of truce. You will accompany Ector, Merlin, Kay and I. Nothing obvious will be accomplished other than an exchange of insults. But it gives us an opportunity to take a closer look at their defenses. Keep your eyes open. Look for chinks in their armor, anything that might give us an advantage. Whatever happens out there, we will fight them today. We have to win or this dream of a united kingdom will be stillborn."

We readied a flag of truce and the five of us cautiously walked our horses out of the cover of the tree line. I fully expected to feel the impact of an arrow in my chest, but nothing materialized. The taunting jeers of the Saxons raised to a crescendo.

The center of their line opened to allow four of their own men to ride out to meet us. These were some of only a small handful of horses I could see. They had nothing resembling a cavalry. That advantage was ours, but the sharpened stakes could end our charge quickly.

The Saxon envoy sat close to their line. They wanted us to come close to them for the parley. It was a small act of defiance; making us advance was an attempt to prove they were the superior force. We went. If we were attacked our troops were ready to charge, consequences be damned.

The four men before us were typical of the Saxon breed. They were shaggy, with long hair and beards. Two of them wore their hair in long braids. They wore a mismatch of armor, mostly hide and leather, though there were pieces of ring mail draped over them as well. Tattoos covered their arms, and each of them carried the scars of previous battles. Their leader was a tall, muscular man, older than those who rode with him, not quite Ector's age, but it was obvious he had led a harder life these past years. He was solid muscle still, not tending to fat the way Ector was. A livid scar drew a line across his left cheek. He raised a hand and the Saxon horde went suddenly still.

"So this is what is sent to fight me?" the lead Saxon said in a broken but understandable version of our tongue. "Children, old men and cripples?"

"Our real warriors thought this was all that is needed to defeat you," Arthur said. "They decided to wait at home until real men were arrayed against us."

The Saxon smiled at this, a smile made hideous by his scar. The left corner of his mouth rose to reveal a sharp tooth, giving his grin a hungry, feral look.

"I am Hengist," he announced. "When I was a child I fought the blue people from the north for your King Vortigern. I was promised land and gold and women. But when Vortigern died his followers denied me my just reward. When I was a young man I fought against your King Uther. I killed his men and raped his women. Many among you are probably the spoiled seed of my loins. In this way I have already conquered your country. I come home now to settle amongst my sons and daughters in this land, the land I was promised. Are you here to challenge my just claim, or are you here to embrace your brother?"

"I am Arthur, son of Uther. I am High King of Britain and I reject your claims. If my people are your brothers and sisters, sons and daughters as you claim then you are guilty of fratricide and the rape of your children. That alone speaks against any rights you have, to live here, or to live at all. Take your people, get back on your boats and go back where you came from."

"High King?" Hengist snorted. "That's a big title for such a child. Your father was much older than you when he claimed it, and he still died like a sheep at slaughter time. You're barely old enough to cut your own meat, let alone wield that big sword against my seasoned warriors."

"I hope they are seasoned," Arthur said. "They will be more tasty for the dogs and crows that feast on them as they litter the ground."

"You should hope your sword is as sharp as your wit, boy," Hengist said. "We are wasting daylight. Will you step aside and command your men to lay down their arms, or do we have to slaughter all of you?"

"The land you stand upon is not yours," Arthur said. "Unless you leave it peacefully, even though it is a small piece of my kingdom, I will claim it back from you at the price of your warrior's lives."

"So be it then, little king," Hengist said. "Bring your men to me so that I may kill them." He turned and walked his horse back into the mass of his men. They immediately began to scream and beat their blades against their shields. We turned our backs on them and rode slowly back to our troops.

"You played his game well," Merlin said, chuckling to himself. "Believe it or not, you won his respect back there by trading insults with him."

"Insults won't beat him," Arthur said. "Bedivere, did you see anything of note while we were there?"

"Their shield wall looks solid enough," I said. "They don't have the discipline we do, so there will be gaps that should be easy to exploit. The problem is that line of sharpened stakes. Not only are they a threat to any cavalry charge, they pose a problem for our infantry as well."

"How so?" Ector asked. I was sure he saw the trouble, but wanted to not only test me but to give me the chance to appear valuable to Arthur.

"If they hold their shield wall just behind the line of stakes," I explained, "our men will have to break their own line to step past them. We will be creating gaps in our own wall just as we are engaging the enemy. With their attacks it will be difficult to close our gaps before they are able to exploit it. The stakes will also be in the way of our line of men directly behind the shield-bearers.

"But," I said, "I think I have an idea. The stakes were placed quickly. They never meant to have this beach be their battleground. We surprised them here, so I believe the defenses were hastily erected."

"So?" Kay said.

"So while Hengist talked I saw a lot of nervous shuffling on the part of those in the front line. Several of them bumped against the butts of the stakes. The ground here is loose and they are not very secure. One of them simply fell."

"So how do we take advantage of that?" Arthur said.

"Here's what I think," I said, and began to outline my plan.

It was close to another hour before new orders could be relayed to our troops. It was approaching midday by then, but it was overcast and gloomy. No hint of sunshine peeked through the clouds. There was no rain, but the air felt damp and cloudy.

I sat on my Arabian with forty other cavalrymen under my command. We had ridden south to take our position along the Glein, blocking any escape in that direction. Our job that day was to be cleanup. No matter how much I had improved I was still not ready for heavy combat with my left hand. The first part of the battle was up to the others and all I could do was watch. Warok commanded the heavy cavalry at the center of our line. If all went according to plan my men and horses would be the final hammer blow against the enemy.

I watched as our infantry stepped out of the safety of the trees and began the long slow march to the enemy line. The Saxons weren't advancing to meet us. We knew they wouldn't. Our plans counted on it. The river protected their rear flank from attack by men or horses. This was an advantage to them, but it also served to crowd them together and limit their range of motion. This would make their shield wall difficult to break, but if we did, there was no real place for them to run.

The noise was thunderous as the Saxons continued their onslaught of screamed insults and riotous noisemaking. Our own men, while more reserved, shouted their fair share of invective. Gawaine's distinctive bellow occasionally rose above the rest.

When the infantry was halfway across the open ground Warok walked his charger out of the trees. A line of warhorses formed on either side of him. The riders carried shields on their left arms but had not yet drawn their swords.

Ten yards from the line of sharpened stakes our men came to a halt. The clamor on the beach was deafening. They were close enough to see the enemy up close, to hear his breath and see his eyes. In mere moments men would be dead on both sides. Energy buzzed along the lines. From my advantage I could see the ebb and flow of the Saxon line. They were impatient. They wanted to break their line and engage. They were not really trained for this style of fighting. They were more chaotic, individual brawlers instead of an organized force. Hengist, or someone, had convinced them that to break the line this early would mean their death. Still, discipline was not their strongest attribute. I could see their desire to leap forward, axes swinging, instead of waiting for the coming assault. The longer our line waited the more I could feel their tension.

Our line stepped forward. The heads of the men in front were directly below the tips of the angled stakes. This was the moment when, to move forward, one in every three men in our shield wall would have to drop his guard in order to walk around the planted shafts. Once that took place, the Saxon line would surge forward into those gaps.

We didn't let that happen. Our line halted once more, eliciting screams of fury from our enemy. Their line almost broke then, but they were in the same position we were. In order to close that final three yards and engage they would have to break their wall to step around the stakes. It caused the same conundrum for their advance that it did for us. They had been told not to step over that line, and were completely confused by our seeming refusal to do so either. They could smell our sweat but we remained a sword length out of reach.

Then, to their complete surprise, my plan went into action. Instead of advancing, the line of men directly behind the shield bearers reached up and grabbed the tips of the stakes and yanked them forward out of the ground. We didn't get all of them. Some were hammered into the earth more securely than others. But most of the dangerously sharpened shafts were pulled free and passed backward along the mass of our troops. Most of the ones we didn't actually steal were knocked to the ground. Before any of the Saxons really comprehended what had happened our shield wall, completely intact with no need to step around the stakes, advanced into the enemy with a resounding crash and the slaughter began.

It could have been a lot more drawn out and dangerous than it was. In any battle the press of men on both sides almost creates a stalemate. Men die, but they drop to the ground at the shield line, creating an obstacle for both sides. Swords, axes and spears are thrust over and under the defenses of the enemy. Wounds are numerous, but serious injury or death takes a long time. It's not until the men begin to tire and defenses drop that the killing begins to take its real toll. It was our plan to cause a diversion before our men began to seriously flag.

I saw motion out of the corner of my eye and before I could focus on it I heard the screams from the rear of the Saxon line. The second and third flights of arrows from Tristan's troops on the far side of the river were in the air by the time I looked in that direction. He and his men from Cornwall had ridden north and crossed the Glein at a narrower and shallower spot. His instructions had been to take position across the water and to wait for our attack. He had thirty men, and they only had thirty to fifty arrows each. They could not keep up the assault for long. But at that precise moment, when the Saxons were focused on us and felt secure in the rear, the attack was devastating.

For obvious reasons I was never able to use the bow, as a

weapon or for hunting. I knew from the military history I had been taught that archers had been used to good effect for centuries, but I had never really taken it very seriously. Watching the chaos it unleashed along the Glein convinced me of its efficacy as a weapon of war. In a few seconds the rear ranks of the Saxons took heavy casualties. Archers didn't need pure accuracy in this type of battle. Simply putting a tremendous number of arrows in the air took its toll. They fell on the beach like lightning from the gods. Not all hit their targets; armor and shields deflected them. Most of them weren't fatal, but the enemy dropped with lengths of wood piercing their arms, legs, and feet.

One arrow in thirty carried flame on its tip. Tristan had told me when we were planning this assault that flame arrows were more difficult to aim accurately and had a shorter range due to the extra weight at the head. Tristan wielded Failnot for this task, and soon the tents and makeshift structures at the rear of the enemy's camp were ablaze. More importantly, many of the boats and their sails began to smolder.

The Saxons reacted quickly to this assault from the rear. Many of them turned and raised shields to protect those in the front line. Impotent though they were to strike back at our archers they did prevent many more of the arrows from doing real damage to the troops. The side effect of this was that it created chaos among their ranks as they were suddenly confronted with an attack on two fronts. Those in the shield wall had no idea what was happening behind them, except that their support had turned and abandoned them. The line began to break apart and then to buckle.

Conventional wisdom said that our own infantry should have surged forward at that moment and broken the wall. We could have done that, but the loss of life for our men would still have been staggering. Instead, our shield wall stepped back just as theirs began to collapse. Instead of pressing an advantage, most of the undisciplined Saxons turned to see what was happening behind them. That was their undoing. As soon as our shield wall saw the Saxons were not advancing they quickly retreated and stepped aside.

The Saxons looked back at our troops in time to see the solid wall of horseflesh hurtling toward them. Warok led the charge. Each of our cavalry held one of the sharpened stakes we had stolen from their line. Instead of our horses being impaled upon the wood we had turned their own defense against them. They started to break in panic but it was much too late. Men were impaled on the lances and trampled under the hooves of our heavy horses. Our men dropped the spears and drew their swords as they rode into the midst of the enemy horde. Our arrows stopped falling and our infantry followed the horses, giving the last stroke to those who were wounded by the charge.

At that point the battle was simply a rout. Saxons attempted to flee into the river. Others ran along its length. I ordered my troop of Arabians to charge and we cut off their southern escape route. Many of the Saxons attempted to flee north along the Glein only to encounter the thick shield wall of Uriens men, marched into position the night before by Owain and Kynon.

It's difficult to describe a battle to anyone who wasn't in it. There are many different battles fought, one by every man involved. There are the plans that are made before the conflict, and then there is the reality of what actually takes place. My position allowed me to see the big picture at the beginning, but once I was engaged the entire war shrank down to a two-foot radius around me. I was only aware of those who were attacking me and those I attacked. I have no idea what took place up and down the river while I was fighting. I have heard the stories from the others. Gawaine tells me that he leapt from his saddle to assist his brother after Agravaine was pulled from his horse. They stood back to back in the midst of the Saxon host and cut down at least fifty of the enemy, by his no doubt exaggerated count. Kay rode next to Arthur for the whole battle, and though he was mute about the details I think he may have saved his brother's life. I have been told by many that Merlin cast spells from horseback and Saxons simply fell dead at his words, though I didn't see anything like that. Tristan and his archers sniped those who were attempting to swim across the river to get away.

Some reached the boats and escaped downriver and there was nothing we could do to stop it. Hengist must have been one of them for we could not find his body in the aftermath of the battle. He certainly returned to plague us again and again.

I have always been amazed at how quickly the chaos seems to end. One moment your soul is a screaming frenzy surrounded by enemies, and one last sword stroke later you are standing alone in a field full of bodies and the battle is over.

It's never quite that clean, obviously. All up and down the river there were still small pockets of fighting, and the cleanup would take forever. But there came a moment along the Glein when suddenly, for me, the battle was over. I stood near a mound of Saxon bodies. I saw hundreds more strewn about the river plain. Crows and seabirds were landing everywhere to claim their spoils. I don't remember getting off my horse. I was drenched in blood and I wasn't sure if any of it was mine. My arm was tired and sore. I felt like I could barely stand. Though I could hear the moans and screams of the wounded, the cries of the carrion eaters, and the continued peal of steel on steel, the world seemed silent compared to the cacophony that had reigned earlier. The sun had slid down the western sky and I wondered how that much time had passed.

It took a few moments for the realization to set in. We had won. The men I saw standing were ours. King Arthur had led the combined troops of the petty kingdoms to a significant victory against the largest gathering of Saxons seen since Uther's time.

CHAPTER NINETEEN

Sitting in my quiet study, the crackling of the fire in the hearth my only accompaniment, it is difficult to imagine the chaos of battle. In my thick, comfortable woolen garments and a warm mug of mulled cider at hand, it is hard to believe I ever stood covered in blood, surrounded by hundreds of dead men, with the reverberations of battle still echoing up my sword arm. Today I am well fed, comfortable, and the only fear I have before me is the death that awaits all old men. Even at my age that prospect feels distant and hard to comprehend. After a lifetime of staring at the prospect of my death a mere arm's length away it is hard to believe it may come to me quietly in my sleep instead of violently on an enemy's sword. I can't believe there are so few of us left who enjoy that option.

We lost men on the Glein. There are no battles of that size that spares men on either side. But our casualties were few compared to our enemies. It was, I now realize as a veteran of many larger battles, a relatively small affair. There were hundreds of men fighting along the river, and while that may sound unbelievable to the common man who never sees more than the dozens of people in his home village at any one time, it pales compared to the thousands of men I would see arrayed against each other in times to come. Still, it was my first. I hate to think I grew that jaded as time went on, but I don't remember ever being as affected by the aftermath of battle as profoundly as that cool, gray day beside the Glein.

Bodies were strewn about in chaotic profusion. The clamor of battle had passed to be replaced by the moans and wails of the wounded and dying. Crows and seabirds found us before the fight was finished and made no distinction between the dead they feasted on and those who were simply too weak to wave them away. There were dogs foraging among the spoils, snapping at each other and any of the living that came too close. I don't know where they came from, but like the birds, there were always dogs at play in the fields of the dead. No one ever talks about the smell of combat, the reek of spilled blood and offal. Many men soil themselves, before and after death. In the hot months it was overpowering. The need to bury or burn the bodies quickly was paramount, and a tremendous amount of work. We often were unable to clean up the field before the stench became too much.

I walked through the carnage, occasionally stopping to slice the throats of those who were too wounded to be saved, friend and foe alike. I ended the suffering of injured horses, their uncomprehending eyes cloudy with pain and fear. I was anxious to discover the fates of my friends, but I was also parched. I went upstream to a place where there were no bodies clouding the water and knelt to drink. I threw up then. I think it was more of a release of tension than anything else, though I'm sure there was revulsion as well. Killing never became easy to me, even though I did it well. We all had our own ways of returning to the world of the living. Arthur immediately began to take reports and organize the cleanup and secure the perimeter. Tristan invariably wept. Lancelot would kneel among the bodies and pray. The aftermath of battle always left me weak and empty, not with remorse for had had occurred, but with the need to purge myself of leftover emotion.

I was on my knees washing the taste of vomit out of my mouth and the stickiness of other men's blood from my skin when I heard my name bellowed. Still on edge, my hand went for my sword, but I relaxed when I saw Gawaine and Agravaine walking along the shore toward me. I stood just in time to be swept up in a rib-crushing bear hug.

"We did it!" Gawaine shouted as he swung me around. "We beat the bastards."

"Yes, we did," I gasped. "Now put me down."

"It was glorious!" Gawaine proclaimed. "I've never felt more alive! I need a drink and a woman! Or two!" He danced around, full of energy. Gawaine was a natural warrior. He never exulted in killing for killing's sake, but he never questioned its necessity the way Tristan or I did. In battle he was a man possessed. The proximity of his own death made him feel alive in ways I would never understand. Agravaine was his brother's contrast, as always. He stood, quiet on the riverbank, a smile on his face his only acknowledgement that he had survived and was pleased by our victory.

Together we made our way back into the center of the carnage and eventually found Arthur and the others. He looked tired, but determined. He was already giving orders for what would come next. Details of weary men made piles of the dead, ours separated from theirs. Weapons were being gathered, as were usable pieces of armor and any other valuables that could be salvaged. He turned at the sound of our approach and a smile lifted the corners of his careworn face. He stepped forward and pulled me into an embrace. For just a moment I felt all strength leave him as he rested his burden on my shoulders.

"Thank you," he whispered. I don't know if he was thanking me, or the gods for sparing me. He stood back and once again he was the High King and not just my boyhood friend.

"You did it!" Gawaine said, and slapped Arthur on the shoulder a little too hard.

"We did it," Arthur said. "All of us."

"We were lucky," Ector said. "Not to take anything away from our victory, but that went too well. Trust me when I say not every battle you engage in will be this easily won."

"Ector is right," Merlin said. "They came here not expecting any resistance. They were not prepared for this sort of confrontation. We surprised them. Your strategy was sound, but don't underestimate the role surprise and luck played. Don't let this make you overconfident."

"But they are defeated," Gawaine insisted. "A measly few of them escaped to run back to wherever they call home."

"They want to call Britain home," Arthur said. "They will be back."

"Probably not this year," Ector said. "It's too late in the season, so we have time to prepare. But they will be back."

"Yes," Merlin agreed. "They will. In greater numbers now that they know what awaits them. With more weapons and organization. They now know they can't come here with small raiding parties. They will start to arrive with armies. Next summer, maybe the next year. But soon. We have much to do to get this kingdom ready."

"We have much to do to clean up this battlefield," Arthur said. "I want graves dug for our men. There will be a service for them once they are buried. The bodies of the Saxons will be burned. Are there any prisoners?"

"Some," Ector said. "Not many. The Saxons would rather die than be taken prisoner. Even the severely wounded are more likely to try to attack us than let us treat them. They're looking for a death in battle."

"What kinds of men are like that?" Kay asked.

"They are a warrior culture," Merlin explained. "Nothing is valued more highly than a valiant death in battle. They believe the warrior is rewarded in their afterlife, but he who dies of old age, or without a weapon in his hand will languish for eternity. The details vary from tribe to tribe, but one thing that remains constant is that being captured by your enemy is the greatest shame that can befall a warrior. It's why they fight so fiercely."

"I will speak with any captives later," Arthur said. "Merlin, you can speak some of their tongue, can't you? Good. Make sure they are well treated. Give them water and food."

"They won't take it," Ector said.

"Try anyway," Arthur said. "Treat their wounds if they will allow it. Right now, we have a lot of work to do."

We followed Arthur into the middle of the battlefield and helped with the disposal of bodies and goods. Arthur worked as hard as anyone there. Covered as he was in blood and gore, sweat running down his face, reeking of sweat, he looked nothing like a High King of anything. But throughout the rest of that day, as he labored like a common man, men came to him. They offered congratulations. They pledged their fealty. They kneeled in the blood-soaked grass and declared they were his.

Owain came by, wearing a bandage around his head. I would later discover it covered a wound across his scalp, the scar of which he would carry for the rest of his days.

"King Arthur," he said to get our attention. I saw him wince in pain when he spoke. Arthur embraced him.

"It's just Arthur to you, my friend," he said. "Thank you. And my thanks to the men of Gorre. Did you take many casualties?"

"Not many," Owain said. "The shield wall is a dangerous place, as I'll be reminded every time I touch my head. But it could have been worse. They were a disorganized rabble by the time they reached our line.

"The men have talked," Owain continued. "They sent me to speak with you. They want you to know that, whatever Uriens may say, they are yours now. These Saxons would have traveled up the

Glein and taken our homes, and there would have been nothing we could have done to stop them on our own. They are convinced that the time has come for all of Britain to unite, and that you are the man to do it. If you wish to overthrow my father, they will side with you."

"I don't wish to overthrow anyone," Arthur said. "I want Uriens to support me of his own volition. Speak with him. Tell him what you just told me."

"Leave out the part about his troops openly rebelling," Kay advised.

"Well, yes," Arthur said. "But if he knows his people are behind me he will surely see his support is gone. We need not threaten him. Simply show him the facts. Let him know the Saxons will return, and Gorre is rich with farms and land. Ask him if he can protect it on his own. Tell him what you saw here and that the numbers of our enemy will only increase. Tell him I consider Gorre a part of Britain, whether he supports me or not, and I will protect it because in doing so I am protecting the rest of us.

"Is there anything else?"

"Yes," Owain said, and I saw the pain in his eyes. "I don't believe Kynon is going to make it."

"Kynon!" I cried.

"Go to him," Arthur said to me. "Help him if you can, but don't let him die among strangers."

I followed Owain at a run, back up the riverbank to where the infantry of Gorre were cleaning up the northern reaches of the battlefield. Wounded men had been lain out in the shade of the trees that converged on the river here. Some slept, others moaned, a few screamed. I saw surgeons stitching up wounds with catgut, others putting poultice-soaked bandages on defiled flesh. I stumbled for a moment as I passed a pile of severed limbs. My stump cried out in sympathetic agony as I realized these had been amputated in an effort to save men's lives.

Kynon was near the end of the line, sequestered with men who weren't dead yet, but soon would be. Some wounds simply cannot be treated and death will not be denied. A length of linen had been wrapped around his midsection. It was now soaked with his blood and the contents of his guts. He was covered in sweat and dirt and writhed in feverish delirium. His agony was obvious and immense.

I knelt by his side and took a trembling hand in mine. I brushed wet hair away from his forehead, and then found a damp cloth and washed the dirt and sweat from his face and neck. He opened his eyes and I saw they were already beginning to focus on the Otherworld more than this one.

"Kynon?" I whispered.

"Bedivere?" His voice was weak, a gurgling ghost in his throat.

"I'm here."

"I should have stayed on a horse," he said. "The shield wall id deadly."

"You brought them here," I said. "You and Owain. This victory is yours."

"My family?" he asked. Kynon had not seen the devastation that had been wrought on our homes. He was the oldest son of an old widower in our village. None of his relatives had been found when we returned. We assumed they were among the ashes of the bone-fire we had found. I wanted to lie to him. I wanted to tell him that they were fine so as not to burden him further. But he was dying, and would soon meet them in the afterlife and know that my last act to him had been a lie.

I shook my head, letting him know they were gone.

"I'll be joining them soon," he said. I didn't know what beliefs Kynon had held in life. We never discussed it. They were probably a mix of Christianity and the old ways, neither fully understood or practiced.

"Will there be horses there?" he asked.

"I'm sure there will be," I said, but I don't think he heard me. By the time I answered, Kynon knew the answer for himself.

I wept then as I cradled his body. It was the first time since we had returned home that I allowed the full grief of everything I had lost to sink in. We were creating a new kingdom, and a new future for all of Britain. But right then all I could see was the emptiness of loss.

I don't know how long I stayed there next to Kynon. Dusk was upon us when I felt a hand on my shoulder. I looked up to see Tristan. He and his men had ridden back north and crossed the Glein to rejoin us. His colorful clothes were unmarred by close combat, but the lines of loss and grief stained his face as well.

"Arthur is looking for you," he said. I nodded, wiped the tears from my eyes, and stood.

I heard Gawaine's shouts long before we reached the makeshift command tent where Arthur and his advisors stood. A line of Saxon prisoners kneeled in the torchlight, hands and legs bound together. They stared at all of us, defiant to the last.

"Kill them all!" Gawaine roared. "If you let them go they will come back to kill our people. Every one of them you send back is someone we will have to kill in the future."

"Give me a blade and I will fight you now," one of the Saxons said in our language. "Let me die a warrior and take some of you with me."

"See?" Gawaine said. "Next summer this man will be right back here, killing and raping. We should execute all of them and let the crows have their bodies."

Gawaine had a point. I didn't know if I had the stomach for summary execution, not after all of the death I had already witnessed. But he was right. Every one of the barbarians we held would return to our shores if we let them go. Any one of them could be the man who would kill us in the future.

Arthur looked tired. He rubbed his eyes.

"Merlin, what would you have me do?" he asked.

"It is your decision, King Arthur. There are consequences either way. If you send them back they will carry the tale of this victory and perhaps their brethren will think twice about invading a country that can now defend itself. By the time any of them return our armies will be bigger. We will be more organized. They can expect more defeats at our hands. But they will return, and they will rape and kill. There are but a few here, so in the grand scheme, insignificant. But any one of them could be the difference in our future.

"However, if you execute them, you begin your reign with an act of cruelty. Justified or not, the tales will say you murdered defenseless men. They may deserve it. As a man I believe they do. As a servant of the gods I think these men's lives were spared for a reason, and that reason is to spread word of the new High King of Britain and of the armies he commands. Of how in his first battle, he destroyed a host of Jute warriors with little preparation. Of what awaits every invader that comes to our shores."

I could see Arthur struggling with the decision. He could kill in battle, but he was not a murderer. Having these men executed went against his very nature. But he knew the risks of letting them go. He could not have the lives of their innocent victims on his hands either.

"I think I have a compromise," I said. I wasn't proud of what I was about to suggest. I'm still not. I'm not sure where the idea came from, and though it was brutal it offered a solution.

"Let's hear it," Gawaine said. Arthur gestured his approval. I held up my right arm so that no one could doubt what I meant by my next two words.

"Cripple them."

Eyes widened all around the circle. I could see the uncomprehending surprise on every face. I spoke quickly so that I could explain exactly what I meant.

"Cut off a hand," I said. "Make sure they can never raise arms against us again. Then send them back to spread word of what awaits those who wish to take our land or threaten our families."

"A hand won't do," Kay said. "You carried a sword today and did just fine. By next summer you will be as good with your left hand as you ever were with your right."

A round of debate followed. The Jutes howled their protests as they began to understand what we were discussing. Arthur believed it was unnecessarily cruel, but he was beginning to realize that as king he would constantly be faced with impossible decisions. What did the least harm and would have the greatest effect? How far could we go to protect ourselves and not lose our souls in the process? These questions have plagued every leader of merit, and man of good character in history.

It was Agravaine's calm and calculating voice that cut through the din.

"Take two or three fingers from each hand," he said. "They will be able to feed themselves, but they will never lift a weapon against anyone ever again. And when they die, as toothless old men, it will not be in battle. Their souls will linger in whatever place awaits those who die with no honor."

It was perhaps the cruelest thing we could do to them, and in the end, the most practical. I watched in stolid silence as Arthur mutilated the men. He would not ask anyone to do something he could not do himself. Their hands were bandaged and then they were taken to the Glein. A group of our men escorted them down river to where the clear water runs into the sea. There the invaders were placed on a boat and set adrift to go back to wherever they came from.

I suppose it could be argued that our treatment of those

prisoners, and of many more who followed, only stoked the fires of Saxon hatred. They saw us as a people to be conquered, and the mutilations surely caused them to think even less of us as a nation. We saw them as barbarians, filled with cruelty and avarice. I'm sure those are the same tales they told of us. Our golden age was built on the deaths of our enemies. Was it just? Probably not. It certainly wasn't humane. But wars are not humane, and whatever the true consequences were, whatever stain was left on our souls, I can say with certainty that those men never killed another man, woman or child of Britain in battle.

Riders were sent out the following morning to take word of our victory to our allies. The men of Gorre began their long march back to their homes. Those too wounded to walk were transported by litters carried by their fellows and by a few of the horses we could spare. We said goodbye to Owain and let him know he was always welcome at King Arthur's court, wherever that would be.

Most of the cleanup of the battlefield was complete. The heavy, moist air kept the odor of burning men and decaying blood close to the ground. We dug a mass grave for our own fallen. Scavengers were already among the dead and we could not keep the birds away. There simply was not time or energy to dig that many individual graves. I was among those young soldiers who felt it seemed disrespectful, but the practicality cannot be denied. The men had fallen together and would now lie together. Over time and many battles I stopped questioning the practice. When the dirt was tamped into place over the bodies Merlin led a brief ceremony to send their souls to whatever fate awaited them.

By noon we were ready to return to our home village. We rode slowly through the thick forest, taking our time not only in consideration of our wounded, but because for the first time in weeks we were able to relax. There was still much ahead of us. We had a kingdom to build, and though our victory would make that task easier it was still going to be a lot of work. A much more pressing concern was deciding where we were going to spend the coming winter. Our home village was too remote to serve as home for the High King of all Britain. Even if that were not the case, the Saxons had ruined it for all of us. There were too many destroyed memories there. Most of the men who had traveled with us to Avalon and Benwick had returned to find their families dead and their homes destroyed. Very few of my lifelong neighbors wanted to stay. Even if we did it would be a difficult winter. Our livestock was gone and most of our crops and grains had been taken or destroyed.

These issues weighed heavily on our minds. But that afternoon the sun finally burned away the morning fog and lit the leaves that were just beginning to turn with an autumnal radiance; we were content in the moment.

For myself, I was weary, and nodded in my saddle. Every muscle in my body throbbed, especially my left arm. It was still unused to swinging a sword. I felt pins and needles in my phantom hand, excruciatingly annoying, and nothing I could do would make them go away. I carried a headache behind my right eye that ran back over my ear and into my shoulder.

We came home to the cheers and applause of those few we had left behind. Our victory had given a sense of safety back to our people. Their need for vengeance had been appeased. I don't think the average inhabitant of our land understood or cared that the war had probably just begun and that far more demanding days lie ahead. All they needed were victorious soldiers, and the belief that those who had attacked them had been destroyed.

In the happy chaos of our arrival I saw Nimué running through the crowd straight for me. She had somehow spotted me in the confusion. She dodged nimbly between the men and horses, and once I saw her dart under one and come up on the other side.

"Bedivere!" she called as she approached. I leaned over in my saddle and grabbed her outstretched hand. I lifted her tiny frame easily and swung her upward to plop down in the saddle in front of me. She turned and wrapped her thin arms around my waist in the strongest hug she could manage.

"I'm so glad you're back," she said.

"I'm sorry if I worried you, little one," I said.

"I wasn't worried." She gave me a look that said she thought I was silly for thinking so. "I knew you would be back today. I'm just happy to see you."

She frowned then, and a tiny furrow creased her brow. She reached up and ran her fingertips along my temple, tracing the path of my headache around my skull and down my tight shoulder. She did this three times, and then smiled and turned back around to watch where the Arabian walked. My headache didn't immediately disappear, but it did start to fade until I no longer noticed it. I wrapped my right arm around her and guided our horse with my left. She placed her hand directly in the empty space where my right hand should have been. I know it was just another of the phantom sensations that I have grown so used to over the years, but the pins and needles disappeared and I swear I could feel her fingers intertwine with mine.

I looked down at my small companion. I had seen Nimué since the night I had brought her back with me, but we had not spent a lot of time together. Merlin's advice had been correct. Her presence had worked miracles on the women who had been so abused by the invaders. Having a child to watch over gave them something to do other than dwell on their own misery. From what I could tell, Nimué was delightful, smart, and precocious.

Her head leaned back against my chest and the sun painted golden highlights in her tangled red hair. Her skin was pale, almost translucent; I could see the blue spider web traces of her veins through it. Her lips were large and not given to easy smiles. Her eyes were huge, almost too much so for her face, and slightly slanted. They were blue, but not the icy color of Morgan's. More like the sky just at dusk. Dark circles formed half moons beneath them, no matter how well rested she was. It was another legacy of her pale skin, but it made her look, even as a child, as though the wisdom in her eyes had already made the burdens of the world visible on her face. She was beautiful, but it was the beauty one recognizes in spite of, or maybe because of, the hardships in life.

I had guessed she was three or four, but she claimed to be five; she held up a whole hand full of fingers when asked. She was simply small for her age. That would hold true for the rest of her life. When she was an adult, in middle age and in the prime of her power, she still looked like a child. Some people are just naturally smaller than others, but I have been told she carries the blood of the Otherworld in her veins so maybe she is descended from the wee fair folk who populate that land. I've never actually seen any of the *Fey*, so I can't say.

Merlin left for Avalon the following morning to make preparations for our return there. I noticed that he actively avoided us when Nimué was with me, which was often. She had bonded with me, and I think, felt safer in my presence. The rest of us stayed at Ector's village for several days; they run together in my head. Our wounded needed time to heal, and I'm sad to say that not all of them survived. We salvaged what we could from our homes and packed our goods for transport. There was some debate about what to do with the remaining buildings. Some argued that they could be used by the Saxons in the future and should be destroyed. Arthur correctly pointed out that we could use them as well, and if the invaders were eventually driven away, someday Britons would live here again. I think he simply couldn't bear destroying what was left of our home.

Finally, we were ready to leave. It was a clear and crisp fall morning when we once again set upon our journey to Avalon. Our breath misted around our faces. Steam rose from our horse's flanks. Nimué, sitting with me on Butter's broad back, snuggled back against me for warmth, tucked under my riding cloak. I had tried to tell her she would be more comfortable and warm in one of the wagons with the other women, but she would have none of it.

By noon we were too warm. It was the time of year when it was impossible to choose clothing appropriately. Earlier in the week the air was damp and cold. The first few days of our journey started out cold but quickly warmed under a bright sun. The leaves were on fire with color and though I knew it was because they were dying, the world appeared vibrant and alive. Nimué was overjoyed with all of the wonders she saw and took great pleasure in pointing out every pretty leaf, odd stone and wild animal we passed.

My tiny companion amused the others. Gawaine started calling her my girlfriend, but there was nothing untoward about it. Agravaine was uncomfortable with her, and she seemed not to like him very much either. She loved Tristan, but then I have met very few women who didn't. Arthur engaged her in conversation, and listened intently as she spoke. Her intelligence, though unformed due to her limited experience, was obvious.

The cold front moved through on the day we reached the Roman road. Freezing rain mixed with snow and blew directly into our faces for the rest of the trip. Nimué's enthusiasm was undeterred.

"It won't last," she declared to me through chattering teeth and shivering bones. "It's going to be a mild winter." I smiled at her optimism and naiveté. Over time I would learn to take her pronouncements more seriously.

Several cold days later we approached the trail through the woods that led to Avalon. I looked forward to a warm fire, a hot meal, and to not being on a horse. I saw lights in the windows in the distant abandoned fortress that stood over the wide bend in the river as we approached the field of Camlann. I was somewhat surprised to see that someone had taken up residence there, but abandoned or not, the fortress could provide shelter to someone over the coming months. It had never crossed my mind that this was the perfect location for our displaced people.

A group of riders approached us on the road. I saw immediately they were envoys from Avalon. Morgan rode at their head, wrapped in a thick, fur-lined cloak.

"Welcome back, King Arthur," she said. "And congratulations on your victory. All of Britain rejoices at your success and mourns the loss of those who died."

"Thank you, Morgan," Arthur replied. I saw the look of pleasure in his eyes as they spoke. "Why are you greeting us here instead of at the lake?"

"Merlin came before you," Morgan said. "We are all aware of your need for winter lodging. The castle of Camelot stands ready... well, not really ready, but serviceable to your needs. There is room there for all of Ector's people to winter. In addition to the fortress there are many houses and barns and stables for your animals. I will not lie; there is much work to be done. It is drafty and dirty and needs much in the way of repair. But we believe it will suffice. The enforced seclusion of winter creates time for that sort of work. If your people wish to truly make it their home there will be no idle hands in the coming months. Those who remained here while you were away have already begun the work. Lucan has proven to be quite the taskmaster in setting up the household."

"How is my brother?" I asked.

"He walks with the aid of crutches," Morgan said. "And I think he will always have a limp and need the occasional use of a cane. It hasn't seemed to slow him down very much. The main quarters of Camelot are already livable thanks to his efforts. This location is a good one for the High King of Britain. Its proximity to Avalon will help bring about the marriage of the sacred realm to that of the worldly. The petty kings and other pilgrims have traveled to this part of Britain for years now to see Excalibur. It will be an easy transition for them to come here to see the one who wields it.

"We met you here to save you the trip to the lake. I'm sure you are all tired, cold and hungry. A feast has been prepared in anticipation of your return. Avalon and the neighboring lands have contributed to your stockpile of food for the winter. Leodegrance sent barges down the river from Cameliard. It will be difficult, and you will need to hunt more than you may be accustomed to, but we expect a mild winter and an early spring."

Nimué looked up at me with a knowing smile.

"Bedivere," Morgan said. "Merlin says you have someone to deliver to Avalon?"

"This is Nimué," I said. Morgan stared at the child. Nimué returned her gaze. They seemed to be studying each other. I saw expressions of wonder cross both of their faces and then they relaxed into smiles.

"Thank you for bringing me home, Bedivere," Nimué said.

"Yes," Morgan said. "Thank you. The Goddess led you to this one."

Morgan brought her horse next to mine. Nimué stretched up and kissed me on the cheek, and then climbed from my lap to Morgan's.

"You won't forget me, will you?" she asked.

"Never," I said.

"Can I come see you?

"Whenever you like."

"You'll come visit me?"

"I promise."

"Bedivere will come to Avalon often," Morgan said. "We have much to prepare for. There must be a coronation, and many plans for the future of our realm must be made. Arthur will be traveling back and forth from Camelot to Avalon regularly. Lady Vivienne wishes to see him as soon as they are settled. Many things must happen in the next few months. Bedivere will always be at Arthur's side."

"Until the very end," Nimué said.

"Let's not speak of that here," Morgan whispered so that only the child and I could hear.

"Leodegrance and his people have returned to their homes," Morgan informed us. "As have King Mark and all of the other delegations. I have been asked to instruct their troops here to return home at their earliest convenience. You are welcome to stay at the lakeside clearing, or with Arthur's permission at Camelot, until you are rested and healed. There is plenty of room for you at either place.

"We have already established a routine of daily messengers. If you need anything from us please let us know."

The various factions in our entourage broke into groups to discuss their plans. Arthur of course said they were welcome to stay as long as they needed to. The consensus opinion was that everyone needed to rest and recover from the cold for a day or so. The men from Cornwall had a longer trip than most of the others, and wished to be on their way so they could be home before winter truly began.

"I have a message for you," Morgan said to me as the others discussed their options. She handed me a scroll that had been tied with a pink ribbon. Morgan gave me a smile and then moved her mount closer to Arthur. I watched them for a moment, the smiles they shared, the way they leaned toward each other. Though they did not touch, their bond and continued desire in spite of their relationship was obvious, at least to me. I didn't know what this would lead to, but I didn't think it was my place to say anything. Not in front of anyone, anyway. If it led to complications I promised myself I would address it with Arthur privately. It was part of my duty to serve the king and not the man.

I untied the scroll and unrolled it. The page was filled with a fine feminine script. It was from Guinevere.

"Dearest Bedivere," it began. "I hope this reaches you in good health. I write this as we prepare to leave Avalon and journey home. I wish to stay until we have news of your victory, but father insists that we have been away too long, and that we will learn the outcome of your battle with the Saxons wherever we are. While I know that is true I had hoped to see you again.

"I am sure I will see you at Arthur's coronation next year. I will think of you often during the cold nights of winter. Please think of me as well. Give our king my highest regards, and give Butter an apple for me."

I was touched, but wary. It was obvious to me that Guinevere harbored more than a friendship for me. In a year or so she would be a marriageable age. Under different circumstances I would have considered it. But I had other duties to consider. While nothing official had been declared, I knew Merlin was considering Guinevere as a wife for Arthur. He would need a queen, and heirs to his throne. Guinevere was a good political match, and personal feelings of love had very little to do with marriages of state. It would do Arthur nor me any favors to speculate on a future for Guinevere and myself, at least until I knew for sure what was planned for the kingdom.

I looked at Arthur and Morgan again as they shared a laugh over a private joke. Whatever the future held for any of us was bound to be complicated.

Eventually it was decided that all of our traveling companions would spend some time at Camelot before continuing their respective journeys home. Everyone would enjoy a hot meal and a good nights sleep at the very least. We bade goodbye to Morgan and the other acolytes. Nimué waved at me until they were out of sight.

We turned our entourage off the Roman highway and crossed the field of Camlann. A forgotten pathway to the abandoned fortress had been rediscovered in our absence. We followed the now well-trod trail until we were among the derelict outbuildings that surrounded the steep hill. If we wished to make this our home these would have to be fixed or rebuilt. As the home of the High King and the center of the kingdom we would eventually attract many more settlers. Farms would need to be established on the floodplain of the crooked river that wended its way around the far side of the hill.

We were met at the broken down gate that led into the grounds of the fortress proper. The cheers of our people were loud and there were many welcoming hugs and tears. It was a reunion of joy for those who survived and anticipated a new life, and one of grief as the fates of those we left behind were recounted.

Warok and I, along with the rest of our cavalrymen, took our horses to the recently cleaned stables. We inspected the buildings as the horses were brushed down and fed and our gear was treated and stored. The barns were filled with hay and oats. While there was still much work to be done to bring everything up to our standards the buildings were serviceable for the time being.

A large outbuilding had been designated as quarters for the troops. Our men joined the infantry there. Lines of cots and straw-filled pallets covered with woolen blankets stood against the walls. Like the barns, much work was needed, but with the fire that already roared in the fireplace this would be paradise compared to where our troops had been spending their nights.

Finally we made our way into the fortress proper. I was surprised at how clean and well lit it was. It was obvious that a lot of work had been done in our absence. On closer examination it was also obvious how much more would need to be done. Cleaning and repairs would keep us all busy during the winter months.

I could smell the divine scent of cooking as I was led toward my quarters. My mouth watered so that I nearly decided to skip changing my clothes and bathing. The tub of steaming hot water that awaited me changed my mind.

I was pulling on a new pair of fur-lined boots when I heard a knock on my door. I looked up to see Lucan entering my room. Wordlessly I stood and embraced my brother.

"It's good to see you," he said.

"And you. Are you all right?"

"Yes, for the most part. And you? You're not the boy who left home last spring."

"No. I've seen too much."

"Was the battle terrible?"

"Worse for them, but yes. Necessary though. And not the last, I'm afraid."

"Welcome home."

"Are we calling this home already?" I asked.

"Where else? And after the work I've put into this place you all better be happy and enthusiastic." I saw the smile play around his mouth.

"As long as there is hot food imminent I couldn't be happier."

"Then follow me," Lucan said. "Prepare to be delighted."

He led me through the corridors to the grand dining hall. His injured leg was still bound, and he used a single crutch to help him walk. I could see the swivel in his hip that indicated his injuries would never heal completely. But Lucan was no more a cripple than I was. More than anyone else, he was responsible for turning an empty, desiccated fortress into the wondrous center of Arthur's kingdom, the castle that legend would call Camelot.

CHAPTER TWENTY

It's getting more and more difficult to get out of bed in the morning. The midwinter solstice and festival has come and gone. We are in the darkest days of winter. It is cold in Mont St. Michael. My old joints protest with every movement. The nest I make in my large feather bed, snuggled under layers of woolen blankets and an old bearskin is much too warm and comfortable to leave. But the inevitable call of nature eventually wins out over my desire to stay put and I have to walk to my chamber pot, breath visible around my head. My knees pop with every step across a floor whose stones are too cold to be completely muffled by the rugs and rushes that cover it.

Listen to the complaints of an old man. There have been many times in my life when I would have begged for these minor discomforts. I have slept in snow and freezing rain, in muddy ditches and dank caverns. I would have scorned the man who complained about any indoor accommodations in January.

True to Nimué's prediction, our first winter in Camelot was mild; though most of our nights were less comfortable than any I have spent in these latter days of my life. We had snowfall, but it rarely coated the ground for any length of time. There were periods of rain and freezing rain that coated the grass and branches in crystalline beauty and filled the air with tingling chimes and fractured crashes.

We said goodbye to most of our guests within a week of our arrival. Tristan and the men from Cornwall were the first to leave. We planned to see them again in the spring when Arthur began his first tour of Britain at large. I was personally sad to see Tristan leave. His personality and his songs filled the empty halls for a few days and made the place seem less empty. I sent a letter to Guinevere with Leodegrance's men when they left the following day. It was short and to the point. I told her that we had won the battle and that I had not been injured. I spared her any of the more horrific details. I was also careful not to write anything she or anyone else could interpret as improper.

Gawaine and Agravaine stayed with us. They weren't sure if they were welcome back in Orkney, even with our defeat of the Saxons. Even if they were, this late in the year their home was far enough north to already be under a thick layer of snow and ice. Extensive travel there would be suicide. In any case, Gawaine had sworn to be Arthur's man, and saw Camelot as his new home.

We had a lot to do to keep us busy. There were always repairs to be made, and buildings that needed either to be fixed or torn down so a new one could replace it. Trees needed to be felled for timbers to make the repairs and firewood chopped for heat and cooking. Walls were scrubbed. Tapestries were hung to keep out the winter air. Chimney's had to be cleaned. Nests of rats and mice needed to be trapped. There were birds and bats in most of the upper rooms. More walls and floors were scrubbed. Our horses had to be tended to, as did the little stock we had– a few cows, goats and chickens we had been given by our new neighbors at Avalon for milk, eggs and the occasional bit of meat. A lot of hunting and trapping in the river took place. New cloth was spun and old clothes were mended.

We were an entire village of people attempting to create a new community in a makeshift situation, and we were trying to do it while still grieving the past and preparing for the future.

Arthur worked as hard as anyone. Though his duties often took precedence, and he did spend a great deal of time with Merlin and Vivienne at Avalon–and Morgan, I assume–he never shirked his share at Camelot. He lifted bundles, sawed wood, hammered nails, laid thatch and scrubbed filth with the rest of us. Many nights he would be covered with a film of sweat, grime and sawdust. He may have been the High King of Britain, but Arthur would always remain a man of the people.

Many of our community had converted to the Christian way over the years. For their worship services we converted an unused outbuilding into a chapel. Leodegrance, through his correspondence, urged us to begin making plans for a great church. As the center of a kingdom that was increasingly Christian it would be a necessity. He also reminded us that we were not sequestered completely away from the larger world. The Christian Church and its Pope wielded great power and influence. For a united Britain to thrive we must establish communication and trade with the rest of the world, and obtaining the official recognition of the Church was a must.

It was during these few months that the roles that Lucan, Kay and myself were to play in Arthur's life became cemented. Lucan had proven his worth at household organization when we were still at Ector's village. At Camelot, with no option of ever being a warrior again to distract him, he flourished. He kept detailed lists of everything; what rooms and buildings needed to be taken care of and the supplies necessary to do the job, how much firewood was being used and how much more there should be, manifests of our food supplies and detailed menus for the cooks so they could most efficiently use what we had at hand. I believe we would have all starved to death or frozen that winter without his guidance. Arthur saw his efficiency and was more than happy to turn the disposition of the day-to-day running of the castle to him. He was officially appointed Butler to the King and to the kingdom. He was no mere servant; the hallways, storerooms and every usable room in Camelot became Lucan's kingdom as much as all of Britain became Arthur's.

There is a long time rumor about Lucan I suppose I should address. It has been said by many that he preferred the company of men to that of women. I'm sure much of the reason for this gossip is simply because he was not a warrior and because he dedicated his life to what many see as "women's work." I don't know the truth of it. My brother and I never discussed personal affairs. If he was a lover of men he kept it discrete. The old religion I know he followed did not have the same proscription against it that the Christians do. I personally don't care. I have seen behavior between men and women who profess to love each other that I understood less. Whatever his private life entailed he was a good man who served his king loyally and better than most, until the very end. I have been known to break the nose and not a few teeth of men who suggested otherwise.

To everyone's surprise, Kay showed a talent for organization as well. While Lucan tended to the needs of the castle and the home, Kay took charge of matters of the kingdom. He proved incredibly efficient at keeping track of Arthur's appointments, organizing the layout of the village that was sure to grow around the fortress, making plans for where our crops would be planted and where our animals would graze. He made detailed lists of our supplies; every weapon, piece of armor, saddle and bridle we had was cataloged. He knew every nail, hammer, and piece of wood. From these lists he determined where our needs were and what should be addressed and in what order. It wasn't long before it was Kay who made the daily work assignments that allowed Camelot to take shape. Arthur appointed him to the role of Seneschal to the King. As a word it meant senior servant, but Kay was no one's lackey. In years to come Kay would organize every major event and keep track of all the myriad details that Arthur simply did not have time for.

Arthur and I were privately amazed and amused. Kay had always been impatient and easily bored with the tedium involved in learning a new task. To see him hunched over his lists long into the night was not only a new phenomenon, but to us a funny one as well. We still saw evidence of his impatience when things didn't happen on schedule or go by his plan. Several of his younger staff, and a few of the older men, suffered his ire. His explosions of frustration were much more entertaining now that they weren't being aimed at us.

I'm not sure what wrought the change we saw. Like Arthur and I, Kay had seen much more of the world that year. It sobered him up to the reality we all faced. I think our new positions gave him a sense of purpose he had never had before. As the son of Ector he would have been a warrior and a knight, but he would have been one of many, and his chances to excel would have been few. As brother to the king he felt far more responsibility. I think Kay was terrified of failing Arthur.

He continued to help with my rehabilitation as well. We sparred every day. I essentially started at the beginning of my training again. I knew all the theory now, so it went much more quickly, but I had to completely retrain my physical responses. I spent hours simply swinging the sword, building up the muscles in my left arm. All of my instinctive movements were still right-handed. I had to think through every step, consciously move in ways that were unnatural to me. I had to do it until it became natural. In battle I would not have time to think, I would have to simply respond, and a misstep would be lethal. I had survived the battle of the Glein, but that was due as much to luck, maybe more so, than any skill on my part. I wouldn't always be that lucky.

My own duties of course revolved around the horses. During the winter there wasn't much to do other than keep them fed, warm and healthy. Since the weather was mild Warok and I would take our cavalry men out frequently to put them through their paces. The fields of Camlann around the fortress hill were large and allowed for us to practice charges and strategy as well as to simply exercise the animals. I had spoken with Warok about my ideas for new tactics based on the dance of the acolytes I had witnessed. At first he laughed, but as he saw what our new Arabians were capable of he began to change his mind. Warok was very traditional in his thinking, and to him a cavalry was a blunt instrument, a moving shield wall of horseflesh designed to hammer the enemy into submission. I spoke about lightning strikes and complex patterns designed to confuse and separate our enemy. I convinced him that the discipline of coordinating such complex movements was worth our time if nothing else was. He was skeptical at first, but as time passed and my knights mounted on the Arabians consistently out rode and outmaneuvered his warhorses he began to see my point. I did not desire to completely replace the old ways; a blunt force charge had its place. But together we began to develop new strategies that would utilize the strengths of both.

We discussed breeding options. If the cavalry was to be the base of Arthur's army we needed more horses. Our mares would not come into season until late spring and early summer, so it would be well over a year before we would have new foals. As a result, much of what we talked about was conjectural. Still, the idea of a united Britain was a long-term vision. If all went well we would have years to put our notions into practical action.

In the meantime we needed to set up a blacksmith shop. There were two abandoned forges within the walls of Camelot. I was not a blacksmith, but I had grown up in my father's shop. I found those who did have the skills and gave them whatever they needed to get the forges working again. We needed horseshoes and nails immediately, and it would not be long before we needed as much armor, weapons and as many shields as could be produced. In time two forges would never be enough, but it was a start.

One of the first pieces made was a metal hook that we affixed to the leather cup that covered the stump of my right arm. It took some experimentation to find a way to attach it in a way that didn't simply pull the whole contraption off my arm when I attempted to lift something with it. Soon though, I was able to wrap the reins of my horse around it, allowing me more efficient use of them than I had previously had. I didn't wear it every day, and there were times when it was simply in the way. But overall, its presence improved the quality of my life.

It was Kay who suggested a system of communication across the kingdom. Part of the problem in defending Britain has always been the distances involved. That is true of every place in the world, I suppose. He suggested a network of manned stations. Somewhere he had found an old map of the entire island of Britain; its Latin markings and Imperial seal betrayed its origins. I suspect Merlin gave it to him. The Roman roads were clearly marked and it was clear to us that they linked most of the key cities and areas of our land. Even if we did not have the manpower or knowledge to maintain them in the Roman fashion they were still our most efficient means of travel. Kay suggested we build guard posts along the highways, each a half days ride from the other. The people of whatever land they occupied would man them. Horses would be maintained at each station so that a messenger could ride in, change to a fresh mount and ride on. Hopefully it would shorten the time it took a message to travel.

We also discussed the possibility of maintaining line-of-sight bonfires across the kingdom. This was a strategy that had been used forever by our people, but never on as massive a scale as we proposed. As soon as we approved the notion Kay began to design its implementation. As with so many of our plans, it would take years for all of it to reach fruition.

We planned the official coronation of Arthur as High King of Britain. It was to take place at the clearing at Avalon, on the very spot where the sword had sat in its stone for so many years. We did not yet have a church that could house all of the guests, and even though the Christian faith was spreading in influence we wanted to acknowledge the old religion as well. As a compromise Arthur agreed to be crowned by Archbishop Dyfrig of Caerleon, with our promise to build a cathedral on the grounds of Camelot. This was arranged through months of correspondence and amounted to nothing less than an official recognition of Arthur's legitimacy in the eyes of the Church and the world outside our shores. As soon as this detail was confirmed invitations went out to each of the petty kingdoms, whether they had formally agreed to support Arthur or not. It was an attempt to bring them into our fold, and to let them know of Arthur's standing. Arthur also informed them that he would be making a tour of the realm throughout the following year and visiting all of the petty kingdoms to discuss their role in Britain's future. We received many letters in return, welcoming our visit at any time. King Ban of Benwick assured us he would make the trip across the Channel to attend the coronation and extended his support to our efforts. Even Lot agreed to meet with us at some point. We heard nothing from Malaguin, Uriens, or from several of the smaller fiefdoms.

As the weather cleared Arthur began to travel. We made a systematic survey of the lands around Camelot that were now under his rule. He wanted the common man to know him, and to discover what they needed from him. I think many were surprised at how knowledgeable he was about the realities of their day-to-day lives. Growing up the way we did gave him insights that no spoiled nobleman could ever know. Added to that was the truth that Arthur was simply a remarkably likable man who was not afraid to get his hands dirty. He showed everyone that he had great plans for our country, assured them of their safety from invasion, and proved to them that he was, in many ways, just like them. There are many farmers who would tell the tale of the day the High King helped to milk their cows or mend their fences.

We planned to begin our tour of the petty kingdoms with a trip to Leodegrance's kingdom of Cameliard, and from there to swing southwest into Cornwall to renew our alliance with King Mark. From there we would return home, hopefully in time for the Beltane celebration at Avalon. May and June would be spent preparing for the coronation ceremony that had been scheduled for Midsummer's Day.

But before any of that took place there was another event, on the night of the spring equinox. It is a tale that has never before left my lips in all the years since. I was witness to an event in Arthur's life very few people were ever made privy to. I was sworn to silence then, and even now I am loath to give voice to what I know. But there have been so many false tales and assumptions, and now nearly everyone and everything involved is gone. No more damage can be done by the truth.

It is the tale of the night Arthur married the land.

CHAPTER TWENTY-ONE

Once again, it has been several days since I have written. I have been suffering from a late winter cold. My body aches, my noses drips like sap from a maple tree. I feel as if a nail has been driven into the bone just under my eyes. A cough has settled in. Isolde has brewed concoctions of willow bark and other remedies. It has helped, but I am not yet well. The weather shows signs of breaking, at least for a short spell. Hopefully the thick morass that resides in my chest will break with it.

As much as I would like to blame my lack of writing on my health I know there is more to it than that. I have been avoiding the topic I must now address. After all this time I hate to shed an unfavorable light on my friends and family, especially Arthur. While I believe his reign will be looked on in the future as a shining radiance of justice and hope in a sea of darkness, there are facts of his life that will be judged adversely. Many will find what I have to say distasteful and abhorrent. The Church, I'm sure, will judge it an unforgivable sin. At the very least, most will never understand the reasons or comprehend the need of the events of that spring night before Arthur was crowned. I do not fully understand, and I was there. Merlin tried to explain it to me. I was asked by Arthur to stand by his side and to bear witness so that someone would know the truth of events. As always, I did as Arthur asked. I supported him and was one of a very small handful of people who would help him bear his secret. But I am a simple man, ignorant still of the world of the gods and destiny and the inner workings of the will of the world, and I still do not comprehend just what really took place.

But there have been rumors and insinuations for years, and at the very least I can lay those to rest.

Arthur came to me early in March of that year. We had spent the afternoon drilling the cavalry in new riding formations and I was in the stables instructing some of the younger boys on the correct method of brushing down the horses. I was just hanging my own equipment on the wall when I saw him in the doorway, framed by the light of a setting sun. He smiled and for a moment we were boys again. I half expected him to invite me on some adventure in the woods. I felt a pang of remorse for what we had lost, what all men lose eventually. Adult responsibilities steal our youth, and even when we were able to relax we would never again simply play in the unself-conscious way of the child.

He walked with me through the stables, inspecting the horses and speaking to the men there. It was casual and friendly, filled with small talk and joking familiarity and I could tell he had something else entirely on his mind. Eventually we found ourselves alone watching the stars appear in a clear evening sky.

"I have a favor to ask of you," he said.

"Anything," I said. "You know that."

"This is important, Bedivere, and I ask you as my friend. Not as your king, not as my Horse Marshall. This is between you and I and the friendship we share."

"Anything. As my king or as my friend. I'm here."

"Will you come to Avalon with me for the spring equinox?"

"Of course." We had gone to Avalon a number of times in the previous months, for any number of reasons. I didn't understand was different this time.

"It will be just you and I on this trip," he said. "Merlin will meet us there. Bring your finest clothes."

"Okay. What's the occasion?"

Arthur actually blushed. He was rarely without words, but here he hesitated, as if weighing exactly what he wanted to say. For a moment I thought he was going to withdraw his request.

"There is to be... a ceremony," he finally said. "It is important to my future as king, and it is important to me personally. I really can't say anything more specific until we arrive there."

"It's a secret?"

"Yes, in a way, I suppose. Lailoken... Merlin says it has to do with the demands of the Otherworld and the gods. As such, we are not to speak of it anywhere except on Avalon, even to him or each other. Not many people would understand or approve; I'm not sure *you* will approve. But Merlin says it has been part of the plan from the beginning."

"If it is good for you, and good for the kingdom, how could I not?"

"We'll see. Lailoken will explain it to you far better than I can. I only know the part of it that feels right to me. There are bigger issues I don't really get either. Lailoken lives in a different world than us, Bedivere, one occupied by gods and goddesses. He is guided by their needs and concerns, and all of us, even me as High King, are little more than fleeting pieces in an eternal game they play. He says this ceremony is essential for my role in what is to come, that I am assuming a role that is bigger than my life here as a man."

"What does that mean?"

"I have no idea," he laughed. "But it feels like the right thing. Even if the world judges me harshly for this, my heart says it is right."

I began to be concerned then. I knew what had been happening between Arthur and Morgan, and when he spoke of his heart I knew she had to be involved. I didn't really approve of their relationship, but more because of what the rest of the world would make of it. I knew Arthur didn't think of her as his sister. They had never had that kind of relationship. He had fallen in love with her before he knew who he really was; and do not doubt that he *was* in love with her. The blood they carried may have been the same, but the hearts that pumped it were those of a man and a woman.

"You are the only man I would ask this of," Arthur said. "You are the only one who might understand. You are the only one I can trust with this."

"I'll stand by you, in whatever way you need," I said. What else could I say to my friend, my brother, and my king?

We left for Avalon near noon on the day before the equinox. Spring officially arrived tomorrow, but winter had already given up the ghost. The sun was bright in a cloudless sky. Colorful flowers formed brilliant constellations on the newly green field of Camlann. Buds were breaking out of their winter's prison on every branch. We passed farmers just beginning their spring labors, turning over the dark soil of the fertile earth. Seeds would soon be planted, putting our faith in a bountiful harvest deep within the soil.

Birdsong accompanied us along the forest path. It felt like the entire world was waking up. Though I still carried some apprehension about the ceremony I had agreed to be a part of it was still a wonderful day. For a few hours Arthur and I were able to put everything behind us and simply enjoy the day. For a brief time we were able to forget that he was the king of Britain and simply be friends. We raced our horses, talked of nonsensical things, and reminisced. We were perhaps too young to have been indulging in nostalgia, but our youth seemed far away. It had been less than year since we had started on our first pilgrimage to the Shrine of the Sword. How the world had changed in that time. We paused by a secluded spot by the lake to eat before going to the clearing where the acolytes of Avalon no doubt were awaiting our arrival. We dined on dried meat, hard cheese, and bread baked that morning. We could not wait for fresh fruit and vegetables, though both were still weeks in our future.

I had refrained from asking anything about the ceremony, or

what my part in it would entail. Arthur had assured me that Merlin would fill me in. As we packed up the debris of our meal and climbed back in the saddle I began to feel more uncomfortable. The long afternoon with Arthur had served to remind me of our closeness, of how it existed outside of the demands of our roles. We hadn't had the opportunity to just be together as friends for so long. I remembered the feeling I had the previous summer when I realized that Arthur and Morgan had first been together. I had felt Arthur, the Arthur I had always known, slipping away from me then. He was bound for places I could never go. The revelation of his true identity and destiny had furthered the gap between us. Though I was assured of his constancy with me by the very fact of my presence on this occasion I still feared losing him to forces larger than our friendship. I was afraid that whatever this ceremony was it would lead to an even wider gap between us.

A small group of acolytes met us at the clearing by the lake. Morgan was not among them. After our horses were stabled in the barns around the clearing we boarded the swan boats and paddled to the island. We had made this trip many times over the winter. The lake had frozen, but the ice had never been very thick during that mild winter. Some years it would freeze solid so that the only way on or off the island was on foot. Many were the times over the years that I tread across its surface, fearful of plunging into its chilly depths.

We were taken to our regular rooms where we stored our gear. I was surprised that Nimué was not there to greet me. On every previous visit she had been waiting at the shore, no matter how cold or uncomfortable the day may have been, to leap into my arms to welcome me and then begin to chatter about all of the wonderful things she was learning. She had adapted quickly, and if she carried any distress over the death of her family I never saw it. I wondered if she even remembered them as anything other than images. I believed the time would come when her life at Avalon would be the only life she recalled at all.

Still, Nimué had connected with me, and I had to be a reminder of where she came from. I suppose I was the closest thing to an adult male in her life. She told me once that even though Merlin spent a lot of his time at Avalon she never saw him. I remembered his reaction when he first saw her and wondered if he was avoiding this delightful child for some reason.

I asked after her, and all I was told was that she was with Vivienne and Morgan preparing for a special occasion. The acolytes seemed to have no more specific knowledge of what was happening than I did. They were used to the hierarchy of their order I suppose, and accepted that there were higher mysteries they were not meant to know. At first that seemed strange to me. I thought I would die of curiosity in their position until Arthur pointed out my lack of interest in the higher mysteries of running the household and the kingdom that Lucan and Kay took for granted. I protested that that was different, but I knew he was right. In my world I accepted my role and counted on others to perform theirs. I assume it was much the same for the acolytes.

Arthur went off to meet with Vivienne. I relaxed in my room

with a very good wine and some wonderful pastries until I was very bored. My salvation came in the form of Merlin.

"Griflet," he called from my doorway. He didn't use my boyhood nickname very often, but it made me smile when he did. The wizard had been a part of my life since before I could remember, and as unsettling as I often found the world he lived in, his presence was always something of a comfort.

"Lailoken," I shot back.

"Come, walk with me," he said. "Arthur has chosen you to be a part of this evening's rite. There is much we should discuss before then. Come with me, and bring me one of those tarts."

I followed him through the hallways while he happily munched his treat. We walked down a length of marble steps and went outside into the late afternoon sun. A path led through an orchard of apple trees. It was still too early for the fragrant blossoms, but the buds were evident. We walked in silence until we came to the lake. A small bench was stationed at the shore. Merlin sat and after a moment gestured for me to join him. I stared out over the calm, deep water and waited for him to speak.

"What do you know about the gods?" he finally said.

"Not much," I shrugged. "I accept that they exist, but I don't understand much more than that. They don't seem to interfere with my life very much, so I've never given them much thought."

"Good answer," Merlin said. "I think that is how most people feel about them. It's only a few of us who are doomed to live with one foot in their world and to address their whims. Why do you think you don't give them much consideration?"

"I don't know. Like I said, they seem very removed from my life. I can't see why a god would care very much whether I have fed my horse or if I am hungry. I can't spare much thought for them when I have so much to do right here."

"Philosophy is the luxury of the well-fed," Merlin said. "Most people are simply working too hard to survive to question the nature of the world."

"Well, yes," I said. "But it's more than that. I think most people just don't understand. It's hard to talk about the gods. It's too... intangible, I guess. It's like trying to describe the wind, or the color of the sky to a blind man."

"And now you've touched on the meat of it," Merlin said. "Language. You're right. The gods and the Otherworld exist in a place where our words fail to follow. We can never speak of these things directly. We have no language for the ineffable. We can only speak of these things through symbols, and symbols can be easily misinterpreted. What do you see in front of us?"

"A lake."

"Nothing more?"

"Water," I said, trying to guess what it was he wanted me to see. "I suppose I could say it is also a place for boats, or a source of drinking water, or a place to get fish. It's a barrier and a protection for this island from anyone without a boat."

"It's all of those things, and what one thinks of when he hears the word 'lake' is dependent on his needs. A thirsty man will not see the distance to the other side until he drinks.

"You see water," Merlin continued, "and several very practical uses for it. I see the lake as a symbol of the Otherworld. It is a gateway. We see the surface of things, and most of what we see is a mere reflection of the world we already know. But there is a whole world just under the surface that we sometimes glimpse. That's what the Sight is. On rare occasions some of us are able to see beneath that surface. That's what the Lady of the Lake truly means. Vivienne doesn't carry that title in reference to this body of water. She is a conduit to that Otherworld, a stream that flows from there to here. The Goddess speaks through her, as she has spoken through every Lady of the Lake. As she will speak through Morgan, and someday Nimué."

"Nimué?"

"She is a gifted child. More so than either Vivienne or Morgan, I dare say. It was more than luck that led you to her. The time to begin training a new heir is now. I fear Vivienne's time with us grows short."

"Why?"

"Vivienne is older than her usual vitality would lead one to believe. She has been Lady of the Lake for a very long time. She grows weary. This past winter she contracted a wasting sickness that all of the powers of Avalon cannot heal. She believes she will not last the year. She is at peace with this."

"So then what? Morgan becomes the new Lady of the Lake?"

"Yes. She has trained for that since she was first brought here. She is a bit young to take on this responsibility, but the Goddess has chosen her for the role. Just as Arthur is still young to be High King, but that is his destiny as well. We do not get to choose what road the gods put us on, only how we travel them."

"Arthur and Morgan," I ventured. "Their destinies are linked by more than their shared blood."

"And we come to the heart of it," Merlin said. "Yes, linked by more than their shared blood, and linked because of it. This is the part that is difficult to describe. Sit back, Bedivere, and listen, for the sake of Arthur and the sake of the future of Britain. There are stories you must hear."

He paused and stroked his beard as he gathered his thoughts. I studied his face, and saw, in spite of the lines there, a vitality to be envied. Maybe it was because I was no longer looking at him through the eyes of a boy, but he looked younger to me than ever before, almost as if he were aging backwards. That is an absurd notion, I know. I think that to the young all adults seem ancient. As you get nearer to them in age they cease to change as dramatically, or at least you stop noticing.

"As I said," Merlin began, "the lake is a symbol of the Otherworld. But it is more than that. Remember, Bedivere, everything I say here is a symbol, an attempt to describe the workings of the divine in our limited tongue. This land, all land, is the body of the Goddess. We all live here by her grace. The foods we eat, the shelters we build, the clothing we wear... all are the fruits of her body. All of us, and everything we see, are children of the Goddess. In religions all over the world this has been seen as true. The earth is our mother. But children need a father as well. In some cultures our father is believed to be the sky. The Greeks believed this. So did the ancient Egyptians. The northmen think so as well. When you look at their stories more closely, it is more complex than that, but in general it is true."

I laughed, and Merlin raised an eyebrow.

"I'm sorry," I said. "I was remembering something Morgan said the day we first saw the sword in the stone. She said it was the Skyfather copulating with the Earth Goddess. I was shocked at her blunt description."

"And more innocent then, I gather? She was speaking in symbols, but she was right. The world is created anew each day by the relationship between the God and the Goddess. The Goddess is eternal. The God must constantly be renewed. We have many symbols of this. You have heard tales of the Green Man, I assume?"

"Jack-in-the-green? Gawaine invoked his protection every day when we were stalking Saxons in the forest."

"Yes, the male figure that stalks the woods and lives in every growing thing. Each spring he rises anew from the earth, reborn, young and vigorous. Each fall he dies and goes to the Otherworld where his seed is planted in the Goddess so that he may be reborn. He is the God of the harvest, and the god of the hunt. He is the great horned god who gives his body to us as meat in the wintertime and is reborn as fawns in the spring. He is the great bear who fights the forces of darkness in the cold months and returns to us again every year when the days grow longer. He is the Christ who the priests tell us was born at midwinter and then died and returned to us in the springtime."

"The Christians say their Christ and their God are the only true gods," I said. "At least that's how I understand them."

"And they are correct," Merlin said. "There is only one god, and he returns to us in many different forms in all the cultures of the world. Their Christ is another story, the same story, among many."

"Leodegrance would argue that with you."

"And he does," Merlin laughed.

"So what does this have to do with Arthur?" I asked.

"In the material world a king is the ruler of his land and of his people. It is his job to protect both, to make and enforce laws that are to the benefit of all. To steward the land to peace and plenty. The earthly king is a representative of a higher ideal. The concept of a High King is that the man in that role is symbolic of the god. Too often, however, the king forgets he is a symbol of that higher power and believes it is his right to do whatever he pleases. Kings become tyrants. They want power and riches, all too often at the cost of the health and wealth of their land. They become petty kings, more concerned with temporal power than with the sacred duty with which they have been charged."

"I doubt most of them have ever considered that they have a sacred duty," I observed. "I can't imagine Uriens thinking in this way."

"Exactly," Merlin said. "They do not know they are sacred, and therefore do not act so. Each man will grow old and die, but the king must live on. Just as the god dies and is resurrected, the King must continue. That which once was must be again in the future. The earthly king is dead, but long lives the High King. The sacred king is at once the lover and husband of the goddess and her son, for his essence dies and is reborn. For this to happen, here and now, Arthur must know what he represents. His must be a sacred kingship, borne of knowledge of the role he plays. He must be High King of the earthly realm, and the physical representation of the god for the Otherworld. He must husband the land. To do that he must symbolically be married to the Goddess."

"Morgan," I said.

"As high priestess of Avalon, and future Lady of the Lake, she is the earthly representation of the Goddess."

"She is his sister," I said.

"Have you ever heard of the *Hieros Gamos*?"

Morgan's words from the previous summer came back to me. I didn't know what the words meant when she uttered them. It seemed I was finally going to learn.

"No, of course you haven't," Merlin said, making an assumption of my ignorance. "It is a Greek word meaning Holy Marriage. It refers to the union of the male and female aspects of the gods. True unity and prosperity can only occur when the forces that govern the universe are balanced. There are stories of sacred unions between the gods in almost every culture. The gods of ancient Egypt, Osirus and Isis were brother and sister. In Sumer the goddess Inanna married the shepherd Dumuzi who was also her son. The Greek gods Zeus and his wife Hera were siblings, the children of the Titan named Cronos. Closer to home the Irish hero-god Cuchulain was the son of Lugh and

Deichtine who were the son and daughter of Conchobar. The Irish still celebrate the Feast of Tara when a new king must be chosen. It is to ensure they choose the right man because they recognize that he is marrying the land and embodying the god. The northmen speak of a race of gods known as the Vanir. Freyr, the god of fertility is wedded to his sister Freyja. All of this speaks to the precedent of familial marriage among the powers of the Otherworld. It is a symbol for us to follow."

"But Arthur and Morgan are not really gods," I said. "None of us are. Are we truly meant to try to live like gods?"

"What are gods but the images of the way we are meant to live? They are our stories writ large. Each of us, if we take time to look, can find the tales of the divine running through our lives. I see this in you as clearly as I do in Arthur?"

"How?"

"You are not the only one-handed warrior to exist. The Northmen tell the story of Tyr. He lost his hand to the great wolf Fenris, yet still is worshipped as their god of justice and single combat. In Irish tradition the first king of the Tuatha De Danaan was Nuada of the Silver Hand. He lost his real hand to a fierce enemy, and then went on to father Lugh. Lugh became king by defeating the one-eyed god Balor, the new god replacing the old. By the way, Goibniu, known to us as Gofannon, the god of the smiths who forged Excalibur was foster father to Lugh. Your father was a smith. Do you see how it all repeats?"

"It makes no difference," I said. "No one, especially the

Christians, will look kindly on incest, no matter what religious stories you trot out to justify it. It could destroy the kingdom before it even begins."

"Which is why no one outside of this island must ever know of it. Avalon is the center of the Otherworld in this world. Morgan will be Arthur's wife and High Queen on these shores and nowhere else."

"And when the time comes for him to take a wife and produce an heir for the rest of the Kingdom?" I asked.

"He will do so," Merlin said. "But that will be a marriage of state. He will marry for political reasons, but it will not be for love. His wife will be his queen. She will rule at his side, she will, hopefully, give him an heir, but she will never have his heart. You've seen. Morgan has that whether we will it or not."

"Will his public queen know about Morgan?"

"She will have to. It will take a strong woman, who understands and is equally committed to the kingdom we wish to build. She will be made privy to everything. It can be no other way."

"Guinevere?"

"Perhaps," Merlin said. "She is certainly to be considered. But there are other possibilities. Bernard of Astolat has a daughter, Elaine, who may serve, though she is yet much too young. There are Irish princesses who may bring them to us as allies. Hoel's daughter Helena would have been a good match if she had lived. Time and politics will make that decision for us. Why do you ask about Guinevere? Do you have your own plans for her?"

"No," I said. "Not really. If she is not to be married to Arthur, then perhaps. But if that is a possibility then I should look another way until the matter is settled."

"You disapprove of all of this," Merlin said.

"Yes. No. Everything you have told me makes sense, given the context of the Otherworld and the needs of the gods. But I do not understand that world, and I daresay very few other people do either. I know Arthur does not think of Morgan as a sister. That is not the relationship they grew up with, nor did he know it when they first set interested eyes on each other. But my instinct tells me it is wrong, and will only bring heartache and trouble to us all. I think my reaction is the one most people would have."

"Will you tell this to Arthur?"

"Yes. That is my duty, to the man and to the King, as charged to me by Arthur himself."

"And if he insists on going through with the sacred marriage?"

"Then I will stand by his side, and keep his secret, and do all within my power to make sure he fulfills the role he has taken on."

And with that pronouncement the course of my life was determined. I returned to my quarters where I bathed in hot water and shaved all but my mustache, an affectation I had grown fond of at the time. I dressed in the finest clothing I owned, packed and brought with me at Arthur's request before I knew the reason. I capped my stump with the leather cup and tucked the sleeves of my shirt into it. I would have no need of my hook for what lay ahead, and though it had its uses I was much more self-conscious of that curved piece of metal than of an empty sleeve.

Arthur came to my room at dusk. Shadows from an oil lamp cavorted on my walls. He was dressed in a long robe and Roman-style sandals. It was an odd choice, I thought. I assumed it was simply a dressing gown and his ceremonial garb was being prepared. He looked sheepish.

"Lailoken tells me he spoke with you," Arthur said. "He says you have questions, or concerns."

"Do you really believe all of that stuff about the gods and sacred kingship?" I asked.

"Yes," he said. "I know it sounds... I don't know. Extraneous? Complicated? Unnecessary to be king? Maybe. But Merlin and Vivienne believe it. They have worked long and hard to make this happen. Uther and Igraine were married here in the sacred kingship. I am the result of that. This has been long in the making."

"The people you rule will never understand, or accept it. I believe if your relationship with Morgan ever becomes public knowledge it will be the end of your kingdom."

"This kingdom has never really existed before. None of the petty kings have been able to protect this land. Whatever passes between Morgan and I, I truly believe our only hope of survival against the invaders, the only way our way of life can continue, is for this land to be united. I stand a better chance of making that happen than anyone ever before. I must unite our people and the tribes. I must somehow unite the Christian path with the ways of the old ones. This ceremony is a way to unite this world with the Otherworld."

"Most people don't even truly believe the Otherworld exists," I said.

"It does not rely on our belief to exist," he countered. I heard this as Merlin's words more than Arthur's.

"Do you love Morgan?" I asked. "And what I mean, is do you love her as a woman?"

"Yes."

"Even though she is your sister?"

"I didn't know that when I fell in love with her."

"And that makes no difference to you now?"

"Of course it does. I have given this much thought. But we could have met and fallen in love and never have known who we really were. I don't mean for this to be insulting, but how many unknown siblings do you suppose we both have scattered around this country. Both of our fathers were soldiers, and neither of us are naïve enough to believe they didn't leave their seed behind all over this land. Gawaine probably already has three or four babies he will never know about in the making. This could happen to any of us."

"But you know the truth."

"I know where my heart lies, and Lailoken tells me this is the will of the gods. I have to believe my encounter with Morgan and all that has passed since was meant to happen. I believe I must marry her for the good of the land."

"And this marriage," I asked. "Will it be a symbolic marriage only, or will she be your wife in the worldly way?"

"She will be my wife, in every way that word implies. But only here. Only on Avalon. This island is an extension of the Otherworld on the shores of the material world. Once we leave this place the marriage will never be spoken of or acknowledged. Out there I will find a woman to be my wife and queen, and we will produce an heir to my throne, but it will be a marriage of convenience and politics. Not one of love."

"And you are willing to perpetrate that deception on whoever becomes your queen?"

"She will know everything. She will have to agree to this before she becomes the Queen of Britain. There is no deception. I must be king of two realms, and only a few people live in both. They are the only ones who can understand."

"I don't live in the realm of the gods, Arthur. Why bring me into this?"

"Because you are my brother," Arthur said. "Because I cannot do this alone. Because, of all men, I trust you to stand by my side."

I looked him in the eyes. I saw his longing there, for Morgan, and for the future. I saw trust, and fear, and desperation. I also saw my friend, my brother, and the person I truly believed was the best hope for all of Britain. I still had my concerns, but as always, I could not tell him no.

"Twice now," I said, "you have asked me to serve the King. Once, at the side of a pond when we were boys, and the second time, last summer at this lake, in front of your new kingdom. You made me promise to always follow his lead as long as it is righteous. To be his conscience, to be his right hand in all matters. To follow him until the end of his days as long as his rule is just and fair. To serve the office and not the man. Do you remember that?"

"Of course."

"In the interest of following that dictate, I want to make sure that you understand. This sacred marriage, no matter how much you believe it is necessary and the right thing, no matter how much you may love Morgan, will never be accepted by the great mass of people you wish to rule. The people here, people at large, the Church especially, will judge you and censure you for this. I believe there is the potential for great harm to you personally and it may pose a threat to your rule.

"But, if you believe in a higher power guiding your destiny, if you believe this is what must happen, knowing the consequences if others discover this, then I will stand by your side. I will guard this knowledge from others to the best of my ability. I will help you build the greatest kingdom in Britain's history, come what may."

Arthur embraced me. There were tears in his eyes as I heard a small whisper in my ear.

"Thank you," he said.

He left my room to prepare for the ceremony. I waited there to be summoned, wondering what I had agreed to, and if Arthur and I had just signed the death warrant of his kingship before it ever began. As with so many things, I decided the issues were much too big for my common brain and decided to leave it in the hands of the gods. They started this mess. It was up to them to see it through.

I ate sparsely from a plate of bread, cheese, and mealy apples left over from last years harvest while I waited. Eventually, well after darkness had wrapped itself around the island, there was a quiet knock at my door. I looked up from where I had started to doze to see Nimué. She was dressed in the plain white shift of the acolytes. Tiny white petals of the common snowdrop, one of the earliest flowers of spring, had been plaited into her cherry-red hair. I expected her to run and jump onto my lap, which had become her usual greeting for me. Instead she stood by the door, a solemn look on her face. She looked healthier since her arrival at Avalon, but the dark rims that underlined her worldly eyes remained.

"It's time," she said, and beckoned me to join her. I was surprised that Nimué would be privy to that night's events, but then I remembered Merlin telling me that she was destined to one day be the Lady of the Lake. If all of our plans for Britain succeeded she would be dealing with Arthur and our kingdom as the representative of the goddess, either as Morgan's aide or successor, for decades to come.

I stood and joined her at the door. She took my hand in her tiny one and led me through the hallways. Only once did she look up at me, and then she giggled, briefly breaking her much too adult demeanor. She squeezed my hand to let me know she was happy I was there and that she was excited. By the time we reached the path to the oak grove her serious face was back in place.

The night was clear and unseasonably warm. I could see torchlight between the boles of the great trees at the end of the path. The lake lapped softly against the nearby shore. A full moon looked down on us through the new buds of spring. Nimué paused at the edge of a clearing. She bade me kneel down so that she could whisper to me.

"You don't have to if you don't want to," she breathed into my ear. "But everyone else will be skyclad for the ceremony."

I didn't know what she meant until she pulled her shift over her head, dropped it to the ground, and walked into the ring of light. Still not sure what to expect I followed her into a circular grove of thirteen large oak trees. The lake met the land here. Torches flickered in the slight evening breeze off the water. An archway had been constructed of wood and decorated with the same flower petals that adorned Nimué's hair. She stood at the archway with Arthur, Merlin, and the Lady Vivienne; Morgan was curiously absent.

The meaning of skyclad became instantly obvious to me. All of them were completely naked. I saw Nimué hide a giggle behind her hand. Arthur merely shrugged, blushing as furiously as I'm sure I was. Merlin and Vivienne were completely at ease. I had the momentary urge to strip off my own clothing, believing I could not possibly be more embarrassed or self-conscious than I already was. The urge passed. Merlin smiled and motioned for me to stand by Arthur's right side. Once I was in place Merlin nodded to Vivienne to begin.

Arthur and I stood still and watched as the three of them stepped through the archway to stand closer to the lake. They stopped by a table on which I saw several objects; there was a ceremonial knife, a metal container shaped like a small cauldron, a wooden staff, and some other vials and containers. There was also an ornate scabbard, made of leather and studded with shining jewels.

I watched Vivienne as she spoke a blessing to the four directions and invited the attendance of the Goddess and the God. I was still uncomfortable with her nudity, but I also saw evidence of the illness Merlin had spoken of. She was thin with deep shadows separating her ribs. Her eyes looked tired, with dark half-moon lines under them. Her breathing was labored and she had a small cough. I thought that being outside at night in March was not a good thing for her, even if she had been clothed.

There are many aspects of the ceremony I do not remember. There were many invocations and she utilized each of the items on the table, except for the scabbard, in some fashion. It was all extremely esoteric to me and so far outside of my experience I couldn't see the significance of most of what was said.

Once the opening benedictions were finished Vivienne faced Arthur through the opening in the archway.

"Arthur," she pronounced. "You, like all men, are the human embodiment of the God. In this manifestation the God is the King of the land. The God and the King came before you. For a time they will live within you. When your mortal body passes the God and the King will live on.

"The King stands in the middle of the physical world. The great wheel of the universe revolves around his throne. He is the lord of the four quarters, the powers of which we have invoked. The King brings order to the chaos of the world. There are other aspects of the God; there is the warrior who protects, the magician who creates, the lover who unites, the father, the brother and the son. All are subservient to the King who gives meaning to every other role.

"But the King does not do this alone. The King must have a Queen. The God must have a Goddess. Neither can exist without the other. They are the two sides of the generative power of the universe. All life comes from the Goddess. She is the womb of the world. All that is, is born from the waters of her body. She is the land. She is the food we eat, the water we drink, and the air we breathe. We live on the body of the Goddess like the newborn babe lives from the milk of its mother.

"It is the King's sacred duty to protect her. To create life with her. To unite with her. He is her father, her brother, her lover and her son. She is his mother, sister, lover and daughter.

"Arthur, as the living vessel of the power of the God and of the King, do you accept the responsibilities of that role?"

Arthur did not hesitate. Unlike me he seemed to know what his role here was and what was expected of him.

"Yes," he said.

""Then step across the threshold into the Otherworld and claim your Queen," Vivienne commanded.

Arthur stepped through the opening in the archway. I did not follow. I had not been asked, and somehow I knew that my presence here was that of a witness. I had no place in the Otherworld, and no desire to go there. I discovered in my years of service, that no matter the strength of my loyalty to Arthur, there were certain places I could not follow him. This was the first such place.

"The Goddess," Vivienne continued, "like all that exists, is born from the womb of the world. She is that world. Like the wheel of the year and the seasons, like the day and the night, it is a timeless cycle. The God and the Goddess are eternal. The King and the Queen are eternal. They live in each of us, wearing our forms like clothing they shed when the fabric of our lives have worn thin. But they will come again, born anew from the intercourse of creation itself.

"The King stands ready. The Queen opens herself to him."

A brilliant reflection of light caught my eye from the darkness of the lake. Torchlight glimmered from something rising out of the water. It grew longer, casting more light as it did so. As the cross-guard broke the surface of the water I recognized Excalibur, water dripping down its length as it continued to ascend. I saw a pale, feminine hand gripping the hilt. The hand became an arm, and then I saw Morgan's head rise above the water as she walked toward the shore. She was naked and wet. Her black hair clung to her voluptuous body as water sluiced its way down her curves.

I thought, at first, that I was witnessing firsthand the magic of Avalon. Had Morgan been under the water all that time? How, without drowning? Had she appeared there from the Otherworld, summoned by Vivienne's words? In the years since I have thought of numerous ways this could have been accomplished without magic. I think my rational mind needed an explanation it could accept, and I convinced myself that what I saw was mere illusion and trickery.

Until the night so many years later when I returned Excalibur to the lake of Avalon.

Morgan walked to Arthur and kneeled in front of him. She still held Excalibur aloft.

"The sword," Merlin said, taking up his part of the ceremony, "is a masculine symbol. It represents the power of the mind, and its power to separate truth from lies, and good from evil. It has two sides. One that will destroy an enemy. The other, if used incorrectly, that will destroy he who uses it. It also has the power to defend. The true power of the sword can only be known when it is no longer needed, when its presence alone assures peace and prosperity. Only when it is sheathed for good can the true kingdom of man be born."

Arthur took the sword from Morgan. She stood and lifted the scabbard from the table.

"The scabbard," Vivienne said, "contains the power of the sword. As long as the King trusts in the peace he preserves he cannot be harmed. It is the union of the two that creates the world."

Arthur slid the blade into the scabbard Morgan held. She belted it around his waist. She turned to face Vivienne and Nimué. Nimué picked up a chalice from the table.

"The cup is a feminine symbol," Vivienne said. "It is the Goddess and the world. It represents the power of the heart. It is the well of life from which we all come from and return to. The entire cycle of life is contained within. From the virgin child, to the fecund mother, to the aged crone and back again, we are all immortal in its embrace."

Nimué drank from the cup and then passed it to Morgan, who drank and passed it to Vivienne. The Lady of the Lake drank and handed the cup back to her youngest acolyte.

Morgan turned to Arthur and took his hands in hers. She spoke words of ritual.

"I am She, the Goddess and the Queen."

"I am He, the God and the King," Arthur responded.

"I am the song."

"And I am the refrain."

"I am the Earth."

"I am the sky."

"I am the cup."

"I am the sword."

"I am she who births the world."

"I am he who protects it."

"Come, embrace me, and live in my heart forever."

"Come, embrace me, and live in my heart forever."

They clasped each other tightly and kissed. It was short and sweet, and even from where I stood I saw the hunger they both had for more. Reluctantly, I thought, they stepped apart, though their hands remained linked.

"Go now," Vivienne said. In this world you are God and Goddess, King and Queen, Husband and Wife. Take these powers with you and step back across the threshold and enter the rest of your lives."

Arthur and Morgan stepped through the archway and came to my side. They smiled and then Arthur took her in his arms again and lifted her from the ground. Their laughter mingled in the warm night air as he swung her around.

"Thank you Bedivere," Morgan said. She leaned in and embraced me. I was uncomfortably aware of her nudity as she kissed my cheek. I was even more uncomfortable when Arthur did the same.

"Thank you, my brother," he said. "For being here at this moment. For witnessing this and for standing by me."

"It was my duty, " I said.

"I hope it was more than that," Arthur chided.

"It was my honor," I said.

"Tomorrow," Arthur said, "we start our tour of Britain. Tomorrow we begin to truly build this kingdom."

With that promise he and Morgan left the circle of oaks and followed the path back to their quarters. When I turned back to the others they were, thankfully, clothed again. Vivienne and Merlin were gathering the implements of the ceremony.

"You can go now, Griflet," Merlin said. "Thank you for your understanding. I daresay this will not be the most difficult thing Arthur will ask you to do for him."

"Nimué," Vivienne said, "can you take Bedivere back to his room?" Nimué clapped and giggled, her solemnity finally giving way to childlike delight. She ran and took my hand and pulled me along the path, chattering the whole way.

I really didn't listen very closely. My mind was on too many things. I turned what I had just experienced over and over in my head, trying to make sense of it. No matter how I looked at it I couldn't find a way we could ever justify it to anyone outside of this island. I feared the consequences of this forbidden love, whatever the gods had decreed.

But that was for the future to decide. We still had much to do.

The kingdom we wished to build was a more immediate concern. We needed to finish Camelot. We needed to have a coronation. We needed horses and men. Not all of the petty kings were yet on our side. The threat of the Saxons loomed.

This sacred wedding I had just attended was not the last thing Arthur ever asked me to do. I was to stand by his side for years. The hardest thing he ever asked of me was to leave his side when he was dying. But that story still lay many years in the future of that night. On that long ago spring evening every possibility still lay before us, and we believed we could accomplish anything. There was still a lot of work to do, and Arthur would count on me being beside him for all of it.

I was, after all, the King's right hand.

End of Book One

About the Author

Wayne Wise is a writer, artist, seeker shaman and magician, or at least claims to be in casual conversation. He has a BA in History and an MA in Clinical Psychology and in his life has worked as a counsellor, an administrative assistant for a state legislator, an inter-office mail courier, a freelance comic book inker, and a department store Santa. He wrote music and comics-based articles for several local news mags and a couple of national magazines. In 1993 he and his business partner/collaborator Fred Wheaton self-published the comic book Grey Legacy. In 2010 he wrote and drew a follow-up called Grey Legacy Tales. Raised in rural southwestern Pennsylvania he is currently employed by the Eisner Award-nominated comic book store Phantom of the Attic in Pittsburgh and recently taught a course in Comics and Pop Culture as a guest lecturer at Chatham University. You can read his Blog at www.wayne-wise.com **or visit his Amazon author page at** http://www.amazon.com/-/e/B0058QJICW.

His other novels (available soon) include;

King of Summer

Scratch

This Creature Fair

Bedivere: The King's Right Hand

9 781466 301481